A WARDEN'S PURPOSE

WARDENS OF ISSALIA, BOOK I

JEFFREY L. KOHANEK

FALLBRANDT PRESS

PUBLISHED BY JEFFREY L. KOHANEK and FALLBRANDT PRESS

www.JeffreyLKohanek.com

ALSO BY JEFFREY L. KOHANEK

Fate of Wizardoms

Book One: Eye of Obscurance

Book Two: Balance of Magic

Book Three: Temple of the Oracle

Book Four: Objects of Power

Book Five: TBD

Book Six: TBD

* * *

Prequel: Legend of Shadowmar

Runes of Issalia

The Buried Symbol: Runes of Issalia 1

The Emblem Throne: Runes of Issalia 2

An Empire in Runes: Runes of Issalia 3

Rogue Legacy: Runes of Issalia Prequel

* * *

Runes of Issalia Boxed Set

Heroes of Issalia: Runes Series+Rogue Legacy

Wardens of Issalia

A Warden's Purpose: Wardens of Issalia 1

The Arcane Ward: Wardens of Issalia 2

An Imperial Gambit: Wardens of Issalia 3

A Kingdom Under Siege: Wardens of Issalia 4

ICON: A Wardens of Issalia Companion Tale

* * *

Wardens of Issalia Boxed Set

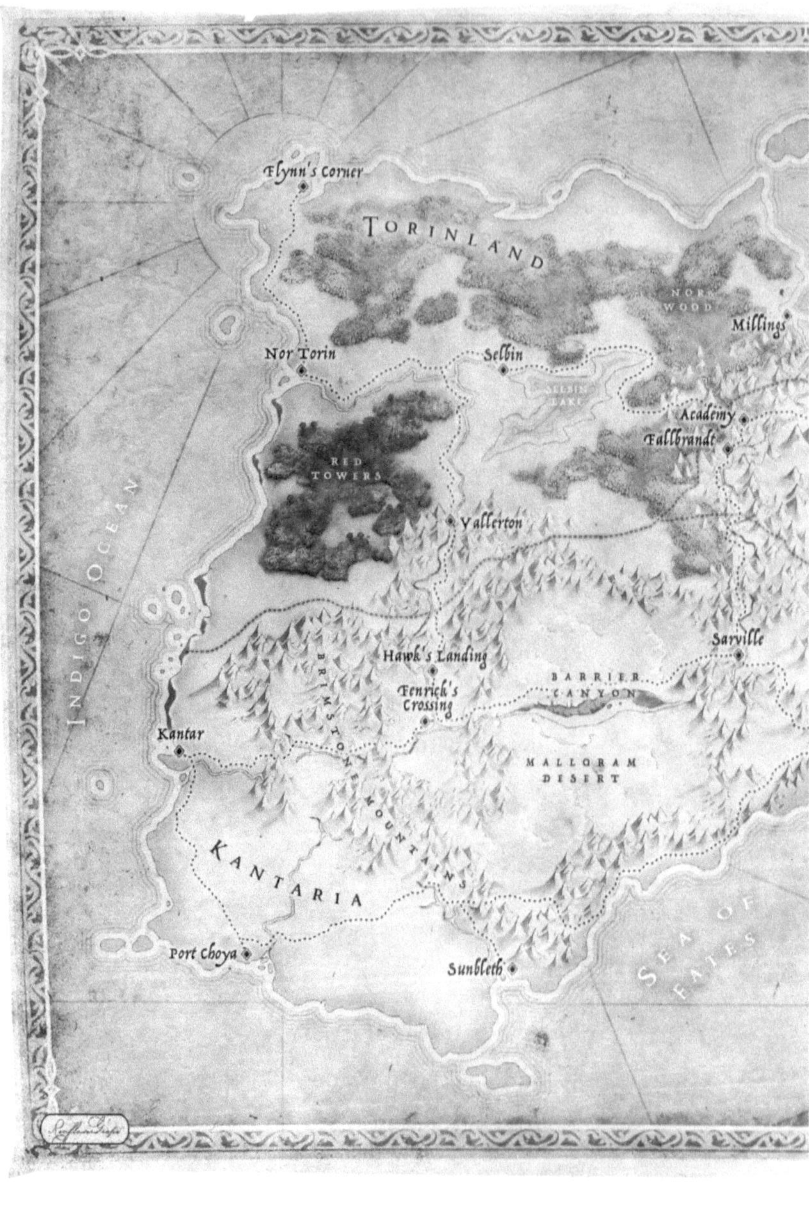

Flynn's Corner
TORINLAND
NOR WOOD
Millings
Nor Torin
Selbin
SELBIN LAKE
Academy
Fallbrandt
RED TOWERS
Vallerton
INDIGO OCEAN
Sarville
Hawk's Landing
BARRIER CANYON
Fenrich's Crossing
MALLGRAM DESERT
Kantar
BRIMSTONE MOUNTAINS
KANTARIA
SEA OF FAIES
Port Choya
Sunbleth

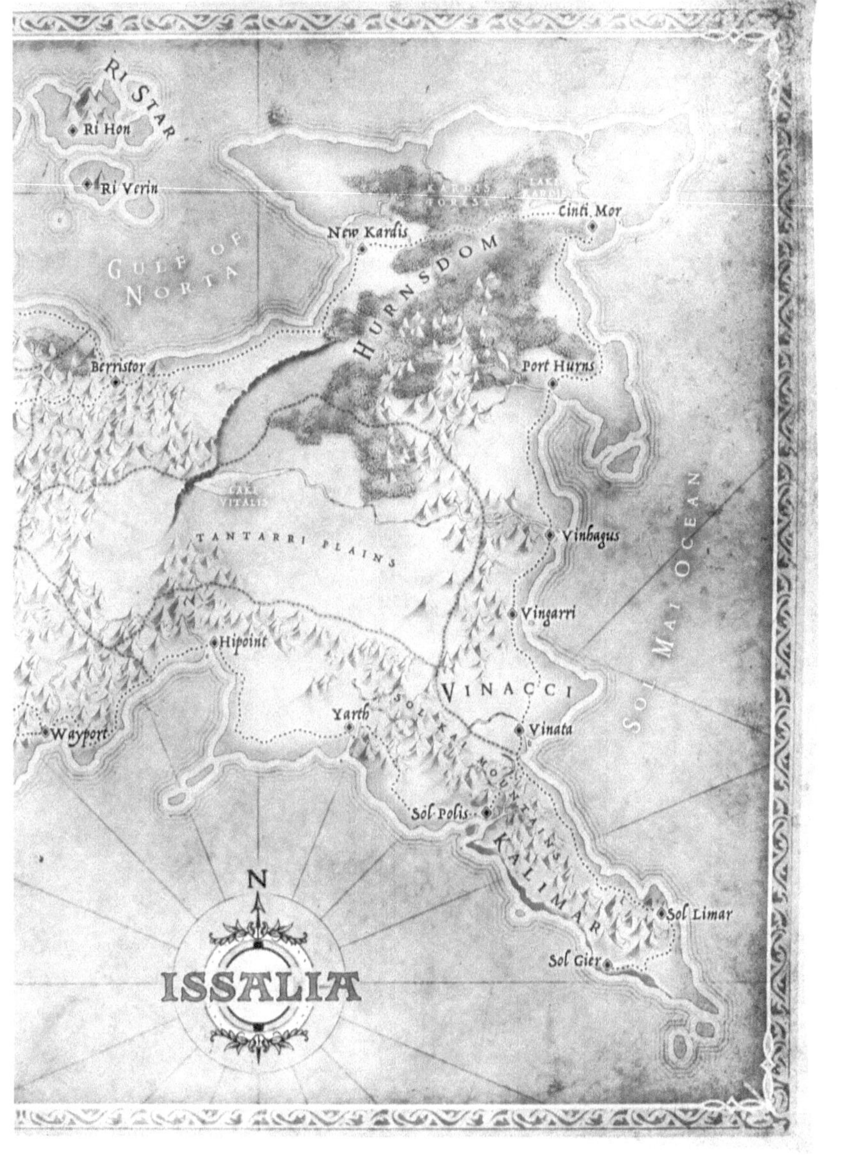
RI STAR
Ri Hon
Ri Verin
GULF OF NORTA
New Kardis
HURNSDOM
Cinti Mor
Port Hurns
Berristor
LAKE VITALIS
TANTARRI PLAINS
Vinhagus
Vingarri
SOL MAI OCEAN
Hipoint
VINACCI
Yarth
Vinata
Wayport
SOL KAI MOUNTAINS
Sol Polis
KALIMAR
Sol Limar
Sol Gier
N
ISSALIA

T ime has passed since the Horde invasion, the collapse of the Empire, and the disbanding of the Ministry. As time is prone to do, our wounds have healed. The kingdoms of the east continue to rebuild but may be strong again one day. The kingdoms of the west – untouched by the ravages of war –thrive under their new regimes. All things considered, the rulers of Issalia could not ask for more.

However, a darkness lingers, hiding amidst our shadows, slipping between them unseen. It has claimed the life of one king and has attempted to take others with it. We know of it, but it appears to know us far better. At such a disadvantage, I fear the plans this shadow will conceive and what bold move might come next.

Accordingly, we cannot sit back and wait for it to strike like the viper it is. We must turn the tide and play the same game or risk losing everything. Thus, I have set in motion something dangerous, and, in that danger, I place my hope – a viper of my own creation. After years of preparation and planning, this viper has been set free in Fallbrandt. It will bring an end to our enemies, or it will take us all down with it. I pray that Issal watches over us.

-King Brock of Kantaria

1

———

TWISTED THOUGHTS

A noise woke Everson. He blinked at the dark wall beside his bed, holding his breath as he listened. The rustle of cloth scraping across cloth left the hair on his arms standing on end. When he rolled over, he found a shadow hovering above him. He gasped as a hand clamped over his mouth – the palm smelled of metal and was damp with sweat. The thump of Everson's heart was a drum in his ears. Unable to breathe, his eyes grew wide with fear.

"Don't make a sound," a female voice whispered as the tip of a blade burrowed into his neck...a prick of pain that carried a dark promise.

The blade held still for a moment before the pressure eased. A trickle of blood tracked down his neck as a reminder. Another shadow loomed behind the first. Rough hands gripped him and sat him upright. Starlight through the open curtain revealed Jonah's empty bed, the covers thrown back against the wall. *Where is Jonah?*

Before he could contemplate the whereabouts of his roommate, his attackers forced a long strip of cloth into his mouth and tied it around his head. Panic took hold. His gaze darted about the room in desperation but he found no escape. One assailant produced a black sack, drew it over Everson's head, and the surrounding shadows slipped into oblivion.

The intruders flipped Everson over and held him face down as they bound his wrists together, the ropes digging into his flesh as they secured them tightly. They then wrapped a blanket about him, lifted him off the bed and hauled him from his room. His imagination began to conjure frightening thoughts – images that included instruments of torture and the use of terrible magic.

With each step, he bounced violently as his captors ran down the corridor. They slowed and he heard a door opening before they carried him through. Wearing nothing but his smallclothes, the brisk night air seeped through the blanket and gave him a chill, but even his involuntary shiver was interrupted as they shoved him into a carriage. Air blasted from his lungs as he landed on his side and an aching pain shot into his shoulder. Two thumps of a fist pounding against the wall followed, and the vehicle lurched forward, the momentum rolling Everson from his side and onto his back.

He sensed the warmth of another human beside him. At the same time, he noticed a familiar sweet scent – one he knew well. Oddly, his anxiety eased, and a sense of faith filled the vacuum. She made no sound, but he felt her breathing. They were together, and she was alive.

Minutes trickled on or maybe passed by quickly. He was unable to tell. When the carriage slowed to a stop, Everson wondered where they might be. His mind began working the calculations, but the door opened and someone grabbed his ankles before his thoughts could reach a conclusion. They pulled him from the carriage and hoisted him up again, carrying him by his armpits and ankles as they headed up a short flight of stairs.

Determined to keep his wits intact, he listened carefully for clues, counting steps and making mental notes of the path taken. A door creaked slightly, clicking as it closed behind them. Fifty paces down a corridor, they turned. Another door opened, this one creaking louder, and he felt himself going downward, his body twisting as they descended a stairwell.

Stone scraping against stone made Everson frown, trying to place the origin of the sound. They carried him forward, stopped, and unwrapped the blanket, the warmth it provided replaced by cool, damp air. A grunt slipped past the gag in his mouth when his rear thumped onto a wooden seat. Rope slid across his bare chest, chafing his skin as it wrapped about him three times before tightening until the pressure made it impossible to take more than a shallow breath.

Boots scuffling and chairs sliding on stone tiles reignited Everson's fear. He tried to move his wrists, to free his hands, but found the bonds tightly secured.

Sounds of movement and shifting briefly surrounded him before settling to silence. The distinctive tap of boots on stone made its way across the room and circled behind him. A hand pressed against the top of his head. The sack lifted away, taking the veil of darkness with it.

Blinding white light invaded and forced him to squint at the intensity. Fingers danced at the back of his head, working the knot until his gag fell away. The dryness in his throat forced him to cough, drawing pain from the pressure of the bonds across his chest. He worked his jaw and glanced about, seeking Jacquinn. Dark gray block walls stood five paces to either side of him. Backed by a shroud behind it, a bright light, white and intense, glared before him. Beyond the bright light were shadowy forms – three people, perhaps more. He sensed that one or two captors hovered behind him.

"Where is my sister? I know you have her," he croaked.

"Silence!" A deep voice echoed off the chamber walls.

Although the intense light made it impossible for Everson to see beyond it, he knew the chamber was not very big. The sound pattern dictated that the room couldn't be much deeper than its width. His focus shifted up to the dark wooden beams that supported the low stone ceiling. *Under the ground. I'm somewhere underground.*

"You have been brought here to answer questions, not to pose threats nor make requests." The male voice sounded rough, commanding – yet old. "Answer our questions, and Jacquinn will remain unharmed. When we have the information required, you will be released…assuming we find your story satisfactory."

"What if…what if it doesn't meet your satisfaction?"

Deep laughter reverberated throughout the room, a laughter that sounded demented. Evil.

"You don't want to know."

Everson's imagination invented a maniacal face for the villain who was speaking, the image hovering within his mind's eye.

"What we require from you is the truth."

Red eyes flared from the shadows, crackling with energy. A rune drawn on the floor began to glow, a rune that Everson recognized. The crimson power of *Chaos* caused the rune to flare brightly, pulse briefly, and fade to darkness. Lies were no longer an option.

"We have been watching you…monitoring your training…tracking your interactions with others. There are things that have come to our attention, things we must validate before we decide what to do with you."

Dark thoughts – twisted, hopeless, and terror-filled – threatened to dominate Everson's will. He fought to contain them, to keep himself from withdrawing. In an odd reversal, Jacquinn's life depended on him. He desperately wished she was with him, wished he could look into her steely eyes. This time, he had to find strength elsewhere. He could not let her down.

"You will tell us about yourself – your story, your life growing up. Everything. Start at the beginning and leave nothing out, nothing that might be of note or interest.

"First, state your name."

"Um…Everson Gulagas."

"When you and Jacquinn arrived in Fallbrandt, you claimed to be brother and sister. That isn't true, is it?"

A heavy silence hung over the room, weighing Everson down. His mind raced at the thought, attempting to divine their intent.

The voice spoke again. "Her hair is a ray of sunlight, yours murky shadows. Her eyes are bright like the sky, yours as dark as the soil below. Who are you, really? Where were you born? Remember that her life depends on your response, and we will have the truth."

Everson bit his lip as uncomfortable feelings surfaced, rising above the tension of the moment. His eyes lowered to his lap and saw pale thighs – scrawny, twisted, useless. He hated his legs and wished he could cover them, hide them away. Closing his eyes, he shifted his focus to the question posed. For Quinn, he dug himself from his shell of fear and insecurity. For Quinn, he forced himself to speak.

"I...hail from Cinti Mor. I was born shortly before The Horde destroyed the city. My...Jacquinn's mother and father were among a small group of citizens who fled the city prior to the attack. If they had not, they surely would have died along with everyone else.

"This group of refugees took shelter in the ruins of Old Kardis. Two days after the attack, Evers Gulagas, along with a handful of other survivors, left the ruins in search of food. It was mid-winter, so the snow was a hindrance, the cold a threat.

"During their journey southward, Evers came across a woman in the snow, lying facedown. When he turned her over, he discovered that she was dead – her skin pallid, her lips blue. She had escaped the horrors of the monstrous army only to fall victim to the frigid weather. Beneath the woman, he found a bundle of rags, and within the rags, he found an infant – cold and hungry but still alive.

"Evers picked me up and wrapped his fur coat around me, holding me tight to his chest to keep me warm. He told the others to continue south in search of food while he returned to Old Kardis. He knew I was close to death, badly in need of warmth, shelter, and nourishment. Since his wife had recently given birth to Jacquinn and was still nursing her, he hoped I might survive if he could get me to her in time.

"Traveling alone, he made his way back to the chamber where they had taken shelter in the ruins. His wife, Polly, fed me and kept me warm. However, they realized that my legs were... malformed. They didn't know if I was born that way or if it was a result of my ordeal.

"Through some miracle, I survived, and they chose to raise me as their son. They named me Everson to honor the man who saved me."

Everson looked down in silence. Being the center of attention made him feel more self-conscious about his legs.

"Very well. That answers one question," the voice from beyond the light responded. "Continue on. We would hear the rest of your story. Tell us of your life, of the path taken that led you to Fallbrandt."

Everson imagined how Quinn would respond. *You don't need to do this, Ev. You owe them nothing.* He smiled at her stubbornness, her spirit. The thought gave him strength. *She is right, but I have nothing to hide. Besides, she needs me this time.*

He closed his eyes and cast his mind back, seeking the beginning.

"My first real memories come after my new family moved back to Cinti Mor, during the rebuilding of the city. King Ulric and his men guided the reconstruction, while ordinary citizens helped wherever they were best suited. Being a blacksmith, my father often found himself forging and constructing metal works for the city, often without commission. My mother was a cook for a local inn, working every day from mid-morning through dinner.

"During those early years, I hardly ventured outdoors. My... disability made moving about difficult. As a result, I focused on things like reading and numbers while other children spent their time playing games in the square. There were days when I would stare out the second-story window of my room and watch them run past. Hearing their laughter made me feel lonely...an outcast.

"If not for Quinn, I would truly be alone. She split her time between remaining indoors with me and playing with her friends, often a result of my insistence that she leave me to my own devices. While I cherished her company, I could not bear the guilt I felt when I would catch her glancing toward the window with longing in her eyes.

"And so, my sheltered existence continued until a non-descript autumn evening during my seventh year. My father returned home from his smithy with a gift for me, a gift that changed my life."

2

———

SMALL VICTORIES

E verson lay in his bed, resting on his stomach with a book spread out before him. Kneeling on the floor beside the bed, Jacquinn carefully stacked wooden blocks into a tower. She pulled a stray lock of honey-colored hair aside and tucked it behind her ear while her other hand placed a block atop the pillar. Each movement was smooth and precise, her blue eyes intense and focused.

The book Everson read from was among his favorites: *The Adventures of Jerrell Landish*. He had read it twice before, but never to Jacquinn.

"...but Jerrell knew that it could not be that easy. Exotic treasures such as this were not attainable for the unprepared...or for those who were foolish. He scanned the room, seeking hidden dangers in the dark recesses. A black millipede scuttled into a crack in the walls, seeking refuge from the torchlight. Wispy cobwebs fluttered at the breeze, appearing alive as they danced in a swaying motion. Broken bricks among the ruins lay in piles, surrounded by walls of natural stone in an odd convolution of man and nature.

"Finding nothing of note, Jerrell's gaze shifted toward the colored mosaic of tiles on the floor, arranged to form the image of a five-headed beast with gaping black eyes and long sharp fangs. Green and blue scales covered the monster's body, its long sinuous tale encircling the image..."

"Wait, Ev."

Everson turned from the book to look at his sister. "What is it, Quinn? I'm just getting to the best part."

She stared at him with her face twisted while holding a wooden block in her hand. "What's that last word you said? Sinnus or something?"

"Sinuous?"

"What does it mean?"

"Mother told me that it means long and curvy…like a snake."

Quinn tilted her head and squinted. "So it's some sort of five-headed snake monster?"

"Well, it's a *picture* of a five-headed snake monster, but on the floor."

She nodded and carefully placed the block atop the tower. Her eyes glimmered with anticipation when the column wobbled. A grin formed when it did not collapse.

Everson turned back to his book, scanning it in search of where he left off. As he moved his finger down the page, the shadow it cast from the light of the glowlamp followed, as did the softer shadow cast from the dying light coming through the window.

"Jerrell was clever, and he knew that the Tantarri created clever traps to prevent others from stealing their treasures. Inspired by his intuition, he pulled his coin purse out and tossed it onto the tiles. Ten tongues of angry fire burst up from the eyes of the monster, creating a wall of flame that forced Jerrell to back away from the heat."

The sound of the front door opening drew Everson's attention. He looked toward the open door of his and Quinn's bedroom, and he listened.

"This is the city watch," his father's deep voice boomed. "I heard that a pair of rascals have been terrorizing this house."

Quinn squealed, stood, and scrambled from the room with her long golden hair trailing behind. Everson slid off the bed and pulled himself across the wooden floor, sliding past Quinn's wobbling tower as the rapid stomp of her footsteps descended the stairs.

"Father!" Quinn whooped as Everson dragged himself through the doorway. When he reached the railing, he peered down to see Quinn jump into their father's arms and give him an enthusiastic hug.

"Did you have a good day at work today, Father?" Quinn asked.

Everson slid over to the stairs and began easing himself down.

"It was a bit quiet at the smithy, so I worked on something special."

"Really? Is it anything for me?"

Everson stopped in mid-descent and pressed his face against the rails, watching for his father's response. The big man grinned and flashed white teeth from within the thick curls of his blond-streaked brown beard. While holding Quinn in one arm, he reached into a sack resting on the table, nestled beside a glowlamp that bathed the room in pale blue light. Clinking and clanking sounds rang from inside the sack, and his hand emerged with a figure fashioned from metal. Quinn's eyes lit up as he handed her a small statue of a female warrior, armed with a sword and shield.

"She's amazing," Quinn said with awe in her voice. "Thank you so much, Father!" She hugged him and kissed his cheek, rubbing her nose when she pulled away – a result of the tickle from his beard.

Everson resumed his descent, his backside touching each step for a moment before he slid to the next one. When he reached the bottom, Evers put the girl down and turned toward his son.

"And who is this rascal?"

"Hello, Father." Everson smiled as he pulled himself over to the man. "Do you have anything for me?"

Massive hands with fingers like sausages gripped Everson beneath his arms and hoisted him up. His Father smelt of the smithy, with fumes from the forge and melted metal embedded in his clothing and his beard. Everson wrapped his arms about the man and squeezed.

"I happen to have something that might be of interest to you."

The big man reached into the sack and lifted a series of metal rings bent into various shapes, all interwoven into a jumbled mess.

Everson's eyes lit up, his mouth forming a big *O*. "A new puzzle!"

He accepted the puzzle, examining it, his eyes following the interwoven sections and calculating which pieces fit over which as he decided on where to start.

"I spent more time creating this one. I hope it takes you a bit longer to solve it."

The man set him on the floor, but with his attention focused on the puzzle, Everson didn't even notice. He gripped a triangle piece and lifted it so he could slide a circular ring around it and onto a rod bent in the shape of a figure eight.

The front door opened, and a woman with brown hair tied in a bun stepped into the room.

"Mama!" Quinn ran over to her mother, holding the metal statue toward her. "Look what Father made for me. Isn't she lovely?"

The woman smiled and kissed her daughter's head. "Yes. She will fit in nicely with the others."

"Hi, Polly." Evers took two big steps toward her and bent to give her a kiss. He then peeked into the sack in her arms. "What's for dinner?"

"I brought some leftover stew from the kitchen and purchased a loaf of bread on the way home." She crossed the room and placed her sack on the table, pulling a black kettle from it before walking the kettle over to the fireplace. "I need a little time to heat the stew up and then we can eat."

Polly grabbed some birch bark from the barrel beside the fireplace and used the fire iron to stir the coals until live embers appeared. She bent and blew on the coals, the glow growing brighter until a flame blossomed, its orange tongue licking the birch until it, too, caught fire. Grabbing two chunks of wood from the barrel, she slid the wood beneath the kettle as the bark crackled and curled, the flames soon spreading to the logs.

During the entire exchange, Everson remained focused on the puzzle, working out the possible angles and dimensions for each piece. He slid the ring around the last bend, lifting, twisting and pulling on the rails that contained it. The ring came free and he whooped at the accomplishment.

"What?" his father exclaimed. "I spent days making that thing, and you solved it in two minutes." The man moved closer and rested his meaty fists on his hips. "What am I to do with you?"

Everson laughed as he stared up at the man towering above him. "I don't know. I just like puzzles." He shrugged. "I like things that make me think."

The man grunted and reached into his sack, pulling out more creations made of metal. Leather straps dangled from the things, binding them together into two sets, open at the front. He knelt down and met Everson's gaze.

"I made something for you, Son. I think...I hope it will help you stand."

Everson stared at the metal bars, leather straps, and buckles in his father's hands. "Really?"

"They are braces for your legs. This part straps to your thighs, while this other part goes on your lower leg. They should keep your knees straight. Do you want to try them?"

Everson looked into his father's eyes and found deep blue pools of compassion, hope stirring the waters. He bit his lip and gave the man a nod.

Gentle hands lifted his leg and slid the brace beneath. His father buckled straps across Everson's scrawny thighs and around his lower leg. Upon closer inspection, Everson determined that the metal bars joining the straps together were intended to prevent his knees from bending. When the man was finished, he gripped Everson beneath the arms and lifted him.

"Stand with your feet spread apart."

The boy spread his legs as the man put him down. His father gripped his hands to hold him steady for a moment, and then...he let go.

Everson's heart hammered in his chest, his breathing coming in rapid gasps. He wobbled and shook, but he did not fall. He looked up and found his mother and father staring at him, Polly with her hands covering her mouth, Evers kneading his thick hands in anxiety. Tears tracked down Polly's face. Evers wiped his eyes and chuckled.

"You did it, Ev. You're standing!"

Hearing Quinn's voice, he turned and gave her a grin. When he tried to move a leg to step toward her, his body twisted and collapsed, sending him crashing to the floor.

"Oh, my!" Polly shrieked and ran over to him. "Are you all right?"

"I'm fine, Mama." He grinned, sitting upright. "I did it. I can stand."

"It looks like I need to make something so you can steady yourself," his father rubbed his chin in thought. "Standing is only the first part. When I'm finished, you will walk, Son."

It was a beautiful spring day on the eve of Everson's eighth summer when he first left his house under his own power. He blinked at the bright sunlight hovering in the pale blue sky. Water dripped from the eve above him and landed on his forehead before trickling down his face – a remnant of a snowfall that occurred just a week prior. Sometimes winter didn't know when to give up.

"Come on, Ev," Quinn waved him forward. "I want you to meet the others."

She weaved her way through the puddles dotting the street, her long blond mane bouncing as she skipped. Everson gripped his canes and pushed himself forward, dropping down the single step to the street. Moving his canes simultaneously, he launched himself forward, two feet at a time, swinging his legs with each step. A winter of indoor practice had strengthened his arms and torso, enabling him to move at a moderate pace. The thudding of his canes striking the cobblestones echoed off the surrounding homes, tall and narrow and tightly nested together.

He reached Quinn as she turned the corner onto a wider street, busy with foot traffic. Everson stopped and watched the people passing by – half of whom were too busy to pay him any attention. The other half stared with raised brows. His breathing grew rapid and his heart began to race. Strangers made him nervous. His braces and canes made him feel self-conscious. *So many people…*

He suddenly realized that Quinn was fading into the crowd, and he hurried to catch her. The thought of being on the street alone terrified him.

The girl weaseled her way down the street, slipping through gaps barely wide enough to see past. Unfortunately, Everson required a wider path, forcing him to wait until one opened or to circumvent the crowd entirely.

When he approached the end of the street, he found that it led to a large square with a fountain at the center. Quinn was already beside the fountain, talking to a group of kids – those who were too young to start school but old enough to be out on their own. All but two stood taller than Quinn.

The thought of meeting other children made Everson nervous. They might be kids, but they were still strangers. He had been so excited to venture outside, he had not considered what it meant. Stopping, he leaned into his canes and watched them from across the square, experiencing a pang of loneliness as they talked and laughed with one another. Four boys sat chatting on the low wall that surrounded the fountain, while three girls and another boy stood in a circle as they listened to Quinn.

Deciding that he had better cross the square and meet them before Quinn forced him to do it, Everson gathered his courage. Once Quinn's mind was set, there was no getting out of it. With a sigh, he set off to do just that.

A boy seated on the fountain wall noticed him approaching. The boy nudged the boy beside him and whispered in his ear while pointing toward Everson. It only took a moment before they had all turned toward him – everyone except for Quinn. As Everson drew near, he heard her talking.

"…play *A King and His Court*. My brother can join us, making two teams of five."

She noticed everyone staring and turned around. A smile crossed her face.

"This is my brother, Everson."

Standing beside Quinn was the prettiest girl Everson had ever seen.

A smattering of freckles dotted her button nose, while her green eyes sparkled in the mid-day sun. With brown auburn curls that framed a pale face, the girl flashed a smile, and he thought his heart might burst.

Quinn put her hand on the girl's shoulder. "This is Rena."

Rena. The name rang within Everson's head as Quinn continued to introduce the others.

One of the boys on the fountain wall stood, rising to a height a full head taller than Quinn. The boy had unkempt auburn hair and freckles. Everson decided that the boy must be a year or two older. Yet, despite being born during Empire rule, no rune marked his forehead. The boy glared at Everson as his lip twisted in a sneer.

"What is this? I thought you wanted to play *A King and His Court*, not *A Cripple and His Court*."

Everson's hopes faded.

Quinn stepped closer to the boy. "Be nice, Torney. Everson might have to use canes, but he's kind and he's smart. Super smart. He already reads books and know lots of stuff – stuff you won't learn until you start school."

"Who cares? It just makes him an even bigger freak." The boy pointed past Everson. "Why don't you crawl on back home? You won't be able to play anything we play anyway."

Everson's gaze shifted to Quinn, his eyes meeting hers. His lip began to tremble as tears blurred his vision. Quinn's expression grew hard, defiant. She turned toward the taller boy and thrust her finger against his chest.

"You take that back, Torney Jacobs. That's a mean thing to say, and my brother has done you no wrong."

Torney slapped her finger away and pushed her backward. "What are you going to do about it, you little runt? If you like him so much, *you* go play with the little disease."

To Everson's surprise, Quinn smiled. Torney's brow furrowed in confusion. He turned toward the boys still seated on the fountain wall and he shrugged. Quinn launched herself at the taller boy, driving her shoulder into his stomach and pushing him backward. His legs hit the fountain wall and he flipped over it. The splash of him striking the water caused the other three boys to scramble clear.

Torney flailed around in the fountain, gasping as he tried to get his feet beneath him. Eventually, he was able to stand, the water merely waist-deep. Quinn glared at him, and the other kids laughed as Torney's wet face gathered into a thundercloud.

"You're going to get it now, you little runt," Torney growled as he began to wade toward Quinn.

Quinn turned toward Everson and panic gripped him. He couldn't run to escape. If she fled, Torney would catch him. Watching Quinn's face, Everson saw her reach the same conclusion. Her grin fell away and her blue eyes seemed to turn the gray of steel, hardening.

Torney reached the water edge, and he lifted a waterlogged trouser leg over the wall. Before he could bring the other leg over, Quinn hit him.

The first punch struck the side of his jaw, knocking it open, leaving his eyes wide with surprise. The second punch hit his nose, and he raised his arms to defend himself, which left his middle exposed. He lifted his trailing leg from the water with his arms covering his face. Quinn lunged forward and kicked with all her might, connecting squarely with the boy's groin before his other foot touched the cobblestones. Torney cried out and doubled over as he collapsed to the ground. Curled up into a ball, the boy whimpered in pain, interrupted by a fit of coughing. Quinn stood over him with her fists on her hips, daring him to stand.

The other kids appeared in shock, their eyes bulging and mouths hanging open until Everson decided to intervene. He didn't want anyone to get hurt…at least not more than what had already happened.

"Quinn. Let's leave," he urged her. "We can come back and play another day."

When their eyes met, the fury on her face slid away, her expression softening.

With a nod, she said, "You're right. Let's go visit father at work instead." She glared down at Torney, who was still crying. Blood oozed from his nose, mixing with the spittle and tears on his face. "We'll be back tomorrow and if anyone tries to pick on my brother, I'll make them wish they hadn't."

Quinn turned and walked away with Everson following close behind.

The ring of a hammer on iron grew louder as Everson approached the building, its sound a guide to anyone seeking a smithy. Quinn gripped the handle on the large door and pulled hard. The sound of the hammer increased as the door slid open. Everson watched the metal wheels above the door with interest. The wheels squeaked as they rolled along a metal rail, protesting at the weight of the door suspended below them. Having only seen hinged doors in the past, he found the design intriguing and began imagining other uses for wheels on tracks to guide them. When the door was open wide enough, Quinn led him inside and he blinked, allowing his eyes to adjust to the dark interior.

A fireplace sat in the corner of the room, lit with the glow of hot coals. *That must be the forge.* On the wall beside the forge, tools dangled from a row of hooks – hammers of various sizes and shapes, clamps, tongs, punches, files, chisels, and more. Upon the bench below the tools, rested various smaller tools.

His father stood over an anvil mounted on a workbench made of stone, placed on the opposite side of the forge from the tools. The man was shirtless, and his hairy torso glistened with sweat. He wore leather gloves that covered his hands and forearms. One hand held a hammer while the other gripped a pair of metal tongs clamped about a sword, its blade blackened. When the man noticed them enter, he rested the hammer on the bench and removed the gloves.

Evers smiled at the children. "Have you rascals come to take over for me? I could certainly use a break."

"Silly. We can't use a hammer that big," Quinn replied with a grin.

The man grabbed a towel and wiped the sweat from his face, working it down his neck and torso.

"In that case, I need to find something else for you to do."

A question burning in the back of Everson's mind made its way to his mouth, passing his lips without him even realizing it.

"Why doesn't Torney have a rune?"

"Who?"

Quinn piped up. "Torney Jacobs."

Evers put his towel aside. "I see. Well, not everyone was marked with a rune back then. Some were…denied."

Everson's brow furrowed. "Why?"

Evers shrugged. "I'm not sure. You should know that those people were…treated poorly. They called them Unchosen." He sat on a stool and looked Everson in the eye. "Remember how I explained my rune?" He tapped the symbol etched in his own forehead, shaped much like the letter Y with two antennas poking up from it. "They call this rune *artifex altus*. It means high craftsman in the old language. From the time I was just a little boy, I knew that I was destined to be a smith, or a jeweler, or something similar. It gave my life definition and purpose but left me without the ability to pursue my own path. Quinn would have a mark today if not for the invasion, which occurred the day before her Choosing ceremony was to take place. You were born even later.

"When we returned to Cinti Mor and began to rebuild it, a new minister appeared, along with King Ulric. They informed the people that the Ministry was no longer, the Empire had been disbanded, and the Choosing ceremony was permanently abolished."

"Abolished?" Quinn repeated. "What's that mean?"

Evers smiled. "It means that they can never do it again. It also means that you children have the right to choose your own path in life, to follow your dreams, and to pursue a future that makes you happy."

"But what about these Unchosen? It seems like they would be…like pieces from another puzzle, pieces that don't fit into the old Empire ways."

His father nodded. "You see to the heart of the matter, Son. Empire law left them with nowhere to go in life. I may not have had much choice in my path, but at least I had a path."

"Is that why Torney can be so mean?"

"I don't know, Quinn. There are still many who treat Unchosen unfairly, but it becomes less so with each passing year." He shook his head. "If everyone you met was mean to you, you might become that way yourself. That or you might become shy and withdrawn."

Everson looked at Quinn, her eyes meeting his as she bit her lip. He suddenly felt guilty for what happened to Torney and suspected that she felt the same. Turning away from Quinn while avoiding looking at his father, he spotted a contraption leaning against the forge. It was as tall as Quinn, pie-shaped, and had two handles poking up from it.

"Is that the bellows?" Everson asked, pointing toward it.

"Sure is. I need to heat this blade again. Would you like to pump the bellows for me to make the fire hotter?"

Everson grinned. "Yes, Pa."

Donning his gloves, his father lifted the sword and carried it to the forge. The man propped a stool beside the fireplace and patted the seat. Everson sat on it and leaned his canes against the workbench to free his hands. His father grabbed the bellows and placed the end with the metal tube on the hearth before setting the handles on Everson's lap.

"I need you to pump hard. The faster you pump, the hotter the fire will grow." He raised the sword. "Mind you, it must be quite hot. The hotter the fire, the softer the metal."

Everson gripped the wooden handles, thick and solid. He lifted them and found the bellows heavier than anticipated, even with the other end resting on the hearth. When he squeezed it together, air wheezed from the far end and the coals grew brighter. He pulled the handles apart and heard the bellows taking a deep breath. Another hard squeeze caused the air to expel, and the coals glowed even brighter. The heat from the forge made Everson's eyes water, and he leaned away from it. His father plunged the blade into the coals and gave him a grin.

"You're doing it, Ev," Quinn said with an edge of excitement in her voice.

He turned to find her standing beside him with a proud smile – a reflection of what he felt inside. *This is what it's like to feel useful.* The feeling was sweeter than honey and tasted better than his mother's apple cobbler. He desperately wanted more.

3
____

A TASTE TO SAVOR

The glare of white light forced Everson to keep his head turned away. He swallowed hard, his throat dry, his armpits damp with sweat. Being held captive in a dark cell was unnerving at best. Terror threatened to overwhelm him but he fought it, stuffing it away for Quinn. With a deep breath, he forced himself to continue his tale.

"As spring continued," Everson told his captors, "I increasingly spent time with the other children, eager for their acceptance and finding that the interaction filled a void. When bored of playing games, we would find other means to entertain ourselves. There were times when our hijinks drew trouble, but none so bad as to draw ire from my parents. The moments that brought us closest to the edge were always led by Quinn, for dancing that line seemed to bring her pleasure."

Everson smiled inwardly as he thought of those simple days, filled with wonder and a sense of adventure that he had missed before the braces and canes.

"A month into this broadened existence, came *Libra Te*. For the first time, cause for celebrating independence was something I understood."

With every shop, inn, and cart closed for the day, the people of Cinti Mor had gathered with other thoughts in mind. Clustered within the city square, citizens of all ages waited in anticipation. Smiles and laughter were prevalent. It was a day to celebrate life and independence from Empire rule. For Everson, it held even more meaning.

In past years, Libra Te was among the few days where he ventured beyond the shelter of his home. Hoisted upon his father's shoulders, he always had a wonderful view – able to see over even the tallest of men. However, the day had always lacked something he had desired…until now.

Everson glanced back and saw his father's thick hair and beard above the crowd, his arm about Polly's shoulder. The man gave a nod and a smile, which Everson returned.

Shuffling forward, he followed Quinn through the crowd, keeping up as best he could. When the fountain came into view, he found Quinn standing on the fountain wall, beside the other children. As Everson drew near, he slowed and bit his lip. He wouldn't be able to see the platform that had been erected at the north end of the square – not unless he could join the others on the fountain wall.

Quinn turned toward him and jumped down. "Come on, you guys. Help me get Everson up on the wall."

Panic surfaced, coming in ragged breaths as Everson stared at the water. "I can't swim, Quinn."

She chuckled. "Don't worry. The water is only waist deep."

Colton and Dillon jumped down and sidled to opposite sides of Everson, each standing a head taller than him.

"Good." Quinn said. "When I count to three, you two lift him up. I'll put his feet on the wall while you hold him." She pointed a finger at each of them, her eyes turning a steely gray. "Don't you dare let go before I say so, or you'll wish you had listened."

Colton glanced at Dillon, their eyes wary.

Circling behind Everson, Quinn gave her commands. "Get ready. One, two, three. Lift!"

With a grunt from each boy, they hoisted Everson up. Quinn grabbed his ankles and placed his feet on the fountain wall. The boys pushed him up, almost overextending and sending him into the water before they could hold him steady. Everson positioned one cane atop the wall and turned toward the other. Once it was placed securely, he gave a nod and the two boys let go. After a slight wobble, he held steady.

While the boys returned to their vacated spots on the wall, Quinn climbed up beside Everson and smiled, eliciting the same reaction from him.

A girl's voice rang out from his other side. "You're doing great, Everson."

He turned to find a bright smile framed by auburn curls. Large green eyes – appearing like precious gems in the afternoon sunlight – stared back at him. Any sense of confidence gained by his success of standing upon the wall faded in a blink. He wobbled, stumbled, and only stayed upright because the two girls reacted, each gripping an arm. Damaged pride aside, Everson was glad for it. Somehow, he choked out a response.

"Thank you, Rena…Quinn."

"There he is!" Torney exclaimed.

Everson turned toward where the boy pointed and saw a tall man – no more than thirty summers of age – being escorted through the crowd. With dirty blond hair that curled at his neckline and a trimmed beard to match, Everson would have been able to identify the man even without the crown upon his head or the regal cloak about his shoulders.

"King Ulric," Everson whispered.

Two guards dressed in plated leather armor, marked with blue and gold stripes, led the man up the stairs to the temporary platform. The guards spread out, each positioned at a front corner of the platform as the king strode to the heart of the dais with hands raised. The crowd quieted and he lowered them.

"Greetings, citizens of Cinti Mor. Another year has passed – a year of prosperity and growth. I'm not much for words, never have been. Therefore, I will keep this brief."

Glancing about, Everson estimated a thousand people occupied the square – a mere fraction of the city's population before it had been destroyed. He recalled his father telling him that the first Libra Te in Cinti Mor had a crowd of less than two hundred. His gaze returned to King Ulric, the man's fur-trimmed golden cloak and blue tunic appearing bright in the afternoon sun.

"We gather today to celebrate life and freedom. Despite the dark army that ravaged our city and others eight years past, we have rebuilt and will continue on…living our lives. No longer under the thumb of the Empire, oppression has been replaced by independence, commerce, and a realization that people matter…every one of you.

"As in years past, the crown has provided a feast for all to share." He gestured to his left, toward the grills and swirling smoke above them. "To this side, you will find grilled fish, freshly caught just yesterday." He gestured to his right, toward butchers with smocks covered in grease, knives held ready, and tables before them with cuts of meat. "Here, we have roasted pigs – three of them. In addition, each local baker has donated two dozen loaves of bread. Farmers have added fresh vegetables. And, of course, we have three barrels of the finest Hurnish Ale, tapped and ready for consumption."

The crowd cheered at the mention of ale. Ulric waited for them to quiet and then waved his arm. "After the meal, the children are welcome to join in races and other games near the temple. For the adults, we will have musicians playing on the stage. I expect you to dance. If ever there is a day for dancing, this is it."

He grinned at the crowd. "What are you waiting for? Let's eat!" He pumped his fist in the air, and a cheer rose up, the thunder of it shaking Everson to his bones.

Everson sat at the table with the bright glowlamp beside him. His tongue wagged across his lips repeatedly as he concentrated on his drawing, tracing the image he saw in his head. Quinn sat across from him, playing with her metal statues. Apparently, her female warriors were battling The Horde, who had once again invaded the land. In this case, The Horde had taken on the shape of a ripe melon, which rolled about the table as she attacked it.

The front door opened, and both children turned to find their father entering the room. His face appeared weary, which was common when the weather grew hot. It was the heart of summer, when even Cinti Mor experienced hot sunny days, sticky with humidity.

"Hello, little rascals," he said.

"Hello, Father," Quinn replied.

A thud sounded and Everson turned to discover the melon on the floor with one side smashed in.

"Oops," Quinn said as she stared down at it.

Evers sighed. "We needed to eat it anyway. I have to wash up and change." He passed the table, and crossed to the open doorway below the stairs. "Please try to have this cleaned up before your mother gets home."

"Yes, Father."

While Quinn picked up the melon and went in search of a rag, Everson returned to his sketch. He finished it minutes later as his father emerged from the bedroom.

"What is that, Son?"

Butterflies tickled Everson's stomach as he slid the paper closer to the glowlamp so it would be easier to see. His father leaned over the drawing, examining it.

"Is that…a bellows?"

"Yes, Pa. I had an idea. It's been in my head for a while now. You know how you have to use both hands to pump the bellows?"

His father nodded. "Yes…"

"Well, with my idea, you don't have to do that." He tapped the paper. "The bellows is mounted on this thing and there is a lever connected to a cam that is connected to a foot pump…you know…like the one on your grinder."

The man's eyes narrowed. "So, I would pump my foot and the bellows would open and close?"

Everson grinned. "Yep. It will be way easier than using your arms, and it will keep your hands free for other stuff."

His father chuckled and patted Everson on the head. "That's a wonderful idea, Ev." He picked the paper up, staring at it. "Can I keep this?"

"Yep. I made it for you."

"Thank you, Son. I'll stop by the mill tomorrow and get some wood for the frame. It should only take me a few hours to build this. Stop by the smithy in the afternoon and you can see how it works."

⎯ ◈ ⎯

"Rena, you may take six baby steps," Everson bellowed.

"Captain, may I?" Her voice rang out from behind him.

"Yes, you may."

He heard her count off six steps, the image of her position clear in his mind as he faced the fountain. In his mind's eye, he pictured Rena now in the lead – a step ahead of Quinn, two ahead of Frieda, Lark, and Norry, and three ahead of Torney, Colton, Dillon, and Travis. *I need to let somebody beside Rena win this time*, he thought. *If not, they'll never let me be captain.*

"Colton, you may take three regular steps."

"Captain, may I?"

"Yes, you may."

The boy counted off three steps. Everson's mental image adjusted, placing the boy in the lead and just two strides from the fountain. Inspiration struck. He knew who should win this time.

"Torney, you may take three giant steps."

"Captain, may I?"

Everson heard the anticipation in his voice.

"Yes, you may."

"One…two…three." Torney slapped his hand down on the fountain wall. "I win. I'm captain!"

Releasing his grip on the fountain wall, Everson grabbed his canes and turned about to find the other kids standing exactly where he expected.

"I was so close, too," Colton complained.

"I need to go," Rena announced. "I'm to be back home for lunch."

Norry nodded. "Me too."

"Yeah. We should go."

"But I just became captain," Torney complained. "And today is my last day before I go to school."

"We can meet here later and play again," Quinn suggested.

"Yep."

"I can come back later."

"Me, too."

"See, Torney." The tall boy flinched as Quinn patted him on the shoulder. "You can be captain for the first game after lunch."

Torney's eyes appeared doubtful as he shrugged. "Now that you mention it, I *am* hungry. I guess I will see you guys after lunch, then."

The kids scattered, each heading a different direction, leaving Everson alone with Quinn. She turned toward him.

"We should run to the inn and eat."

"Can we stop by the smithy first? I want to see how the…how father's work is coming."

Quinn smiled. "You want to see if he built your invention, don't you?"

A guilty grin crossed his face. "Um…I guess."

She laughed. "Fine. Let's go. It's only a few blocks out of the way, anyhow."

The two children crossed the square and melted into the foot traffic. Men and women with carts lined the sides of the square, while people crowded around the carts to inspect and purchase the wares for sale. To avoid the crowd, Quinn circled around and slipped through the gap between a cart and the wall. Everson followed, finding the narrow space difficult to navigate with his canes. A woman with scraggly hair appeared to block his path.

"Hello, boy. I see that you've got sump'in wrong with your legs. What happened to ya?"

Everson did not reply. His tongue wouldn't allow it. She bent down, lowering her face until it was even with his. Panic gripped him as he stared at her bloodshot eyes and the toothless gaps in her terrifying grin. The rancid smell of her breath made him hold his.

"What's a matter, boy? You mute or dumb or sump'in?"

His eyes darted about, seeking a way to escape but the woman had him cornered. He tried to back up, but his cane got stuck in the spokes of a wheel. It felt as if his lungs might burst.

"Leave him be!"

The woman stood upright and turned to find Quinn standing behind her.

"And who might you be?"

"I'm his sister."

"What's wrong with him?"

"There's nothing wrong with him. He's super smart. Way smarter than a hag like you."

The woman's ruddy face became a darker shade. "Maybe I should teach ya' how to speak to your elders."

Raw defiance flared on Quinn's face. "You touch me, and you'll regret it." She glared at the woman, who glared back in return. "Come on, Ev. Let's go to the smithy. It smells better there."

Seeing the opening, Everson hurriedly slipped past Quinn as she stared daggers at the woman. A moment later, she caught up to him. He turned toward her and she smiled. His anxiety slid away, replaced by her confidence and strength.

"Thanks."

"She's a nasty woman. Don't listen to her. She doesn't know anything."

A grateful smile crossed his face. "Thanks, again."

Without a word, she hurried forward, turned the corner and made her way to the smithy door. By the time he reached it, she had it slid open enough for him to enter.

Evers turned toward the door and smiled when his children entered. He put down the kettle in his hands and shed his gloves.

"I was hoping you would stop by soon. I finished it about an hour ago and ate a quick meal so I would be here when you showed up."

Everson didn't respond. He shuffled toward the contraption that held his attention. It was as if his imagination had solidified into something tangible. He stopped before it and leaned a cane beside a workbench as he reached out and gripped the frame his father had built. Oddly, he found the cool wood against his palm surprising. A part of him had wondered if it was real or some sort of dream. Something he had invented in his mind was now a thing – a thing that was useful.

"Do you want to see how it works?"

Everson turned toward his father and nodded.

"Quinn, would you please give the foot peddle a few pumps?"

"Me? Oh, yes!"

She hurried over and put her foot on the wooden foot peddle, her shoe appearing tiny on something made for their father's feet. With a grunt, she pushed the peddle down and the bellows opened. When the peddle raised up, the bellows huffed a stream of air into the forge, waking the sleeping coals. Everson grinned. Quinn laughed. She pumped it again and again, gaining momentum as the heat flared within the forge.

"It works just like you said, Son." Evers put a hand on Everson's shoulder. "Wait until I present this to the guild. I have calculated the cost of materials, and I plan to start taking orders at the next meeting."

"What?" Everson turned toward his father. "You're going to sell this?"

The man laughed. "Yes. An invention like this is worth something. It'll make smithing easier and forging faster. People will pay for that. You just watch and see."

"Does that mean you could make these and sell them in other cities?" Quinn asked.

The man shrugged. "I don't see why not. I'm not much for traveling, but I bet I can find a trader who will buy them and sell them elsewhere at a profit." He squeezed Everson's shoulder. "Just think, Ev. An invention created by an eight year-old being used throughout the kingdoms of Issalia."

"The idea that something I had created might be used by blacksmiths everywhere awakened something inside me. Despite my..." Everson's gaze flicked down to his gnarled legs, "challenges, I found a sense of purpose – a sense of self-value that I had never known before. I realized for the first time that I could be more than a burden to others."

A tear tracked down his cheek and he turned away from the light. He thought of Quinn, seeking her strength to fuel him as he continued his story.

"My daily life rounded out after that. Quinn and I spent our mornings with friends. Torney and Travis joined the older kids at school in the temple, while a boy named Hillis and a girl named Bari joined our group. The next year, Rena, Norry, and Colton left the group to attend school, and again, new kids joined our group to take the place of those who had left us. It was a wonderful time, filled with precious memories."

Everson smiled as he thought about those years, when everything was simple, new, and exciting. Sometimes when he looked at Quinn, he caught glimpses of the girl she used to be – effervescent, enthusiastic, and bold. Turning toward the light, Everson resumed his telling.

"In the afternoon, Quinn and I would visit our father at the smithy. He taught us to heat and shape metal, to file, punch, grind, and cast it. With the money earned from selling the foot-powered bellows, he would purchase extra raw materials for us to shape metal into something new.

"The first few works that Quinn and I created were rough, clumpy messes. With time, our skill increased as our understanding of the process expanded. Within a year, Quinn was creating her own figures of warriors and placing them on the shelf beside those created by our father. At the same time, I created a series of my own puzzles and set my father to the task of solving them.

"The joy of creating puzzles soon faded. While interesting, those creations lacked that satisfaction I had tasted with the foot-powered bellows. As a result, I set my mind to building a better *something*. I just needed to decide what that something was.

"An afternoon visit to my mother at the Foxtail Inn stoked the embers of an idea for my next invention.

"While watching her use a whisk to beat eggs into a batter, I noticed how hard she worked. I then made it a goal to make the task easier. For days and days, I drew sketches and tweaked my designs until I had something I believed I could produce. Over the next eight weeks, I created castings for a large gear and two small gears. Then I shaped narrow steel rods into a crank, two heavy whisks, and a body with a wooden knob at the top. When I assembled the shaped rods and the gears, I had created a blending tool that caused the whisks to spin when the crank handle was turned.

"I created a half-dozen other inventions over the next year, with varying degrees of success. When I reached the end of my tenth summer, my life changed again."

4

PITY

Despite the early hour, the sun was hot, the air sticky. Everson stopped in the middle of the street and leaned against his new, longer canes – the result of a recent growth spurt. His father had wrapped rabbit fur about the handles, making them more comfortable to grip than the previous set. Those canes had served him well, lasting him nearly three years.

He stared at the building that would become his home away from home for the next six years. The sight stirred a distant memory, one of his father carrying him into the temple, of his mother pleading with the ecclesiast to help her son. Everson remembered the heat of the woman's palm when she placed it on his forehead, recalled the somber look in her eyes when she opened them and shook her head. His mother had thanked the woman and wiped the tears from her eyes.

"Please don't be sad, Mama," little Everson had said, not under-standing why she was crying.

She smiled at him and cupped his cheek. "I'm not sad, dear. I'm crying because I love you so much."

He frowned, not understanding why loving him would make her cry. His father kissed him atop the head and carried him out of the building while little four-year-old Quinn trailed behind him.

As his reverie faded, Everson turned toward Quinn and found her staring at him.

"Are you all right?" she asked.

He shrugged. "I'm fine. Let's go in."

She led him up the stairs, waiting at the top as he methodically lifted his dead legs from step to step. When he reached the landing, she opened the door and he scooted past her, into the dark building.

Everson moved forward, past the entry and into the interior of the temple. A vaulted ceiling stood high overhead as colored light filtered through arched stained-glass windows. Row upon row of benches filled the room, all facing the glowstone altar upon the dais at the front. A black banner covered the far wall, marked by a circular symbol intersected by an eight-pointed starburst. The circular symbol was sewn in blue, the starburst a bright red.

A sign marked *classroom* graced a door to the side of the room. Quinn led Everson toward the door, glancing at him with a grin as she opened it.

Conversation and laughter greeted them as young voices filled the room, some of whom had undergone the change, some teetering on the edge. Rows of tables and chairs stood to each side, occupied by boys and girls ranging from ten to sixteen summers. Everson took a deep breath and led Quinn down the aisle, seeing unfamiliar faces mixed with ones he knew.

"Hi, Everson," Dillon said as he passed by.

Everson gave him a nod in return. He swallowed hard at seeing her turn toward him, the girl appearing more beautiful than ever.

"Hi, Rena," Everson's voice croaked.

"Hello, Ev, Quinn," Rena chimed as they passed her.

He then spotted Torney Jacobs, sitting with two older boys whom Everson didn't know. It had been two years since he last saw Torney. In that time, the boy had grown significantly, which left his body long and lanky as the growth of his limbs outpaced the rest of him. The boys seated beside him were of a similar height, one thinner and the other heavier than Torney.

When Torney spotted him, he pointed and said something to the other two boys, causing a fit of laughter among them. Everson turned toward Quinn and found her face clouded over, her eyes gone gray. Hoping to avoid trouble during his first day of school, he intervened.

"Hey, Quinn," she turned toward him as he used his cane to point toward a table in the front row. "Those two seats appear to be open."

Without waiting, he shimmied down the narrow row and sat in the farthest chair, his rear dropping down into it with a thump. Quinn took the chair beside him as a middle-aged woman dressed in a purple cloak entered the room, trailed by a woman and man, both of whom were far younger. The older woman's dirty blond hair – marked with a single streak of gray – was tied back in a bun. Age lines marked the corners of her blue eyes and a circular symbol marked her forehead – a mark Everson knew as the rune of Issal. He recalled the memory of his childhood visit to the temple and decided that she was the woman his parents had met.

The woman was a little shorter than the younger female instructor and nearly a full head shorter than the man, who stood tall with a thin frame, brown hair, and green eyes. His female counterpart also had brown hair and green, albeit much larger, eyes. Both were dressed in dark clothing and black cloaks.

"Everyone take your seats," the older woman commanded in a firm voice.

She stopped at the fore of the room and waited while the students shuffled about, causing a ruckus as chairs slid across the stone tiles. When they had settled into place, the woman shared an inviting smile and gave them a nod of approval.

"Welcome, students. I'm Master Lomisse. The two instructors beside me are Pastor Birch" she gestured toward the woman, pausing before she turned toward the man, "and Pastor Dardis."

"I hope everyone had a good break. I know how fast it passes." She clapped her hands together and smiled. "Let's begin our school year by meeting our new students.

"I'd like each new student to stand and tell the class your name and a little about yourself."

She pointed at Quinn. "Young miss, would you please begin?"

Quinn stood, turning toward the class. "My name is Jacquinn Gulagas, but everyone calls me Quinn. My father is a blacksmith and my mother cooks for the Foxtail Inn."

"Thank you, Quinn."

As Quinn sat down, the woman turned toward Everson. "What about you young man?"

Everson's pulse throbbed in his temple as his stomach twisted. Everyone was looking his direction. He gripped his canes and pushed himself up to stand, wobbling a bit as he got his feet beneath him.

"My…" he coughed, finding his throat dry. A smattering a laugher dotted the room, making him feel even more self-conscious. "My name is Everson. I'm Quinn's brother."

The woman raised one eyebrow. "Are you twins? You don't look it."

He shook his head. "No ma'am. My…birth parents died when The Horde took Cinti Mor. I was adopted by Quinn's family."

"Pity."

Everson turned toward the voice. "What?"

Torney shrugged. "They took you in because they pitied you is all. Why else do it?"

Quinn bristled. "Everson is part of my family, Torney. We love him."

"If you say so."

"That will be enough," Master Lomisse scolded.

As she moved on and had the next student stand to introduce himself, Everson plopped down into his chair. He had hoped that he would find himself welcome at the school, but Torney wouldn't have it. Everson feared that the old bully had returned.

Later that evening, Everson lay in his bed, thinking on where things had gone wrong. His side was sore, his chest bruised. He turned toward Quinn's bed and found her lying in the same position. With the way her eye had swollen shut, he couldn't tell if she was awake.

The door opened downstairs, and Everson held his breath, trying to discern if it were his mother or father. Footsteps crossed the room and began climbing the stairs. The small tap of each step made it clear. His mother was home. Master Lomisse had, indeed, notified her as she promised she would. He swallowed hard, anticipating the worst.

Polly stepped through the door and crossed her arms over her chest. Quinn sat up, and Polly's demeanor softened when she saw the girl's face.

"Oh, my." Her concern for her daughter was apparent by the look in her eyes. "I heard you were in a fight. Are you all right, Quinn?"

Quinn grinned. "This is nothing. You should see the boys who started it."

Polly arched a brow toward Everson, who shrugged. He pushed himself up, grunting and gritting his teeth at the soreness in his torso. His mother sat on his bed and patted the spot beside her.

"Get over here."

Quinn stood and crossed the room to join Everson. The anger he had feared seemed to have fled from her voice, now replaced by a worry that matched her expression. When Quinn settled beside her, she made the request that he was expecting.

"Tell me what happened."

"It was Torney Jacobs, Mama," Quinn was animated as she spoke. "He was mean to Ev for no reason at all. It's like he wanted to be mean just to be mean."

Polly sighed. "Torney has...issues. His mother died during his birth, and his father...let's just say that Timothy Jacobs is not a nice man. I suspect that has had an effect on Torney. Your father and I try to teach you and your brother to have compassion, to be kind to people, and to be thoughtful of their feelings. I have a suspicion that Torney's father treats him badly, which teaches him nothing but do to the same to others."

"That makes sense, I guess," Quinn admitted. "But, it still isn't right."

Polly shook her head. "No. It certainly isn't right. I just thought it might help if you understood him better." She hugged Quinn and kissed her forehead. "Now, tell me what happened. I should know in case someone from the school comes hunting me down at work again."

"It started with me, Ma."

She turned toward Everson. "Okay. Speak up."

"When the day began, Master Lomisse had everyone take a simple reading test. I finished it before everyone else, and she put me into a group with the oldest kids. Quinn was grouped with the middle group, the same one as Torney even though he's two years older. Some of the others, the ones who couldn't read much, or at all, were placed into a third group.

"Things were fine for a while. I learned a few things and even found a new book to read, but then we broke for lunch.

"Quinn took my food and hers to a table to eat. As I was making my way to the table, Torney kicked one of my canes out, and I crashed to the floor. I landed on my side, and I hit so hard, I couldn't breathe. I rolled over and saw Torney laughing with his friends. Quinn ran over and asked if I was all right. She helped me sit up and noticed my cane across the room. *Did Torney do this*? She asked. I didn't respond, but she knew it anyway.

"Quinn turned toward him, and she grabbed his hair with both hands, pulled his head back, and slammed his face down into the table, right into his meat pie.

"The boy seated across from Torney jumped up and tackled Quinn, falling to the ground on top of her. Then Torney stood, his face appearing furious with a gash on his forehead and chunks of meat stuck to his cheek. He knelt beside Quinn and punched her in the face. I was afraid for Quinn, desperate to save her. So, I swung my cane at Torney's back. He cried out and turned toward me. I was so scared, I swung again and hit him upside the head."

Everson's eyes were downcast. "The crack I heard when the cane struck him sounded horrible. Torney's eyes rolled up and he tipped over like a lumberjack felling a tree. He just lay there, not moving – like he was sleeping or something.

"The next thing I knew, Quinn was on top of the other boy, hitting him in the face over and over and over.

"That's when Pastor Birch ran in and pulled Quinn off the boy. Master Lomisse appeared, and she knelt beside Torney. The woman placed her hand on his cheek and closed her eyes. I watched in confusion until the cut on his forehead suddenly closed – all on its own! Torney's body shivered, and he gasped for air, opening his eyes as if waking from a dream. I saw it, Mama. She healed him right before my eyes!"

Polly nodded. "Ecclesiasts can do that."

"That's amazing," Everson noted. "Anyway, Master Lomisse was super angry with us. She told us that we needed to leave, all four of us. We were told to come back tomorrow, and that she would seek out our parents to tell them what happened. If we get caught fighting again, she said we may be expelled."

Polly put an arm around each child, hugging them. "I'm glad neither of you was seriously hurt." She released her hug and looked at Quinn. "Although, you'll have a black eye for a few days."

Quinn grinned. "It's not as bad as the other kid. I gave him two black eyes, and a cut lip…maybe even a broken nose."

Polly chuckled. "While I don't condone the fighting, I'm glad you're looking out for your brother." She turned to Everson. "I'm proud of you for helping your sister, too. However, don't make it a habit to use your canes as weapons. They are meant to help you walk, not to hurt others."

"I know Mama. I didn't care much for how it felt to hit him anyway, even if he is a mean kid."

"Just remember what I told you about Torney and his family. Try to think about how *he* feels. Maybe you can find a way to help him be less mean."

"Yes, Ma'am."

"Okay, Mama,"

The door downstairs opened, closing hard. Everson gasped. His father was home early. Master Lomisse had spoken with him as well.

"You two stay here." Polly stood and walked to the door. "I'll deal with your father."

The door closed, muffling the sound of her footsteps treading down the stairs. Both children stared at the door for a long time, hopeful that they had dodged further trouble.

5

POWERED BY MAGIC

Master Lomisse paced in front of the classroom as she recited the tale. Everson and the other students listened closely, even the older children who had heard the story before. After all, the events described were the stuff of legends, but these legends were real history – history that had occurred only a decade past.

"Consisting of giant monsters whose horrible wails strike mind-numbing fear into the hearts of mere mortals, The Horde crushed every city in their path. The Kalimar province fell to them in a handful of days, Vinacci in a matter of weeks. They then turned their might upon Hurnsdom, taking Port Hurns before a winter storm struck the coast. The snow slowed The Horde, the cold killing a fair number of the monsters in the process. This enabled the Holy Army to catch them from behind as they attacked Cinti Mor. Taking the evil army by surprise, the paladins caused The Horde great damage and offered the city hope – hope that lasted only minutes. When the wails began, the Holy Army began to crumble. Worse, horde arcanists used fireballs and other magic to blast away sections of the city walls so the monsters could invade. Only a smattering of lucky citizens escaped before the city was lost."

Everson glanced at Quinn, who watched Master Lomisse in rapt attention. Her parents…his adopted parents were among those who had fled the city.

"With the Holy Army crushed, a handful of surviving paladins fled Hurnsdom with The Horde in pursuit. They headed southwest, toward the Tantarri Plains to join the armies of man, who had gathered to stop The Horde, or die trying.

"With fewer than a hundred inexperienced Paladin trainees, two hundred Tantarri warriors, and a handful of Holy Army survivors, this force was to face two thousand blood-thirsty giants in a struggle to save humanity. However, they had a secret weapon – an ancient magic that they were still learning to wield.

"In a contest of mind and magic versus raw might and sheer numbers, the human army faced The Horde on the Tantarri plains in a desperate gambit to save humanity from certain annihilation.

"With powerful magic on display, wielded by both sides, death and destruction dominated the battlefield throughout the night, leaving the plains scorched and blood-soaked. When all appeared hopeless for the human army, a flying machine appeared and rained fire upon The Horde, shifting the tide. This final onslaught broke the enemy, and the humans were able to rally and overwhelm the evil army.

"When dawn broke, thousands of dead monsters littered the plains. Some of these giants roam the countryside still, their corrupted hearts stalking the night in search of prey. So, if you venture beyond the walls of the city, beware the darkness, for that is when they feast upon the bodies of men, women, and children. For they care not who they kill…or who they eat."

An oppressive silence fell over the room, its weight palpable. Master Lomisse closed her eyes for a long moment, speaking again as she opened them.

"With the armies of man victorious, the Tantarri returned to their home while Empire forces marched west to Fallbrandt with the hope of a new beginning.

"The Empire was disbanded, and the kingdoms of old were reformed anew, each with its own government and own army to protect them. Under the Pretencia Accord, these kingdoms signed a treaty to act as an alliance, agreeing to honor political borders and free trade for the benefit of all.

"The Tantarri nation is now an ally of the other kingdoms, with free trade between them and us after years of enmity during the existence of the Empire.

"In addition, the Ministry is no longer. The church of Issal is once again what it was founded to be – the human conduit of Issal's teachings and mankind's guide to higher knowledge. This is why you children attend school. Armed with knowledge, your generation will be the catalysts for a better tomorrow. In addition, a select few of you will head to Fallbrandt during your seventeenth summer, where you will train to become warriors, engineers, healers, and magic users. Testing for those roles will take place during the end of your sixth year. Those who do not pass will be encouraged to apply for the trade apprenticeship of their choice."

The woman continued speaking for some time, discussing other changes that occurred during the founding of the kingdoms, but Everson stopped listening. He found himself intrigued by the concept of going to Fallbrandt. Of course, he had heard of the *Fallbrandt Academy of Magic and Engineering*. But, until now, he had never considered it something he could pursue. His dream to change the world with his inventions began to coalesce into something more. He now knew how to make it a reality.

With his mind still filled with thoughts of joining the wondrous academy, Master Lomisse dismissed them for the day.

Everson slid his books into his pack and slipped it over his shoulder. As he gripped his canes and pushed himself into a standing position, Quinn circled the table and approached Torney. A pang twisted Everson's stomach and he bit his lip in fear of what she might do.

"Hi, Torney," she said, causing the taller boy to turn toward her.

When Torney saw her, he flinched visibly, his eyes shifting nervously. "Oh, um…hi, Quinn."

"I'm sorry about what happened yesterday. I shouldn't have done what I did." She held her hand out. "Let's be friends…like we used to be."

He stared at her hand with a furrowed brow, his eyes shifting toward her face with a look filled with trepidation. Finally, he reached out and shook her hand.

"All right."

Quinn smiled. Everson mirrored her grin, feeling relieved.

Torney's eyes settled on Everson. "I'm…sorry, Ev."

Everson shuffled around the table. "Let's forget the past. I agree with Quinn." He stopped before the larger kid and held both canes in his left hand as he extended his right. "We should be friends."

Torney shook his hand and gave a hesitant grin.

Everson found himself hopeful. "Now that we are friends, maybe I can help you."

"With what?" Torney appeared doubtful.

"It seems that doing numbers and figures isn't that easy for you." Everson glanced toward Quinn before looking back at Torney. "It's nothing personal. We all have things that we do well, while there are other things that don't come so easy. For me, math is something that I do well. I'd like to share a few tricks that might make it easier for you."

The doubt melted from Torney's expression, replaced by a hopeful grin.

"I'd like that."

"Great. Let's go sit outside, and I'll show you the table I made for Quinn to help her memorize multiplication."

"All right, but only for a bit. If I'm not home before my pa, he'll get real mad."

As the last to leave the classroom, the three kids passed through temple, careful to remain quiet and not disturb those who prayed there. They stepped outside to find the afternoon sun behind a puffy white cloud. Everson plopped down on the top step and rested his canes beneath his legs before taking his pack off. Torney sat to one side of him, while Quinn sat to the other side.

Everson pulled his sketchbook from the pack and opened it to the first page, showing a handwritten grid filled with numbers. As he did so, the sun emerged from the cloud and shone brightly on the page.

"See the numbers on the left and across the top?"

Torney nodded.

"They…"

A buzzing sound arose, distracting Everson. He searched the southwest horizon for the source. The noise grew louder and a dark shape glided across the sky, briefly eclipsing the sun as it flew past.

Bleached hides stretched tautly across wings that must have been ten strides from tip to tip. A wooden frame held the wings together and secured them to the body of the flying machine. Everson spied a person in the cockpit, peddling wildly as ropes drove pulleys and gears in tight rotations, forcing the two propellers on the rear of the machine to spin furiously. In moments, the flying machine crossed the exposed sky and disappeared beyond the rooftops across the square.

Everson stared in the direction of the flyer, transfixed. It was the most beautiful thing he had ever seen. The buzzing sound faded in the distance as it headed toward the Citadel. "What was that?" Quinn asked.

"That was a Hedgewick Flyer," a woman said from behind them. "I'm afraid of what this means. The machines are used for only the most urgent of issues."

Everson turned to find Master Lomisse staring at the sky as he had. He squinted at her and found his curiosity unsatisfied.

"How does it work? How can they make it fly?"

After a quiet moment, the woman shrugged. "Those flyers come from Fallbrandt, but they didn't exist during my time there." She stared in the direction the flyer had gone. "I suspect that magic is somehow used to make them fly, but I don't know how it works. The magic I speak of… was unknown when I attended the school."

Everson turned back toward the Citadel, speechless in the firm grip of his wild imagination. Inventions powered by magic offered entirely new possibilities. He would surely meet his destiny in Fallbrandt.

6

UNRELENTING DETERMINATION

Quinn counted three shadows beyond the bright light in her cell. Her ears told her that three others stood behind her, one likely a girl based on the light tap of her footsteps. The room could not hold much more than that, regardless. Judging by their words, Everson was nearby. She hoped that they were treating him well. The thought of these people hurting him caused anger to flare within her, anger that she immediately stifled.

Rather than show the emotion, her face remained placid while she spoke. Dressed in only her shift, she ignored the cold and relayed her tale, hoping they wouldn't notice her fingers working the knots binding her wrists.

"It turned out that the flying machine was on its way to Fallbrandt with an urgent message that King Talvin of Vinacci was dead." Quinn recalled the moment she had heard the news…and the stories that followed. "There were numerous rumors in the streets regarding how the king had died – it was an assassin; he fell from a horse; he acquired an incurable disease; he had a bad heart; and a few others that were even more outlandish. I have always wondered what really happened to him."

As she finished her answer, the room fell still for a long moment, until the voice beyond the light broke the tension.

"That answers some of our questions." The man's voice sounded young, no more than thirty summers. "Tell us what brought you to Fallbrandt and of your interactions at the academy."

A frown passed her face as she considered the request. Inside, frustration seethed. She hated the situation in which they had placed her – ceding control in this manner. Thoughts of Everson returned. They were holding him captive and demanded her compliance. While she was uncertain if they would actually kill him, she had little choice...until she could free herself.

She sighed audibly, hopeful that they would read into it.

"By the end of our first year of school at the Cinti Mor temple, it had become obvious to others what I already knew. Ev has a unique mind...a mind that would be wasted anywhere but Fallbrandt. I am not as brilliant. School was not overly difficult for me, and I was an above-average student. However, to compare us is like comparing an ocean to a pond. Both are wet, but the latter is not nearly as impressive. Ponds are plentiful, while oceans are few.

"Knowing that my brother was destined to train as an engineer, I needed to find another means to be there with him...in case he needed me. As we neared the end of our last year at the temple, my anxiety increased.

"I felt hopeful when I was tested for my potential to wield magic, but sadly, hope was not enough. I was denied entrance to the academy where Everson was headed, and I feared I would be stuck in Cinti Mor, apprenticing with my father or some other craftsman in the city. That is, until I heard about the new school."

Quinn stared at the altar as her mind drifted, void of coherent thought. She felt calm in her resolve.

"Are you sure about this, Quinn?"

Everson's voice echoed in the temple, the building empty other than the two of them. She turned toward him with her lips pressed together.

"Okay. I know that look," he sighed. "I just hope you don't get hurt."

"Getting hurt happens when you fight." Quinn shrugged. "Avoiding pain isn't my goal. Winning is."

"You do know that this man is trained, right? He's been dueling for years, against opponents far more experienced than you."

"I know, but he wouldn't be here if untrained opponents didn't have a chance. Besides, I have something they don't have."

"What's that?"

"Unrelenting determination."

Everson chuckled. "Hard to disagree on that one."

Quinn stared into her brother's dark eyes and noticed a red-tinted ray of light shining on his disheveled dark hair, giving it an auburn hue. The classroom door opened and Master Lomisse patted Dillon on the shoulder as he exited. The boy stared at the floor, his eyes reflecting dejection. Things had gone poorly for him. Without a word, he headed toward the temple exit, his feet dragging as if heavy weights trailed behind them.

"Jacquinn." Master Lomisse announced. "You're next."

Quinn stood and her gaze shifted to Everson, his eyes showing concern. She patted him on the shoulder and walked toward the open door, past Lomisse, and into the room.

With the tables pushed to the walls and the chairs stacked atop them, the heart of the room stood open and empty – save for the man standing there.

Perhaps ten years her senior, the man had dark hair and a thin mustache to match it. With tawny skin and dark eyes, he had the swarthy look of a southerner, perhaps Kalimarian or Kantarian. He wore a sparring vest, leaving his muscular arms bare to the shoulders. Those arms were crossed against his chest as he watched Quinn cross the room to stand before him. She looked up at him, finding him a half-head taller. Of average height for a woman, Quinn had reached her full height during her thirteenth summer. Since then, her body had filled out a bit, yet remained lean and strong. Time spent in the smithy saw to that.

She heard the door close behind her, and the man gave her a shallow bow, which she returned.

"My name is Severs. I am here to test students who believe they have a future in the physical arts." His glare was intense, leaving Quinn feeling as if he were staring into her soul. "I understand that you wish to be tested."

Quinn nodded firmly. "Yes, Sir."

"Why do you pursue this path?"

"Truthfully, I wish to go to Fallbrandt because my brother is bound for the academy of magic and engineering. I do not possess his mind for inventions, so I must take my own path. I belong with him."

"Very well." The man gestured toward the wall to his left. Quinn's gaze followed and she found wooden staves, swords, and shields lying on a table. "You may choose any weapon."

The options offered spun in her head, but considering each, she knew she lacked training in any of them.

"May I duel without a weapon?"

"Yes. It is an unusual request, but it is allowed."

She flexed her fingers, loosening them as she turned toward Severs. "That is my choice."

"Very well. Prepare yourself."

Quinn pushed the sleeves of her tunic to her elbows and took a ready stance as her father had taught her.

"Let's begin."

He held his hands before him, left fist in front of the right. She adjusted herself to mirror his stance and met his eyes.

Severs jabbed at her face, and she dodged. He swung toward her midriff, and she swatted his hand aside. Suddenly, he attacked with a flurry of punches as Quinn blocked and dodged. One hit her stomach, and she bent with it. The next struck her forehead, and the world jolted as pain shot through her skull. She found herself on her hands and knees, blinking at the pain in her head.

"You do not have to continue if you are hurt."

Rising to her feet, she smiled at Severs. "You can quit if you're scared."

He frowned and lifted his fists into a ready position. Quinn edged closer to him and waited until he lunged forward. She ducked beneath the blow and punched hard. When her fist struck his groin, he grunted and doubled over. Quinn grabbed his shirt and pulled herself up as fast as possible, slamming the top of her head into his face.

She stumbled backward, wincing at the pain as the world tilted and stars invaded the edges of her vision. Blinking, her focus returned to find blood oozing from Severs' nose. He wiped his face with the back of his arm and stared at the bloody streak in surprise.

Quinn raised her fists again and smiled, "You do not have to continue if you are hurt."

The man grimaced and raised his fists, edging toward her more carefully this time. He jabbed. She dodged. He jabbed again, but she knocked it away and threw a punch of her own. Lightning quick, Severs grabbed her wrist, twisted, and threw her over his shoulder. Quinn landed hard on her back and quickly rolled over twice to create space. Despite the pain, she stood and he attacked. His foot struck her stomach and she clutched it. A fist to her cheek followed, and she spun a full circle before landing on her rear. The metallic taste of blood filled her mouth, and she spit crimson liquid onto the floor. She worked her jaw. It clicked each time she moved it and sent spikes of pain into her throbbing head.

"We can stop if you are hurt," the man panted.

Stumbling, she rose to her feet although the room wobbled and spun this way and that. She spit blood again and grinned.

"You can quit if you're scared."

He frowned, his face blood-streaked from the nose to his chin. Blood splatter dotted his sparring vest, now in serious need of a wash.

With a shake of his head, Severs raised both fists and eased toward her. The left side of Quinn's face had gone numb, and her vision blurred on that side. She realized that her left eye was swelling shut and tilted her head to the left so her right eye could focus on her target as she edged toward him.

Quinn faked a high strike and the man reacted to block it. Ducking, she lunged toward his legs and grabbed them, lifting as she continued to drive forward. Despite his heavier frame, she lifted him off his feet and drove him to the floor. He hit the stone tiles with a grunt, but reacted by wrapping his legs about her neck. Pressure built in her throbbing head as he squeezed tightly. She tried to push his legs apart, but found them immovable. The edges of her vision began to blacken, forming a tunnel as she struggled for air. With a narrow view, she saw only the man's thigh directly in front of her face, so she bit him. Hard. Severs cried out in pain, and his grip eased enough for Quinn to slide her head free. As she gasped for air, she hit him in the kidney three times before he rolled away.

They both stood and faced each other with Quinn swaying as she heaved deep breaths, the vision in her right eye slowly returning while the left remained swollen. He touched the back of his head with one hand and it came away bloody. The man's eyes narrowed as he stared at her. She grinned in reply.

"That's enough."

Quinn turned toward the voice and found Lomisse approaching.

"If you two keep this up, you'll end up doing something that I can't heal."

"The girl bit me. She bit me! Who does that in a duel?"

"You didn't say I wasn't allowed to bite."

A frown crossed his face. Lomisse chuckled as she put her hand on Quinn's forearm.

"She has a point, Severs."

The woman closed her eyes and all fell still. Quinn's chest contracted, and a shock of cold wracked her body, creating a violent shiver that drove the air from her lungs. As warmth returned, Quinn's lungs regained their function and she gasped. Her stomach growled noisily, demanding food. She ignored it as she realized that her head, face, and back no longer hurt. When she worked her jaw, the clicking sound was gone.

Lomisse moved to Severs and performed the same process. The man's eyes grew wide and he gasped for air before nodding to her.

"Thank you, Master Lomisse."

"You are welcome, Master Severs."

The man turned toward Quinn, frowning again.

"Clearly, you are untrained in combat. In fact, you fight dirty."

Quinn shrugged. "Unless there are rules, I'll do whatever it takes."

Severs snorted. "That much is apparent."

He turned from her and crossed the room before taking a drink from a tall mug waiting on the table. When he finished his drink, he pointed toward the door.

"You are dismissed."

Quinn frowned at Lomisse, her confidence waning. "I don't understand. Did I pass?"

Quinn gripped the handle and the wheels at the top squeaked noisily as the door slid open. She scurried into the smithy as Everson trailed behind.

Bright orange sparks flared into the air, fading as they fell in a trail created by the knife blade pressed against the grinding wheel. Her father glanced up and stared at her through the odd spectacles he wore while grinding metal. The man pulled the blade from the wheel and ceased pumping the pedal. As the wheel lost momentum, Evers set the knife aside and lifted the spectacles to his forehead, which had expanded greatly over recent years and now nearly reached the back of his head. His hand absently cleared tiny metal shavings from his thick brown beard, now streaked with gray.

"I did it, Father! I passed!" Quinn proclaimed excitedly.

Concern reflected in his eyes. "Are you hurt?"

"What?" She looked down at her tunic, the front splattered with streaks of red. "No. This is nothing…Master Lomisse healed me…us, after the duel."

"Duel?" He stepped closer, his concern still apparent.

Quinn sighed. "Yes, Father. They aren't going to invite me to an academy that trains warriors unless I can prove myself."

Evers nodded. "That makes sense, I guess."

"Anyway, I passed. I'm going to Fallbrandt with Everson!"

A moment passed before a smile appeared on his face and he held his arms out. She ran to him and gave him a hug as his big arms offered a gentle embrace.

"I'm glad that you two will be together, but I'm afraid of how your mother might take it. She will find it difficult to see you both leave."

"She won't try to stop me, will she?"

Evers chuckled. "No." He shook his head. "Your mother would never stand between you and your dreams. If this is what you want, she will support you, as will I."

"Thank you, Father."

Everson appeared beside her. "You should have seen the instructor, Father. When he exited the classroom, blood covered the front of his white vest and the leg of his breeches…even worse than Quinn's tunic."

"Is that so?"

"He didn't specify any rules before the duel." Quinn shrugged. "It's his fault."

Evers chuckled and wrapped his arms around both teens. "You two are quite the pair. I believe that Fallbrandt valley will soon discover that they have signed up for more than anticipated."

A blue nimbus from the charged glowlamp beside Everson's bed provided light to the dark room. Quinn sat on the edge of his bed, while Everson lay on his stomach. Her gaze followed his finger as it slid across the map to settle on a dot near the most northern point of the east coast.

"This is Cinti Mor." His finger meandered to the left, across Hurnsdom until it reached a spot marked as New Kardis. The path then angled southwest to a city named Berristor before turning south, meandered through what appeared to be a mountain range, and ended at a city beside a lake, nestled amidst the mountains. "Here is Fallbrandt."

Quinn squinted at the map, focusing on their destination at the heart of the continent. "That seems far."

"It's far for sure. Hundreds of miles."

She frowned, thinking that Everson could barely cross the city. *How would he ever make it to Fallbrandt?*

"You can't…We can't walk there. It's too far."

He sighed. "I know."

"Can we take a carriage?"

"Those cost money." He shrugged. "I don't know if we can afford it. Mother and Father are discussing it now. That's why they sent me up here with you."

"We are to be in Fallbrandt in three weeks. That's not much time if the journey is so far."

He turned toward her, his dark eyes meeting hers. "I know."

The thump of footsteps on the stairwell drew their attention toward the door. It opened, and Polly entered the room with Evers a step behind. Quinn sat upright while Everson swung his legs off the bed to sit beside her. The two teens stared at their parents with Quinn biting her lip, Everson kneading his hands. They both sensed the moment as something meaningful.

"We have something to tell you," Polly glanced up at Evers. He nodded and she continued. "Your father and I have discussed your upcoming journey to Fallbrandt."

"Please don't say no, Mother," Quinn blurted. "Everson belongs there. Everyone knows it. I want...I should be there with him...to help him."

Polly put her hands on her hips. "Are you through interrupting?"

"But..." Quinn sighed. "Yes."

"Good." Polly's hands shifted from her hips to clasp before her lap. She glanced at Evers again, and her expression softened. "You may not be aware, but we have saved up a fair amount of money the past few years, much of which was the result of selling Everson's inventions.

"When Cinti Mor was destroyed by the Horde, we lost every family member besides you two. Yes, we have some friends here and your father's smithy, but those roots are not so deep. As a result, there is nothing that tethers us to Cinti Mor."

"What are you saying?" Quinn asked.

"Can't you see?" Everson nudged her in the ribs. "They plan to come with us."

Polly chuckled softly as a tear slid down her cheek. "You were always clever, Everson. Yes, we plan to come with you."

"What about the smithy?" Quinn asked.

Her father's deep voice replied. "I can be a smith anywhere. Where there are people, there is need for a blacksmith."

"We intend to purchase a wagon and horses with the money we have saved," Polly informed them. "With them, we will move the smith tools and ourselves to Fallbrandt. When we get there, we will sell the wagon and horses to use that money to buy a house and a new smithy."

Quinn smiled and jumped up, hugging her mother fiercely. "I'm so happy! You're the best parents ever."

7

MOMENT OF DESPERATION

The sun hovered low in the eastern sky, its bright rays reflecting off the deep blue waters of the Sol Mai Ocean. The cliffs across the bay cast long shadows, making it difficult to see anything below but white foam among rocks that cut the water's surface.

Quinn stared down at the bustling harbor – the docks filled with activity as men unloaded goods from two ships that had arrived that morning. Most slips stood empty, vacated by fishing boats that were somewhere beyond view, seeking their daily catch.

She heard a snap when her father flicked the reins.

"Get," he barked, and the wagon lurched into motion.

Seated backward on a bench in the wagon bed, Quinn gripped it to prevent herself from falling forward. A glance toward Everson revealed a grin on her brother's face, one she mirrored. After ten agonizing days of preparation, their journey had finally begun.

The rumble of wagon wheels soon drowned the crashing waves and whispering breeze. Rolling fields of yellowed grass spread out to each side of the road they traveled down. Wildflowers in shades of white and purple and yellow dotted the fields, drawing bulbous bees that bounced from flower to flower in search of nectar. A loud rush of squawking drew

Quinn's gaze toward the sky as a wave of blackbirds emerged from the forest to the south, briefly eclipsed the sun, and continued northward. Motion on the hillside that led to the docks then drew her attention.

Two workhorses, pulling a wagon filled with crates, trudged up the road from the docks. A minute later, the wagon passed through the city gate and disappeared from view, leaving a trail of dust stirred from its passing.

Pale sections marked the dark and weathered rock of the walls that surrounded the city. Quinn knew that those sections had been rebuilt during her childhood – repaired after The Horde had destroyed them. Seeing them from her position seemed odd. Just being outside the city seemed odd…yet exciting. Watching the city – the only home she had ever known – fade into the distance brought on a brief wave of sadness, countered by the hope and expectations that the future might hold.

They reached an incline and the wagon began to rise, further expanding the view behind them. Another wagon loaded with goods departed from the docks and made its way up the curving road that led to the city. As Quinn watched it, the driver stiffened and tumbled from the seat, falling face-first onto the dirt.

She said, "Did you see that man fall off his wagon?"

"He didn't fall!" Everson pointed in alarm.

Men with bows rose up from the tall grass south of the city and ran toward the walls. A horn blared from the woods and horses carrying warriors in burgundy and green burst from the trees. *Vinacci soldiers*, she thought. The rolling thunder of three dozen horses galloping across the field rose above the rumble of the wagon wheels.

"Father!" Quinn yelled. "Look!"

The man turned in his seat and became visibly alarmed when he saw dozens of armed warriors on foot, following those who were mounted. The soldiers sprinted through the long grass and onto the road, most brandishing a sword and a shield. The rest held gripped bows in one hand, a ready arrow in the other.

"Issal save us," Polly gasped.

"Get!" Evers shouted as he snapped the reins, causing the wagon to increase in speed.

A Cinti Mor guard appeared atop the city wall. As the man turned to shout something, a volley of arrows darkened the air, arcing to rain down on him. The man staggered and disappeared from sight.

The portcullis began to lower, slowly closing as the marauders raced toward it. The mounted men closed on the wall, and Quinn feared that the gate might not close before the vanguard reached it. When halfway down, the gate suddenly dropped and slammed closed, loud enough for Quinn to hear it despite the distance.

A man waved his arms, and the other riders moved away from the gate. He then threw something and kicked his horse into motion, away from the wall. A burst of green flame shot up at the gate, blasting away a portion of the surrounding wall. The thump of the explosion reverberated in Quinn's chest and she heard her mother cry out in fear.

Distant screams came from inside the wall. The flames turned orange. The gate shuddered…and fell.

Locked in a state of horror, Quinn watched the Vinacci riders charge through the destroyed gate and engage with the city guards inside. The sound of swords clashing ensued, and Quinn imagined a fierce battle occurring beyond the broken gate and dying fires. Moments later, two riders rode back out as the invaders on foot reached it. The riders turned their horses, and Quinn realized that they were heading in their direction. The wagon crested the rise and began to descend the backside of the hill, obscuring her view of the gate. In the passing of two breaths, even the top of the walls and the Citadel to the north faded from view.

Fear held Quinn hostage, unable to think, unable to move. She stared hard at the road behind them, praying that the men would not appear.

Until they did.

The first man crested the hill, riding hard. Morning sunlight reflected off his helmet and the sword he held out to his side. His pockmarked face twisted into a grimace and determination reflected in his dark eyes. Quinn's own death reflected in those eyes.

She turned toward Everson and saw horror on his face. Upon seeing her brother in danger, the terror slid away from her. Like a morning fog evaporating to the warming rays of the summer sun, a moment of clarity obliterated her feeling of helplessness. *They will not hurt my brother.*

Her eyes narrowed and her lips pressed together as she turned toward the first rider, now nearly upon them while his companion crested the hilltop.

Quinn turned and pushed Everson aside, knocking him off the bench. "Woah!" he cried out as he fell onto a crate covered by their tent.

"Quinn! What are you doing?" her mother shouted.

Ignoring her, Quinn climbed behind the workbench and lifted it with all her might, tipping it up and over the back of the wagon. The bench hit the ground with a thud, sending splinters into the air as two of the legs snapped. The first rider's eyes grew wide, and his horse tried to leap over the tumbling bench, but it was too late.

The horse stumbled, and one of the splintered legs pierced its chest as the stallion smashed into the gravel road and launched the man forward. He landed headfirst beside the wagon – his neck bent in an unnatural position before his body rolled over him, tumbling in a massive cloud of dust. The horse cried out as it attempted to stand before stumbling and falling back to the ground.

Without pausing for his companion, the second rider circled around the broken bench and the dying horse. He drew his sword and made ready as he neared the wagon.

Desperate, Quinn began searching for something, anything that might help. She then spied the handle of her father's massive hammer. Scrambling over a large chest, she gripped the handle and lifted the hammer with a hearty grunt. She turned to find the soldier almost upon them.

With all of her might, Quinn swung the hammer around. The man raised his sword arm and prepared to strike. She released the hammer and it sailed through the air, barely clearing the horse's head. A clang sounded as the heavy hammer smashed into the metal armored plates on the soldier's chest. The sword fell from his hand, and he slid backward off the horse, his legs flipping over his head as he landed face-first on the road. His horse slowed and angled away from the wagon as the man squirmed in pain.

The wagon then reached the forest edge, and a wall of pines – thick with dark needles – obstructed the view of the wounded soldier and his riderless horse. Engulfed by shadows and surrounded by tall, dark trees, they continued west on the narrow road with nothing but a tail of churned dust following behind them.

8

THE HAPPY CROWSTER

The fire crackled and popped, sending a burst of embers that floated upward in a twisting motion toward the darkening sky. Quinn stared into the flames as she thought about the friends she left behind in Cinti Mor. *What has become of them?* She suspected that her brother and parents shared similar concerns but those concerns remained unspoken. Barely a word had been said during the long day on the road. The morning's events had left them in a mood as dark as the forest surrounding them.

Quinn glanced toward Everson, seated on the log beside her. The fire-light flickered on his face as he stared blankly toward it. Her gaze shifted toward her parents, both sitting on another log a quarter-turn around the fire pit. Polly held tight to Evers' arm and her head rested against his shoulder.

"Father," Quinn broke the silence. "Why did Vinacci attack Cinti Mor?"

When the man looked toward her, she found somber eyes that lacked their usual spark.

"I don't know, Quinn." He shook his head. "Perhaps they seek to expand their borders. The Issalian Alliance, under the Pretencia Accord, has held true for seventeen years, maintaining a state of peace and prosperity across kingdoms. However, the Vinacci king who signed them died a few years ago. Since King Talvin had no children of his own, the succession was a nasty bit of business. Eventually, Vinacci appointed a council to govern the country. I would not pretend to guess at their ambitions."

"Do you think the other cities know of what happened?"

Her father shrugged. "I suspect that Port Hurns fell days ago since it lies between Cinti Mor and Vinacci. New Kardis and Berristor reside on the gulf side, beyond this forest. That's quite a distance for an army to travel unnoticed, particularly before they captured Cinti Mor." His brow furrowed. "Ships might bring the news, but it takes three or four days to sail from Cinti Mor to New Kardis, around the north coast. Our route is far shorter, a straight line between the two cities. Even at a slower pace than what we traveled today, we should reach the city by nightfall tomorrow."

"We must warn them," Everson said with conviction.

"You're right, Son. They must know what happened so they can prepare. Even if the Vinacci forces advance no further, I expect that our city is lost. Despite the years that have passed since The Horde invasion, the population of Cinti Mor is a fraction of what it once was. The only hope is that word reached the Citadel in time to secure it."

"What about that explosion?" Quinn asked. "What was it? Can the Citadel stand against something like that?"

Her father shook his head. "I don't know, Quinn."

Quinn looked into the fire and realized that the flames had grown weaker, as if exhausted from a long day. Feeling her own exhaustion, she rubbed her dry and weary eyes.

"The tent is ready. Why don't you children go to bed?" Polly suggested. "We will join you shortly."

"I...think it best if I sleep under the wagon, Polly," Evers said.

She turned toward him. "Why?"

"While I think it unlikely for them to pursue us this far, I should watch for Vinacci soldiers. They sent those two men after us for a reason. Besides, there is always the threat of bandits."

Concern reflected in her eyes, mirroring what Quinn felt inside. She recalled the fear she felt when the Vinacci soldiers had chased after them. While her actions had saved her family, she knew that luck had played a significant part in her success. Things could have easily turned out far worse. The thought made her shudder.

Everson grabbed his canes and pushed himself to a standing position. "Come on, Quinn. Let's go to bed. I'm exhausted."

Without a word, she stood, circled the fire and opened the tent flap to allow her brother inside.

Quinn's eyes flashed open and she sat upright, the nightmare lingering. The tent was dark, still under the shroud of night. Her brother slept beside her and her mother beyond him.

A distant wail echoed in the night…the same horrible sound from her nightmare. She gasped, her heart racing. Her brother woke with a start, as did her mother. A shadow appeared outside the tent, tall and imposing. Quinn stared at the silhouette in fear.

"Quiet, now," her father said in a hushed voice from outside the tent.

"What is it?" Quinn whispered.

"Banshee."

Polly gasped audibly. Quinn and Everson looked toward each other.

While Quinn had never seen a banshee, the stories were plentiful. The Horde was an army made of the giant beasts, their voices laced with dreadful magic that drove the most courageous of men to despair. Mindless monsters, banshees were known to eat anything they found…dead or alive.

"What should we do?" Polly whispered.

"Unless it finds us, we stay here and remain quiet," Evers' hushed voice carried through the tent wall. "If it finds us, don't leave the tent. I'll do what I can to draw it away."

His shadow moved away from the tent, the crunch of his footsteps fading until Quinn only heard the sound of her own panting breaths. She lay down and pulled the blanket to her chin, listening to the night while praying that she would hear nothing of note. Hours passed, yet the banshee did not come...nor did sleep.

New Kardis was familiar and unfamiliar at the same time. The architecture and design held much in common with Cinti Mor but was in better condition. The city walls appeared original and intact, three stories tall and encircling the city save for the gates to the east and west. When their wagon passed through the eastern gate, Quinn gazed in wonder at streets covered in shadows cast by the setting sun.

Dressed in everything from rags to finery, crowds of people milled about, heading toward their destinations or conducting business. Carts and shops lined the streets, selling food and wares to eager patrons. Guards strolled past, their shoulders marked with blue and yellow stripes. She had never seen so many people.

The wagon slowed, easing down the main boulevard as the foot traffic gave way to the workhorses. They happened upon an inn, the sign above the door marked with the image of a fat bird with a red head, black neck, and brown body. The words *Happy Crowster Inn* were etched below the image of the bird.

Evers drove the wagon into the alley beside the inn and into the courtyard at the back. As the wagon came to a stop, a skinny man appeared, his back hunched at the shoulders from his slouching posture. He wore a stained tan tunic, which may have been white at one point. Black suspenders held his trousers up – trousers that sagged between the straps as they threatened to abandon him. The man gave them a toothy smile from a hatchet face crested by a mess of dirty blond locks.

"Hello. Are you staying for the night?"

Evers nodded. "Yes. We need a room for four along with some food and water for our horses."

"My name is Stigg. I'll be taking care of your horses." He thumbed toward the stable at the back. "I can lock your wagon inside, so you needn't be worrying about your things getting stolen or anything."

Evers climbed down from the wagon before turning to help Polly down. "Good idea. See that nothing happens to our goods and it's worth a silver piece for you."

Stigg's blue eyes brightened. "Yessir!" He stepped back with a bow and held his hand toward the back door of the inn. "Step on inside and ask for Trudy. She's the owner, and she'll set you up like royalty, she will."

Quinn leapt from the wagon bed and turned to take the canes from Everson. Her father lifted the boy from the wagon, grunting at his weight. He stood Everson beside the wagon while Quinn handed the canes to her brother. Led by Evers and Polly, the four of them entered the inn.

A corridor led them to a common room with a vaulted ceiling supported by open beams. Quinn searched the room and found it filled with men drinking ale, women sipping wine, and a smattering of folks eating dinner. The scent of smoked fish and roasted corn teased her senses and left her stomach complaining. She noticed a bar at the far end of the room – lined with patrons – while an open stairwell stood to her other side with a dark wooden railing that led to the rooms upstairs.

Evers turned toward them. "Wait here."

Without waiting on a response, he crossed the busy room to lean against the open end of the bar. After a quick conversation with the short woman behind the counter, he returned across the room.

"I paid for a room and dinner." He turned toward Polly and held a key out toward her. "Our room is upstairs, at the end of the hall. You should stay with the children, but I must meet with the duke to tell him what happened."

Polly appeared doubtful. "Will he believe you?"

He shrugged. "I don't know. I have no proof, but I must try."

"I can go with you, Father," Quinn suggested.

He turned toward her, his blue eyes meeting hers. After a moment, he acquiesced. "That might help, and it certainly cannot hurt."

"Is that safe?" Polly's voice rang with concern.

"Quinn appears fairly capable of taking care of herself if need be, but I doubt anything bad can come of this."

Polly turned toward Quinn. "Mind your tongue, dear. Like a tail that wags the dog, you have a tendency to let it lead you to trouble. When talking to a duke, it might draw more trouble than we can manage."

Quinn smiled. "Don't worry, Mother. I'll be on my best behavior. I promise."

Polly gave her a hug before turning toward Evers and hugging the big man. Quinn's gaze shifted to Everson's dark eyes, which locked on hers.

"You must make them believe you. These people," Everson turned toward the crowded room, "are counting on you."

He then turned and followed Polly to the stairwell, easing himself upward one step at a time while Quinn and her father headed out the front door.

When they stepped outside, twilight had given way to nightfall, leaving the area dark beyond the blue nimbus of the glowlamp mounted beside the door. The crowd had thinned, but dozens of people still occupied the street.

"I saw the Citadel after we passed through the gate, at the heart of the city." Evers turned and led her down the street as Quinn hurried to catch the tall man.

They passed numerous shops, most closed, their interiors dark. A wagon rolled past, heading out of the city as the farmer driving it returned home. The dirt streets turned to cobblestone at the next corner, leaving Quinn feeling as if someone had forgotten to finish paving the city. A glowlamp on a post lit the intersection, shedding light down a street that curved in both directions. Quinn spied two armed guards with strips of blue and yellow on the shoulder of their leather jerkins.

She tugged her father's sleeve. "Father! Look!" She gestured toward the guards. "Guards with Hurnsdom colors. Maybe they can get us in to see the duke."

"Good idea." The man switched directions.

He approached the two men, in the midst of a quiet discussion. The shorter guard, a man with a stocky build and closely shorn hair, noticed Evers approaching and elbowed his companion. The other guard, tall and lanky with long straw-colored bangs combed to the side, turned and eyed Evers warily. A *custos* rune marked both guard's foreheads. *Not paladins*, Quinn thought.

"Excuse me," Evers held his hands out, his palms empty. "I have just arrived from Cinti Mor, and I have grave news to report."

The shorter guard rested his hand on the pommel of his sword. "It is late. Court will be held tomorrow, two hours past sunup. I suggest you get yourself some sleep and show up at the Citadel in the morning."

"I understand," Evers said. "But you must know that this is a matter of import. Waiting could cost lives…or perhaps the entire city."

The shorter guard moved closer to Evers, thrusting his chest out as he stared up at the big man. "Are you threatening me or my city?"

With a roll of his eyes, Evers replied, "No, you idiot. I'm trying to tell you that Hurnsdom is under an invasion."

The taller guard put a hand on the shorter man's chest and pushed him back as he turned toward Evers.

"What are you talking about? Who would do such a thing?"

Quinn couldn't wait any longer. "It was Vinacci. They attacked Cinti Mor while we were leaving the city." Her words came out in a flurry. "They sent men after our wagon to kill us so we couldn't tell anyone."

The tall guard grimaced at his companion before turning to face Quinn. "If this were true, girl, how is it that you yet live?"

She glanced toward her father, who gave a slight nod. "I dumped a workbench from our wagon, and one of the soldiers died when his horse fell over it. The man landed with his neck bent in an ugly way and…he didn't move again."

The guard chuckled. "What of the other soldier?"

"My father is a smith. I grabbed his hammer and swung it hard as I could. The hammer hit the man in the chest and knocked him from his horse. He didn't die though…at least he was still alive last we saw him."

The man's eyes narrowed. "When did this happen?"

Evers said, "Yesterday morn. We spent two long days traveling through the Kardis Forest to get here and just arrived moments ago."

The two guards stared at each other in a long moment as Quinn held her breath, waiting on their response.

Finally, the tall guard sighed. "Follow us."

Quinn had never been inside a castle. She thought about the Citadel in Cinti Mor, recalling the time during her ninth summer when she had tried to sneak inside. It had required some of her best convincing to get Everson to agree to her plan.

Sent in alone, Everson had used his canes to shuffle his way up the flight of stairs before the gate, struggling as he ascended one stair at a time. Quinn crossed the square during this process, monitoring the guards stationed at the top as they watched her brother. The male remained stoic while concern clouded the face of the woman beside him. Everson reached the top as Quinn reached the bottom. He stumbled, fell sideways, and rolled down the stairs past her. The female guard gasped and ran past Quinn to help the boy. When the male guard moved to the top stair so he could see what transpired below, Quinn slid behind him and darted through the gate.

With her back to the wall, she stared in wonder at the well-tended shrubs that lined the brick path that led to the gray castle. The front of the building was four stories tall with two sets of double-doors at the base. Rows of windows and balconies dotted the upper levels, the ones on the eastern face overlooking the ocean. A square tower stood at each end of the building, jutting up two stories taller than the rest of the complex. *The view from the towers must be amazing.*

Quinn's focus shifted, looking around to find another path that led to her left, toward a domed temple of sorts, with stained-glass windows inlaid in gold and a massive symbol of Issal on the front. Quinn beamed and decided she would start there.

"Where do you think you're going?"

She turned to find the male guard looming over her.

"Um…I just wanted to see…"

"I'm sorry, but this is no place for children." He grabbed her arm and escorted her through the gate before he released her. "Go on and find something else to do. Mind that you avoid trouble. Don't make me report this to my captain."

Quinn gasped before turning to descend the stairs, passing the female guard as she joined her brother. Dejected at their failure, the duo headed back to meet their friends at the fountain.

When she heard her father clear his throat, Quinn blinked, her mind returning to the present. Evers appeared calm until she noticed his thick hands kneading each other. She turned toward the stocky guard who shared the chamber with them. Beside him, the dull blue of the waning glowlamp in the open doorway shed just enough light to reach the corners of the waiting room.

Two intricately woven tapestries adorned the walls at each end of the room, one depicting a battlefield of men on horseback fighting giants and another showing a likeness of Issal bestowing blessings upon his flock. She moved closer to the second tapestry and squinted, trying to see a face beyond the halo of light that encircled Issal's head. Someone cleared her throat, drawing Quinn's attention.

She turned to find a short woman with dark hair. The lines around her angular eyes marked her as middle-aged and the rune of Issal marked her forehead. A thick robe of blue velvet covered the woman's body, yet she appeared to have a small frame. The tall guard who had escorted Evers and Quinn to the castle stood beside her.

"Good evening. I am Duchess Chinu Mae." Her dark eyes focused on Evers. "I understand you have something to report."

Evers bowed his head. "Pardon us for the intrusion, Duchess. We would not bother you if not for news most urgent. We…"

"I would hear it told from the girl."

Her father blinked at the interruption and bowed again. "Of course."

Everyone turned toward Quinn. Her stomach fluttered, leaving her nauseated in an instant.

"What is your name?" the duchess asked.

"It's Quinn…Jacquinn Gulagas. But everyone calls me Quinn."

"Thank you, Quinn. Can you tell me what happened in Cinti Mor? Don't leave out any details."

"Yes Ma'am." Quinn took a deep breath and recited her tale, telling the woman of the family leaving Cinti Mor for a journey to Fallbrandt and relaying the attack on the city. When she told the woman of the soldiers who pursued them and what Quinn had done to thwart them, the woman's brows shot up in surprise. Not one word was said during the telling, not until Quinn concluded her tale with their checking in to The Happy Crowster Inn and heading to the castle.

The duchess frowned and turned toward Evers. "This is true?"

He nodded.

"Do you have anything to add?"

He shook his head.

"Thank you for sharing this news. It is certainly dire. Go back to your family and continue your journey to Fallbrandt. I will take the necessary action, so you no longer need worry." She smiled at Quinn. "You focus on your training. Our future will one day be in the hands of your generation."

9
———

TACT

Two long days later, they pulled into Berristor, a port located along the southern shore of the Gulf of Norta. As the most western point of Hurnsdom, Berristor was bordered by a forest to the east and mountains to the south and west. With buildings made of red-tinted bricks, the city almost appeared sunburnt in the light of the setting sun.

After spending a night at a local inn and restocking their supplies, they once again took to the road, which soon entered a wooded valley that ran between mountains to the north and the south. Despite it being well past the heart of summer, snow remained on the towering peaks that surrounded the road. Quinn stared at the view in wonder and decided that she had never seen anything so majestic.

A barren strip of gray and brown earth ran between the snowcap and the thick green forest that stretched upward from the bottom. The forest itself consisted mainly of dark pines, with occasional clumps of leaf trees scattered here and there. Quinn found herself repeatedly glancing toward the mountains for the remainder of their journey, one that remained happily uneventful.

After a day and a half of travel through valleys surrounded by giant peaks – on a route that changed directions from westward, to south, and finally eastbound after circling a massive mountain – the family reached the outskirts of Fallbrandt.

With the afternoon sun behind them, buildings began to appear in the forest that enveloped the road. At first, the buildings were sporadic, as if small bits of civilization were invading the grandeur of nature. This lasted for a while until Quinn realized that they were inside the city. Unlike other cities that she had visited, there was no wall surrounding Fallbrandt. Without such a boundary, she found herself unable to tell where the forest ended and the city began.

The wagon reached an intersection and turned north on a gravel road. Two riders, a man and a woman, rode past them at a trot. The man tipped his hat as he passed, while the woman flashed a smile when Quinn waved.

A driver with a loaded wagon came toward them, the man staring blankly at the road ahead as he rode past. A strange looking metal oven stuck up from the wagon bed. Quinn glanced toward Everson, who grinned and shrugged.

Two teens on strange contraptions sped past them, each sporting two wheels secured to a wooden frame. The riders pumped cranks with their feet, seemingly to propel them forward.

"What are they? Why don't they tip over?" Quinn asked.

Everson replied, "Like rolling a coin, they are likely easy to balance when moving. As for what they are, I have no idea."

Shops with second-story apartments above them bordered the road as people on foot strolled down the wooden boardwalk that ran along the buildings. A man exited one shop with a loaded sack that seemed to float above his shoulder. Quinn's brow furrowed, but when she looked toward Everson, she found his eyes wide with wonder.

Smaller streets crossed the road with a dormant glowlamp mounted on a pole at each intersection. She caught a glimpse of a lake in the gaps between the trees at the end of one such road.

The wagon turned, and her father drove the team around a building to a fenced yard that waited at the rear. As they pulled through the open gate, Evers pulled the reins, and the horses came to a stop before a stable with a shed built on the back. A thin man with dark hair, dark eyes, and a brown tunic emerged from the shed.

"Hiya, folks." The man approached the wagon and gave them a toothy grin. "I'm Ned. I can tend to your horses and watch your wagon. Are you here to eat or are you staying the night?"

"Hello, Ned. My name is Evers, and this is my family. We'll be staying the night and possibly longer, depending on how long it takes to find a suitable home."

"You're planning to live here?"

Evers climbed down from the wagon. "Yes. At least for a few years. You never know where life might take you next."

Ned's gaze shifted to the wagon, scanning the contents. "You wouldn't by chance be a blacksmith?"

Evers frowned. "As a matter of fact, I am. Why do you ask?"

Ned shrugged. "We have a bit of a need. Used to be that the academy helped with our smithing jobs, but things have changed of late. They don't seem to have time for us common folk as they're focused on their fancy inventions. Just getting a horse shod is tough, with only one smith in town. The man is too busy, and you have to pay extra to get anything done in a timely way."

Evers smiled as he helped Polly down. "Seems I came to the right place, then."

Quinn jumped over the side of the wagon and landed softly in the gravel.

"Seems right, indeed." Ned nodded in agreement. As the man spoke, Evers had helped Everson from the wagon. "Go on in through the kitchen. Ask for Dory. She owns the place. Tell her that you're the new smith, and you need a room 'til you find a place of your own."

"What's this place called, anyway?" Quinn asked.

"Why, you are at the finest inn in Fallbrandt," Ned said proudly. "Welcome to The Quiet Woman."

The song of a starfetch lilted in the air, a sweet serenade to the morning sun. As Quinn and Everson approached the massive oak, she searched the sprawling branches – thick with dark green leaves – but was unable to locate the bird. They passed the tree and her focus shifted to the massive structure ahead.

It soon became apparent that the complex was made of numerous independent buildings that had been interconnected over time. Two large, blocky buildings stood in the center with long sections stretching out to the sides, each end culminating with a circular tower. Parts of the complex consisted of three levels while the interconnecting portions had just a single level. At the rear of the academy, a massive square building reached toward the sky and was far taller than the surrounding structures.

As they approached the stairs at the front, Quinn read the alabaster plaque above the door, etched with the words *Fallbrandt Academy of Magic and Engineering*.

Everson stopped and Quinn turned toward him.

"This is it." Everson looked toward the building. "My new home."

Quinn put her hand on his shoulder. "Don't worry. You'll be fine." She looked back and found herself unable to see through the trees that lined the road. The sister school, her school, waited beyond the trees and across the fields. "I'm close by if you need me."

She pressed her lips together and resisted speaking her concerns. This would be their first time apart, even if their separation were to be a mere two miles.

"I know." A grin spread across his face. "I'm sure you'll get in trouble without me there to look out for you."

Quinn laughed. "Without a doubt." When her focus shifted toward the sky, she found the sun well above the mountains to the east. "I'd better go. I'm already late."

"You didn't have to walk with me. I know I move slowly." His eyes were apologetic.

"Nonsense. I wanted to see you all the way here."

Their slow pace had frustrated her all morning. Normally, she accepted the issue, knowing that Everson would move faster if it were possible. Today was different. The fact that dozens of other students had passed them during the journey made it that much worse.

A distant light flared at the edge of her vision. Quinn turned toward the school and saw two balls of fire arcing from the rooftop of the square tower at the back. Everson noticed and turned to watch the fireballs streak through the sky until the building obscured them from view.

"What was that?" Quinn asked.

"Magic, I guess." His voice betrayed a sense of wonder.

Her concern for him resurfaced at the mention of magic.

"You had better go," he reminded her.

"You're right."

"I'll see you soon."

Giving his shoulder a squeeze of affection, Quinn spun about and broke into a run, heading south on the gravel road they had just taken from Fallbrandt. As she ran with her pack over one shoulder, she wiped her eyes dry.

Her thoughts returned to their brief stay in Fallbrandt. Only two nights had passed at The Quiet Woman before her parents were able to sell the wagon and horses in exchange for a new home. The house was smaller than their home in Cinti Mor, this one with just a single bedroom. However, she and Everson only needed to stay there a few days.

During that time, she helped her father clean out and repair the shed behind the house. They then spent nearly two days building a new forge using rocks and mortar. By the time the new smithy was functional, Evers had secured enough business to keep him busy for months.

Despite the fact that the more distant of the two schools was only three miles away, their mother was crushed when Everson and Quinn left Fallbrandt that morning. After warning them days earlier that she might cry when it came time to say goodbye, Polly proved her ability to predict the future – at least in this case. Yes, Quinn would miss her parents, but her larger concerns centered on Everson.

She reached the driveway that led to the other school and turned, heading east toward the structure. Similar to the academy for magic and engineering, the combat school consisted of many interconnected buildings, all constructed with pale stone blocks.

Quinn slowed to catch her breath as she approached the school. The path led directly to a blocky building, two stories tall with a row of windows near the roofline. A stable yard and a massive stable stood to the right of the main entrance. She approached the double-doors and gazed up at the plaque, reading the words engraved there – *Torreco Academy of Combat Training*. Gripping the knob, she pulled one of the heavy wooden doors open and stepped inside.

An open hall stood before her, its ceiling built with open beams that stood two stories above. Morning sunlight streamed through windows at the far end, above a corridor that led deeper into the complex. Doors lined both sides of the hall, and a massive statue of men fighting a giant monster drew her attention to the heart of the room.

"You're late, Cadet!"

Quinn turned to find a man approaching. He stood a half-head taller than she and had broad shoulders, a barrel chest, and thick arms. His sleeveless black leather jerkin left his arms bare save for the leather bracers on his forearms.

"The instructions clearly said that you were to arrive within an hour of sunrise." He frowned at her with dark eyes below a strong brow, the rune marking his forehead partially covered by brown bangs.

"I'm sorry...I needed to..."

"I don't care what you need!" He stepped close and glared at Quinn. "You better learn to follow directions if you expect to remain here. Can you do that, soldier?"

"Um...yes."

"The proper response is *yes, Sergeant!*"

"Yes, Sergeant!"

"That's better." A grin formed on the man's face. "You missed bunk assignments, but we can deal with that later. For now, you are to head to the Coliseum for your debriefing." He gestured toward the corridor at the back of the hall. "Hurry along, it's about to start."

With a nod, Quinn rushed across the room in the direction indicated. Just prior to reaching the center hallway, she noticed two other corridors, one to her left and the other to her right. She entered the hallway, lit in blue light despite having no windows. Somehow, the thick wooden beams that supported the ceiling glowed blue like a glowlamp. Not having time to inspect them, she hurried past and made her way to the double-doors at the end of the corridor, ripped them open, and darted inside.

She stopped at the top of a row of stairs as hundreds of faces turned in her direction. The Coliseum was a huge chamber, oval in shape. Rows of seats encircled the building, save for a straight wall at one end. Below the seats was a dirt floor surrounded by a ten-foot tall wall, which made the room appear like a giant bowl.

"Take a seat, Cadet!"

Quinn's focus shifted to the man who had bellowed the command. He stood in the center of the dirt floor, his arms crossed over his chest as he stared in her direction. Students filled the seats between her and the floor, many of whom stared in her direction. Moving down a number of steps, she found a spot in one of the middle rows and slid past three other students before sitting on the bench.

"If you're finished interrupting, I will continue." The man uncrossed his arms, revealing a sleeveless leather jerkin, bleached white. In his mid-thirties, the man had a shorn head of brown hair and trimmed beard to match. "As I was saying, you have been sent here by your respective kingdoms because someone saw potential within you. Be aware that life here is not easy. You are nothing but lumps of iron today – formless, raw, and largely useless. However, if you dedicate yourself and commit to the program, we will mold you anew, forge you into weapons."

He began to pace, his long legs striding in a measured and purposeful manner. "Why, you may ask. Why go through the pain of combat training? Why endure the hardships of a soldier without pay? Why would you wish to become a weapon?"

The man's eyes lowered for a moment before he lifted his head to face the crowd.

"Because somebody must protect the innocent." His manner grew more animated. "You all saw the sculpture in the central hall. Those warriors are heroes. That monster you see them fighting was real. In fact, there were thousands of others just like it. Without men and women like them, trained for combat – brave, fierce, determined – we would not be here today. All of you, and everyone you know, would be dead. That battle occurred just seventeen years ago. Many soldiers died that day, but humanity survived. Someday, you may be called upon to save mankind...or to protect your king...or simply to capture bandits who prey upon the innocent. Regardless, the path is the same. You must train yourself for combat in order to survive it.

"We will train your mind so that a bit of awareness and a lot of cleverness might help to save lives. We will prepare your body for the rigors of combat in the event that a physical confrontation cannot be avoided. We will train you to shoot, to ride, to hunt…to survive.

"Know that we will ask much of you, but in return you will find a new sense of purpose. You will become the protectors, the shield against tyranny and darkness."

Quinn could not help feeling inspired. She already knew her purpose. This man merely confirmed it.

10

———

MAKING ENEMIES

A cluster of girls funneled through the doorway in small, shuffling steps. Quinn moved aside to survey the room as the other girls moved purposefully toward their respective stations.

Two rows of bunks lined the walls, ten bunks on each side. Between each set of beds was a window, the open curtains allowing sunlight to illuminate the room. A chest sat at the foot of each bunk and left the middle of the room empty. Girls hurried to stand at attention to each side of a chest. As the last of the girls settled into position, a firm voice startled Quinn.

"Attention!"

She turned to find a woman in a gray sleeveless jerkin standing beside her. The woman had a dark complexion and black hair tied into a bun behind her head. Matching Quinn in height, the woman had a lean, yet muscular, build. When she turned toward Quinn, the woman gave her a firm glare with her dark eyes.

"Get to your station, Cadet!"

Quinn looked down the length of the room, toward the girls who lined each side, their eyes staring straight forward. "I…arrived late and missed bunk assignments."

The woman frowned. "When you address me, you are to use the term

Sergeant or *Sergeant Jasmine.*" The woman moved closer to Quinn without the hint of smile in her glare. "Now, go find an open bunk and get into position!"

Quinn nodded. "Yes, Sergeant."

She scrambled across the room, seeking an open spot. At the far end, she noticed a swarthy girl with black hair standing alone beside a chest. The girl was the tallest in the room, broad of shoulder with thick arms. Quinn reached up to put her pack on the top bunk until the girl's hand shot out to grab her wrist, squeezing it tightly.

"That bunk is mine," the girl growled. "You're on the bottom."

Quinn yanked her hand free and set her pack on the bottom bed before taking position. Although her wrist hurt, she refused to let it show, unwilling to give the rude girl the satisfaction.

Sergeant Jasmine strolled the length of the room, her gaze inspecting each girl as she walked past. The thump of her boots on the hard floor was the only sound in the room, matching the woman's methodical pace. When she reached Quinn, the sergeant grimaced before turning to retrace her steps.

"You heard Captain Goren's message. I suggest you take it to heart. Your training will be difficult and will require discipline, dedication, and perseverance." She stopped and smirked. "And it begins now."

A rumble arose from beyond the open door as a cart, pushed by a female cadet, rolled into the room. Pairs of tall leather boots occupied the shelves of the cart, the boots shaking violently from the vibration. Another girl then pushed a second cart into the room, this one with clothing piled atop it. The carts stopped and the two cadets began handing out black boots, green tops, and brown breeches to the girls in line.

"Try on the sparring vest, breeches, and boots that you are provided to ensure they fit." Sergeant Jasmine commanded. "If you need a different size, swap it out now. Store the clothing you are wearing, along with personal belongings, in the chest beside your bed." She crossed the room and stopped beside the open door. "You have fifteen minutes to complete your fitting and meet me in the Coliseum."

The sergeant exited the room, closing the door behind her as the girls scrambled to change.

—·◆·—

Every movement required effort. Quinn's muscles were worn, her joints sore. Although her body longed to lie down, her stomach wouldn't allow it – at least not without dinner.

She followed the other students to the mess hall and found herself in a line that methodically inched through the kitchen. When she reached the front, she accepted a small meat pie and a glass of milk from a serving woman before turning to find a seat.

Boys clustered at some tables, girls at others. She spotted a table with an open seat beside her bunkmate. Taking a deep breath to steady her nerves, she put on a smile and approached the table.

"Hello. We weren't properly introduced earlier. My name is Quinn."

The girl's dark eyes scanned Quinn for a moment before landing on her face. "I'm Darnya."

"Pleased to meet you, Darnya." Quinn moved toward the bench, intending to sit beside the girl.

Darnya's hand slapped the bench right where Quinn had intended to sit.

"This spot is taken. Find another table."

Quinn frowned. "Um…sorry. I didn't realize someone was sitting there."

"Oh, nobody's sitting here. I just like it open. It gives me more elbow room." The girl grinned at the other girls, some of whom laughed.

Anger flared inside Quinn, yet she maintained restraint. *I don't need to make enemies already,* she thought.

"No worries. I'll find another table." She smiled before adding, "One that smells better."

Darnya's face darkened and Quinn turned from the table, walking away as if nothing happened. *So much for not making enemies.*

Moving past a full table, she found an empty one and set her bowl and mug down before sitting. The food was hot and the first bites burned her tongue, but she was too hungry to care. She ate with fervor, using her fork to scrape the bowl clean.

"May I sit here?"

Quinn looked up and found a boy standing across from her, the rune of Issal marking his forehead. He was tall and muscular, but in a lean way. With olive-toned skin and black hair, his eyes shone with the amber of sunlight in a shallow stream.

"If you wish," she responded with a shrug. "I won't stop you."

He smiled, and Quinn decided he had a nice smile.

After setting his bowl and mug on the table, he held his hand out toward her. "I'm Ikonis. My friends call me Iko."

She pulled her hand from beneath the table and shook his. "Call me, Quinn."

Iko sat and began poking his meat pie, steam rising from where he pierced the crust. "I'm first-year, so today's my first day here. How about you?"

"Same."

"Where are you from?"

Quinn considered the harm in responding, but not finding any. "Hurnsdom. I grew up in Cinti Mor."

His eyes narrowed. "That's a good distance away. When did you leave?"

"A couple weeks back."

Iko hesitated before he spoke again. "Are things still good in Cinti Mor?"

Quinn shrugged. "I'm not sure. The city was attacked while we were leaving."

Her thoughts shifted to the friends she had left behind. She said a silent prayer to Issal for them.

Iko appeared surprised. "Attacked? Attacked by whom?"

"Vinacci soldiers."

"What? Are you sure?"

"Yes. At least they wore Vinacci uniforms."

"I can't believe it." He shook his head. "Why would they do such a thing?"

"I...don't know."

"I'm sorry, Quinn. I hope your parents are safe and well."

She snorted. "They were fine when I left them this morning." When his brow furrowed, she added, "They moved to Fallbrandt to be close to me and my brother."

"How fortuitous."

Iko took a bite of his food while Quinn looked around the room. Tables of boys and girls surrounded them, their busy conversations filling the room. She then noticed another table that was empty but for a single girl. Focused on her food, the girl had dark hair, dark eyes, and tanned skin. There was an exotic nature to the girl and odd markings covered the upper portion of one arm. Quinn frowned upon noticing the body art, unused to seeing it save for a rune that often marked people's forehead.

"Tantarri."

Quinn turned toward Iko. "What?"

He bobbed his head toward the girl sitting alone. "That girl. She's Tantarri."

"What do you know of them?"

Iko shrugged. "They are a race of savages. They live in the wild, east of here. Body art and other oddities are commonplace to them."

Quinn glanced toward the girl again and felt a string tug at her heart, urging her to go over and say hello.

"I can't believe they allow Tantarri here," Iko muttered.

She turned toward Iko and found him frowning.

"They believe in false gods, and they refuse to follow the word of Issal."

She turned back toward the girl as she considered his words. Thoughts of introducing herself to the girl dissipated, but Quinn's curiosity remained.

11

———

DANGEROUS WEAPONS

Simone's leg lashed out, and Quinn dodged the kick with a twist of her body. She lunged with a punch, but Simone blocked it with a forearm swipe. The other girl kicked again, her knee connecting with Quinn's ribs, forcing her backward with a grunt.

Quinn held her hand to her side and stared at her opponent. Simone's face appeared emotionless, her eyes measuring Quinn. The two were of a similar size, but as a second-year cadet, Simone had training that Quinn lacked.

Ignoring the pain from her ribs, Quinn raised her hands before her and reset her stance, mirroring her opponent. They both eased forward, and Simone threw a jab toward Quinn, who slapped it away. Another jab lashed out, and Quinn dodged it before throwing a counterpunch that missed when Simone spun away. The girl ducked with her spin, and her leg thrust out behind her, striking Quinn's midriff. Quinn doubled over, and Simone's fist smashed into her temple. The world spun and Quinn found herself on her hands and knees.

She blinked and rose to her feet, turning toward Simone in anger.

"Match," Sergeant Jasmine called out.

Quinn turned toward her. "I'm not done. I can win."

Jasmine's brow rose.

"Um…Sergeant," Quinn added.

"She had you beat, Quinn." The woman shook her head. "You can try again another day."

Despite the urge to do otherwise, Quinn pressed her lips together and said nothing more. After six weeks of hand-fighting training and duels twice a week, she had yet to win. The frustration inside her was unbearable.

"Take positions!" Jasmine shouted.

The girls, forty in all, lined up along the arena floor in two rows – second-year cadets in front, first-year students in the rear.

With her hands clasped behind her back, the woman paced along the line as her dark, almond-shaped eyes measured the students before her.

"It is time to move beyond hand fighting." Jasmine waved a hand in the air. Her two assistants, Vi and Lissa, opened the doors at the far end of the arena to expose a room below the stands. "You will each be provided training weapons, something that best suits your physique and skillset." As she spoke, her assistants each pushed a cart filled with wooden weapons onto the dirt floor of the Arena. "Second-year cadets, you already know your weapon set. Remain in line and advance to the cart on the left where Soldier Vi is waiting. Tell her what you need and get yourself armed."

Led by Darnya, who stood at one end of the line, the second-year cadets jogged over to the cart and began to request their training weapons.

Jasmine turned toward the first-year students, addressing them. "Come along. Let's get you outfitted as well."

She then led the students to the other cart, where Lissa waited. Jasmine picked out a wooden longsword and shield and handed it to the first girl. The second received a quarterstaff. The third, a short sword and shield.

When Quinn reached the front of the line, the sergeant held a quarterstaff out toward her. Rather than accept it, Quinn stared at it for a long moment.

"What are you waiting for, Cadet?"

"Which weapon set is the most dangerous, Sergeant?"

"What?"

Quinn's eyes locked with Jasmine's hard gaze. "The weapon set that best suits me is the one that is most dangerous."

The sergeant's eyes narrowed and her lips pressed together. After a moment, she replaced the staff into the rack on the cart, grabbed two short swords, and held them out to Quinn.

"While being the most dangerous, you best be aware that fighting with dual blades also provides the least defense."

Quinn shrugged as she accepted the wooden swords. "I won't have to defend myself if they're dead, Sergeant."

With her training weapons safely stored and her body bathed, Quinn set off to grab dinner. As she strolled down the windowless corridor, lit by the glowing beams above, she contemplated a plan.

For the safety of students, the Coliseum and sparring areas were off limits in the evenings. However, she wanted to become an expert with her weapons as soon as possible. Based on her experience with hand fighting, that only came with practice. Her natural quickness and agility would help, but skill required something more in battles when her life was on the line.

The subject occupied her mind as she entered the mess hall, passed through the kitchen, and sat at an open table. She had a mouth full of grilled fish when movement in the periphery caught her attention. She turned and found Iko approaching, tall and handsome and grinning. Beside him was a slightly shorter boy with brown hair, green eyes, and a similar build.

"Hello, Quinn."

She swallowed. "Iko. Hi…how are you?"

"I'm fine. Thanks for asking." Iko gestured toward the boy beside him. "This is my friend, Percilus."

The other boy's brow furrowed, and Quinn noticed his rune, the same as Iko's. "But nobody calls me that." He turned toward Quinn and smiled. "I'm Percy. It's great to meet you, Quinn."

Quinn nodded. "Hi, Percy."

"We got our weapons today," Iko said.

"Us, too," she replied.

"I went with a longsword and shield."

"Classic combination. You're tall enough for it, too," she noted.

Iko grinned. "My thoughts as well."

"I chose a quarterstaff," Percy said. "However, the longbow is my first choice."

Iko laughed. "No doubt." He leaned closer. "You should see him shoot. Percy's adopted father is a hunter." Iko thumbed toward Percy. "He learned some serious skills from that man. The art of the longbow is just one of many."

The mention of Percy's adoption steered Quinn's thoughts toward Everson. She fell silent, thinking about her brother and wondering how he fared at his school. It would be weeks yet before she would be allowed time off so she could see him.

There is nothing you can do about it, she told herself. *Don't forget why you are here. Focus on your training and time will pass quickly enough.*

Iko gave a nod. "I'll see you in the morning, Quinn."

She stared at both boys with a furrowed brow. "What?"

"Tactics training begins tomorrow. While Seventh Day remains a day of rest, we'll be spending half the day in a classroom – first-year students in the morning, second-year's in the afternoon. I'll see you there."

A nod was Quinn's only response.

"Bye, Quinn," Percy said as he turned away.

Iko gave her a smile before turning and following his friend. Quinn's thoughts turned to the aforementioned Tactics class, wondering what it involved.

"As you can see, by positioning themselves along the edge of the upper plateau, the human army was able to gain a distinct advantage."

Tactics Master Trijia pointed at the center of the oversized map secured to the wall as she spoke. Scarred on one side of her face and sporting short-cropped golden hair, she had the look of a soldier who had seen her share of combat.

"The cliff walls that stood over the lower plains enabled them to fire projectiles down upon The Horde. The narrow slope that connected the lower plains to the plateau acted like a funnel. Despite vastly superior numbers, The Horde could only attack with a portion of their army at a time."

She turned to the class, striding toward the students seated in a half-circle that faced her. Quinn sat in the third row, two steps above the classroom floor. All eyes were on Trijia, the cadets listening intently.

"The Battle at the Brink is just one of many conflicts we will study over the course of the year. As you can see from this example, entering a battle with a competent strategy can compensate for deficiencies and provide a tactical advantage, especially if you can neutralize key strengths of your opponent. Please note that pre-planning will only get you so far. You must also consider all possible responses from your opponent, ensuring you have a counter-strategy for each. Even then, success on the battlefield requires the ability to adjust on the fly. Battles are unpredictable. If you cannot display tactical agility when the unforeseen arises, even the most brilliant battle strategy can result in defeat."

Trijia spun about and sauntered toward a nearby table. A map painted on a board sat on the table. Overlaying the map was a grid consisting of hundreds of cells. Wooden figures, about five inches tall, stood upon the board, half of which were dyed blue, the other half black. Each piece had a small rod jutting up from the top. Some had two yellow disks on the rod, others held five, and one piece on each team held a stack of ten.

"On this table is a game called Ratio Bellicus. You'll note that each game piece includes disks that represent their remaining life. The Captain of your army is the one with ten disks. The game features various other types of pieces, each possessing a military unit and applicable attributes.

"Cavalry units can move five spaces per turn, but they are vulnerable to archers at a distance and infantry pikemen at close range. Foot soldiers, armed with swords and shields, possess effective melee attacks and have inherent defensive advantages against archers but are susceptible to cavalry unit attacks. Arcanists can wield powerful ranged attacks or can empower fellow warriors, turning them into killing weapons for a short time. Note that the use of magic renders the arcanist useless for five turns, leaving that unit unable to move or counterattack. Each team has two ecclesiast units, able to restore life disks to any game piece that hasn't been eliminated. In addition, each game piece has an element unknown to your opponent." She picked up a piece and showed the bottom to the classroom, revealing a small cavity. "A black disk can be inserted in this opening, turning one unit into an assassin – a piece that can kill the opposing Captain with one hit despite the ten health disks that accompany that piece.

"The game board comes with terrain markings, limiting how you can move the pieces. The board before you is marked differently than the one in the Cadet lounge, for each board is unique.

"Taking turns, you move one piece at a time to position your units and take out enemy forces. If your Captain dies, you lose. If all of your pieces are eliminated, you lose.

"The intent of this game is to develop your thinking as you consider different strategies and respond tactically to your opponent's moves."

Quinn chewed her lip as she stared at the game board, eager to play. She was determined to learn the game and found herself wishing Everson could play with her. If anyone could master the game, it would be him. With that thought in mind, she decided to seek out the most challenging opponent and play until she won.

12

———

FAME

A shiver shook Everson, and his teeth chattered. He heard hushed whispers pass between two of his captors as he tried to reason through his situation. *Why did they kidnap me? Why are they asking these questions? What are they after?*

Cold and thirsty, he found himself wishing for a hot cup of caffe and a nice, warm bed.

"Everson." Hearing his name, he tried to look toward the man speaking, or at least toward his silhouette. "How did you meet Jonah Selbin? We would know of your interactions with him."

"Well…as I explained, Quinn and I set out from Fallbrandt early that morning. She walked me to my school, although it was two miles beyond her destination."

Everson's eyes drifted toward the floor as he recalled their discussion. "I told her I would be fine traveling there on my own, but she wouldn't have it. That's how Quinn is. She puts others before herself. Besides, I knew there would be no changing her mind." He shook his head. "You'll have better luck moving a mountain than getting my sister to veer off course once her mind is set.

"I met Jonah just moments after Quinn left me. At the time, I had no idea what the future held, or who Jonah really was…"

Everson watched Quinn run down the long gravel road, passing through the long morning shadows cast by the trees that lined it. Beyond the trees, far across the massive lawn, stood the sister school – Quinn's new home. Yes, she would be close, but he wouldn't see her for weeks if not longer. For the first time in his life, he was alone. His heart fluttered and his stomach roiled in a moment of panic. He closed his eyes and took a long calming breath. With a clear mind, Everson extended his senses.

Birds chirped in the distance, the chatter of nature. Morning sunlight warmed his face, cooled by the soft mountain breeze. His nose caught the hint of a sweet bouquet floating past. When he opened his eyes, he noticed purple wildflowers swaying in the fields to the west. Beyond the fields, dark trees bordered the lawn – the edge of a thick forest that ran up the sides of the surrounding white-capped mountains. As he drank in the harmony of nature's embrace, the tranquility of the moment settled his nerves and warmed his heart. *All right. I'm ready.*

He turned and shifted both canes to one hand as he opened the door. Moving quickly, he grabbed a cane with his free hand and used it as a doorstop. Beyond the doorway, he found a short line of students, all of whom had passed him during his journey to the school. He shuffled inside and let the door close behind him as he surveyed his surroundings.

The students in line were talking amongst one another, their voices echoing off walls standing over one hundred feet apart. An upward glance revealed a high ceiling supported by two rows of brick pillars that interrupted the otherwise open space. Rows of doors dotted the interior walls, and dark railings lined two terraced levels that overlooked the hall.

Everson shuffled forward when the line advanced a stride. A teen glanced back at him and whispered to his neighbor. Everson turned away, feeling self-conscious. The door behind him burst open, a boy darting inside and slowing as he reached the back of the line.

With a mess of strawberry blond hair, freckles, and green eyes, the boy leaned forward with his hands on his knees as he caught his breath.

Odd. I don't recall seeing anyone on the road besides Quinn. The other boy stood upright, a bit taller than Everson.

"Whew. I was afraid I was late."

Everson glanced away, deciding if he should respond. Finally, he forced himself to speak.

"You're not late…at least, I don't think you are."

"Good." The boy smiled and held his hand out. "My name is Jonah. And you are…"

Everson stared at the boy's hand and bit his lip. "I'm…Everson." He shifted both canes to his left hand and shook Jonah's hand.

"I overslept, so I ran all the way here." Jonah gasped for air. "I only arrived in Fallbrandt last night, and I was pretty exhausted from the journey."

Curiosity flickered inside Everson. "Where are you from?"

"Nor Torin."

Everson imagined the map he had reviewed before traveling to Fallbrandt, recalling the image in his head. In his mind, he pictured Nor Torin along the northern portion of the west coast of Torinland. He quickly calculated the distance.

"Nor Torin must be nearly two hundred miles from here."

Jonah grinned broadly. "That's right."

"That's a long way to walk."

Jonah sighed. "There's no denying that. It took me five long days to reach Fallbrandt." He pointed past Everson. "You're next."

Everson turned around as the boy in front of him stepped aside and headed toward the corridor at the back corner of the room. When he approached the table, a girl with dark hair glanced up at him. Framed by long lashes, the girl had large eyes, brown like Everson's.

"Name, please."

"Everson Gulagas."

She looked through the papers, her finger trailing across them until she found his name.

"Here you are." She frowned. "Have you requested a roommate?"

"Um…no."

"What about me?" Jonah asked. "You could room with me."

Everson turned toward Jonah. "Are you sure? You don't mind

that…" He gestured toward his legs.

Jonah shrugged. "Not as long as you don't care that I'm a ginger."

Everson frowned. "A ginger?"

Jonah's big grin returned. "Yeah." He gestured toward his head. "You know…the red hair."

Everson frowned. "Why would that matter?"

"Exactly."

Everson's frown turned into a smile, driven by a rush of gratitude. He felt glad to have met this boy.

"All right, then." Everson turned toward the girl. "I guess he's my roommate."

She looked toward Jonah. "And your name is…?"

"Jonah Selbin."

She flipped the page and scanned the list before nodding. "You two can have room 1021. It's the closest one that's open."

The boy behind her turned toward a cart that included a series of wooden pegs, keys hanging from each peg.

"I thought you would rather not have a room at the far end of the wing." Her eyes flicked toward Everson's canes. "It's a bit of walk."

Everson gave a weak smile. "That's considerate…but don't worry about me. I can get around fine."

The boy appeared beside her and held out two keys, each dangling from a brown leather cord. Everson grabbed one and looped the cord around his neck as Jonah grabbed the other.

While pointing toward a corridor that led east, the girl spoke again. "The boys' wing is down that hallway. You'll find your room on the first floor." She pointed toward the center hallway. "The dining hall is the first door down that corridor. Lunch is served at noon. There's a mandatory meeting right afterward, so don't be late."

Jonah grinned at the girl. "Thank you, my dear…"

"Stella," she said with a smile at the corner of her lip.

"Thank you Stella." Jonah bowed to the girl. "I hope to see you again, soon."

He then turned and crossed the tiled floor, toward the boys' wing. Everson hurried to follow, catching Jonah as he entered the wide corridor.

Although the hallway was windowless, there was plenty enough light thanks to a blue glow emanating from various tiles in the floor. Everson stared at them in wonder, having never seen so much glowstone in his life. He paused and tentatively tapped one with a cane before continuing on.

When his focus shifted to the walls, he noticed tapestries filling the empty spaces between closed doors. The nearest pair of doors were stained a deep walnut color and marked with a plaque that read *Hall of Truth*. He frowned and considered what the room's purpose might be.

Jonah spoke, drawing his attention. "So, where are you from?"

Everson shuffled faster to catch his new roommate. As he reached him, they both resumed their trek toward the narrow hallway ahead.

"I'm from Cinti Mor."

"Hurnsdom?" Jonah raised one brow. "I expected you might say Vinacci, or perhaps Kalimar."

"Why do you say that?"

Jonah shrugged. "Most Hurns have lighter hair with green or blue eyes. You clearly are not like most Hurns."

Everson's thoughts turned to his family and his friends in Cinti Mor. He had never acknowledged it, but Jonah was right. His dark hair and dark eyes made him different.

"What is your talent?"

"What?" Everson looked at Jonah. "What do you mean?"

"Why are you here?" Jonah shook his head. "They don't let just anyone into *FAME*."

Everson's brow furrowed. "FAME?"

"Yeah. Fallbrandt Academy of Magic and Engineering." Jonah grinned. "FAME."

"I haven't heard it called that, but it makes sense."

"I'm here to learn magic." Jonah's eyes glowed as he said it.

A pang of jealousy quivered within Everson, more so than when he saw other kids running or jumping or doing other physical feats that were beyond his capabilities. The idea of magic excited him like nothing else.

"That's...amazing." Everson hoped he sounded supportive.

The hallway narrowed, becoming just wide enough for the two boys to walk in tandem comfortably. Glowing tiles continued to light the way, intermixed with the dull gray of standard stone. Every few strides, they passed a closed door on each side.

"You still haven't told me why you're here."

"Oh, sorry. I'm here to become an Engineer."

"You're smart, then."

Everson shrugged, "I guess."

"Have you invented anything?"

He nodded absently as he peered through an open door and found a boy sitting on a bed, reading something.

"I knew it." Jonah smiled, his excitement apparent. "Maybe we can invent some new stuff together. I've heard that FAME holds the secrets to enchanting."

Everson stopped outside the door marked 1021 as Jonah used his key to unlock it.

"Enchanting?"

Jonah opened the door and stepped aside. "After you."

Everson shuffled past him and into a room with two beds – one along the left wall, the other to the right. Sunlight shone through a gap in the dark blue curtains covering the window opposite the door, providing a bit of light. A desk and a chair sat below the window, while a wardrobe stood beside the door as the only other furniture in the room.

Jonah rested his pack on the bed near the door and moved to the window, parting the curtain. "Enchanted items have magic embedded in them, forever. They are objects of power, rare and valuable."

"I don't know anything about magic." Everson backed up to the other bed and sat before sliding his pack off his shoulder. "They tested me for it before I left Cinti Mor, but I don't have the talent."

Just thinking about it caused Everson pain. He desperately wished to learn magic – dreamt of discovering what impossibilities it might make possible. He then considered Jonah's words, and the concept of inventing something enchanted by magic suddenly gripped him. In his mind's eye, a mysterious corridor appeared, filled with a shifting purple haze. A closed door waited at the far end, beyond which, new possibilities awaited him. Somewhere within the Academy, he would find the key.

13

THE MAN IN BLACK

An ocean of students dressed in long blue coats filled the Dome. Circular in shape, the massive building was divided into eight sections of benches, each section facing the raised dais at the core. Everson sat at one end of a crowded bench. Jonah sat beside him, chatting with Garien, another first-year student they had met in the dining hall during lunch.

Everson stared up at the crystal suspended from the center of the domed roof, its angular facets refracting the rays that streamed through skylights. The effect caused diamond-shaped rainbows to drift through the audience as the crystal slowly rotated. Everson found himself admiring the design and its ability to convert simple sunlight to an array of colors.

Above the buzz of conversation that filled the air, Everson heard a commotion behind him. He turned to find a procession of fifteen people pass by, all dressed in purple and black coats, save for the man who led them.

The silver panels in his black coat had a metallic effect that reflected light, although it was fabric. A well-trimmed brown beard and short brown hair framed the man's face, narrow to match his squinty eyes. He appeared serious and confident as he climbed the stairs to the dais.

When the entire procession arranged themselves in the chairs behind the man, he stepped to the podium and the crowd quieted. As the din fell to a hush, an odd series of scraping and thumping sounds echoed from the aisle. Everson and everyone else turned to find a man hobbling toward the dais with the support of a cane.

Dressed in black with a black flowing cloak to match, the man's long graying hair was tied in a tail that dangled to his shoulder blades. When he reached the stairs rising to the dais, he edged up them one step at a time, eventually cresting the top before he shuffled toward the last open chair. The grimace on the man's face eased to the look of relief as he sat. Everson noticed that the man lacked a rune, unlike his comrades – every one of whom was marked with the rune of Issal.

The man in the silver-paneled coat nodded to the men and women seated behind him before turning to face the podium. Tall and thin and middle-aged, the man wore the cloak of authority with practiced ease.

"Welcome to the Fallbrandt Academy of Magic and Engineering. My name is Abraham Ackerson. As I begin my seventeenth year as Head-master of this fine institution, I find myself reflecting on how the academy has evolved over time.

"Founded over four centuries ago as a bastion of knowledge, the academy has forever existed with the mission to foster the natural talents of our students. With our help and guidance, academy graduates leave here to become the leaders of tomorrow.

"Time passes. Seasons change. New babes enter this life while others die and move on to the next. Even kingdoms and empires come and go. Yet, the academy remains. This institution is not defined by individuals or nations, for it exists beyond borders and politics. By becoming a student of the academy, you take an oath to never abuse the knowledge you garner inside these walls. Rather, you must pursue the highest of ideals, for you have an obligation to humanity. Your life-long mission will be singular in nature, one that will foster a better tomorrow.

"You and your fellow students have traveled here from all corners of Issalia with dreams of magic and inventions and new possibilities. Here, we will help you harness your abilities so you may use your skills to achieve things never before dreamt possible.

"Some of you now take your first step on the path to becoming a master, while others find themselves nearing the end of their quest. The master instructors seated behind me will be your guides on this journey. Regardless of your specialty – be it ecclesiast, arcanist, or engineer – remember that the tools you develop here come with responsibility. You must never use your power with the purpose of taking innocent lives nor for pure personal benefit. Life is the greatest gift of all. Use your abilities to improve lives, to prolong lives, to enrich lives, and to save lives. In doing so, you will help usher in a new age.

"The remainder of the day is your own. Enjoy the freedom, for tomorrow class begins after breakfast. You are dismissed."

Applause flooded the air, the cacophony dimming to buzzing chatter as the students in the room began to rise. As they poured from the benches, the herd gathered in the aisle and filtered through the door at the back of the room.

"Come on," Jonah prodded Everson. "Let's go."

Everson shook his head. "No. I'll wait a bit. I don't want to slow anyone down."

"Okay. I'll wait with you."

Everson twisted his body, pulling his legs aside so that others could pass by. Garien and the other students in the row shuffled past before following the others toward the door. Everson glanced at Jonah, who appeared ambivalent about needing to wait while the others departed.

Just when Everson was about to get up, he noticed Headmaster Ackerson descending the stairs with the school instructors following. Again, the gray-haired man in black trailed the group, leaning heavily on his cane. The man's face clenched as he descended the stairs, one step at a time. He reached the bottom and began up the aisle, the man's hard eyes meeting Everson's as he passed. Everson's breathing stopped in a moment of exposed fear – fear that this man spied his weakness, the chips and cracks that lined his very soul.

The man passed by and Everson exhaled, suddenly realizing that he had been holding his breath.

"Everyone's gone now. Let's go." Jonah said as he stood.

Everson pushed himself to standing position.

As he trailed behind the school leaders, Everson watched the man in black, his gait twisted and uneven, his weight leaning hard on the cane in his hand. Everson glanced down at his own canes and found himself wondering what others saw when they looked at him. *Do they see an invalid? Does anyone think I'm capable?*

They emerged into the hallway, illuminated by glowing tiles amidst the dull gray stone floor. While everyone else headed toward the front of the school, the man in black turned left at the first corridor. When Everson reached the intersection, he stopped and watched the man approach an ominous pair of black doors at the end of the hallway. A single word marked the plaque above the doors, piquing his interest. *Forbidden.*

The man opened one of the doors and slipped through, closing it behind him.

"I wonder where that door leads," he muttered.

"That's the entrance to the Arcane Ward, the big square tower at the back of the school."

Everson turned toward Jonah. "How do you know?"

A look of surprise flashed across Jonah's face, disappearing in a blink. "I've heard of it." He shrugged. "I heard that it took fourteen years to build, with nearly three hundred people working on it the entire time… and it was built with the assistance of magic."

"It sounds incredible."

Jonah leaned closer and spoke in a hushed tone. "I also heard that the tower is restricted – no students allowed."

Everson turned toward the doors, black and ominous. "Why?"

"That's where the master arcanists live."

With a nod of thanks as Jonah held the door open, Everson shuffled outside, squinting in the bright afternoon sun that shone upon the lawn before the academy. He then methodically worked his way down the stairs until he reached the gravel at the bottom. Two students – a boy and a girl – walked past him and recognition struck Everson so hard that he almost stumbled.

Almost four years had passed since he had last seen her. In that time, she had somehow become even more beautiful. Without even knowing it, her name slipped between his lips and sang in the air.

"Rena?"

The couple stopped in mid-conversation. The girl turned toward Everson, her green eyes coming alight and she wrapped her arms about him.

"Ev! It's great to see you!" Rena exclaimed.

As she released him, her companion patted Everson on the shoulder. "I thought you might end up here. You always were the smartest kid in Cinti Mor."

Taller than ever, the boy towered over Everson. His auburn hair had been tamed, now combed to the side. He shared a friendly smile as Rena took his hand. Everson was stunned as pleasant and troubled memories of his past resurfaced in simultaneous contention. After a few seconds, he gathered himself enough to respond.

"Torney?"

Torney grinned. "Yep. It's me."

Jonah stopped beside the trio. "You guys know each other?"

Everson turned toward Jonah, thankful that someone else was present to divert the conversation…to hide his awkwardness.

"Jonah, meet Torney and Rena." Everson nodded toward them. "They're both from Cinti Mor. We…grew up together."

Jonah smiled and held his hand out. "It's nice to meet you. I'm Everson's roommate."

Torney shook Jonah's hand and replied in kind before Rena did the same.

Everson turned toward Rena. "What are you doing here? I heard that your parents moved to New Kardis."

"When they tested me at the temple in New Kardis, they discovered I had some talent with magic." She smiled. "I came here last year and began training."

Everson looked at Torney. "What about you, Torney?"

The boy shrugged. "I've been here two years. Like Rena, I'm training in magic, both *Order* and *Chaos*."

Curiosity stirred inside Everson, hungering for information. "*Chaos*? What is that?"

Torney gave a knowing smile. "You'll find out."

A frown crossed Everson's face. He hated leaving his curiosity unfed. The hunger of it gnawed at him, consuming his attention until he spied Rena's hand clasped with Torney's.

Confusion caused Everson's head to tilt and his brow to furrow. Realization rushed in and an aching feeling flooded over his curiosity, leaving it drowned and forgotten.

Rena followed Everson's eyes, and she glanced at her hand. "Oh, yes. I...um...we should tell you that Torney and I began seeing each other last year." She smiled at the tall boy. "Torney's my boyfriend, now."

Everson wanted to respond, but found his tongue locked within a chest, the key nowhere to be found.

"That's great!" Jonah patted Rena and Torney on the shoulders. "I'm happy for you." He turned toward Everson. "Everson is, too. Right?"

With a forced smile, Everson gave a weak nod. His hands shook, causing his canes to wobble. He prayed that he would not fall over. Not now. Not in front of her.

14

CHAOS THEORY

Noisy chatter permeated the dining hall, the tables filled with anxious students. Everson sat alone at a bench, his table empty amongst the crowd. As other boys and girls walked past him, his gaze would flick up toward them, only to flash back toward the table when they looked in his direction. None sat at his table.

Eventually, Everson spotted Jonah approaching with two bowls in hand and two cups held against his torso with his forearms. A wave of relief struck at his roommate's arrival.

"Take a bowl." Jonah nodded toward his left hand. "It's porridge. My guess is that their dogs rejected it, so we have to eat it."

Everson reached for a bowl and a cup, setting them on the table. "Thanks again. I...don't know what I'd do without your help."

Jonah sat on the bench opposite from Everson. "You haven't tasted the porridge. You might find yourself cursing me instead of thanking me."

Everson returned Jonah's grin. "Fair enough."

Steam rose from the bowl as Everson scooped a spoon full, blowing on it before taking a taste. It was hot, but not scalding.

"Ugh." Jonah scrunched his nose. "I knew it. Nasty."

Everson shrugged. "I've had worse."

Jonah shook his head. "What's worse than porridge?"

Everson grinned. "Cake."

"What? Cake is delicious."

"Not when my sister makes it."

"How so?"

"She messed up the recipe. Rather than using a teaspoon of salt, she used a tablespoon full."

Jonah frowned. "That sounds bad."

"Oh, it was bad."

"Ugh."

"That wasn't even the worst part."

With a raised a brow, Jonah asked, "Okay. What else?"

"She accidentally used salt instead of sugar when mixing the frosting." Everson shook his head at the memory. "The cake tasted like the salt licks that farmers put out for cattle."

Jonah chuckled. "Okay. You win. Your sister's cake is worse than porridge."

Everson took another bite of the porridge and found it cooled enough to eat. Alone at their table, he and Jonah ate in silence. When he finished, Everson looked up to find Jonah's bowl clean.

"For hating porridge, you sure ate it well," he noted.

Jonah shrugged. "It might be disgusting, but it's food. I want to make sure I have energy for my first day of class."

"I can buy that," Everson said. "Speaking of class, we have our first class together. Let's head there now, so we can get decent seats."

"Good idea." Jonah grabbed the bowls and cups as he stood. "Head for the hallway, and I'll meet you there after I drop these off."

With a nod in response, Everson fished his canes from below the table and pushed himself into a standing position. He shuffled down the aisle between tables, toward the door. A glance to the side caught sight of Rena, sitting at a table with Torney and four other students. She looked gorgeous with her auburn curls pouring over the shoulders of her white-trimmed navy blue coat. She laughed at something said, and her green eyes sparkled with mirth. When she turned toward Everson, he realized he had been staring at her.

Panic struck and he hurried forward. In his haste, he collided with an empty bench and fell over it. He desperately grabbed the table's edge to stop himself from falling, which caused the far end of the table to flip up, launching the bowl of porridge sitting there.

Everson landed hard on his hip and released his grip from the table, which fell to the floor with a loud *thud*. A crash on the tabletop caused Everson to look up as the bowl of porridge bounced, flipped, and dumped its contents onto his head.

Wiping the hot porridge from his face, Everson looked around in shock. The boy who had been eating alone at the table still held his spoon as he stared at his breakfast all over Everson. In fact, dozens of students stared in his direction, many standing, most with eyes wide. Everson's gaze shifted toward Rena, and he found her looking at him, her eyes filled with pity.

Laughter erupted throughout the room. Fingers pointed in his direction. Everson wished he were anywhere else. Anyone else.

He turned around and found his canes a few paces away, in opposite directions. Clenching his teeth as he struggled to hold his tears back, he pulled himself toward the nearest cane. When he reached it, he found two sets of boots before him. He looked up and found Rena looking down with sadness in her eyes.

"Oh, Everson."

He swallowed hard, not knowing what to say. He turned toward the boy at her side and found Torney smiling down at him.

"You sure made a fool of yourself, Ev." Torney shook his head. "Here. Let me help you up."

The tall boy bent and put his arm about Everson, lifting him as he got his cane into position.

"Um…thanks." Everson mumbled.

"Are you all right?" Rena asked with a concerned expression.

"I'll be fine." He said, his voice shaky. "Nothing injured…except my pride."

"Here's your other cane."

Everson turned to find Jonah holding his cane and sporting a wry grin.

"I leave you for one minute and look at what happens." Jonah shook his head. "I'd be hard pressed to invent a better way to get everyone's attention. Well played."

"What?"

"You can't shine like a star if nobody ever looks your way." Jonah patted Everson's shoulder. "You got their attention. Everyone here will notice you now. All you have to do is show them something."

"Um…okay."

Jonah turned toward Torney and Rena. "Thanks for helping him. I can take it from here."

Everson made his way toward the door as a hurricane of humiliation swirled inside him, buffeted by waves of confusion.

When they reached the hallway, he turned toward Jonah.

"I didn't do that on purpose."

Jonah shrugged. "I know that." He glanced back toward the dining hall. "Hopefully, what I said will give them pause. It might even work out, provided you follow with something more spectacular sometime soon."

Everson gave a weak smile. "Thanks. I'll see what I can do."

Jonah patted him on the back. "For now, I suggest we head back to the room so you can clean up before class." He paused and cocked his head to the side. "That is, unless you prefer to wear porridge for the day."

Everson put on a shaky smile. "No. I think I'll pass."

Dressed in a navy coat that was still damp from rinsing away the porridge, Everson followed Jonah into the classroom. Rows of tables filled the room, split by an aisle down the center. Four chairs sat beside each table, facing the front of the room. Students within were chatting busily until a bell rang in the corridor outside. Everyone turned toward the front of the room as the instructor rose to her feet from her desk.

The woman's black wavy hair shone with a luster, complementing her large brown eyes. She wore a form-fitting purple and black coat, unbuttoned at the neckline. Where exposed, her mocha skin appeared smooth and youthful despite Everson's suspicion that she was far older than he was. Where covered, her body had curves that men noticed and women envied, regardless of age. The woman sauntered down the aisle in her black breeches and tall black boots as Everson and Jonah stared. She arched a brow in question.

"Aren't you two going to sit?"

Everson blinked and glanced at the tables, finding two open seats – one in the front and the other near the back.

"Yes. Sorry, Master…"

The woman smiled. "Alridge. Master Salina Alridge."

Jonah turned to Everson. "Why don't you take the seat at the front?"

Everson shuffled across the room to the open chair. Only after he and Jonah were seated, did Master Alridge speak.

"Good morning, Novices. My name is Master Alridge. I will be you instructor in Chaos Theory."

She paused, glancing about the room with her eyes narrowed. "Yes, I see confusion and curiosity on your faces. This is good…and expected.

"Chaos is a relatively secret thing, something you will hear very little about beyond this valley. In part, this is because the discovery, or more accurately, rediscovery of this magic occurred less than two decades ago. The larger truth is that Chaos is very powerful…and very dangerous. Its misuse can be fatal. When wielded with evil intentions, it can be devastating."

She stared at the students with intensity in her eyes.

"You must never take Chaos lightly. It should be treated with much consideration and handled with delicate care."

Again, she paused to allow the students to absorb her message. After a moment, she clasped her hands together and gave a firm nod.

"Now that you have been warned, I shall begin."

She strolled down the aisle as she spoke. "Chaos is a term used to describe the energy that exists all around us. Heat, light, kinetics, grav-ity…any source of latent energy other than life. Life is different and relates to Order, which in many ways is the opposite of Chaos. However, that is for another lesson in another class.

"On the most basic level, arcanists are individuals who have a natural ability to gather ambient Chaos, drawing into themselves by force of will. Be aware that an arcanist cannot hold this energy for long, or it will destroy them. Instead, they channel the gathered Chaos into a rune, giving the energy purpose. The runes themselves are the most important aspect of Chaos Theory. Without a properly drawn rune to harness the energy, to give it shape and definition, the Chaos will destroy anything or anyone near the rune. It will fry people's brains, burn out their eyes, and leave them an empty husk."

Everson swallowed hard as he imagined this unknown power lashing out and killing those who stood too close.

"Many of you have come to this school in hope of learning to wield this magic I speak of. You dream of unimaginable power and supernatural abilities. Others have come to the school with the knowledge that they cannot wield Chaos, but either have some affinity for wielding Order or have the imagination and intelligence required to excel at Engineering. Those who can never tap into Chaos themselves may wonder why they attend this class."

Everson found himself nodding, and he noticed others doing the same.

"We teach everyone the theory because understanding is required in order to respect the power. In addition, Engineering students may discover new means of combining Chaos augmentations with inventions, tools, and weapons in some way that others have yet to conceive."

Enchanting, Everson thought.

Master Alridge stopped at the front of the room and picked up a small chunk of glowstone. Using it, she then began tracing a symbol on the black wall at the front of the room. After a minute, she stepped back and nodded in approval.

Pointing at the symbol, she turned toward the class. "This is the rune for Light, and it is the rune we will focus on for now."

She moved to her desk and picked up a stone the size of her fist. When she held the stone up, Everson noticed a rune drawn on it, the same rune as she had drawn on the wall.

"Watch and learn." Master Alridge closed her eyes.

The room fell silent, the very air dripping with anticipation. The woman's eyes flashed open, and Everson gasped. Red energy crackled in her pupils, glowing brightly. She stared at the rune, which lit up with a red glow, pulsed, and faded. Everson's attention returned to Master

Alridge, and he found her eyes had faded back to brown. The rock in her hand flared into white light, so bright that Everson had to turn away. When the bright rays dimmed, he turned to find Master Alridge covering the light with a black cloth.

"As you can see, the effect the rune exhibits is very singular in nature. Please note that effect and application are not the same. We will explore various applications over the next two weeks before we move onto the next rune."

Bright white light still leaked from beneath the cloak, illuminating the floor below. Everson stared at it as his mind began to race, considering the possibilities of how to put this magic to use.

15

COINCIDENCE

Tall workbenches arranged in columns ran the length of the Engineering classroom, with three stools beside each workbench. Everson chose a stool at a bench in the middle row, beside a girl with rectangular spectacles. Tall and thin, her dark hair fell straight and lifeless over her shoulders. The girl's furtive gaze flicked in his direction, her amber eyes widening when she noticed him looking at her. She looked away and Everson did the same.

A pudgy boy with square-cut bangs walked past, as did a girl with a long blond braid and nervous blue eyes. A short boy, barely five feet tall sat across from him, beside a girl of the same height but twice his weight.

Everson turned toward the door as a tall boy entered and stopped to survey the room. With dark brown hair and eyes to match, the boy had the shoulders of a warrior and carried a calm confidence. His eyes met Everson's and he smiled, his white teeth a stark contrast to the golden hue of his skin.

The boy circled a row of benches and approached Everson with an affable grin.

"You're the porridge boy, right?"

Everson frowned, recalling the incident well.

The boy held up his hands in surrender. "Don't worry. I'm not trying to make fun of you. It's just that it was my porridge you spilled." The boy smiled. "I actually want to thank you. I despise the stuff."

"Um…you're welcome?"

The boy's grin widened and he extended his hand. "I'm Donnell."

Since he was sitting with canes resting below the bench, Everson's hands were free to shake the other boy's hand.

"I'm Everson. It's good to meet you, Donnell."

"Is this seat taken?" Donnell pointed toward the third stool at the workbench.

Everson shook his head. "No. Please, sit."

Donnell slipped past Everson, sat on the stool, and slid his pack onto the bench. The chime of a bell arose and echoed in the corridor beyond the open door. Two male students scurried into the room, one short and portly, the other tall and stick-thin. They scrambled to claim the last two open seats, leaving all eighteen stools occupied. As they settled, the room fell into a state of silent expectation.

Everson glanced toward the open door, toward the cold and silent hallway beyond. His focus shifted to the desk at the front of the room, which remained unoccupied. A glare in the corner of his eye drew his attention to the window, toward the glinting sunlight reflecting off the glass panels of the domed temple roof. Nearing mid-day, it would be warm outside although it remained cool within the stone block walls of the school.

An odd series of sounds came from beyond the open door, drawing everyone's attention. A thud, a footstep, a scuffing – like something being dragged across the floor. The series of sounds repeated, growing louder until a shadow appeared, bent and hunched over.

Stepping into the room was a wizened old man with thin wisps of white curly hair scattered about his balding head. The man's eyebrows were so long that they curled around the frame of his thick, rounded spectacles. Even if he stood upright, the man was small by any measure. Bent over as he was, his head barely cleared the top of the workbenches as he shuffled past. Everson's attention was drawn to the man's cane, made of metal but for the leather-wrapped handle and the odd foot at the bottom. As the man headed toward the desk at the front of the room,

Everson wondered at the weight of a cane made from metal. *How can this decrepit little man carry such weight?*

The man reached the front and sat on the low stool that waited beside the desk. A long sigh slipped out as he visibly relaxed with his cane in his lap.

"And so. It begins," the man said in wheezing voice.

Everson glanced about the room and found others appearing as confused as he was.

"Sixty-two years ago, I began this journey. In that time, I have seen many amazing things come to light – inventions, discoveries, victories, and change. Things always change.

"I have witnessed the horrors that only an army of monsters can inflict and have basked in the glory of their defeat. I watched an empire crumble, and I helped build a new regime. My name will remain among the histories when I pass – at least until mankind sees fit to erase even that – for such is the way that man treats the past. And then, I will be forever lost and forgotten like so many ghosts before me. For now, it is time for me to sleep…forever."

The man fell silent, his eyes drifting closed. Not a word was whispered. Not a person moved. A tension filled the air as the still moment carried on. In subconscious reaction, Everson held his breath, gasping when the man's eyes flashed open, and he hoisted his cane above him.

"Got you!" The man's cackling laughter filled the room.

Everson found himself grinning, but had no idea why.

As his laughter died down, the old man rested his cane across his lap and spoke.

"I am Master Pherran Nindlerod." He nodded. "Yes…THAT Pherran Nindlerod."

He looked about the room, seeking something. He frowned.

"Doesn't anybody know my name?"

Everson raised his hand.

"What's your name?"

"Um…Everson. Everson Gulagas."

"Well, *Um Everson*. What do you know about me?"

"I…um…you invented the pedal-driven grinding wheel."

Master Nindlerod smiled. "Yes. That's good. Anything else?"

Everson gave a weak shrug, unsure of what to say.

Nindlerod sighed. "Well, at least you got one of them." He shook his head, and then his bushy white brows furrowed. "Does anyone know why we are here?"

A smattering of hands raised, and Nindlerod pointed toward the girl sitting beside Everson.

"Yes, miss…"

"I…," she mumbled.

"Could you repeat that? I didn't quite get your name."

She cleared her throat. "Ivy. My name is Ivy, Sir. Ivy Fluerien."

"Good. Now, tell me, Miss Fluerien, why you are here?"

"I'm here to learn. To learn and to invent…things that might make the world a better place."

Nindlerod laughed, cackling as his head bobbed eagerly. "Very good. Very good, indeed. If I were a decade younger, I'd dance a jig for such a response.

"Each of you is here because you have demonstrated a high level of intelligence. I suspect that each of you is used to being the smartest person in the room. However, you cannot all be the smartest person here, can you?"

He paused as the students glanced at each other.

"In fact, one of you is the dumbest person here!" Nindlerod's laughter cackled again as he slapped his leg. "The dumbest," he mumbled, shaking his head with a big grin on his face. When he recovered, he spoke again.

"Since there is no sure way to quantify who is smartest and who is dumbest, I suggest that you forget your pride and stop worrying about such things. There will always be someone smarter than you. In fact, the truly intelligent person remains cognizant that there is far more to learn than he or she can ever know.

"Instead, focus on absorbing everything you can from your instructors, from books, and from each other. But remember that being an engineer is not just about learning, it is about creating. It is about dreaming up new ways of accomplishing ordinary tasks and about accomplishing tasks never dreamt of before. So, use your intelligence to feed your imaginations so they might give birth to inventions that will change the world."

While Nindlerod continued speaking, going on about the principles of physics that he would teach in class and the fabrication skills that the students would practice in the Foundry, Everson's mind drifted higher and higher, soaring above the school, the mountains, and even above the clouds. Inspired by Nindlerod's words, he knew that, for the first time, he had found a place where he could maximize his abilities. Here, he would learn everything he could learn. Here, he would experiment, create, and invent something special. Here, he would show the world that he was capable. Here, he would make a difference.

Boys emerged from their rooms and fell into the flow of bodies in the narrow hallway as they headed toward the dining hall. Everson did his best to avoid hitting others with his canes as he shuffled along, a half step behind Jonah. As he made the journey, his mind drifted to the afternoon he had spent training, or more specifically, to the wonders of The Foundry.

He and the other first-year Engineering students had met there after lunch and were introduced to the skill specialists who would be training them. Having grown up with a blacksmith as a father, Everson thought he had a solid grasp of what to expect. He had never been more wrong.

A twisting maze of pipes ran the length of The Foundry, connected to pumps, lifts, winches, and presses. Everson had heard of steam power, and he had even seen two steam carriages on their journey to Fallbrandt. Yet, when he discovered that these tools would function with a simple pull of a lever or the turn of a valve, he had been quite impressed. This fact did not account for the size of such machines nor for the amount of force they could muster.

A number of forges, each three times the size of his father's, were built into one of the long Foundry walls. Scrap metal piles and work-benches filled with hand tools dotted the room. Everywhere Everson looked, students melted steel, bent pipes, blew glass, and assembled their contraptions. The smells of burnt metal and sulfur made some of his fellow students cough, but it didn't affect Everson. He had grown up with it.

In his reverie, he recalled the musical notes he heard when first entering the Foundry, the heavy clang of an iron hammer ringing throughout the room with the whistle of released steam filling the gaps between strikes. Everson grinned as the sound replayed in his ears – a sweet melody that only he could hear. He ached to create something in the Foundry.

"Are you listening to me?"

Jonah's voice pulled Everson from his musings.

"What?" Everson turned toward Jonah.

"I was telling you of the rest of my day."

"Oh. I'm sorry…my mind was elsewhere."

The crowd slowed as they funneled into the dining hall. As Everson broke away from the cluster, Jonah turned toward him.

"I'll go get us some food. You find a table."

"Good idea."

Everson considered his situation as he watched Jonah head toward the kitchen, deciding that it was a massive stroke of luck to have met him. He genuinely liked Jonah, and his manner put Everson at ease. Even the way Jonah helped him seemed natural – not forced, nor out of pity.

He shuffled between the rows of tables and noticed Rena sitting with Torney at a table with three other students, each wearing navy coats with white piping on the shoulders. An image of the morning spill flashed in Everson's head. Wishing to avoid another incident, he looked away from Rena and focused on navigating the tight rows.

When he broke free of the occupied tables, he found an open table and settled onto the bench. A shadow loomed over him and he glanced up to Donnell holding a plate of food in one hand and a mug in the other.

"Hello, Everson. Do you mind if I join you?"

Everson shrugged. "Not at all. Please. Sit."

Donnell sat on the empty bench across from Everson. "Where's your food?"

Everson turned toward the kitchen. "My roommate is grabbing me a plate." He turned back to look at Donnell, who appeared worried. "Don't worry. He's quite friendly. I'm sure you'll get along fine."

Donnell stared at his fork as he stirred pasta about his plate. He lifted his head, his eyes meeting Everson's.

"So, where are you from?"

"I'm from Cinti Mor," Everson replied.

Donnell's brows rose high. "Cinti Mor?"

"Yeah. That's where I grew up. My family moved here just a few days ago."

"So they…left the city with you?"

Everson shrugged. "Yeah. My parents purchased a new house in Fallbrandt, and my father has enough work to keep him busy for some time."

Donnell looked side-to-side with nervous eyes. He leaned forward and whispered. "I heard…I heard that Cinti Mor was attacked."

"Oh." Everson brows rose up. "You know about that? Well, I was there and I can tell you that it's true."

"You were there? How…how did you get away, then?"

"The attack struck as my family was leaving the city. Men came after us, but my sister stopped them."

"Your sister?" Donnell appeared doubtful.

"Yeah. It's hard to believe. In truth, despite her actions, it required a stroke of luck for us to escape."

"What about the city?" Donnell leaned forward, appearing anxious. "Were the Vinacci forces able to take it?"

"I'm afraid so." Everson's voice grew quiet. "They took the gate after an explosion and…their soldiers charged through the gap. I don't know what happened afterward, but it did not look good."

When Donnell looked up, Everson turned to find Jonah approaching with two plates.

"I grabbed an extra sweet roll for you," Jonah said with a grin. As he set the plates down, Jonah asked Everson, "Who's this?"

"Jonah, this is Donnell. He's studying to be an Engineer." Everson turned toward the boy across the table. "Donnell, this is Jonah, my roommate. He's here to learn magic."

"Hello, Donnell." Jonah extended his hand.

Donnell appeared to hesitate before extending his hand. They shook, and Jonah turned back to Everson.

"I need to grab something to drink." Jonah stepped back from the table. "I'll be right back."

Donnell's eyes narrowed as he watched Jonah head toward the kitchen.

"How did you meet Jonah?"

Everson shrugged. "He showed up at the school right after I did."

Donnell turned toward him, looking Everson in the eye. "He walked in right behind you? Was it his idea for you to be roommates? Was it his idea to get your food for you?"

Everson's brow furrowed. "Yes. Why?"

Donnell stared at his plate as he poked at his pasta. "This boy you don't know appears from nowhere, volunteers to be your roommate, and now helps you get your meals. That seems mighty convenient and a bit too coincidental." Donnell's eyes met Everson's. "I don't believe in coincidence."

16

RANGER OUTING

"In addition to gaining access to melee weapons, our training expanded in other areas." Quinn peered past the light to count the shadows again, finding three silhouettes. "Three times a week, we spent our afternoons on the archery range. After testing a longbow, flatbow, and crossbow, I settled on a shortbow. The weapon felt less awkward than the longbow and faster to reload than the crossbow. While my skill with the bow seemed better than most of my fellow cadets, there was one girl whose expertise stood out.

"I'll never forget the first time I watched Chuli Ultermane shoot a longbow. Her precision was uncanny. When I watched her grab three arrows at a time, hold them with one hand, and fire them off in rapid succession, I asked Master Hammerton if we would learn the technique. Her response was a frown, and she told me it might take months to master. I noticed the pride and appreciation in the woman's eyes whenever she watched Chuli shoot."

Quinn grunted as she tugged on the knot, grinning when she felt it begin to give.

"On the afternoons when we weren't training as an archer, we spent time in the stables to work on horsemanship. Unfortunately, I discovered that caring for a horse also included mucking the stables – a job I detested. Feeding, grooming, checking shoes, and tacking the horse were all skills we had to learn before our first ride. After two weeks of this torture, I found myself upon the saddle for the first time." She grimaced at the memory. "The thrill I experienced when first riding the horse was soon tempered by the soreness of my rear and thighs. That soreness grew worse the next day, leaving me wincing in pain each time I tried to sit.

"Despite these new activities, each morning began with physical training that varied between running, calisthenics, rope climbing, agility training, and boxing with hay-stuffed sacks. Every day ended with a session in the arena or training yard, where we would practice and perfect our forms, sometimes in hand fighting, and other times armed with their training weapons.

"Hand fighting duels still took place once a week, but something had changed. I began to win my duels as the attacks and responses came more naturally. Still, I longed to try my skill with the swords against a real opponent. One can only beat a sack of hay so much before it becomes redundant.

"Seventh day remained our designated day of rest, with half the day spent in Tactics training. During the other half, we were expected to study historic battles, geography, recorded strategies, or play Ratio Belli-cus. Once every four weeks, we were tasked with planning an attack or defense under a given set of circumstances.

"This cycle continued for weeks, until Sergeant Jasmine took us to a field near the archery range. There, we joined her assistants, who waited beside a pile of tents. The sergeant announced that we would depart on our first ranger training session the next day, and we had best learn to pitch a tent or we would find ourselves sleeping without shelter. Unaware of what exactly a ranger did, I wondered about what came next."

With the weight of a loaded pack on one shoulder and a short bow and waterskin on the other, Quinn stared across the shadowy field. A puff of steam swirled from her mouth when she sighed – a sign of the chill hanging in the predawn mountain air. Quinn's quill, a bedroll, and a tent big enough for two filled the pack on her back. Hirna, her tent mate, carried their food in lieu of a tent.

Jasmine strolled past the two girls and continued down the line as she inspected the cadets. Quinn chanced a glance to the side and found her fellow first-year cadets standing at attention in a straight line. Each girl was clothed in a brown leather coat, tan breeches, and tall boots. With a pack and a bow strapped over each shoulder and a knife strapped to one thigh, they appeared ready for their first outing.

"When we depart, we will keep a brisk pace through the forest, not slowing to a walk until we begin our ascent. You are to keep up despite the weight you carry. We will spend five nights in the mountains, moving each day and setting up a new camp each night. The afternoons will be spent teaching you ranger skills." She stopped and smirked. "You're lucky because the weather is mild this time of year. When we embark on our first winter session, you'll find yourself wishing for warm and dry weather."

With the flick of the sergeant's staff and nod of her head, her assistants scrambled to the fore with one girl standing to each side of her.

"Vi will lead the first-year cadets, Lissa has the second-year cadets," Jasmine commanded. "You will follow in tandem lines, and I will trail the squad to ensure that none of you dally. Prepare to march."

Jasmine waved her staff and her two assistants moved to the far end of each row, placing Quinn in the lead position of her group and Darnya leading the other. "We're off!" she barked, and Vi began jogging across the field, heading southeast. Following the leader, Quinn ran with her heavy pack bouncing far too eagerly for her liking.

They circled around the archery range and through the knee-high grass. When the group approached the forest edge, a narrow gap to a trail appeared, well-worn and wide enough for two to run astride, yet too small for a wagon.

Quinn soon found herself panting as she ducked beneath low branches and leaped over downed trees. They ran up hills and down through gullies split by trickling water. After twenty minutes, the density of the forest thinned and a lake came into view. There, they reached an old road that hugged the shoreline and turned east.

Glancing to her right, Quinn gazed at the placid waters, mirroring the purple mountains to the east and the pale breaking dawn above them. Rather than dwelling on the tiring run, she allowed herself to become numb to the effort and sink into the peaceful view. The sight of the still surface beneath the glowing sky was breathtaking – if she had the breath to spare.

Darnya suddenly rammed her shoulder into Quinn's, sending her stumbling onto the rocks at the shoreline. Quinn tripped, wobbled, and fell face-first into the lake.

The shock of frigid water fed by snowmelt left Quinn gasping for air as she struggled to regain her footing. She stood in the waist-deep water, dripping wet as the other girls in her squad ran past. Some girls laughed at the sight. Others stared. Within her mind, she recalled the image of young Torney standing in the fountain. Shame for having done that to him struck her but was washed away by the anger she had toward Darnya.

She looked down at herself. Her clothes were sopping wet, leaving her travel gear as heavy as plated armor. As she sloshed toward shore, the last girls ran past and Sergeant Jasmine slowed to a stop.

"Falling in the water won't make this easy, Cadet. If this were a dangerous situation, such a misstep might cost you your life." Despite the heavy pack Jasmine carried, she did not appear winded. "We are not waiting for you, nor are there any excuses for not keeping up with the squad."

Unable to restrain her anger, Quinn snarled back. "Darnya did this! She pushed me in!"

Jasmine's eyes narrowed, matching her frown. "You are forgetting who you are addressing, Cadet."

Quinn pressed her lips together and held back her retort. "Sorry, Sergeant."

With a nod, Jasmine broke into a run, shouting back over her shoulder. "Hurry and catch up, Cadet. I highly suggest you don't get yourself lost."

—◆—

Soon after passing the lake, the ground began to rise and they slowed to a walk. Two hours later, they reached a saddle between two peaks and stopped for a brief rest. The sun above them warmed the air, but the chill brought by the elevation caused Quinn to shiver in her damp clothing. She didn't talk to anyone, and nobody said a word to her. As she drank from her waterskin, she surveyed the view to the east, gazing over a valley floor surrounded by tree-covered mountainsides. Peaks near and far defined the horizon, many retaining snow on the north face despite it being well beyond the backside of summer. The land appeared wild, untouched by man.

When the squad began the descent to the valley east of the saddle, they resumed their slow run down a narrow trail, requiring them to travel in single file. Branches swatted at them as they ran past. Undergrowth was trampled beneath their feet. Startled birds took flight at their approach. All the while, the sun slowly rose in the sky, toward its apex.

Moving swiftly, the squad soon reached level ground and turned north. For another hour, they ran, not slowing until they reached a small glade among a sea of leaf trees. Pale purple flowers dotted the waving yellow grass of the glade, drawing gold and black butterflies that flitted from flower to flower. The peace of the quiet meadow was soon disturbed as Jasmine declared that they were to set camp.

As they had practiced the previous day, their tents were arranged into two straight rows, the flaps facing one another with a gap five strides apart. Once the tents were raised, they took a quick break to eat a meal consisting of trail rations, dried beef, and hard rolls. With their hungry stomachs adequately tempered, but certainly not full, the real work began.

Quinn found herself among the largest group - twenty girls assigned to collect strong saplings that they would carve into stakes. Four other girls were tasked with digging a fire pit at one end of the field, using small spades supplied by Vi and Lissa. Five girls were sent to find firewood. Another group of five had the task of hiding the trail left behind. The last six girls were split in two, with one following Lissa and the other following Vi. Armed with only their bows, quivers, and knives, those two groups were to hunt down dinner.

With the stakes collected, Quinn and the rest of her group used their knives to carve sharp points and then thrust the stakes into the ground around the perimeter of the field, creating a simple, yet somewhat defensible barrier. The process took three hours and left Quinn wondering why they would spend so much time creating the barrier when they were to leave early the next day.

As the sun edged below the peaks to the west, the fire was lit. A dinner of roasted jackaroo and dry bread followed. Soon after eating, the exhausted girls crawled into their tents to sleep. This is when Quinn realized that her bedroll had not dried from her dip in the mountain lake. Despite the dampness of her bed and the chill in the air, exhaustion won out and she fell into a deep sleep.

The next four days seemed a blur as they traveled about the northern valleys of the Skyspike Mountains. How many miles they covered, Quinn couldn't begin to guess. Each day, when the sun reached its apex, they would stop and set up camp. The groupings changed each day, but the results were the same. Dig a fire pit, collect wood, hide the trail, hunt for dinner, and construct a barrier of sharpened stakes as a defense. Once camp was set, they would work on various ranger skills – navigation the first day, tree climbing the second, foraging the third, and tracking on both the fourth and fifth days.

On the sixth day, they broke camp early – as they had done every other morning – and found themselves crossing a saddle by mid-morning. At the peak, Quinn found herself looking over a valley to the east, one with a complex of buildings at each end of a vast field. Somehow, their journey had circled around both academies and placed them opposite from where the journey had begun.

Two hours later, they emerged from the thick forest and onto the western edge of the lawn. With the academy now in sight, Quinn found herself longing for a night of sleep in her bunk. It wasn't particularly comfortable, but it would feel like a dream compared to sleeping on the hard, uneven ground.

17

THE ESCARP

Wooden swords swept through the air in parallel arcs, spinning and slicing before Vi reclaimed a ready stance. Quinn and three other girls watched her closely and repeated the young woman's moves as if dancing with invisible partners. Their shadows, cast by the mid-day sun, mimicked their movements obediently. A bead of sweat tracked down Quinn's forehead and into her eye. The sting caused her to blink twice, but her attention remained focused. Such distractions now had little affect on her.

For the first week, Quinn had found it difficult to follow the woman, not fully understanding the intent of the exercise. However, repetition is an odd thing, shaving the unfamiliar away until it becomes natural. As her body grew used to the movements, she found herself executing them without the need to think.

By the third week, Vi had doubled her movement speed, forcing Quinn and the other girls to do so as well. Surprisingly, Quinn found the faster speed easier to perform, as if she had been fighting to restrain herself when executing the forms at a slower pace. Now, after eight weeks of practicing, Quinn found the beauty in the form, like poetry in motion...if one viewed a dance with death as poetry.

"Stop and take positions!" Sergeant Jasmine's voice echoed throughout the training yard.

Quinn relaxed her stance, wiped her forehead with the back of her hand, and fell into line. The other groups – the girls who had been training with the quarterstaff and those who trained with a sword and shield – joined hers as they formed two rows. Vi and Lissa stood to the side as Jasmine stood before the female cadets.

The sergeant gave them a nod of approval. "You are progressing well. I suspect that you long to test your skill against another. Beginning tomorrow, we will end each week with a dueling session, which will allow you to test your mettle against a real opponent.

"Yes, there will be injuries, some significant. This is why there will be a crew of ecclesiasts from our sister school ready to heal your broken bones.

"As a reward for the hard work you've put in these past fifteen weeks, you will have the subsequent three days off. Free time is a precious commodity. Use it wisely.

"I'm going to release you early today so you can rest before your duel. But first, I thought it would be fun to have a bit of competition."

The woman walked toward the wall that stood beside the training yard. Built from rectangular rocks mortared together, the face of the wall was hundreds of feet in length and stood four stories tall. A wooden scaffolding stood at the end of the wall that did not intersect with the academy.

Jasmine patted one of the rocks that jutted out from the wall and turned toward her audience. "When this wall was constructed, it was intentionally designed with random rocks jutting out more than others, providing natural handholds. As the second-year cadets are aware, we call this wall *The Escarp*."

As she strode toward them, Jasmine explained. "We use The Escarp as a little test – a chance to put your strength and agility on display. You've been improving both aspects of your body since the day you arrived here, so climbing this wall should be no trouble. As incentive, whoever can do so the fastest earns a reward. Unlike the other duels where I will assign each pairing, the winner of this challenge is allowed to select their opponent themselves."

She stepped aside and pointed toward the wall. "Second-year Cadets, you know what to do. Go!"

The front row of girls bolted toward the wall and began scaling it. Moving at varying speeds, they worked their way up the wall like a nest of freshly hatched spiders.

Simone and Darnya separated from the pack, rising faster than the other girls. In a close race, Darnya reached the top a half step ahead of Simone. Quinn frowned as she watched Darnya stand to raise her fist in the air, pumping it as she said something to Simone. She then jogged to the scaffolding at the far end and descended the series of ladders with ease. By the time the last girl stood on the rooftop, Darnya was on the ground, striding proudly toward Jasmine.

"Very good, Darnya." The sergeant nodded in approval. "I think you're even faster than last year."

"Thank you, Sergeant."

Darnya, Simone, and the other second-year students settled into a line behind the first-year students. With them all in position, Jasmine addressed the squad.

"First-year Cadets, you have seen how it's done. Get to the top as fast as possible, but don't fall. It may not kill you, but it will cause a great deal of pain, and you'll find yourself in the infirmary." She moved aside to leave open ground between the students and the wall. "Ready…and…go!"

Quinn sprinted toward the wall, slowing just before reaching it. She extended her arms and found a handhold, pulling herself up while pushing up with the opposite foot. Keeping her eyes above her, she continued upward, working as quickly as she dared. When she reached the top, she pulled herself onto the roof and stood.

The height seemed much higher than it did when standing on the ground. A glance to one side showed the roof empty save for the Tantarri girl, who was pulling herself to her knees. A glance to the other side revealed a short girl named Yvette doing the same. When she realized that she had won, elation forced a grin onto Quinn's face. As the Tantarri girl approached, Quinn nodded to her.

"That was a tough race, Chuli. You did well."

Chuli's eyes narrowed. "Thank you, Jacquinn Gulagas."

She continued past Quinn and climbed onto the scaffolding to begin her descent, trailing behind Yvette. After a glance toward the other girls cresting the roof edge, Quinn scrambled down the first ladder.

When she reached the ground, Quinn joined Chuli and Yvette to take position in line behind the second-year students. The other girls soon joined them, lining up as Quinn considered whom she might choose to fight in tomorrow's duel. With everyone assembled, Sergeant Jasmine again addressed the group.

"That was not a bad first attempt. In particular, I was impressed by the speed of Cadets Quinn, Yvette, and Chuli."

For the first time since her arrival at the academy, Quinn felt the warmth of praise. Like a parent hugging a child, the embrace of approval provided comfort and a sense of accomplishment.

"Darnya and Quinn, since you each won your heat, I need you to step forward so we can settle this."

"What?" Quinn muttered as she watched Darnya stand at attention beside Jasmine.

"What are you waiting for, Cadet?" Jasmine asked as she crossed her arms over her chest. "I'm sure the others would like to head to the baths so they can take advantage of this glorious autumn afternoon."

Realizing that everyone was looking at her, Quinn shuffled forward to take her position beside Darnya. Standing beside the girl made her feel small. Having everyone watching sent her heart racing.

"This is it. Winner chooses their opponent for tomorrow." Jasmine shouted, "Ready…go!"

Quinn darted forward, matching Darnya in speed despite the other girl's longer stride. They reached the wall simultaneously and began scaling it with Darnya slightly ahead due to her added height. Discarding caution, Quinn climbed faster than she thought was possible.

As Quinn neared the top, she found herself gaining on the other girl. With a few feet remaining, she sensed herself passing Darnya…until her grip slipped. Panic struck, and Quinn scrambled to grab something – anything – when her fingers clamped around the tail of Darnya's hair.

"Argh!" the other girl cried out as her head snapped backward.

Quinn released the girl's hair and was able to grab ahold of a rock.

She resumed her climb, but Darnya was a step ahead and crested the rooftop just before Quinn reached it.

Pulling herself to her belly and rising to her knees, Quinn caught her breath while glancing up at the other girl.

"You tried to pull me off the wall!" Darnya bellowed.

Quinn shook her head. "I slipped. I didn't mean to."

"Liar. You're a liar and a cheater."

Quinn rose to her feet. "No. Really, I…"

"I don't want to hear it." Darnya jabbed her finger into Quinn's chest. "I'll teach you tomorrow in front of everyone, because you'll be my opponent…or, more accurately, my victim."

18

—————

I SEE YOU

The smell of spiced mutton teased Quinn's senses and sent her stomach rumbling. She carried a plate of steaming meat and vegetables in one hand and a big mug of milk in the other as she crossed the mess hall. Ignoring the taunting comments from Darnya as she passed by, a smile tugged on the corner of her mouth when she noticed Iko and Percy seated alone at their table. When she approached, Iko looked up from his meal and smiled.

"You're here," he said.

"I am? I hadn't noticed." Quinn raised her eyebrows. "I wonder how that happened."

Percy chuckled at the comment.

"Funny." Iko's face twisted in a half-grin. "What I meant is that I haven't seen you at dinner lately. In fact, not for weeks."

Quinn sat across from him and picked her fork from her plate. "I've been...busy."

"Too busy to eat?"

She shrugged as she stared at her plate, watching her fork shift the steamed potatoes and carrots. "No. I just stop by the kitchen later at night. There's always something left to eat."

He frowned. "Are you avoiding me?"

Quinn shook her head. "No. Not anything like that. I'm just spending extra time on other things."

"Okay. But if I've done anything to upset you, you'd tell me, right?"

She shrugged. "Sure, but don't worry. It has nothing to do with you."

He flashed his white teeth, his amber eyes sparkling. "Good."

Although she was drawn to his smile, her stomach rumbled, forcing her to acknowledge her hunger. As she ate, she glanced up to find Iko finishing his meal, his plate cleared as he scooped the last bit of potato. He smiled again when their eyes met.

"We have our first sparring duel tomorrow," Percy said.

Quinn nodded. "Us as well."

"I know," He replied. "We go first. When we finish, we'll get to watch your duels."

The hunger in her stomach suddenly turned sour. She glanced toward Darnya's table. The girl pointed in Quinn's direction and laughed as she said something to her companions. Quinn's eyes narrowed as anger began to stir inside.

"What's the deal with you and Darnya?" Iko asked.

"She's a bully. Skilled, but still a bully."

Iko shrugged. "Yeah. There are likely a few of them here. This is a school for combat, you know."

Quinn's voice grew angry, "I have no time for those who mistreat others for no reason. Bullies seek to build their own reputation by tearing down the reputation of others. There is no call for it, and I don't like it!"

By the time her speech ended, Quinn was shouting. Iko appeared taken aback and held his hands up in surrender while Percy looked around as if seeking a place to hide.

"Woah. I give. You win." Iko grinned.

"May I sit here?"

Quinn turned to find Chuli standing beside the table with a plate and mug in her hands.

"Yes," Quinn said. "Of course."

As Chuli sat, Quinn noticed the dark look on Iko's face. He picked up his plate and mug as he stood. Percy mirrored him without speaking a word.

"Sorry to eat and run, Quinn, but we have to go." Iko gave her a small nod. "I'll see you tomorrow."

The two boys turned and retreated toward the kitchen with empty dishes in hand. Quinn tore her eyes from Iko to look at Chuli.

"They do not like me, I think."

Quinn's face remained stoic. "Why would they not like you?"

"I know not, Jacquinn Gulagas," Chuli said as she shook her head. "It was not so long ago that your Empire was at war with my people. Although the Empire no longer exists, some wounds are deep and take much time to heal."

"I suppose." She turned toward the kitchen, thinking of Iko. "But they are my age and were only infants when the Empire was disbanded."

"Some hold tight to the past because of the effect it has had on them." Chuli took a sip of her milk. "For instance, my uncle hated the Empire until the very end, for the Ministry betrayed him twice. The first betrayal came when they took the life of his wife, my mother's sister, and the second time was even worse. They assassinated both him and his father, who was the leader of our people."

Quinn's eyes widened in shock. "I had no idea. That's horrible."

Chuli eyes shifted toward the table, her tone one of musing. "Time passes and things change." She looked up at Quinn. "Consider me, for instance. I am the first Tantarri to attend this school. Perhaps many others will follow."

"You are the first?"

"It's true." Chuli nodded.

"Why did they choose to send you?"

"My aunt has argued for years that the Tantarri send someone. She and her husband convinced my parents to let me come."

"Well, you are amazing on a horse," Quinn noted. "I could barely sit the week we started riding. Yet, you appeared completely at ease and natural."

"Of course." Chuli shrugged. "I am Tantarri."

Quinn frowned. "What's that mean?"

"Tantarri are born to ride, and we begin as soon as we can walk."

"I heard that you have the best horses, but I didn't realize that it was such a part of your life."

Chuli's mouth twisted in thought. "Perhaps there is much we can learn from each other."

"You're probably right about that." Quinn nodded. "If you weren't sent here because of your riding skill, why did they choose you?"

Chuli arched a brow. "Have you seen me shoot a bow?"

Quinn laughed. "Yes. I should have known. You are quite the archer."

Chuli smiled and took a bite of food while Quinn worked on the last of her meal.

Chuli leaned forward, her eyes narrowed at Quinn. "I see you."

"I know." Quinn shrugged. "I'm sitting right in front of you."

"No. I see you training…in the evening." Chuli put her fork down. "You sneak into the training yard while everyone else goes to dinner."

Quinn frowned. "Are you going to report me?"

It was Chuli's turn to frown. "Why would I do that?"

"If you don't plan to report me, why tell me this?"

"I wonder why you do this. You do not have to."

"I want to get better." Quinn hesitated before finishing her thoughts. "I need to get as good as possible, quickly."

"This is a good thing, Jacquinn Gulagas."

"Please, call me Quinn. But, why do you say that?"

Chuli leaned closer, her eyes intense. "We have a saying among my people. Crops may grow sufficiently on their own, but a well-tended field will flourish."

"I…see."

Chuli shook her head. "No. You only see part of it. What you don't understand is that I wish to join you, to help you. And, in helping you, I will get better as well."

19

SURVIVAL

While the other girls cheered, Quinn quietly watched the two boys on the Coliseum floor. For over an hour, she and the other girls had witnessed their male peers face off against one another, the duels lasting anywhere from a few seconds to a few minutes. This particular fight was closer to the latter.

Her gaze shifted toward the side of the arena, where Iko sat on a bench, watching his friend. Only one other boy remained on the bench, a large boy who would be Iko's opponent.

A shout drew her attention to the center of the floor as Percy flipped his quarterstaff, striking his opponent's leg before spinning away. The other boy wore a grimace, clearly a result of repeated attacks by Percy, all inflicting pain but none sufficient to end the duel.

The boy raised his shield before easing forward, appearing to favor his right leg. Percy lunged with a feint, which was blocked. When his opponent swung his sword toward Percy's open side, he ducked beneath it and swept his staff through the boy's legs, sending him onto his back. The boy's sword tumbled across the floor and Percy stood over him as Sergeant Khallum called the match.

While the girls surrounding her clapped and cheered, Quinn watched Iko slide his helmet over his head and stand. Armed with a wooden longsword and shield, he matched his opponent in weapons but not in stature. The other boy stood at well over six-feet and outweighed Iko by a fair amount. Despite the calm look on Iko's face, Quinn found herself worrying about how he might fare. She soon discovered that her worry was misplaced.

When Sergeant Khallum called for the duel to begin, the larger boy moved closer to Iko and took a massive, powerful swing toward Iko's midsection. With a fluid motion, Iko lifted his shield at an angle while ducking. The strike slid harmlessly over his head as Iko lunged and drove his sword beneath his opponent's arm, eliciting a cry of pain when the wooden blade slammed into his ribs and drove him to the dirt.

Khallum called out, "Match."

Iko stood back while a boy in a blue coat ran onto the floor and knelt beside the downed cadet. The sergeant raised Iko's hand and the crowd cheered. By the time Khallum walked away, the other boy was rising to his feet, his injuries healed. Iko clapped the boy on the shoulder and shook his hand as the two walked to the side of the floor.

Iko had won handily, not even breaking a sweat. The boys' duels were finished. Quinn took a deep breath, knowing that the girls were next.

Quinn glared at Darnya, mirroring her opponent, refusing to blink until the other girl looked away. Five strides separated them…a divide of little consequence, yet as vast as an ocean. One girl was tall, powerfully built, and of dark shadows – the other lithe, agile, and as sunny as a midsummer day. Yet, both girls offered nothing but intense glares for each other.

Sergeant Jasmine strolled between them, interrupting the stare-down. Quinn stood to one end of the first-year line, Darnya to the end of the second-year line of cadets. With her hands clasped behind her back, Jasmine strode down the gap between the two lines and addressed the group.

"You just watched the boys duel, so you should know how this goes. Just to ensure the rules are clear, I will repeat them.

"After I call out each pairing, you will face each other within the center circle. As judge, I will declare a winner if any of the following occur." Jasmine held a single finger up. "A combatant is rendered unconscious," she raised two fingers, "a combatant breaks a major bone," three fingers, "we deem a fighter unable to proceed," and four fingers, "or a fighter is knocked outside the circle."

Jasmine's hands rejoined one another behind her back as she spun about to pace in the other direction. "You might wonder why we contain the fight inside a circle. Rather than a strip of paint on a dirt floor, I ask you to imagine the fight occurring atop a tower and that circle represents a drop of a hundred feet. You step off the edge, you lose, and you die. Same here. Combat often has boundaries or obstacles that can kill as easily as the blade you are facing. This is but another aspect of the discipline we seek to instill within you."

Jasmine withdrew a sheet of paper from the waist of her breeches, unfolding it before reading two names aloud. Those girls stepped forward and donned their sparring helmets, while the others drifted to the benches at the side of the Coliseum floor.

Quinn found a seat at one end of a bench, wishing to be alone as she considered how to best fight Darnya. Hugging her sparring helmet with one arm while resting her wooden swords across her lap, she allowed a sigh to slip out. After spending much of the previous night considering how to defeat her bigger and stronger opponent, she didn't expect any insightful revelation now.

Inside the circle, Simone faced another second-year cadet named Bronwyn. The latter had an advantage in size and reach, but Quinn knew that Simone was faster and more agile than the girl she faced. Simone gave her staff a quick twirl, while Bronwyn smacked her sword against her shield with a loud *clack*.

"Begin!" Jasmine shouted.

Bronwyn darted forward with an aggressive attack, the air filling with thumping *clacks* of wood striking wood. The staff in Simone's hands flicked from side-to-side as she expertly blocked a barrage of sword strokes before swiping toward Bronwyn's legs. The larger girl jumped back and blocked a following strike with her shield. Both girls then separated, circled a few steps, and reset with a ready stance.

The pause did not last long as Bronwyn lunged with a stab, a slash, and then closed the gap further with the swing of her shield and a sweep of her sword. Lightning-quick, Simone ducked beneath the strike, spun, and jammed the butt of her staff into Bronwyn's exposed midriff. Quinn heard the girl's ribs crack from ten strides away.

"Match!" Jasmine called as Bronwyn fell to her knees.

Cheers and the sound of clapping hands came from behind Quinn. She turned to find the male cadets filtering into the stands, having finished their duels and a subsequent trip to the baths. It took but a moment before she found Iko, who smiled and waved when their eyes met. Her heart fluttered and butterflies stirred her stomach.

A girl in a blue coat descended from the stands and approached Bronwyn, the cadet's face twisted in a grimace of pain. The ecclesiast placed her hand on Bronwyn's arm and closed her eyes. Both girls stood rock-still for a long moment until Bronwyn shuddered, her eyes going wide as she gasped for air. After a few heavy breaths, a look of relief crossed Bronwyn's face. She gave a nod to her benefactor before rising to her feet.

As the girls retreated to the benches, Jasmine called the next two names. Over the next hour, the process repeated again and again, with each match lasting no more than a few minutes. With each match, Quinn's anxiety steadily grew more intense. Knowing that Iko would be watching her duel only made it worse.

When Jasmine announced the final pairing, Quinn slipped her helmet on, gripped her swords, and stood to follow Darnya to the circle at the center of the floor. The room grew silent but for the crunching of dirt beneath their footsteps and the pounding of Quinn's pulse in her own ear. Upon reaching the circle, Darnya stood to one side of Jasmine, while Quinn stood to the other side.

"Prepare yourself for battle, Cadets." Jasmine strode from the circle, leaving an open gap between Quinn and her opponent, five strides across.

Darnya glared at Quinn with a sneer. "I'm going to embarrass you."

Quinn glared back at the girl in silence.

Tall, strong, and athletic, Darnya possessed natural gifts that placed Quinn at a disadvantage. Her opponent's extra year of training created a gap far more severe. Yet, Quinn refused to succumb to fear or accept any excuse. She found the thought of losing to Darnya intolerable.

"Go!" Jasmine's voice echoed in the Coliseum.

Darnya snarled and jumped forward with a wide slash. Quinn jumped back and smacked her opponent's sword aside. With a lunge, Darnya stabbed at Quinn, who twisted and spun, coming around with both swords at her opponent's exposed backside.

Rather than striking Darnya, the swords struck her shield when the girl spun around backward. Darnya's longsword followed, and Quinn ducked, but too late. The impact of the sword striking her helmet knocked Quinn to her hands and knees, her head ringing as spots danced in her vision. Darnya's boot then struck her midriff with a hard kick, sending a sharp pain through Quinn's ribs and the wind blasting from her lungs.

Quinn rolled with the kick and found herself at the edge of the circle. Her head felt as if it might explode, her ribs on fire. She looked up and found Darnya advancing. The girl had a gloating grin on her face as she raised her sword. Raw anger filled Quinn. With a backhand swipe, she flung one of her short swords.

The wooden sword smashed into Darnya's mouth as her overhead strike descended. Quinn rolled toward her attacker and slammed against her legs as Darnya's longsword crashed into the dirt, barely missing her target. Hard as she could, Quinn jammed her remaining sword upward into Darnya's crotch. The girl's eyes and mouth opened wide, a scream of pain blasting out as she doubled-over. While still lying on the ground, Quinn reached up, grabbed a fist full of Darnya's sparring vest, and pulled down with all her might, wincing at the knife of pain coming from her ribs. Darnya stumbled forward to land on her hands and knees, with both hands beyond the circle's edge.

Jasmine shouted, "Match!"

A gasp slipped through Quinn's lips, a result of the stabbing ache in her ribs at each shallow breath. Wiping her face, her fingers came away red with blood and she realized that her helmet had cut her cheekbone when struck by Darnya's head blow.

A boy's face, framed by yellow hair, appeared in her view. His blue eyes were accompanied by a friendly smile.

"I'm Jurgan. I'm here to heal you. Are you ready?"

When she nodded, he placed a warm hand on her arm and closed his eyes. A shock of cold struck Quinn as a shiver shook her body and her lungs compressed, forcing her breath out. She scrambled for breath, which refused to come until a deep gasp finally refilled her lungs. Amazingly, it no longer hurt to breathe. Her stomach rumbled with the hollow growl of deep hunger, longing to be sated.

Quinn sat upright and found herself whole, her head no longer thumping, her face no longer bleeding. She then spied a girl in a blue coat kneeling beside Darnya as she gasped for air.

Darnya sat upright and glared at Quinn, her face filled with fury. She scrambled to her feet and turned to Jasmine while pointing toward Quinn.

"She cheated!" Darnya snarled. "She threw her sword at me! And did you see where she struck me?"

A frown appeared on Jasmine's face. "I believe you forget who you're speaking to, Cadet."

Darnya's mouth drew a thin line, her lips pressed tight together. "Sorry, Sergeant." As Quinn rose to her feet, the girl pointed toward her again. "She should be disqualified for cheating."

Jasmine shook her head. "She broke no rules, Darnya. In fact, I believe she did you a favor." Jasmine put a hand on the tall girl's shoulder. "Issal blessed you with physical talent, but I have been waiting for someone to beat you. No matter how good you become, you'll never be invincible." Jasmine turned toward Quinn. "Combat is about survival, and there are no rules on the battlefield. Oftentimes, the line between life and death is drawn in an act of desperation. Yes, Quinn's actions were unconventional, and you may even find them despicable. However, following some unwritten code of honor matters little if you are dead."

20

A MESSAGE

Everson stared at his lap as he recited his tale. From time to time, he would look up and squint in an attempt to see his captors beyond the bright light. However, those attempts yielded little more than shadowy forms. Drops of nervous sweat ran down his ribs and he shivered before forcing himself to continue his tale.

"I settled into a daily routine, one that some might consider monotonous…but not me." Everson recalled the sense of satisfaction he carried with him during those days. "Each morning, I would wake, dress, and go to breakfast with Jonah. We would eat and leave the dining hall before most other students were awake. We occupied the extra time before class by poring through books in the knowledge center, in search of information about Chaos and recordings of its use.

"In Chaos Theory, things did not proceed as we hoped they might. Hopes are often left underfed, and Master Alridge was sure to leave us wanting for more. We would spend weeks on a single application of Chaos, covering the many uses of one rune while she reiterated the dangerous nature of the magic and the harm it could create in the hands of the undisciplined.

"Engineering classroom sessions went far better, as did the skill training in the Foundry each afternoon. I eagerly consumed every bit of information placed before me and often presented leaps of thought that left the rest of the class rushing to catch up. At the same time, years of training in my father's smithy gave me a distinct edge in working metal, particularly fine works that required finesse and an understanding of managing the heat and carbon applied.

"The things I built consistently won me praise but also required long hours spent in the Foundry, and I often missed meals. Evening baths became a regular event since I tired of Jonah complaining about the smell of burnt iron and sulfur and sweat. Afterward, I would pour myself into bed and fall asleep in moments, only to wake for another day – each as glorious as the last.

"This pattern continued for weeks until one day in my Engineering classroom, Nindlerod informed us of a new challenge."

"And in conclusion, the mathematical embodiment of time can be represented by various units of measure. Eons, centuries, decades, years, weeks, days, hours, minutes, all can be broken down into seconds – or the passing of a breath.

"Now, can anyone tell me when time first began?" Nindlerod gestured toward a boy near the front. "Sakan?"

The tall, heavy-set boy glanced about the room. "Um…at year one?"

Nindlerod's brow furrowed. "And what year is it now?"

Sakan smiled, pinching his ruddy face. "That's easy. 1467."

Unable to restrain himself, Everson blurted "What?"

Sakan turned toward him. "It's the year 1467. You can't deny that."

Everson snorted. "No. However, that's just a number defined by man. Time began far before we started tracking the years. In fact, it began eons before man even existed."

"Very good, Everson." Nindlerod smiled. "The years that Sakan referred to are merely a construct of mankind. Many additional zeros must be added to represent the true span of time."

Sakan's face grew redder than his hair, and he flashed a grimace toward Everson. Master Nindlerod rose from his stool to stand before the class.

"Time is infinite, never ending, and completely oblivious to the passing of man. Yet, time remains the most fascinating of concepts, and mankind has forever tried to capture it, define it, and track it, with the hope that, one day, we might master it."

As with most concepts covered in engineering training, Everson was enthralled with the concept of time – something so nebulous yet intrinsically core to the lives of everyone who had ever lived. The human definition of time was just that and nothing more. Yet, the concept of time captured his attention and made him feel as if it could be further defined, monitored…tracked.

Nindlerod lifted the hourglass off the desk, its white sand now nearly gathered at the bottom. "Our lives are finite, as is this class session. The sand will soon stop falling, and our session will end. Similarly, one day the hourglass of our lives will run out of sand, and we will leave this life to join Issal and perhaps return to start anew. Think on this. Consider how you will spend your time among the living and what mark you might make on the world. Don't waste your grains of sand, for you cannot know how many remain."

As he ended the sentence, the sand stopped falling, and all that remained was the static mound at the base.

"We are now at the end of your ninth week. You possess a firm grasp on the primary principles of engineering and have been taught the basic skills required to create things in the Foundry. Of course, your knowledge and skill will continue to increase with time, but you need no longer wait to apply what you've learned.

"Hopefully, you have some ideas of things you hope to create, whether it be a completely new concept or a better version of something that already exists. Regardless, I now present your first opportunity to invent something and to compare your creative skills against your fellow students. Prepare yourselves for the annual Autumn Inventor's Challenge!"

As he ended the sentence, Nindlerod held his hand above his head with his finger aimed at the ceiling. The old man's eyes were bright, matching his maniacal grin.

Nindlerod lowered his hand. "I suggest that you form a team and collaborate as needed, for this contest includes apprentice and adept-level engineering students. However, there are rules.

"This competition is limited to creations that function naturally, without any form of Chaos augmentation. You may use any material you choose, and you will be provided full access to the Foundry to construct your creation.

"Your inventions will be presented in the Arena seven weeks from today, to be judged by a panel of academy masters with scores awarded in five categories including originality, practicality, presentation, execution, and function. The winner will forfeit his or her design to the school for the price of five gold marks."

The announcement caused a stir among the classroom. Five gold marks was a significant sum for anyone, especially a student.

Everson turned toward Donnell, who leaned toward him and whispered, "Do you have something in mind? I'd love to help if you think you can win."

Everson chewed his lip and considered the idea that had been forming. "I need some time to think on it." He turned back toward Nindlerod to find the man grinning as the students quieted.

"Yes. The winning team earns five gold pieces, a hefty prize to be sure." Nindlerod rose to his feet, groaning as he leaned on his cane. "I look forward this year's batch of creations. Class dismissed. Enjoy your lunch. We will reconvene in the Foundry for a session on casting metal."

The door burst open and Everson sat up in a lurch. His heart pounded in his ears, and he wiped the sleepiness from his eyes. Jonah stood in the doorway, his grinning face lit by a strip of orange light as the setting sun streamed through a gap in the curtain.

"You startled me," Everson said. "I was dozing I think…" He noticed the look on Jonah's face. "You missed dinner. Where were you tonight, and why are you smiling like that?"

Jonah put his pack down and sat on his bed as Everson swung his legs around until his feet thumped to the floor.

"I was out on the lawn by myself, working on something, and…I did it. After weeks of trying, I finally did it!" Jonah's face appeared as if might break from his grin.

"You did what?"

"Magic. Chaos. I made it work."

Everson's eyes narrowed. "Tell me about it. What's it like?"

"Well, I had to get myself real angry to feel it. They say fear works, too, but I haven't had luck trying that route. Today, I focused on anger. Real, hot anger. When I felt enraged, I closed my eyes and sensed something feeding the anger, something around me. It was almost tangible. With my mind, I reached out and grabbed onto it and drew it inside of me."

Jonah's tone softened. "I had no idea how it would feel." He shook his head in wonder. "It was as if I had swallowed a thunderstorm. The heat, the energy...I feared I might explode. I then concentrated on the Light rune, and it flared to life. The next thing I knew, the rock I held shined so brightly, I couldn't look at it."

"How did you feel, you know...afterward?"

Jonah sat back on his bed with his shoulders against the wall. "It left me drained. Exhausted. I sat on a bench until the sun approached the horizon while I waited to recover."

Everson's brain worked the puzzle, tilting and twisting it as he sought to determine what was possible...and what was not.

"So, you could not perform this type of magic again for some time without rest." He stated it as a fact. "Could you perform more than one augmentation at a time by pouring some of the energy into one rune and the rest into another?"

Jonah's blinked at the question. "I...I don't know. Maybe."

Questions spun in Everson's head. "Well, how long does the effect last?"

Reaching for his pack, Jonah dug out a stone the size of his fist. It emitted a dull blue glow, dim as a dormant glowlamp. "This was a bright light over an hour ago, perhaps an hour and a half."

Everson stared at the rock. "When did the rock begin to dim?"

Jonah shrugged. "After about an hour, I guess."

Everson's eyes narrowed. "When we first arrived here, you mentioned enchanting – a way to make the magic last forever."

Jonah shrugged. "That's what I've heard, but I don't know how it works."

"What else have you heard? Do you know how it's been used?"

"Well, I heard that enchanting an oven can make it hot forever. No need to even light a fire or feed it with logs."

"Interesting." Everson considered the idea. "I wonder if the ovens here are enchanted."

Jonah's eyes went wide. "I bet they are."

Everson's grin matched Jonah's. "We should investigate."

"My thoughts…"

A knock on the door interrupted their conversation.

"Are you expecting anyone?" Jonah asked.

Everson shook his head. "Who is it?"

A muffled voice came through the door. "Messenger. I have a letter for Everson Gulagas."

Jonah slid off his bed and opened the door. A boy, tall and thin and dressed in a blue coat with white piping stood in the doorway.

"Everson Gulagas?"

"That's me." Everson said, waving from his seat on the bed.

The boy moved past Jonah, handed an envelope to Everson, and disappeared down the corridor. Jonah closed the door and turned toward Everson.

"Who's it from?"

Everson read the outside of the envelope, seeing his name written in poor handwriting. He smiled. "It's from my sister."

He opened the letter and scanned the contents. After a bit, Jonah spoke, interrupting the quiet moment.

"I don't suppose you care to share what it says?"

Everson lowered the letter and glared at his roommate. "Is your curiosity so strong that you would ask about my private family business?"

Jonah shrugged. "No sense in denying it."

Everson chuckled. "In that case, she says that things are going well. Like us, she has three days off after the fifteenth week of training. She plans to come see me during the first break."

"I can't wait to meet her."

"Don't get any ideas, Jonah. I'd hate to see you hurt."

"Are trying to protect your sister?"

Everson grinned. "Not at all. I'm trying to protect you from her."

Jonah laughed and Everson joined him. He then grabbed the desk chair, slid it out and lifted himself onto it.

"What are you doing?"

"I need to write a note back to her."

Everson pulled a pen from the drawer, its glass body half-full. He tested the ball at the tip, which left a black streak on his thumb. As he stared at it, he considered the convenience of not needing an inkwell. The pen was another creation of Nindlerod's, invented years earlier.

"What about the ovens?" Jonah asked.

Everson turned toward him. "Don't worry. We're definitely sneaking into the kitchen tonight."

Jonah smiled. "That's what I wanted to hear."

Holding the paper up to the glowlamp, Everson read the letter to ensure he had not forgotten anything.

Quinn,

Thank you for writing me. It was wonderful to hear from you and I look forward to seeing you during our break. Perhaps we can journey to Fallbrandt and visit Mother and Father for a couple days.

I'm glad that your training is going well. Things are going well for me, too. My roommate, Jonah, and I are becoming fast friends. To my surprise, Torney and Rena are here, and I see them a few times a week. Both are training to be magic users, as is Jonah. I have even become friends with two fellow engineers – a boy named Donnell, and a girl named Ivy.

In the mornings, I attend Chaos Theory class, where I learn about magic abilities and how to utilize them with engineered creations.

Engineering training consumes much of my time. I spend half my morning in a classroom each day and my entire afternoon in The Foundry. You would love the place. It's like father's smithy, but a hundred times larger and far more impressive. I have learned numerous new skills, and I plan to craft some amazing things.

Take care of yourself and stay out of trouble. I will see you soon.

-Everson

With a nod, Everson folded the letter and slipped it into the envelope. He put the envelope on the desk, turned toward Jonah, and poked him in the shoulder.

"What?" Jonah jerked awake with a start, blinking as his head rose from his pillow.

"You fell asleep."

Jonah rubbed his eyes and sat up on the bed. "What time is it?"

Everson grabbed his pack and opened it. "It's time to go. The sun set over an hour ago, so the kitchen should be quiet."

Standing, Jonah arched his back as he stretched. Everson grabbed the glowlamp and slid it into his pack, plunging the room into darkness. He then gripped his canes and stood as Jonah opened the door. The blue light of the glowing floor tiles in the corridor lit the opening as Everson shuffled through. With the door closed and locked, the two boys headed down the hallway.

Despite the illuminated tiles to light the way, the cold interior of the massive building felt eerie and lonely – an empty husk bereft of a pulse. They passed through the main hall, entered the central corridor, and tested the doors to the dining hall.

"Locked," Jonah whispered as he dug into his pockets. He pulled out a long needle and a flat strip of metal.

"You know how to pick a lock?" Everson asked in a hushed voice.

Jonah shrugged. "Effects of a misspent youth."

He then knelt and slid the needle into the slot, twisting and wiggling it. Everson glanced down the hall nervously as the sound of metal scraping metal echoed in the quiet of night. A click sounded and Jonah slid the flat metal piece into the lock, grimacing as he used it to turn the bolt.

"Done." He turned the knob and the door swung open.

A voice came from behind them. "What are you guys doing?"

Everson stared at Jonah with alarm in his eyes and swallowed before turning. With arms crossed, Donnell stood a few strides away.

"Donnell," Everson stammered. "What are you doing here?"

"I was studying in the lounge, and I spotted you two heading down the corridor as I was returning to my room. Are you breaking into the dining hall?"

Jonah stood and turned toward Donnell. "It's no big deal. We aren't stealing or anything like that."

"So, why do it?"

Jonah glanced at Everson, who shrugged.

"We want to investigate the ovens."

Donnell's eyes narrowed, his head tilted to the side. "The ovens?"

With an exasperated sigh, Everson waved Donnell forward. "Just come with us and you'll see. Regardless, we need to get out of the hallway."

Everson shuffled inside, as did Donnell, while Jonah pulled the door closed behind them.

When the room fell dark, Everson handed his pack to Jonah.

"Take the lamp out so we can see."

Jonah extracted the glowlamp and blue light bloomed, casting long shadows across the room. The three boys slipped past the tables and made their way to the kitchen. They circled the long counter that normally divided the students from the cooks, and the ovens came into view. The air grew warmer as they edged closer. Three massive brick ovens hugged the back wall, each with a heavy cast iron door. Jonah reached for the nearest oven door and yanked his hand back with a yelp.

"Ouch!" His fingers went to his mouth. "I burnt myself."

Everson found a pair of heavy leather mitts on a nearby counter. "Put one of those on."

Jonah slipped a mitt on his hand and he tried again. The door squeaked as it opened and blue light filtered into the opening as raw heat poured out. No fire could be seen. In fact, there was no chamber at the bottom to allow a fire.

The interior was large enough for Everson to squeeze inside, rows of metal racks dividing the oven into four even levels. With the lamp held beside his head, Jonah peeked in.

"Do you see anything?"

"Yes. Come and look."

Everson squeezed in close to Jonah as Donnell did the same. The heat made Everson blink at its intensity. And then, he noticed what Jonah was pointing toward.

Runes marked the metal interior walls of the oven, dozens of them. All the same.

"Do you know that rune?" Everson asked.

Jonah shook his head. "I haven't seen it before."

Donnell added, "Me neither."

Everson stared at one of the runes for a moment, memorizing the lines and storing the image away in the vault of his mind. He then stepped back, relieved to be away from the heat.

"Close the door. We're done here."

As Jonah closed the door, Donnell looked at Everson in confusion. "What is this about? I still don't understand."

"You saw the runes, right?"

Donnell shrugged. "Yeah. So what?"

"You felt the heat?"

"How could I not?"

"Where's the fire? Where are the coals?"

Donnell frowned while staring at the oven. "I...don't know."

"That's because there is no fire. There are no coals."

"Where's the heat coming from, then?"

"From the rune-marked steel plates." Jonah grinned. "They're enchanted."

21

QUARRY

A bead of sweat clung to Everson's forehead. He resisted the urge to itch it as he focused on his task. The bead broke loose and tracked down, past his brow, and into his eye. The sting forced him to squeeze his eye closed and blink in an attempt to clear it. All the while, he watched the forge's heat attack the bronze ingot. What began as a solid chunk of metal soon liquefied, filling the heavy cast iron ladle. Lifting it carefully, Everson turned toward the adjacent workbench and poured the melted bronze into the casting, filling the cavity to the top.

"Okay, Donnell." Everson wiped his brow dry with his sleeve. "Set the casting into the water. Please don't drop it. That casting took hours to machine."

Donnell gripped the casting with a large pair of tongs. He placed the metal block into the shallow tub of water and a hiss of steam rose into the air.

While the casting cooled, Everson slid off his stool and shuffled to the next workstation. With her long dark hair tied back and pair of magnifying spectacles strapped to her head, Ivy leaned over the benchtop as she worked. Everson eyed the hard wire strand as she heated it and coiled it about the rod.

He grinned at his idea taking form. "You're doing great, Ivy. It was clever of you to use the rod as a core for the coil."

The hint of smile flickered at the corner of her mouth, but there was no other reaction. Movement in his peripheral vision caught Everson's attention. He turned to find Jonah approaching with a grin.

"What crazy ideas are you guys bringing to life?"

Everson shook his head. "It would ruin the surprise if I revealed it before we're finished. Besides, I'm not positive it will work."

"I figured you might play it that way." Jonah shook his head. "You and your secrets."

"I guess we all have secrets," Donnell said.

Everson glanced at Donnell and found him staring at Jonah. "What are you doing here, Jonah? Aren't you supposed to be meditating or something?"

Jonah shrugged. "You know the rune we learned this morning in Chaos Theory class?"

Everson tilted his head. "The one that increases gravitational effects? What of it?"

"I thought you might like to join me outside, and we can test it before dinner."

Having never seen arcane arts in use, Everson's curiosity demanded that he accept Jonah's invitation. Grasping for restraint, he tried to hide the anticipation churning inside.

"We are about done for the day, anyway." He shrugged. "Why not?"

Jonah smiled. "Great." He then turned toward Donnell. "Do you want to join us, Donnell?"

The boy's eyes narrowed as he visibly considered the offer. After a moment, he shrugged. "Sure. That would be great."

Everson turned toward Ivy, still busy coiling the heated wire. "Would you like to join us, Ivy?"

The girl removed the wire from the flame and stared into space for a long moment. She then gave a slight shake of her head. "No. I'll finish this. You boys go on."

"All right. Please join us if you change your mind." Everson turned toward two boys. "Let's go. We can exit through the Foundry Yard."

Shuffling down the center aisle of the long building, Everson led

Jonah and Donnell toward the exit. The boys passed clusters of students working throughout the building, crafting components and assembling creations. One particular invention caught Everson's attention.

Similar to his father's grinding wheel, the creation contained a foot pedal attached to a cam and a rod. Above it was a benchtop and a metal armature that held a needle. When he noticed a rod beside it holding a spool of thread, Everson realized that the contraption was designed to make sewing easier. The lead student on the project was Henrick Todd, a third-year student. Everson nodded in admiration, thinking that the creation was quite useful and would win Henrick much praise.

They reached the end of the building, and Jonah opened the door, holding it as Everson and Donnell passed by.

A chill autumn breeze struck them, cooling the sweat in Everson's damp tunic. He had forgotten to grab his academy coat and briefly considered heading back to retrieve it. The sun hovered in the western sky, above the high mountain peaks. Its rays balanced the breeze enough that Everson decided he could survive dressed as he was.

"Come on. Let's move farther from the building."

Jonah waved them forward as he headed past the stockyard of raw building materials and toward the engineering outbuilding.

"Why do we need to be out here?" Donnell asked. "The augmentation seems harmless enough. We could have done the experiment inside."

Jonah spun around, walking backward as he grinned at his companions. "That's true, if we were using an approved rune."

Everson's eyes narrowed. "You want to try the rune from the ovens, don't you?"

With an even wider grin, Jonah nodded.

"Are you sure it's safe?" Donnell asked. "I don't really trust any of this Chaos stuff…it seems so…unnatural." Everson looked at him with a furrowed brow, as did Jonah. Donnell quickly added. "Besides, we don't even know what this one does exactly."

Spinning about to face forward again, Jonah spoke over his shoulder. "Don't worry about it. We'll take precautions."

They circled behind the outbuilding and passed by the closed stall doors. Everson noted that the end stall was twice the width of the others, marked with the number fifty. A plaque beside the number said. *Birthplace of the Hedgewick Flyer*.

"That must be where Master Hedgewick built the first flying machine," Everson said.

"I guess." Donnell shrugged.

"Have either of you seen him yet? Have you met him?"

Jonah shrugged "When would I have met him?"

Donnell shook his head. "Not me."

Everson wondered what kind of man Master Hedgewick might be. "I hear that he does guest lectures and sometimes holds Engineering classes for the senior students."

"You'll meet him eventually," Jonah said. "I'm sure of it."

They passed over a small rise and descended into what appeared to be an old quarry cut into the base of a mountain. Surrounded by pale gray rock that matched most of the buildings within the academy, Everson determined that this is where those walls originated. Geometric corners and depressions gave an unnatural shape to the quarry, an indication that man had claimed dominance to the location.

Jonah crossed the rocky ground and stopped before a stone twice the size of his head. He reached into his coat pocket and pulled out a small chunk of pale blue rock from one pocket and a folded piece of paper from the other. Everson immediately recognized the paper as Jonah unfolded it, marked with a rune he had drawn himself.

Kneeling, Jonah began tracing the rune upon the flat face of the rock. When done, he turned toward Everson, whose nod confirmed that the rune appeared exactly as he remembered. Jonah stepped back as he pocketed the chunk of glowstone.

"In Chaos Theory, we were told that an incorrectly drawn rune is dangerous and could be deadly." Jonah thumbed toward the direction they had come. "Let's go up to the rim of the quarry and I'll try to charge it from there. I think it'll work as long as I can see the rune."

Jonah and Donnell climbed to the top of the hill, where they waited patiently as Everson inched his way up the scattered steps and the rocky incline. When they were all out of the bowl, Jonah closed his eyes.

A cool breeze gave Everson a chill again, and he held his elbows against his torso to try and warm himself. He looked down at the rock, now a hundred paces away, yet with the rune still visible. Beyond the quarry, was a view of beauty – a view that had transformed over recent weeks.

Dark green pines stood out among the reds, oranges, and yellows of the leaf trees. With gray rock and a white snowcap above the trees combined with the purple mountains in the distance, it appeared as if Issal had gone wild and had created a pallete of color to test Everson's ability to concentrate. Regardless, he found the view incredible.

Another gust teased Everson's hair and sent an involuntary shiver down his spine. He turned toward Jonah, who still had his eyes closed. Everson frowned, wondering how long it might take his friend to tap into this magic. Other questions began to stir within his mind. *What if he needed to use this magic during battle? Would he have time? What deaths might result from such a delay? Does it come faster with practice?*

Jonah's eyes flashed open and red sparks sizzled within them. Shocked by the sight, Everson backed up and almost fell, catching himself with his cane just in time.

As the red energy faded from Jonah's eyes, Everson turned to find the rune pulsing red on the distant rock. The glow of the rune faded, and he wondered if something had gone wrong. Suddenly, the rock burst into flames, flaring bright and hot and angry. A thump of warm air hit the boys, sending them back a step.

Even at a hundred paces, Everson felt the warmth of the burning stone. If he had closed his eyes, he would think that he was sitting before a warm fire...or his father's forge. To feel such heat from this distance was incredible. He had never seen stone burn before and would have doubted it possible without the use of magic.

Donnell's eyes were wide, his face filled with fear. "That is...horrible."

Everson's brow furrowed. "Horrible? It's a bit dangerous, but it's hardly horrible."

"How...how long will it last?" Donnell asked.

Jonah scratched his chin. "Based on what I know, the rock will burn like this for about an hour and then slowly die out."

Everson's mind struggled to balance the facts between what he witnessed before him and how the academy ovens functioned. "This kind of heat would turn metal to liquid. How did they make the oven plates perpetually hot, yet not so hot that they melt?"

Jonah shook his head. "I don't get it either. The plates inside the ovens have numerous runes, yet they're not nearly as hot as this single rune."

"In addition, their effect lasts far longer."

Jonah nodded. "There's a secret to enchanting that we haven't learned yet."

Everson's gaze fell on the burning rock. "Yes. I wonder when we will learn that secret. I have some ideas of how I might use it."

22

CAUSING TROUBLE

A fountain of sparks shot into the air as Everson pressed the gear tooth against the grinding wheel. He concentrated through the narrow view of the lens strapped to his head, careful to remove only the unwanted glob of metal. He pulled it back and gave it close inspection before nodding in satisfaction.

"You can stop pumping now," he said, grunting as he slid the massive gear on the bench beside him. He then lifted the goggles to his forehead and turned toward his companions. Donnell wiped the sweat from his brow. Ivy appeared oblivious as she filed a rounded end to a metal rod.

"Good." Donnell sighed. "My leg was getting sore anyway."

Motion of someone approaching drew Everson's attention. He turned to find Jonah heading toward him. "What are you doing here?"

"It's late." Jonah replied. "The sun will drop behind the mountains within the hour."

Everson grinned. "I'm touched that you're concerned about me. Did you think I would skip dinner?"

Jonah snorted. "It wouldn't be the first time you missed dinner because your head was buried in the Foundry."

"You're right," Everson sighed. "We only have two weeks left before the competition. The parts are almost finished. However, we still have to assemble it and test it. If it doesn't work, we'll have nothing to show."

"Don't say that," Donnell chided. "After all the work we've put into this thing, it had better work."

"It will work just fine, Donnell." Ivy's voice carried a fierce edge to it, an unspoken threat. "Everson knows what he's doing."

Everson bit his lip as a wave of guilt washed over him. She had placed her faith in him…faith he hadn't yet earned.

"Enough of your crazy inventions for today." Jonah gestured toward the door. "Let's go. I have something to show you."

Donnell's head shot up with an expectant look on his face. "Should I come as well?"

Jonah shook his head. "Not this time. This particular surprise is only for Everson."

Donnell appeared crestfallen but said nothing. Ivy remained quiet as usual while Everson grabbed his canes and stood.

"Our break starts tomorrow. I may go to Fallbrandt for a day or two." Everson dreaded leaving the Foundry with his project unfinished, but the next break was another fifteen weeks away.

Donnell turned toward Everson. "I may do the same. I have an uncle who lives there."

"Don't worry, Ev." Ivy shrugged. "I'm not going anywhere, so I'll keep working on it."

Everson glanced toward their cart of completed components. Images of them assembling into something useful danced in his head.

"I'll see you guys soon…a couple days at most," Everson said, his mind distant.

As he and Jonah headed toward the door, Everson thought of the work that he, Donnell, and Ivy had accomplished – of the hours and effort expended on an idea he had conceived. The concept was sound and the benefit great, but it remained untried, untested, and the results unknown. He prayed for it to function when they assembled it. Even beyond the satisfaction he would gain, he didn't want to let his companions down.

Jonah held the door open, and Everson shuffled into the hallway, dark and empty save for the periodic glowing floor tiles. As they headed toward the heart of the school, they sporadically encountered students and faculty members, some passing by while others headed in the same direction.

When Jonah walked past the dining hall, Everson stopped.

"Aren't we going to eat?"

Jonah shook his head. "No. There's something else I need to show you…in our room."

Curiosity, combined with a touch of confusion, kept Everson quiet as he followed along.

Upon reaching the room, Jonah put his hand on the knob and grinned.

"You didn't lock it?" Everson asked.

Jonah shook his head. "No need."

When the door opened, Jonah moved aside to give Everson a clear view.

With the curtains pushed open to allow light from the low sun to filter in, Everson spotted yellowed fields outside and the colored mountainside in the distance. Eclipsing the window was the silhouette of a girl, the edges of her golden hair illuminated by the bright view beyond her. The girl turned toward the door and smiled. Everson's heart leapt. He hadn't realized how much he missed her.

"Quinn!"

He hurried into the room, and she wrapped her arms about him in a hug. With his head buried in her hair, he was hit by the recognizable scent, smelling faintly of flowers – the fragrance contained a hint of sweetness, yet airy and confident, like her personality. Unbidden, a tear slid down his face. When she released him, he rubbed it away with the shoulder of his coat and blinked his eye dry.

"It's good to see you are well." She gave him a smile.

"Me? Of course, I'm well. I'm not the one who's fighting others on a daily basis."

Her smile widened. "And to think, this time, you aren't even the cause."

Everson laughed.

"This is touching," Jonah said from the doorway.

Everson turned toward Jonah and rolled his eyes. "Are you going to give me a hard time about this?"

Jonah chuckled as he closed the door. "It seems like too good an opportunity to pass on."

In a flash, Quinn lunged forward and drove her fist into Jonah's stomach. An *oof* burst out as Jonah doubled-over. Quinn wrapped her arm about his head and squeezed.

"I suggest you leave my brother alone." Quinn grimaced as Jonah's face reddened, his eyes bulging.

"Quinn! What are you doing?" Everson cried out. "He's my friend!"

She looked at Everson, and the steel in her eyes cooled…softening. When she let go, Jonah coughed and gasped for air.

"Um…I'm sorry." Quinn patted Jonah on the shoulder and he flinched. "I sometimes can be…over protective. Especially when it comes to my brother."

Everson rolled his eyes. "I can take care of myself, Quinn. You can't go around assaulting people because of things they say." The volume of his voice lowered, his tone earnest. "Yes, words can be sharp as knives, but I've developed some armor against them and the wounds inflicted are quick to recover. Each becomes a hardened scab, more difficult to penetrate than before."

"You're right." Quinn turned toward Jonah. "Again, I'm sorry, Jonah. Everson says that you've been a good friend. I should respect that and trust that you'll treat him as such."

Jonah chuckled. "Apology accepted…so long as you don't tell anyone that I was beat up by a girl."

Quinn's face clouded. "What's that supposed to mean?"

Jonah held his hands up in surrender. "Nothing. I was joking."

Everson decided to save his roommate by changing the subject. "Quinn, I assume you are here for reasons other than to accost my friends."

She turned toward him. "Yes. In your letter, you suggested that we visit Mother and Father. You have tomorrow off, as do I. If we leave now, we might reach Fallbrandt by dusk."

Everson smiled. "Perfect. I'll pack my stuff and we can leave."

—+ φ +—

The sun had dipped beyond the peaks to the west, its waning light painting the clouds above in red and purple hues. Shadows covered the gaps in the trees to either side of the road, leaving the forest dark and foreboding. A blast of wind shook branches and coaxed dying leaves from their host. The leaves drifted toward the ground until another gust sent them scurrying across the road. One crunched beneath Everson's boot as he planted his feet and stretched his canes forward for the next step. The whistle of the wind was accompanied by another sound – that of Everson's laughter at Quinn's story.

"You hit her there?" he asked, incredulous.

Quinn grinned. "Yeah. Hard. I'm sure it hurt like nobody's business."

Everson chuckled. "Is that even allowed?"

"Darnya didn't think so, but Master Jasmine thought otherwise."

"So what happened?"

"I was able to pull Darnya forward, and she fell outside the circle. Master Jasmine declared me the winner and then an ecclesiast came out to heal me." Quinn shook her head. "It's a good thing, too because it felt like daggers just to breathe."

"So what of Darnya? She doesn't sound like someone who's used to losing."

"Oh, she was upset. Outraged, even." Quinn frowned. "She already had it out for me before the match, and I suspect that beating her in front of everyone won't sit well."

Quinn fell silent, likely occupied by her thoughts. Everson had been glad to hear her tale, if just to give him something to think on beside what might lurk in the surrounding forest. The banshee wail they had heard in the Kardis Forest replayed in his mind. An edge of fear had him searching the ominous surroundings.

Darkness obscured the forest beyond the trees nearest to the road, and apparitions moved within the gloom, lurking without emerging. When Everson blinked, they faded away. Realizing that his imagination was getting the better of him, his gaze shifted toward the darkening sky and found that the purple within the clouds had eaten away at the red, the latter now nearly absent as both chased the setting sun.

154

The duo then rounded a bend in the road, and the forest's dark embrace relaxed, opening to a wider view. Beyond that opening, the first buildings appeared, lit by islands of blue light from nearby glowlamps. A sigh of relief slipped out when Everson realized that they had made it to town before nightfall.

Deep into autumn, the days were growing shorter, the air cooler. Despite the darkness, the streets of Fallbrandt were busy.

Horse-drawn carts passed by, followed by two soldiers on horseback as they circled to the back of The Quiet Woman. Four ladies, busily chatting, crossed the road and headed toward the entrance of the inn. Everson thought of his time there, of the amazing food prepared by Saul, the inn's cook. Having not yet eaten dinner, his stomach rumbled. The rumble grew louder, and Everson turned when he realized it was not coming from him.

Black smoke poured from the vent atop an approaching steam carriage. Quinn and Everson moved aside before the steam carriage passed by, its wheels rumbling noisily on the hard road. Puffs of white steam trailed from the machine's exhaust and mixed with the cloud of dust from the stirred gravel. Those on foot gave a wide berth to the carriage as it continued through town until it turned a corner and disappeared from view.

"I wonder how those things work."

"Steam carriages?" Everson shrugged. "It's quite simple, actually. You start with a boiler filled with water and you heat it with a fire until the water turns to steam. The steam creates pressure, which, in turn, moves a piston inside a cylinder and…"

"Enough." Quinn rolled her eyes. "I'm sorry I asked."

"But you…"

She shook her head. "I know what I said. In truth, I don't really want to know."

The disappointment on Everson's face must have shown because Quinn stopped and put her hand on his shoulder while sharing a sympathetic expression.

"I'm glad you understand how it works and that's good enough for me." She gave him a caring smile. "Knowing how things work is your thing. You keep doing that, because you're good at it. I'll do my own thing."

"Which is…"

Her grin widened, her eyes alight. "Causing trouble."

He laughed. "Oh, you're good at that, for sure."

They resumed walking, passing by two men carrying hand tools as they discussed meeting at a local alehouse. At the next intersection, the siblings turned and trailed behind a woman who was dragging a crying girl by the hand. The woman entered the second house on the left, slammed the door closed, and shouts arose from inside.

Quinn chuckled. "Someone's in trouble."

"It's not even you, this time."

They both laughed as they angled toward the next house on the right. Quinn knocked and then hurriedly put her back to the wall.

"What are you doing?" Everson asked in a hushed voice.

"Remember my old trick."

He sighed and waited for the door to open.

"Coming." He heard a deep voice from inside.

Moments later, the door opened. A male figure eclipsed the pale light coming from inside. "Everson?"

"Hello, Father. I came home to see you…and perhaps to eat a bit of Mother's cooking. That is, if it's not too much trouble."

The man burst forward and hugged Everson, squeezing the air from him as he hoisted him in the air. "Welcome home, Son."

Evers set Everson down and stepped back, grinning.

Quinn jumped out and shrieked, "Ha!"

The man stumbled back and put his hand to his chest. "Quinn! Are you trying to scare an old man to death?"

Laughing, she replied, "You're not that old."

She held her arms out as Evers hugged her. After a moment, she stepped back and looked up at him. "Did I really scare you?"

He chuckled. "A bit. I suspected you might be around, so my heart was spared the brunt of your attack. Your mother will be home any minute with dinner. Let's go inside, and you both can tell me of your time at school." With his arm still about Quinn's shoulder, he led them both inside.

23

SOLDIERS LEFT BEHIND

Quinn heard whispers from the shadows beyond the bright light, but she ignored them and continued the telling of her story, reciting the events that led to her current situation.

"I knew the late autumn break spent with Everson and my family would be the last I'd see of them until spring. That reunion refilled my heart and hardened my resolve, something I would need for what occurred during the winter session.

"When I returned to the academy, I settled in for another fifteen weeks of hard training. In addition to my normal schedule, I began training in private with Chuli. After dinner, we would sneak into one of the private training rooms near the Coliseum." Quinn's focus shifted from her shadowy inquisitors to the floor as the recalled the past. "On the third night of sparring, we found that doing so without a healer was a bad idea."

Vi counted out loud as she walked past Quinn, the crunch of her boots in the dirt fading as the distance increased.

Tears clouded Quinn's eyes as she pushed herself up. Her breaths came in shallow gasps, each feeling like a thousand knives in her ribs. Despite the attempt to hide her injury, performing pushups with cracked ribs made it impossible as her pace lagged behind the called count.

"Cadet Quinn," Jasmine's voice came from above Quinn as the woman's boots settled into view near her right hand. "You appear to be having trouble. Is there something wrong?"

Quinn stopped, brought her knees to the dirt, and held her arm against her sore ribs. "I'm...not sure, Sergeant. Perhaps the kick I received when hand fighting with Hirna yesterday did more damage than I thought."

The other cadets continued with the push-ups as Jasmine called out, "Healer!"

Quinn closed her eyes and thanked Issal. Moving gingerly, she opened them and rose to her feet. When she turned toward the stands, she found a familiar face approaching.

"Rena?"

"Hello, Quinn." The girl smiled. "It's good to see you."

"What are you going here?"

"Healer duty. Both Torney and I signed up for it during the winter session." The girl reached out and placed a hand on Quinn's shoulder. "Now hold still and I'll see what I can do."

Rena closed her eyes and her brow furrowed in concentration. Quinn watched her childhood friend and it occurred to her that Rena had become quite beautiful. Yes, she had always possessed cute features, but as the woman inside her began to blossom, so did Rena's beauty.

A shocking chill shook Quinn's body and the air expelled from her lungs. She gasped to reclaim it and realized that her ribs no longer hurt. Her stomach growled loud enough to drown out Vi's count.

Rena opened her eyes and gave Quinn a warm smile. "Your ribs were fractured, but they shouldn't give you further trouble." She withdrew a hard roll from her pocket. "Here. I'm sure you're hungry."

Quinn accepted the roll with a nod. "Thanks."

As Rena turned and walked away, Quinn considered the injury and decided she needed to speak with her. When she turned, Quinn found Jasmine staring at her with a frown, her hands on her hips.

"How did you get the injury?" Jasmine asked.

Worry twisted Quinn's stomach. "Hirna. She kicked me yesterday while we were hand fighting."

Jasmine's eyes narrowed. "Funny, I don't recall you having any problem."

Quinn shrugged. "I guess I didn't notice while filled with adrenaline from the fight."

By the time Quinn reclaimed her spot, pushups were finished and they moved on to balancing on one foot with arms spread out like a bird. With balance being among Quinn's strongest attributes, she easily stepped into the pose and held it, feeling Jasmine's glare the entire time.

Quinn faced her opponent, both familiar and fierce. Chuli fought hard every time, never giving an inch. With an advantage of height and weapon length, Chuli's reach far surpassed Quinn's – even approaching that of Darnya. While Quinn knew that Chuli and Darnya each fought with their own techniques, the hours spent sparring with Chuli would help prepare her for her next duel with Darnya.

Leaping forward, Quinn slapped Chuli's practice sword aside and aimed a strike at her midriff. Chuli's shield caught the wooden short sword and knocked it aside as she wound for a lower swing. Quinn twisted with a desperate block and kicked backward, striking Chuli on the thigh. The girl grunted, shifted, and swung again. Quinn raised her left arm and knocked the strike aside with her sword. She feigned another low swipe with the other sword, but when Chuli shifted her shield, she altered her stroke upward and caught the girl in the chin. Chuli's head snapped back and she stumbled, falling to her hands and knees. She spit a gob of blood onto the dirt and tried to stand before staggering and falling onto her hip. Chuli groaned and squeezed her eyes closed, her chin torn open, blood dripping onto her vest.

Torney ran in and knelt beside her. "Hold on. You'll feel a chill."

Quinn watched the skin on Chuli's chin meld itself together, appearing normal but for the trail of dried blood that remained.

"Thank you, Elder."

Torney frowned. "I told you, my name is Torney." He reached into his pocket and handed her a chip of dried meat. "Here. Eat this. It will help."

Chuli accepted the meat and stood, brushing the dirt clean as she chewed.

"I'm sorry about hitting your face, Chuli. I aimed for your shoulder, but missed."

Chuli shook her head. "If it were a real fight, missing is bad. However, in this case, you would have cut your opponent's face in half." She smiled. "I suspect that means you would win and they would be dead."

Quinn smiled before turning toward Torney.

"We're done here, Torney. You can head back."

He shook his head. "Since it's late, I'll stay for another day. I don't have any scheduled classes tomorrow. Besides, you need one of us around here because you're a walking disaster, ready to rain pain on others."

Quinn chuckled. "Fine. Just be careful to keep this a secret. If anyone asks why you're here so late, just say that you got snowed in."

Torney gave her an incredulous look. "Are you kidding? There is no way I would tell anyone and risk upsetting you. You were feisty when we were kids. Now, you're downright scary."

This time, Chuli laughed. "You are correct, good healer. The look on her face when she fights is that of a cornered badger – frightening to anyone who realizes what they face."

With sparring practice finished, the girls retreated to the baths to clean away the sweat, dirt, and blood. Chuli remained in the baths, opting to soak her sore muscles while Quinn exited the women's baths and headed toward the mess hall to get food. When she turned a corner, she heard a voice behind her.

"I feel a bit hurt that you didn't tell me."

She turned to find Iko standing behind her, his arms crossed as he leaned against the corridor wall.

"Didn't tell you what?"

He gave her a small smile, uncrossed his arms, and edged toward her. "That you are spending extra time sparring. I won't tell anyone, you know."

Quinn sighed. "We aren't supposed to be in those rooms after hours. I figured that not telling you meant that you wouldn't have to lie if asked."

Iko's brow furrowed. "You don't think I can lie for a friend?"

"Well, I didn't want to put you in that position."

"I'd prefer you tell me everything and let me handle the repercussions. Friends do that for each other." He took her hand and stared into her eyes. "We're friends, right?"

The heat of his hand as it held hers sent Quinn's heart racing, the thump in her chest distracting her thoughts. "Yes. We are friends."

He put his other hand on her chin, sliding it to her cheek as she stared into the amber pools of his eyes. When he leaned in close, her eyes drifted closed and her lips parted in anticipation. The rush of the kiss made her slightly dizzy. As he pulled his lips free, her eyes flickered open. Iko gave her a warm smile, and she smiled in response.

"Are you heading to the mess hall?" he asked.

The spell broken, Quinn stepped back and gathered herself. "Um… Yes. I need to get a quick bite before I study the Battle of Yarth."

"Good. I'll go with you. We can talk while you eat."

He grabbed her hand and they walked toward the mess hall. Upon arriving, Iko waited at a table while Quinn visited the kitchen. She soon emerged with leftover mutton stew and a chunk of bread and began eating the moment she sat across from him.

Iko cleared his throat. "We are in the Coliseum tomorrow for another duel with practice weapons. Are you girls dueling as well?"

Quinn swallowed and took a drink of her milk. "Our duels are scheduled for next week. Tomorrow, we are off for a ranger field session."

Iko nodded. "Our trip is next week. I'm afraid that it'll snow and make for a nasty outing."

Quinn shrugged. "I grew up in Cinti Mor. Snow isn't a big deal, provided you dress appropriately."

Chuli entered the mess hall and nodded to Quinn as she headed toward the kitchen. Iko frowned as the Tantarri girl passed by, his expression darkening.

"If you allow yourself to get to know Chuli, you would like her."

Iko turned toward her but didn't respond.

"She's my friend, Iko. If you want to spend time with me, you need to try."

He sighed. "Very well, I will try."

"Good."

Standing, he glanced toward the kitchen. "I must go. Percy is waiting for me to study battle tactics together. Besides, I need a good night of sleep before my duel."

"I'll see you when I return from the ranger outing."

He smiled. "I'd like that very much."

With a bow, he turned and exited the room. As Quinn watched him leave, she felt something stirring within, something she had never felt before.

As they reached the meadow, the squad slowed to a stop. With most of the leaves now settled on the ground, Quinn found the view into the surrounding forest extended much further than on previous outings. The formerly green undergrowth had wilted and yellowed – a byproduct of cold evenings.

Quinn slid her pack off and untied the rolled tent. Working with practiced precision, she and Chuli quickly pitched the tent, stuffed their gear inside, and waited at attention for their next instructions.

A layer of gray blanketed the sky, obscuring the sun although it was mid-day. The clouds carried the threat of snow – a threat that might come to fruition should the temperature drop. In preparation for the weather, the travel gear worn on this outing was heavier than during the previous three trips. They still wore the long, gray cloaks that blended with the forest, but beneath them were layers to keep the girls warm when night fell.

When the last of the tents were pitched, and the girls were standing at attention, Jasmine strolled down the gap between them, nodding in approval.

"You're getting better. A few of you can still improve the coordination of pitching your tent, but most have the process in hand." The woman's gaze swept over each girl as she walked past. "Despite increasing our pace on this trip, you kept up well and none of you appear worn. This is good. It proves that your training has honed you, leaving your bodies fit and your endurance greatly improved."

She spun about. "You have five minutes to eat and then we will break you into groups as we have done in the past." With a wave, she dismissed them.

Quinn waited as Chuli grabbed her pack and handed her a pouch filled with nuts and dried fruit. They ate quickly, finishing the nuts and fruit before following it with two strips of dried beef and a hard roll. With their rations consumed and washed down with a few drinks from their waterskins, Quinn and Chuli resumed positions before their tent and waited on their instructions.

When Jasmine designated the squad that was to hide their trail, Chuli's was among the names called. A group was assigned with cutting stakes and assembling their perimeter defense, while smaller groups were assigned to dig the fire pit and collect wood to burn. When she found herself among the last to be assigned, Quinn knew her task before it was announced.

"Simone, you are to lead a hunting party and head west. Darnya and Quinn are with you. Bronwyn, take Hirna and Vanessa. The three of you are to hunt to the east."

Quinn watched Simone as the girl grabbed her longbow and quiver. Since Simone was among the best with a bow, Quinn was happy to have the quiet girl in her party. Darnya was another matter.

With her quiver over her shoulder and shortbow in hand, Quinn followed the two second-year cadets into the woods as they headed toward the tall peak to the west.

Remaining silent other than the soft crunching of leaves beneath their boots, Quinn and Darnya trailed Simone through the forest. After ten minutes, Simone paused and waved Darnya to one side, Quinn to the other. Once spaced with a ten-stride gap between each of them, they again advanced, moving with caution and careful stealth.

Quinn ducked around saplings and beneath branches, using her bow to gently push undergrowth aside as her eyes scanned the forest for movement. Continuous glances toward the forest floor helped her find clear spots to step, careful to avoid fallen twigs and dead leaves that might announce her approach. The bare branches provided a much greater viewing distance than on previous hunting trips, but she wasn't sure if it was a good or bad thing. If she could see farther, so could their quarry.

They soon came upon two thick copses of pine trees – one directly ahead and one to the far side of Darnya. Simone held her hand up, and all three girls stopped and listened. Simone slid an arrow from her quiver and nocked it without drawing her bowstring. Quinn and Darnya mirrored the action.

The *crack* of a twig sent Quinn's pulse racing. With the echo, she was unsure from which clump of pines the sound had originated. Simone edged forward, moving cautiously and visibly scanning the area while Quinn and Darnya did the same.

A *twang* sounded from Quinn's right. She glanced toward her companions to see who had fired, but both still held their bows with arrows nocked. Her brow furrowed in confusion as Darnya fell to her knees. The girl dropped her bow and clutched at her chest, drawing Quinn's attention to the arrow in Darnya's back, the point sticking through the breast of her coat. Another *twang* sounded and Simone stumbled when an arrow pierced her throat. Quinn's eyes widened when she spied the arrow head protruded from the side that faced her. A glob of dark blood gurgled from Simone's mouth, and she collapsed. Panic struck.

Quinn crouched low, and she scanned the dark pines beyond Darnya, seeking the attacker. The forest seemed unnaturally still – quiet save for a whimper from Darnya, who lay in a pile of damp, dead leaves. The girl's dark eyes stared toward Quinn and blood covered the hand she held around the shaft sticking from her chest. With Simone dead and Darnya dying, Quinn felt naked and helpless. Fear fought to overtake her as she considered her options.

Another twang sounded from the shadows, and an arrow flew past, just a few feet above Quinn's head. The mere sound of the missile passing set fire to the fear that had been smoldering inside, urging her into action.

Quinn turned and ran, throwing all sense of stealth aside in favor of speed. To make a more difficult target, she ducked and weaved among the trees. She stumbled and fell to her hands, a few arrows tumbling from her quiver. Driven by panic, she blasted forward without giving the arrows a second glance.

When she thought that enough obstacles blocked a clean shot for the hidden attacker, she sprinted as fast as she dared, knowing that another fall or twist of an ankle might define the line between survival and death. All the while, images of her dying comrades flashed in her head: Simone's empty gaze, the blood running from Darnya's mouth as it dripped on the forest floor.

After ten minutes of panicked running through the woods, she spotted the clearing where her squad was camped. Not slowing until she passed the first row of tents, Quinn stopped and rested her hands on her knees, gasping for air. Flanked by Vi and Lissa, Jasmine approached with her hands on her hips.

"Where are Darnya and Simone? You know the rules. Stick together at all times."

Quinn stood upright, breathing heavily. "Someone shot at us, Sergeant." She took a breath. "At least one attacker, maybe more. I couldn't tell because they were hidden within the trees."

Jasmine's eyes reflected alarm, although her stern expression remained. "Your fellow cadets, where are they?"

Quinn turned toward the woods. "They were shot. Simone…is surely dead. Darnya might be as well."

Jasmine ran to her tent and came out with a short bow and quiver. "Vi, you're coming with me. Lissa, you're in charge here until I return." The Sergeant waved Quinn forward. "Don't just stand there, Cadet. Lead us to the soldiers you left behind."

Quinn stared at Darnya with a strange mixture of feelings. While she had hated the girl, she had never wanted her dead – not really. Seeing her still staring into space made Quinn feel like Darnya was playing a cruel joke, just waiting for Quinn to step close so she could startle her and laugh about it. However, Jasmine had checked and confirmed the girl was dead, as was Simone.

Turning, Quinn saw Jasmine materialize from the pines. The sergeant's dark features somehow seemed even darker – her face grim. Vi emerged from another gap among the pines. When Jasmine turned toward her, Vi shook her head. Both walked toward Quinn with Jasmine in the lead.

"Are you sure that's where the arrows came from?" Jasmine asked as she approached Quinn.

"Yes. The last one even flew over my head." Quinn pointed past Simone's body. "I was over there. The arrow should be somewhere beyond."

Jasmine knelt beside Darnya and examined the arrow in the girl's back. The frown on her face deepened as she stood and moved closer to Simone. After a brief inspection, she turned toward Quinn.

"Did you fire any arrows?"

Quinn shook her head. "No. When I realized we were under attack, I ducked low among the saplings over there. I searched the woods, but I couldn't see the target within the shadows. When an arrow flew past me, I…I ran." Her eyes were downcast in a moment of shame.

Quinn had spent her life facing her enemies, not backing down to them. She discovered that an invisible assailant was something different, particularly one who had killed her companions before her eyes. The fear of dying had been something Quinn wasn't prepared to face.

She turned toward Jasmine and found the woman glaring with the weight of judgement. The sight made Quinn want to run and hide. It made her miss home – miss her family.

"These are academy arrows," Jasmine said.

Quinn frowned. "What?"

Jasmine took a step closer, while Vi raised her bow and aimed a nocked arrow at Quinn. "Hand me your weapon, Cadet."

Quinn stared at Jasmine's outstretched hand. "You…you can't believe that I did this."

"The bow. Give it to me. Now."

When she held the bow out, Jasmine snatched it from her.

"Now, your quiver."

"I didn't do this, Sergeant." Quinn slid the quiver off her shoulder. "I would never shoot a fellow soldier."

Jasmine examined the quiver. "Why are there only eight arrows? Each cadet had a full dozen when we left the academy."

Glancing past Simone's body, Quinn stared at where she had been crouching before she fled back to camp. "I had an arrow nocked. I dropped it over there when I ran." She recalled falling during her flight. "I also stumbled once, and a few more fell out of my quiver."

Jasmine glanced at Vi before responding. The other girl kept her bow aimed at Quinn.

"We found no tracks among the trees. No broken branches. Nothing that would indicate anyone had been there." Jasmine had never appeared more serious. "Other than your story, we can find no proof of this attack you describe. The only thing I can confirm is that two cadets are dead. Whether you are the one who murdered them is the only thing in question." She nodded firmly. "Yes. This was murder."

Quinn stared at Jasmine in shock as she realized the gravity of her situation. At that moment, white flakes began to fall. Yet, the weather was balmy compared to the looks upon the faces before her. Suspicion of betrayal hung in the air like a cold, dark blanket that threatened to smother her.

The group walked back to the camp with Jasmine in the lead, Vi following Quinn from behind. When they arrived, Quinn was placed under the watchful eyes of Vi and Lissa while they waited for the other girls to return. The day was cut short and they soon struck camp, stopping to gather the two dead cadets before heading back toward the academy.

Trapped between frustration about her situation and fear of what might happen to her, Quinn fell into a daze that left her numb. The journey back to the valley passed without her even noticing. As they arrived at the school, thick white flakes were gathering on the long grass and dotting the gravel paths – the first snow of the year.

The squad entered the building, led by Lissa while Vi and Jasmine took Quinn to the Infirmary. Russel, the enforcer on duty, opened a cell door, and Quinn shuffled inside a tiny room furnished with nothing but a small bed. Turning to face the door, she found Jasmine wearing a grim expression, her eyes reflecting a mixture of disappointment and disapproval. That was the last thing Quinn saw before the heavy door slammed closed. A key slid into the lock, securing it with an ominous *click*.

Quinn sat on the bed – alone and without any idea how she might prove her innocence. She pulled her knees to her chest, wrapped her arms about her shins, and rested her head and cried.

24

THE ARCANE WARD

E verson paused his story and found himself wishing for clothes, or a blanket, or anything to cover himself. The cell was cold and his smallclothes were little protection against it.

He took a deep breath and resumed his story.

"When I returned to the school after visiting my parents, Donnell, Ivy, and I focused on completing our creation with the Inventor Challenge fast approaching." Everson recalled other events and his tone grew somber. "At the same time, I had other...issues. Some of which offered motivation to win...to prove myself."

"Hand me the large gear."

Everson held his open hand out and waited. When Ivy placed the cool metal disk in his palm, he shifted it until he held it between his finger and thumb. Moving carefully, he held it toward the assembly.

Through the magnifying lenses strapped to his head, the gear entered his field of vision, the circular shape appearing four times larger than reality. He slid a small rod through the hole in the center and through two washers before inserting the rod into the hole he had made in the assembly wall. When he pushed the gear down, he turned it slightly until the teeth aligned with the neighboring gear. The fit was perfect.

Gripping the magnifying lenses, he pulled them off his head and put them on the bench. A sigh slipped out as he gazed upon the assembly. It was coming together, but there was no way to test it until it was complete. He looked up and found Ivy staring at him. She blinked in surprise and turned toward the bench.

"The washers were a good idea. If the gears become misaligned, the friction of rubbing on the assembly housing could be problematic." He smiled at Ivy as she looked at him again. "Thank you for that."

The girl shrugged and stared toward the floor as she spoke. "It was nothing. I'm sure you would have thought of it yourself when you began assembling it."

He frowned. "You should be more confident in yourself, Ivy. You're a smart girl. You belong here as much as anybody else does."

A smile quivered at the edge of her mouth. Her eyes flicked toward his face, and she quickly turned away again.

"Thank you, Everson," she mumbled.

Everson turned the opposite direction, toward his other partner in this venture.

"How's the housing coming?"

Donnell looked up from his carving and shrugged. "Fine I guess. I almost have it hollowed out enough."

"Keep up the good work," Everson said. "Appearance is nearly as important as function."

Everson sat back and took stock of the parts piled upon the workbench, waiting to join the assembly. He turned toward the partially assembled mechanism and imagined the gears turning. The mere thought brought him excitement, despite his weariness. Scooping up his canes, he pushed himself into a standing position.

"It's late. We can reconvene tomorrow after class."

"The competition is only a few days away," Donnell noted.

Everson nodded. "True. Other than the housing, we have all the components crafted. If you can finish it tomorrow, we can complete the assembly and should have it up and running the next day."

Donnell eyed his work for a moment. "I'm sure I can get it finished tomorrow."

Ivy smiled. "We will finally get to see it working."

Doubt flashed across Donnell's face, but he said nothing. Everson decided to let it pass.

"I'm off for a late dinner and then to bed." Everson began shuffling his way toward the door. "Goodnight, you two."

When he stepped into the hallway, he spotted someone who looked like Jonah walking down the Arcanist Wing corridor, a hundred paces away. He stared at the student, attempting to determine if it were Jonah. Dressing in a blue novice coat, the boy approached the black doors at the end of the hall, opened them, and disappeared outside. Everson frowned. *Was that Jonah? Regardless, no novice student would be allowed in the Arcane Ward.*

Curious, he shuffled forward, passed the central corridor, and entered the opposite hallway. He glanced toward the closed door to his Chaos Theory classroom as he passed it. *It's late and the classroom is likely empty…as empty as the hallways.* He approached the black doors at the end of the corridor, and his gaze shifted toward the sign above them. Seeking resolve, he took a breath, pulled the door open, and shuffled through.

Brisk evening air struck him, cold enough that his breath visibly steamed from his lips. He stopped and looked around, open-mouthed as he gazed up at the massive tower.

It stood twelve stories tall, wide and square and windowless – a dark and ominous monolith that blocked much of the starlit sky from Everson's view.

Everson's gaze lowered, and he noticed two armed guards standing fifty-feet away, before a pair of massive black doors. Glowlamps to the side of each set of doors lit the alcove. When he glanced to the left, he found a wall, two stories tall and built from the same stone as the tower. Another guard stood outside the wall, beside a glowlamp and a black door that matched the others.

Light from the glowlamps behind him and across from him illuminated the cobblestone covering the ground between academy, the tower, and the wall. To his right was a road that rounded the south side of the tower and ran between it and the Arena.

Jonah – or the student who might be Jonah – was nowhere in sight.

With lips pressed together in determination, Everson shuffled forward. The thumping of his boots and the thud of his canes were the only sounds he heard, the sound echoing loudly as he knew it would. To counter his nervousness, Everson imagined the soundwaves bouncing off the hard surfaces of the narrow space as they found their way back to his ears.

When he approached the two guards, he gave them a hopeful smile.

"Hello. I was just coming to meet a friend. Did you see him pass by?"

The guard on the left, a woman dressed in black leathers with metal plates and a shiny metal helm to match, frowned.

"You cannot enter without a writ."

"Did you see my friend? He was wearing a blue academy coat, like mine. He just passed this way."

The other guard responded, the man's deep voice drawing Everson's attention. "We saw nothing. Now, if you don't have a writ, I strongly suggest you return to the school before you are arrested."

Everson glanced toward the black doors as he struggled with his curiosity. Beyond those doors were secrets…

After a moment, he turned around and retreated to the school. As he crossed the open space again, he thought about what he had observed. *It is impossible for a student to sneak across this space unseen. There is too much light. It is too open. Any sound is amplified and sends echoes throughout.* His mouth turned down in a frown as he considered the situation.

Upon reentering the building, he headed toward the dining hall with the conundrum still turning inside his head.

When he entered the room, Everson found a group of fellow engineering students eating together – two girls and two boys. He collected his courage as he approached the table.

"Hello Freya, Juni," he said to the girls before turning toward the boys. "Hi, Sakan, Yeldin."

The boys nodded toward him, while the girls replied, "Hello, Everson."

"I'm sorry to intrude, but I was wondering if one of you could help me get food from the kitchen." Everson found himself biting his lip as he waited for a response.

Freya glanced toward the others and shrugged. "Sure. I'll..."

"No." Sakan put his hand on her shoulder before she could stand. "If he's so smart, I'm sure he can figure it out himself."

Freya frowned. "Sakan..."

The boy ignored her. "Go on, stick legs. Get your own food."

Everson swallowed the lump in his throat and turned away before the tear could surface. He shuffled toward the kitchen, blinking to clear the moisture from his eyes.

The server approached the counter, and Everson gave her a weak smile. "I'm late for dinner. What you have you got for me?"

She wiped the sweat from her brow. "I have jackaroo stew and hard rolls."

"That sounds wonderful."

Spinning about, she faded into the kitchen and soon returned with a bowl of stew in one hand, a plate with two rolls in the other. She rested it on the counter, spun about, and walked away.

Everson stared at the bowl, considering how to hold it while using his canes. Bending, he looped his right arm about the bowl and pulled it against his hip. Using his other hand, he squeezed the plate with his thumb and forefinger while still gripping the cane. Moving cautiously, he shuffled out of the kitchen.

Hearing laughter, he looked toward the occupied table and found Sakan pointing toward Everson, Yeldin laughing with him. The girls, however, appeared upset. Everson squeezed harder when he felt the bowl slipping. He stopped and shifted, but was unable to stop it from tipping forward. Hot stew poured down his leg and into his boot.

"Argh!" he cried as it burned him. The bowl slipped the remainder of the way, crashed to the floor, and shattered. With his attention on the stew, he dropped the plate in his other hand. It collided with the stone tile, chipped, and sent the two rolls tumbling across the floor.

Loud laughter came from the two boys watching. Embarrassed by his inability to perform a simple task, Everson refused to look their way.

"What's wrong with you two?"

Hearing a male voice, Everson turned to find Torney standing over their table.

"It won't kill you to help him."

Sakan stood and faced Torney. "Leave off, Torney. If you like the turd, you go help him. In the meantime, stay out of my face."

Torney's eyes narrowed. "I believe your face could use a few adjustments, Sakan. I find it difficult to look at."

Sakan's cheeks grew red, his lips pressing together until they were white. Freya put her hand on his arm. "Just let it go, Sakan. You should have just let me help Everson in the first place."

Looking at his companions for support, Sakan found none. With a grunt of disgust, he pushed past Torney and headed toward the door.

Torney walked over to Everson and shook his head. "You made a mess again, I see." He gestured toward an open table. "Go ahead and have a seat. I'll get you another bowl of stew and someone from the kitchen to help clean this up."

Everson shuffled toward the table. In the back of his mind, thoughts of young Torney bullying him resurfaced. The boy had changed for the better. He hoped that Sakan would someday do the same.

After eating a bowl of cold stew and a hard roll, Everson headed to his room. He found the door locked, the room dark and empty when he entered. A quick shake of the glowlamp on the desk brought it to life, lighting the room in a soft blue light.

Exhausted from a long day, Everson sat on his bed and began to undress, tossing his soiled clothing into the laundry bin. Thankfully, each student had been provided multiple uniforms. One such set remained clean and waited in the wardrobe. As he slid under his covers, the door opened and Jonah entered.

"You were out late," Everson noted.

"I…um…went to meditate…you know…for ecclesiast training."

"Where did you go?"

"I was in the dining hall. It was empty and quiet since it's late."

"Funny." Everson said in a flat voice. "I was just there to eat a late meal. I didn't see you."

Jonah shrugged as he began to unbutton his coat. "I must have left before you were there."

"Where did you go after that?"

A frown crossed Jonah's face, and he turned away to hang his coat on a hook, "Why all the questions?"

Everson pressed his lips together, feeling a moment of frustration. "Did you go into the Arcane Ward?"

Jonah's head shot about, his eyes wary as he stared at Everson. "Why would you ask me that?"

"I saw you go through the black doors."

"You saw me do what?" Jonah's brow furrowed.

"I was leaving the Foundry late, and I watched you pass through the doors that lead to the tower. I tried to follow, but the guards stopped me."

Jonah shook his head. "I don't know what you think you saw, but I wasn't in the Ward. Like you said, it's off limits. The guards would have stopped me, too."

"But..."

"I don't appreciate being accused." Jonah sat on the bed and pulled his boots off. "I thought we were friends, Everson."

"Of course we are."

"Well, you're not being very friend-like right now. I told you I was practicing meditation and then I went for a short walk on the lawn. That's it."

A stab of guilt made Everson think of losing Jonah as a friend. He didn't have many friends and surely didn't want that to happen.

"You're right. I'm sorry. I guess it was someone else."

25

TIMEKEEPER

Everson sat between Donnell and Ivy, the three of them on the third row of benches arranged at one end of the Arena floor. Opposite from them were seven academy masters, seated among nine chairs near the center of the massive building.

Students dressed in blue coats filled the benches that encircled the oval-shaped floor, engaged in noisy chatter. When he looked toward the stands, Everson judged the front row of benches to be ten feet above him and the back row three times that.

Master Nindlerod descended a narrow flight of stairs to the Arena floor and hobbled toward the center. Upon reaching it, he held a cone-shaped object to his mouth and bellowed.

"Be still!"

The rush of the crowd eased to a whisper and the man nodded.

"Thank you all for coming. You are about to witness the latest creations from some of the brightest minds in the academy. Each year, we challenge our students to imagine and create something that might change the world.

"These seven masters will join me and one other in judging today's contest. Who is the other, you ask?"

The man chuckled and gestured toward the far end of the floor. "I present to you, the man who created the Hedgewick Flyer, the Hedgewick Rider, the Perpetual Oven, and many other inventions, Master Benedict Hedgewick."

Applause filled the air as a man appeared from one of the doors at the end of the building. With a mess of dark brown hair atop his head, the middle-aged man waved to the crowd as he strolled toward the heart of the floor. Everson had heard of Benny Hedgewick, but this was his first time seeing the man. Sporting a wry grin and rectangular spectacles to go with his rumpled purple and black coat, the man appeared amazingly…normal.

When he reached Nindlerod, the two men gripped the other's shoulder and said a few quiet words to each other. Nindlerod then handed the cone to Hedgewick before hobbling over to his seat.

The crowd quieted, and Hedgewick lifted the cone to his mouth. "Welcome, everyone. I don't have time for many appearances any longer, but I make it a point to attend this event.

"Since I was a child, I have firmly believed that the minds of mankind can be used to enrich people's lives and make this world a better place." The man rocked his shoulders in a quirky manner as he spoke, his face squinting and twitching now and then. "Like myself, Master Nindlerod, and those who came to the academy before us, these students represent the embodiment of that belief. I look forward to discovering the wondrous ideas they have brought to fruition."

Reaching into his pocket, the man withdrew a folded piece of paper and read off the names of the first team. Sakan, Yeldin, Freya, and Juni rose from the bench in front of Everson, the two girls heading toward the middle of the floor as the boys walked toward a cart at the side of the Arena. A black sheet covered a bulky object resting upon the cart, similar to other carts waiting nearby. Everson's gaze fell upon the sheet-covered object, and he tried to determine what creation hid beneath.

The crowd fell silent as the cart rolled toward the center of the floor. Wooden wheels squeaked in protest to the weight, accompanied by grunts coming from the boys pushing the cart.

When all four students met in the center of the floor, the two pushing the cart stood beside it, each boy gripping a corner of the sheet. The girls turned toward the seated masters. Freya cleared her throat and spoke loudly.

"We present to you an invention that will change the world forever."

She turned toward Sakan and gave him a nod. He opened his mouth and tried to speak, but choked on the words. His bravado appeared to have faded before the multitude of eyes watching him. After noisily clearing this throat, he tried again.

"You already know the steam engine, the steam cleaner, and vegetable steamer. We are here to show you that steam can do more."

Juni stopped before the cart and smiled as she gestured toward the object behind the sheet. "Presenting…steam blades."

With a flourish, Yeldin and Sakan pulled the sheet back, but it hooked on something that tore a hole in the sheet, leaving a shiny metal blade sticking through the fabric. After fighting with it a bit, the two boys were able to unhook the sheet and remove it to reveal their creation.

The bulk of the unit consisted of a metal stove and boiler with two cylinders at the top. A series of levers and two cams connected a pair of butcher knives to the cylinders. Yeldin opened the stove door and flue, poked at the coals, and added a chunk of wood. Dark smoke oozed out of the small chimney and white steam puffed from the exhaust. As the fire grew hotter, the steam increased until the pistons began to move up and down, and, in turn, moved the knives up and down. With each rotation of the cam, a knife would thump against a cutting board located on the front of the unit. Sakan pulled the cutting board out and placed a carrot upon it. He then slid the cutting board in and the knives began to chop the vegetable into tiny slices.

A few of the masters watching the scene nodded. Some even smiled. Master Hedgewick frowned and leaned forward with narrowed eyes.

Freya turned toward the masters and announced, "Behold how rapidly this machine can slice five potatoes."

Yeldin adjusted a lever and the machine whistled with increased pressure. The pistons began to pump faster, and the rate of the chopping knives increased. He then placed five potatoes on the cutting board and stood back as Sakan eased the board beneath the fast-chopping knives. As the knives grew louder, so did the chatter and applause from the crowd.

The whirling blades hacked the first potato into thin disks in moments. During the third slice of the second potato, a crack sounded. The fifth brought a louder crack. When the knives dropped for the seventh slice, a blade broke free and flung forward, striking Sakan. He staggered back and looked down in surprise at the blade buried in his shoulder. The machine continued unaware as it frantically chopped with its remaining blade and the bladeless handle.

Stunned, the crowd fell to silence. Sakan's eyes rolled back and he fell backward, fainting on the dirt floor.

Freya screamed. "Sakan!"

The crowd erupted with cries and shouts.

Everson leaned forward to see better, trying to determine if the boy were dead. He then spotted Rena racing down the stairs to the arena floor with Torney a step behind. She ran to Sakan's side and knelt beside him with her hand on his forehead. Torney knelt to the boy's other side as he hastily wrapped a handkerchief about his hand.

She said something Everson couldn't hear. Torney grimaced, gripped the knife blade with his wrapped hand, and yanked it out.

Blood spurted from the wound, but Rena's eyes already were closed. A moment passed, and the blood settled as a violent shiver shook Sakan's body. His eyes flashed open, and he gasped a deep breath as Rena opened her eyes.

Rena and Torney each grabbed an arm as they helped Sakan stand. He glanced down at his navy coat, the breast turned dark purple from the blood. His face turned a shade whiter and his knees gave. Rena and Torney caught him and helped him regain his footing before walking him to the side of the Arena.

Inventions of numerous applications were presented to the panel. Some, Everson found to be ingenious and useful. Others displayed little to no innovation – merely stale copies of someone else's idea.

After the first ten teams had presented, Everson knew that his primary competition was the stitching machine built by Henrick's team. The idea itself was not particularly inspired since it only involved applying existing ideas a new way, but its usefulness was undeniable.

Master Hedgewick lifted the cone to his mouth and his voice rang throughout the Arena. "The next team to present includes Everson Gulagas, Ivy Fluerian, and Donnell Banks."

Everson glanced at his teammates and found them watching him. He gave them a nod as he gripped his canes. They peeled off while he stood and shuffled toward the heart of the Arena. When he settled before the seated panel of masters, he turned to find Donnell and Ivy pushing a hand cart with a covered object resting upon it, the top of which was roughly even with Donnell's head.

Everson turned from his companions to the crowd and his breath caught. Raw, irrational fear had squeezed the air from him and left his heart racing, his palms sweaty. *So many people staring at me, waiting for me to speak.*

He squeezed his eyes shut and sought rational thought. Past moments of fear resurfaced, moments where Quinn had been there to save him. Her face appeared in his mind's eye – smiling, strong, confident. Air refilled his lungs as they regained their function. Holding on to the thought of her beside him, he opened his eyes and found Donnell and Ivy standing nearby, each to one side of the parked cart. Everson gave them a nod and turned toward the panel of masters.

"Time. It is what man values most, but controls least. We are born. We live. We die. The moments that pass are ephemeral and intangible.

"As mankind is prone to do, we have created definitions for time. From seconds to centuries, we have this idea for how time functions, yet our ability to track it is pathetic at best.

"*Meet me at noon,* you say to a friend. How do we define noon? By the position of the sun with little else to inform us.

"*Be back in an hour,* you are told. To do so requires an hourglass or sundial, yet both lack accuracy or practicality.

"We present to you an invention that changes how you will view time...forever."

Everson turned toward Donnell and Ivy and nodded. They each grabbed fists full of the black sheet and pulled it back, revealing their creation. Standing three feet tall, three feet long, and a foot deep, was a wooden structure with rounded corners and stained panels. Three bronze disks covered the front of the invention. The edge of each disk was lined with teeth that interlocked with the neighboring disk and the face of each disk was marked at the edges. The lower two disks held sixty marks, while the upper disk contained twenty-four marks.

"Presenting: The timekeeper," Everson announced loudly to the crowd. "Donnell, please wind the coil."

Donnell gripped a knob that stuck from the side of the machine and began to turn it, the thing making a series of clicks with each motion. As the boy wound the coil, Everson explained the concept to the audience.

"Tracking time, down to the second – the mere blink of an eye – is now possible with this machine." He shuffled toward it, pointing at the bottom disk. "This wheel represents seconds and will turn a full revolution every minute. When it does, it will trigger the middle wheel to move a single increment, representing that minute. After sixty minutes, the upper wheel will move a single increment to show the passing of an hour."

Ivy pulled an hourglass from beside the timekeeper and held it up for all to see.

"Behold. This glass measures a single minute. When I say the word, Donnell will start the timekeeper and Ivy will flip the hourglass."

Everson's heart fluttered, and his stomach twisted in a moment of doubt. They had only been able to test it a few times, a result of the final assembly taking longer than expected.

"Go."

Donnell stopped winding the coil and flipped the lever as Ivy flipped the hourglass. Loud ticking filled the silence of the room as the crowd watched on. When the wheel reached half a rotation, Everson stared at the hourglass and tried to determine how much sand remained. The moment seemed to linger – time seemingly teasing him, toying with him. Suddenly, ten seconds remained. Then five. Then one.

"Stop." Everson shouted.

A moment later, the last bit of sand fell into the bottom chamber. He frowned when he realized that the timekeeper had finished first. Only by a second, but still off.

"Very good, Mister Gulagas," Nindlerod crooned with a nod. "Please do it again, but without winding the timekeeper."

Everson looked at Ivy and Donnell. She shrugged. He nodded. "Go!"

Donnell flipped the lever, and Ivy flipped the hourglass. Again, the crowd watched in silence and the tension wrapped itself about Everson, squeezing sweat from his armpits, his hands, his temple. With ten clicks left on the timekeeper, Everson grew even more nervous. At five, his heart cried out. At three, the hourglass had already stopped. When a full revolution completed, Donnell flipped the lever, and Everson turned toward the masters.

"One more time, please," Nindlerod requested.

The third time was even worse. The hourglass ran out a full eleven seconds before the timekeeper. Everson stared at it as he attempted to divine the cause of the discrepancy.

"The coil must have stretched," he muttered.

Master Hedgewick stood and approached Everson with a sad smile. "While the idea is unique and the intended application commendable, the execution is lacking. The only way such an invention can hold value is for it to be accurate and reliable." Hedgewick looked Everson in the eye and placed his hand on his shoulder. "I'm sorry, but you have failed on both accounts."

26

CHANGE THE WORLD

The novice lounge in the Boy's Wing Tower was quiet but for the tapping of Everson's fingers on the table. He flipped the page and continued to pore over his notes. His hand strayed to the side and gripped the handle of his mug, raising it to his lips. A noisy sip later, he grimaced. The caffe had gone cold. It had taken him a few months to become used to the bitter drink, but he liked it far better when it was hot.

Motion in the periphery drew his attention, and he looked up to find Jonah approaching.

"I was wondering where you were hiding."

"I needed a quiet place to think."

When Jonah saw Everson's notes on the table, he shook his head. "You won't let it go, will you?"

Everson leaned back with a sigh. "It should work. I just need a reliable power source. The coil worked fine when we tested it, but it began to break down from the tension and became too weak to keep time."

"What other options do you have?" Jonah sat at the end of the table.

"That's what I've been thinking on." Everson pulled out a list. "Manual methods such as pedals or cranks are out because that defeats the purpose. Steam is a possibility, but it also requires someone to feed the furnace so the water boils. Plus, the smoke from the fire is less than desirable."

Jonah nodded. "I'm with you so far."

"Then I began thinking about Chaos. It's a form of energy itself. When you gather it and charge a rune, the energy becomes defined into a specific physical effect."

"Yeah," Jonah shrugged. "But is doesn't last long before the effect dissipates."

"Exactly." He leaned forward. "If I can figure out a way to somehow capture it so it lasts forever, I'll have my answer."

"Enchantment?"

Everson gave his friend a big smile.

"But we don't know how to make that work. The only evidence that it's even possible are the ovens."

Another sigh slipped from Everson. "I know. We tried an augmentation using the exact same rune, but got different results."

"I don't get it either."

"I want to try again." Everson's eyes met Jonah's. "Tomorrow is seventh day, so we don't have class in the afternoon. I was hoping you would join me in the quarry again for another experiment."

Jonah smiled. "I feared you might never ask."

Snow crunched beneath Everson's boots. As always when snow was present, he moved slowly, carefully placing his canes with each stride. Even so, winter had caused many falls over the years. He hated the snow…and especially the ice.

Jonah stopped at the edge of the quarry and waited as Everson eased his way forward.

Concern was apparent on Jonah's face as he watched Everson struggle through drifts that came past his knees. "You can wait up here while I go trace the rune on the rock."

Everson drew even with his friend, breathing hard from the exertion. "That's fine by me. You remember the rune, right?"

"Chaos runes are the key to arcanist magic." He grinned. "I'll never forget one of them."

Spinning about, Jonah climbed down into the quarry, slipping once and almost tumbling before he caught himself. When he reached the blackened rock – its surface so dull and flat that it appeared to absorb all neighboring light – he dusted the cap of snow from the top. Kneeling before the rock, Jonah reached into his pocket and withdrew a chunk of glowstone.

As Everson watched, pale blue markings on the ebony surface began to take shape, ending in the form of the Heat rune – for that is what Everson named it after discovering it in the ovens and subsequently setting the boulder ablaze. Once finished, Jonah pocketed the glowstone and retraced his steps to the quarry's edge.

"How's it look?" he asked as he approached Everson.

With a nod, Everson said, "It appears correct to me."

Jonah turned toward the stone and closed his eyes. A thin layer of gray clouds passed before the sun, darkening the day and stealing away the warm touch that had been keeping Everson from growing cold. A chill shook his body and he grimaced. *I despise winter. Why couldn't the academy be somewhere beyond winter's grasp?*

Jonah's eyes flashed open, glowing an angry red. Everson turned toward the blackened rock as the rune upon it flared, pulsed, and faded. Anticipating the rock to burst into flames, Everson frowned at the result...or lack of it.

Crimson energy sizzled where snow contacted the rock, hissing and steaming until only bare earth remained within two feet of the stone.

"Why didn't it burn like before?" Jonah muttered.

Everson shook his head. "I don't know. Let's get closer and see if we can figure it out."

Moving carefully, Everson eased down the steps that led to the quarry floor. When he settled beside the rock, he glanced back and found Jonah following the path made by his dragging feet and the tracks left by his canes.

Everson looked down at the rock, appearing merely as plain black stone. He shifted his canes to one hand and leaned forward. Moving tentatively, he extended his hand toward the rock, holding his palm a foot away as he tried to determine if it were hot. When he sensed no heat, he drew closer and a red spark of energy arced from the rock, crackling as it singed his fingers. Vibrating pain, hot and angry, stung his entire hand.

"Ouch!" he squealed as he yanked his hand back and stuck his fingers in his mouth, trying to suck away the pain.

"What was that?" Jonah stared at the rock in surprise.

Everson pulled his fingers from his mouth and stared at them, finding no visible damage although a strange discomfort lingered in his throbbing fingertips...like a painful memory too fresh to move beyond. His gaze shifted toward the rock, his brow furrowing in thought.

"I don't know what it is exactly, but I have some ideas." He gave his friend a sidelong glance. "Can you try the augmentation again?"

Jonah shook his head. "No, not for a while at least. Each time I use Chaos, it leaves me feeling as if I just ran up a mountain. I need time to recover."

Everson gave the rock a final glance while thoughts spun in the back of his head. "Let's head back to the school for now. I need to think on this. We'll come back later today and try again."

—·◆·—

"What's the saucer for?"

Everson grinned at Jonah. "You'll see."

Jonah rolled his eyes as Everson slipped the towel-wrapped ceramic plate into his pack, nestled beside the small hand pick. He tied the pack closed and slipped it over his shoulder before giving a nod.

"Let's go."

The two boys passed through the Foundry and stepped out into the wintery weather.

Snow falling at an angle caused both boys to pause and raise the hood on their grey wool cloaks. Jonah then set off across the Foundry Yard, leading Everson toward the rock quarry. They moved slowly, paced by Everson's limited ability to move through the snow. As they neared the quarry, Everson looked back and found the Academy difficult to see through the falling flakes. He turned forward again and watched the ground closely to prevent from falling. Jonah stopped and Everson stopped beside him, realizing that they had reached the lip of the quarry.

"That's strange," Jonah's brow furrowed.

Everson followed Jonah's gaze to the black rock, its dull surface a harsh contrast to the white snow surrounding it – except for a ring of bare earth that encircled the rock.

"You're right. Snow is piling up elsewhere, but not around the rock." Jonah led Everson into the quarry again and stopped beside the rock, staring at it in amazement. As Everson neared his friend, he heard the sound of zapping, as if a swarm of bees were blinking in and out of existence. He then noticed the flakes striking the rock were disappearing in a tiny flash of red, accompanied by the zapping sound.

"It's been hours, yet it still retains magic," Jonah said.

"You're right. We were out here right after lunch and now it's nearly sunset."

Everson lowered his pack and handed it to Jonah.

"Take the pick out and hit the rock."

"What? Why me?"

Everson sighed. "Do you really need to ask? Don't worry. I think you'll be fine as long as you don't touch it."

Jonah frowned. "You *think*? That doesn't exactly instill confidence."

Despite his reluctance, the boy opened the pack and removed the pick. He held it up, glanced toward Everson, and smashed it into the rock. The clang it made as it bounced off the rock echoed throughout their little corner of the valley. With a grimace, Jonah raised the pick again and slammed it down, breaking off a chunk that struck the metal brace on Everson's leg before falling into the snow. Sizzling sounded from the spot where it fell as steam filled the air. Within moments, the area surrounding the shard was free of snow, leaving the chunk of black rock visible in a bowl with white sides and an earthen bottom.

"Now grab the plate and use the pick to slide the broken chunk onto it."

"Is that safe?"

"Again, I can't be sure, but I suspect that the plate will insulate you from the energy, as the pick handle does."

Jonah rolled his eyes and dug in the pack. "What does that even *mean?*"

"It means that you *should* be fine."

With the plate in one hand and the pick in another, Jonah crouched beside the rock, glanced up at Everson, and his lips formed a line of determination. The end of the pick dug beneath the shard of blackened stone and flipped it onto the saucer. Jonah then lifted the small plate up to show Everson their prize.

A grin spread across Everson's face as the pieces came together in his head.

"Great. Slip the pick back into the pack, and I'll carry it while you carry the plate and rock piece to the Foundry."

"What are you going to do with it?" Jonah said as he handed Everson the pack.

The grin on Everson's face widened. "I hope to change the world."

27

A MURDERER AMONG US

Quinn paused her story as she relived the frustration of being trapped in a situation beyond her control. That moment had felt even worse than the one she was in now – kidnapped, tied up, and under interrogation.

"I understood why Sergeant Jasmine suspected me of Darnya's murder." Quinn grimaced. "Everyone knew that she and I had a contentious relationship. Despite my insistence that I would never actually kill her, I had no way to prove my innocence." She closed her eyes and recalled the gloom that had fallen over her heart while locked in that dark cell. Squeezing her eyelids tight, she dammed back tears that longed to break free. "Hope is a funny thing. It was something I had always possessed, forever believing that things would turn out fine as long as I put in the effort. Jailed and presumed guilty, my thoughts drifted toward despair – turning as dark as my surroundings. For the first time in my life, hope was beyond my grasp, lost beyond the veil of melancholy draped over me. That lack of hope left a gaping hole inside me – a chasm I had no way to cross."

She swallowed and looked up toward the light. "The next day, I had my first encounter with an arcanist – an encounter that changed everything."

—+ φ +—

Noise within the Infirmary woke Quinn. She sat up, looked toward the small window in the door, and found the light of a glowlamp moving about the room outside her cell. Footsteps outside the door were accompanied by an odd rhythmic tapping and hushed conversation. Moments later, keys jingled, joined by the click of a lock disengaging. The door opened, and Russel appeared, holding a lamp in one hand and a cudgel in the other.

"Remain on your bed. If you get up, you'll regret it."

Quinn nodded in silent response.

The man moved aside and another man hobbled past him, leaning heavily on a cane and reminding her of Everson. A throb of loneliness wracked Quinn. She missed her brother fiercely and wished they were both back in Cinti Mor, safe and together…if Cinti Mor were even safe any longer.

"Good day." The man gave her a nod.

He was old – easily sixty summers, perhaps older than that. His long, graying black hair was tied back in a tail and he wore all black, from his clothes to his cloak. Despite his advancing age, the man had no rune upon his forehead.

"My name is Elias. I'm here to prove your innocence…or your guilt. Whichever holds true."

Another man entered the cell, a man Quinn knew but had never seen this close.

"Captain Goren," she said, not realizing the words had escaped her lips. She attempted to stand and salute, but stopped when Russel raised his cudgel.

"At ease, Cadet." Goren gave her a nod. "We are not here for proprieties. We seek the truth, so I ask that you drop all pretense and protocol. Just give us straight answers."

Quinn grimaced. "Everything I've been saying is the truth. I didn't kill anyone."

Goren nodded. "If that is true, then all will be well."

Elias dug in his pocket and fished out a chunk of glowstone. With obvious pain, accompanied by a low grunt, the man knelt with one knee on the tiled floor. He then began to draw a rune, one Quinn had never seen before. When he finished, a deeper grunt emitted as he stood. The man closed his eyes with Russel and Goren watching in anticipation.

Quinn flinched when the man's eyes flashed open, red energy crackling inside them. The symbol on the floor bloomed with a crimson glow, mixing with the glowlamp to bathe the room in purple light. With the glow in the man's eyes gone, the rune pulsed and began to fade as well. Elias sagged against his cane, clearly struggling to stand.

"I'll get you a chair." Russel blurted before running out the door. When he returned, he placed the chair behind Elias and stood back as the arcanist took a seat.

"Ahh. That's better." Elias swept sweat from his forehead and then ran his fingers down his face, as if wiping his weariness away. "Getting old is a difficult thing, my dear. And I happen to be far older than I look. In fact, it's safe to say that you'll never meet anyone who is quite so long in the tooth."

Quinn felt confused by his statement, thinking that she had met numerous others who were older, some beyond eighty summers. Despite the odd declaration, there was an earnestness about it that was undeniable, a rightness that she could not quite pinpoint.

"Now, let's get down to business." Elias glanced at Goren, who gave a small nod. "The rune you see here is…special. You see, the rune represents Truth. Any lies told inside this room will cause a high degree of discomfort. Truth, on the other hand, will feel pleasant and quite convincing."

Again, the benevolence in his words carried a conviction she could not deny.

"Just to ensure that you understand what I mean, I ask that you tell us a lie. It matters not how significant, so long as it is an untruth."

Quinn frowned at Goren, his expression stern as he stared, waiting.

"Most people don't know it, but I can spit gold."

As the words came out, the room dimmed as a wrongness enveloped her. The taste it left made her gag, the lie impossible to swallow. Revulsion reflected on the faces of Russel and Goren, but Elias remained stoic until a small grin appeared.

"Interesting choice of a lie," he noted. "I believe you now know what truth and falsehoods feel like in the presence of this rune. I suggest that your answers remain honest and as close to candor as possible. Ambiguity will do you no good, so say it plain and straight so we can get to the bottom of this quickly."

Quinn nodded in silence. Afraid to speak, should the revolting feeling return.

"State your name."

"My name is Qui…Jacquinn. Jacquinn Gulagas."

A feeling of goodness filled the room and Elias gave a slow nod. "Good. Where did you go yesterday, Jacquinn?"

"I was with my squad. We set off on a ranger outing, into the mountains to the east, but returned here by nightfall."

"Why did you return early?"

"I was assigned hunting duty with two fellow cadets. While we were searching for game, the two girls with me were shot and killed. Their deaths prompted Sergeant Jasmine to change our plans and return to the academy."

The rightness of her words rang within the room.

"Is it true that you considered one of those girls your enemy?"

Quinn hesitated a moment before responding. "Yes. Darnya. She and I have had issues since I arrived at the school."

"Did you hate her?"

"Yes."

"Did you kill her?"

"No."

Like a warm blanket, the truth of her words felt right, but the men frowned.

"If you didn't kill her, who did?"

Quinn shrugged. "I…I don't know."

"Was there another attacker? What happened?"

"Yes. It was someone else, hiding among a copse of pines. They shot Darnya, killed Simone, and then fired an arrow at me."

"You didn't see this attacker?"

Quinn shook her head. "No."

"How did you respond to the attack?"

"I…I tried to locate the archer and was prepared to fire an arrow back at them, but I panicked and ran." Shame twisted inside Quinn, despite the soothing stroke of the truth she told. She hated admitting that she had run in fear rather than facing her enemy.

Goren said, "That was the best response, given your situation. Your fellow soldiers were dead. If you had died as well, it would have amounted to nothing, and we would be faced with more questions than we have now." He glanced toward Elias. "We've determined that Quinn is not guilty. Thus, we must expand our search. Let's begin with the other girls and see where that leads. We must find the truth, for a murderer lurks among us."

When Quinn entered the mess hall, she found it filled with boys. The girls had already eaten and were likely in the Arena, where she was to join them after her meal.

The smell of roasted pork filled the air, making her mouth water and causing her stomach to growl at having missed breakfast. As she headed toward the kitchen, she noticed boys turning toward her, many pointing. The heat of their glares carried silent condemnation. She knew they suspected her guilty although she had been freed from her cell.

After passing through the kitchen without speaking a word to those who filled her plate, she emerged to find Iko approaching, relief apparent on his face.

"I'm so glad they set you free. How are you feeling?"

She slid past him and walked to a table with him following. "I'm fine. Just hungry."

He sat down across from her. "I told them you would never do what they claimed."

Quinn shrugged and took a bite of the steamed cabbage. As she chewed, she glanced about the room and found numerous cadets looking her direction.

"They're staring at me like I'm diseased or something."

Iko grabbed her hand and held it. "Don't worry about them. What happened is fresh news, something that buzzed through our barracks just this morning. They'll forget about it after a few days." He frowned. "How did you prove your innocence, anyway?"

Quinn swallowed and looked up at him, meeting his amber eyes. "They sent in an arcanist." Iko's eyes widened and he visibly recoiled. "The man used some sort of magic that ferrets out truth." She grimaced as she recalled the feeling. "There can be no doubt when it's used. It caused truth to feel like a loving embrace, so right and compelling that you know it for fact. Lies, on the other hand…" She shuddered.

Iko grimaced. "That sounds…awful."

She shrugged. "It wasn't so bad. I'm actually quite thankful. I knew how bad it appeared. Anyone would have thought me guilty, and I had no way to prove the truth until the man showed up."

He shook his head. "Not me. I knew you were innocent."

She smiled. "Thanks."

"Did they say what they plan to do? You know, about the murder of those two girls?"

Swallowing her bite of pork, she nodded. "It looks like they will continue to investigate, starting with the other girls. My guess is that they will use that same magic and sort through everyone until they find the guilty party. Regardless, they are convinced that the killer came from the school since academy arrows killed those girls."

Iko stared at Quinn for a long moment, not saying a word. She ate as the two sat in silence, filling her stomach as he contemplated something. Realizing that the conversation had only been about her, Quinn posed a question.

"How did your duel go?"

"What?" Iko blinked.

"Your duel yesterday….how did it go?"

"Oh, that." He frowned and shifted his eyes again.

"Well, aren't you going to tell me?"

"I…didn't duel." He shook his head. "Percy and I both woke up sick yesterday. I think it was from the cheese he and I ate last night…something he had been saving. "

"That's too bad. How did the others fare?"

"I don't know. We were so sick, neither of us was able to attend."

"Where did you go? I was in the infirmary, and I didn't see you there."

"No, we spent the day...in the jakes. I was so sick, I thought my insides would come out."

Quinn's brow arched. "I see."

"Yeah. I'd rather not talk about it anymore."

"Fine." She restrained her grin as she finished her meal.

Rather than reflecting mirth, Iko's face remained clouded.

28

BENEATH THE STARS

The next day, Sergeant Jasmine and her assistants entered the room after breakfast. As they had done every day since their arrival, Quinn and her fellow cadets fell into line before their bunks. With straight backs, stiff arms at their sides, and heels pressed together, they waited as she strolled past. The examination had become routine, now lacking the stress of when they first began.

Jasmine reached the end of the line, turned about and addressed them.

"Death is a risk every soldier must accept, be it their own or that of a comrade. However, soldiers taken from us in the form of murder rather than in the line of duty is something this academy is unwilling to accept. The idea of a murderer hiding among us disgusts me and is something I wish to prove or disprove as soon as possible."

She continued to stride between the two rows of cadets, speaking as she walked. "We have arranged for each of you to undergo a private interrogation. Once complete and proven innocent, you are free to train as you wish for the day, and we will reconvene tomorrow morning."

"Chuli, we begin with you." Jasmine gestured toward her assistants. "Vi and Lissa will escort you to your meeting with the arcanist. The rest of you are to remain here until called."

She turned toward Quinn. "Quinn, you are free to leave since you have already been proven innocent."

Quinn grabbed her training gear and left the barracks.

Chuli lunged at Quinn with a kick. Twisting, Quinn avoided the taller girl's foot and swung a backhand strike. Chuli blocked it with her shield, spun, and swiped at Quinn's legs. After leaping over the girl's sword, Quinn swung one sword at Chuli's head, the other toward her waist. Able to block only one sword, the lower strike grazed Chuli's stomach while the upper one bounced off her shield.

With a grin, Quinn stepped back, breathing heavily from the exertion.

Chuli shrugged. "You got me. If it were a real sword, I'd be scrambling to keep my insides from spilling out right now."

"You certainly don't want that," Quinn agreed. "We have no healer today, so perhaps we should stop before one of us injures the other."

Quinn pulled her helmet off and shook her head vigorously, freeing the damp hair that clung to her head.

"Agreed." Chuli removed her helmet and wiped her brow.

"I wonder if they found the killer today."

"If it were one of us, I'm sure they did. The magic they used will ferret out the truth one way or another."

Quinn waved toward the door. "Come on, let's get cleaned up and grab some dinner."

They left the training room and traversed the hallway to the girls' baths. After soaking for twenty minutes, they dressed and exited the changing room, where they found Iko waiting.

He stepped forward, glanced at Chuli, and addressed Quinn. "I'd like you to join me for dinner."

Quinn's gaze settled on the cloth-covered object in his arms.

"What's in the basket?"

Iko gave a hopeful smile. "Dinner."

"Why did you bring it here?"

He shrugged. "I thought we might have a picnic."

"There's a foot of snow outside. You want to have a picnic in that?"

"I have a plan."

She stared at him for a moment and then chuckled. "Fine." She turned to Chuli, handing over her practice swords and sparring gear. "I'll see you in the barracks later tonight."

Chuli nodded. "Be well. You two enjoy yourselves."

Iko watched Chuli as she walked away. Only after the girl turned the corner and was out of sight, did he turn back toward Quinn.

"Take my arm."

Quinn glanced toward his elbow, shrugged, and grabbed ahold, allowing him to lead her down the corridor. They turned before the mess hall and took the south corridor to the academy stables. Curiosity gripped Quinn as he led her through the door.

The stable was large, containing enough individual pens to house forty horses. Not every pen was full, but it was full enough.

Thurmond – the stable hand who cared for the horses – was squatting beside a carriage, inspecting the underside. When he noticed them enter, he stood and wiped his hands on his grey cloak as he approached the couple.

The man flashed a toothy grin. "Good evening, Jacquinn." He bowed and turned to Iko. "Are you two ready?"

Quinn frowned. "Ready for what?"

"I've arranged for a carriage ride." Iko turned toward the stable hand. "Thurmond has agreed to take us for an evening tour of the valley while we eat."

Thurmond strolled toward the carriage and opened the door, holding it as he waited for the couple to climb inside. Iko slid the basket of food in and held his hand out to help Quinn. She hesitated for a moment, reluctant to accept assistance until she realized that his intent was not to slight her.

Thick blankets waited for them on the bench inside. Quinn sat on a blanket and Iko sat beside her before pulling another blanket over their laps. She heard the stable door slide open and the carriage lurched into motion as Thurmond led the horses outside. Once the stable door was closed, Thurmond climbed upon the carriage – rocking it slightly as he did so – and snapped the reins. The carriage began its trek down the starlit road.

Iko pulled the blanket back from the basket and handed Quinn a glass. She was surprised when he removed a cork from a bottle and poured wine into her cup.

"Wine?" she asked. "I don't drink wine...at least, I never have before."

He smiled, his white teeth noticeable in the dimly lit cabin. "Well, now is the time. I made sure to get a fine wine, so I doubt you'll be disappointed." He poured himself a glass and held it toward her. "To us, may we live well and prosper."

Quinn tapped her cup against his with a nod and then took a sip. The wine was cool, yet it warmed her throat when she swallowed. The flavor was strong, a hint of sweet followed by a dash of bitterness. She took another sip and gave him a smile. The smile on his face stretched into a grin of delight.

"I knew you would like it."

The carriage bounced as it went over a bump in the road, and Quinn almost spilled on herself. As a result, she held her glass level for future occurrences.

Iko dug into the basket and handed her a plate filled with slices of dried sausage and cuts of cheese. He then drew out of loaf of bread and tore off a piece before handing it to her. The bread was still warm, and it smelled wonderful.

They ate in silence for a bit, enjoying the meal and the passing scenery through the open curtains. Dark trees – both pine and bare leaf trees – lined the road. Countless stars above shined down, lighting the fields of snow beyond the tree line. Quinn gasped when a star shot across the sky with a trailing streak of light. The moment felt perfect.

Iko cleared his throat, breaking the silence. "Tell me something of yourself, perhaps of your life growing up in Cinti Mor."

Quinn turned toward him and considered where to begin. "My father was a blacksmith, my mother a cook. With both of them away, my brother and I were left to our own devices much of the time. His legs... never functioned properly, so he spent his early years indoors, and I often stayed with him. Once he got his braces and canes, he was able to join me and the other children, although there were few of them since the city had not fully repopulated. Cinti Mor was destroyed during the war, and construction was a never-ending presence – whether it was a build-ing, a city wall, the streets, or the docks.

"Everson and I would often visit my father's smithy, where we learned the basics of shaping metal. I showed some skill, but he displayed ingenuity, the kind that was rare – the kind that awed adults even when he was too young to go to school. When we came of age, we began our training at the local temple. I got an education and eventually found my way here, to train as a soldier. My brother, on the other hand, was forever smarter than any of my schoolmates – smarter than anyone I have ever met. He was obviously bound for Fallbrandt to become an engineer. My path was one that required extra effort.

"Regardless of the hardships, it was a good place to live. My home was always filled with love. I had friends, a family, and found ways to create enough mischief to make memories to smile upon."

Iko took her hand in his and gave it a small squeeze. His palm warmed her fingers, which had grown cold.

"Your childhood sounds wonderful. It seems like you love your family, too."

Quinn gave a sad smile. "Yes. I miss them. They are close, yet I see them rarely."

Iko sighed. "My family is not so close."

"I'm sorry. I should not only be thinking of myself." She squeezed his hand, tugging it slightly. "It's your turn. Tell me of your life before you came here."

The look in his eyes grew distant, and he turned to stare out the window. After a minute of silence, he turned toward her.

"I grew up not far from Hipoint. My childhood…was particularly difficult. My mother raised me alone after my father died during my fourth summer."

"I'm sorry. That must have been horrible."

"The years have clouded my memory of him. I now barely remember his face."

Quinn leaned close and kissed his cheek. He gave her a sad smile.

"I was forced to work, even at a young age. While most kids spent their time playing games, I would labor each day until I dropped from exhaustion. This went on until my thirteenth summer when we…moved.

My mother and I wound up in Yarth, where she sent me to train at the local temple. Like you, I found that an education and the toughness I had built up as a means to a better life."

"Does your rune count as nothing?"

He shook his head. "No. Not any longer. There was a time - when the Ministry ruled – when I would have been revered. My life would have been easy, my path clear. However, such is not the case today. Perhaps things will change, and it will become so in the future."

Quinn shook her head. "I don't know. Under the old way, people had no choice as to what they might do with their lives. Rather than following their passion, they were assigned a role – one they might despise. It may be wonderful for people like you, but it would be horrible for others."

He glared at her with his lips pressed together. After a moment, he nodded. "You are probably right." His eyes softened as he stared at her. "I find you very insightful, Quinn. You're smart, brave, kind, and loyal. To find a strong woman who retains such beauty is a remarkable thing. If I could dictate my future, you would surely be in it."

Quinn found herself at a loss as she considered how to respond. When he leaned close, the urging of her body made her decision for her. His lips met hers, warming them as her eyes drifted closed. Her pulse thumped and her head swam in the rush of the kiss. When their lips parted, she opened her eyes and stared into his. She found herself wishing for their carriage ride to never end…and then the horses slowed to a stop. When Quinn looked outside, she realized they were back in the stable yard, with Thurmond sliding the stable door open. Disappointment sank in as he walked the horses inside.

When Thurmond opened the door, Quinn and Iko exited, thanking the man for his kindness. Iko then took her hand, led her inside, and walked her through the corridors that led to the barracks.

Later that night, Quinn lay in bed, the room dark as she relived the evening in her head. Being with Iko made her feel special – made her feel happy to be herself and nothing more. She longed to see him again.

29

WICK AND FLAME

With breakfast finished, Quinn and the other girls headed toward the indoor training rooms. Chuli walked beside her, quiet and focused. Quinn remained quiet as well, but nowhere near focused.

As it had numerous times during breakfast, the previous evening with Iko ran through her mind. She held it fast to her heart, longing to relive the evening again and again. Lost in her reverie, she almost didn't hear the hushed whisper.

"Quinn."

She turned toward the doorway she had just passed and noticed it open a crack.

"Iko?"

The door opened a bit wider to reveal his face. "Yes. It's me. I need to speak with you."

Quinn turned toward Chuli. "Go on without me. If Jasmine asks, tell her that I forgot something and had to run back to the barracks."

The excuse would buy some time, but Quinn knew she would pay for being late. Jasmine wouldn't allow it to go unpunished.

She stepped into the room and realized that it was an office, empty but for Iko and herself.

"I'm glad I caught you."

Quinn frowned. "Why?"

He edged closer and grabbed her hand, holding it to his muscular chest. "I wanted to see you before I leave."

She stared into his eyes. "Leave?"

"Yes…it's my mother. I received word that she is ill." Pain reflected in his eyes. "I must go see her. They say she may die. I would never forgive myself if she…passed while I made no attempt to see her first."

Quinn glanced toward the window to gather herself. White frost on the limbs of the oak tree outside glistened in the morning sunlight. The tree's grey bark stood out against the white snow surrounding it.

She looked at him and thought of their evening carriage ride. "Traveling back to Yarth will be difficult with winter upon us."

He replied, "I know. I have enough coin to purchase a ride to Wayport. There, I will find passage on a ship heading for Yarth."

Quinn swallowed her own concerns and thought of Iko. "I pray that Issal will give your mother the strength to recover."

A sad smile spread across his face. "It is kind of you to say so. I pray it happens as well, and soon." Stepping closer, he stood just a breath away, holding her captive with his amber eyes. "I will miss you dearly while I'm away."

He leaned close, him a flame, her a wick, unable to resist. Quinn's eyes drifted shut as their lips met. The room faded in the distance as she gave herself to the moment, to the racing of her heart. When he drew back, she wrapped her arms about him and gave him a fierce hug, which he returned. She closed her eyes and willed them to remain dry. Opening them, she released her arms, him doing likewise.

"Be well, Iko." Turning about, she moved to the door, staring at it as she spoke. She did not trust her reaction should she look at him again. "I hope all is well and that you will return soon."

When the door closed, Quinn paused with her back to it. A deep breath followed, one she almost choked on as she exhaled. Remembering that she was late to calisthenics, she ran down the corridor.

—⏀—

Quinn slowed as she neared the door, her breath coming in puffs of steam in the cold air. When she reached for the doorknob, her hands resisted her will. Unprotected in the frigid weather, her fingers had grown numb. After some fumbling, she was able to grip the knob with the heels of her palms, turn it, and step inside.

She stamped her feet on the thick rug. Clumps of snow fell from her boots while a shower of smaller flakes rained from the legs of her breeches. With her hands held to her mouth, she blew warm air to thaw them. As they warmed, they began to sting as if she were holding them in water that was a bit too hot.

A rumble in her stomach reminded her that she needed food. After wiping her boots on the rug, she headed down the corridor.

When she arrived at the mess hall, she found her fellow cadets eating, some already finished. A trip to the kitchen yielded her a plate of steamed vegetables and pasta covered in melted cheese. As she passed occupied tables, she caught a sense of anxiety in the conversation, the way they leaned toward one another, the look in their eyes.

Chuli smiled as Quinn neared the otherwise empty table. "You did not freeze to death, I see."

Quinn snorted. "Not quite, but it was cold enough. I'm glad it was only one lap."

"Running in snow is not so easy."

A chuckle escaped as Quinn sat. "So, I noticed."

Chuli took a bite of her food. Quinn glanced toward the other tables and noticed something odd as she watched the other girls.

"What's going on? Everyone seems…like they've caught wind of some great rumor."

Swallowing, Chuli nodded. "Yes. We heard that the search for the murderer resumed today."

Quinn frowned. "But they already interviewed all of the girls. We passed the test."

"They are apparently now interrogating the boys."

"Interesting." Quinn stirred her food, the steam from it teasing her tongue into watering.

Chuli leaned closer. "The boys were here that day. The murder happened fifteen miles from here, and on the other side of a mountain saddle." She shook her head. "I don't know how they think anyone could have snuck away long enough to run that distance, kill Darnya and Simone, and return here without notice."

Quinn took a bite of food, chewing as she considered Chuli's words.

Chuli's voice interrupted her thoughts. "Are we to train tonight?"

Blinking, Quinn drew herself back to the conversation. "No. Trijia agreed to another game of Ratio Bellicus. I am to go there directly after dinner."

"Have you won a match against her, yet?" Chuli scooped the last of the food from her plate.

Quinn grimaced as she thought about Trijia. "That woman is relentless."

A grin appeared on Chuli's face. "Sounds like someone I know."

"Fair enough," Quinn sighed. "Every time I believe I have a winning strategy, she counters it with tactics I have never seen before."

"I know you. Defeat is not something you willingly accept. The frustration must be gnawing at you." The look in Chuli's eyes was one of knowing.

Quinn stared back for a moment before responding with a chuckle. "You know me too well." She shook her head. "The woman is good, but tough. When I told her I wished to become an expert, she took it to heart and continually tells me that an opponent on the battlefield will display little mercy. She shows that same mindset on the Bellicus board."

Finished with her meal, Chuli stood. "Well, I wish you luck."

As Chuli walked away, Quinn stirred her food as thoughts tumbled in her head. Life at the school would be different without Iko. *With him away, I will focus on my training. I will get better faster. And when I'm the best, I will train even harder.*

30

AUGMENTATION

Everson blinked at the light in his face. "With Winter's grasp firmly taken hold of the valley, I remained indoors for the next ten weeks. My...disability makes walking through snow overly difficult – sometimes impossible."

Licking his lips to wet them, he found his tongue dry. "May I have a drink of water? I'm quite thirsty."

He heard shuffling behind him. A moment later, a hand appeared before his face, holding a cup of water. When they pressed it against his mouth and tipped it up, he drank eagerly while water dripped from his chin, onto his bare thighs. With the cup empty, the hand withdrew. Everson tried to wipe his mouth on his shoulder, but found it ineffective.

Feeling a bit refreshed, he continued his tale.

"I had a theory about the power contained within the blackened rock, a theory that I needed time to prove. Accordingly, I spent weeks working alone, crafting a new mechanism for the clock, one that would replace the coil. Inside that mechanism, I placed the chunk of Chaos-charged stone."

He found himself smiling at the memory, a moment he would remember forever.

"Not only did it work, it was more effective than I had anticipated. The clock now ran on its own, with no need to wind it. For days, I tracked the clock's accuracy, making timing adjustments until I had it just right. A week later, the time remained exact.

"However, I remained reluctant to reveal my discovery of this new power source." Everson sighed and stared at the floor in shame. "You see, it presented me with a new opportunity – an opportunity to change my life. While I knew my idea might help others, my true intent was to help myself."

"...know the basics of fluid dynamics. With it, we have been able to create wonderful inventions ranging from simple pumps that move water to complex pistons that multiply the force input of a press."

Master Nindlerod placed the hydraulic piston on his desk and turned toward the class.

"Tomorrow, we will meet in The Foundry to dissect a number of real-world applications in fluid dynamics. I expect it to be another thrilling day that spurs new ideas." He grinned. "These ideas could become the fuel for another great invention – one that might gain you recognition and a bit of gold." He cackled in laughter. "You see, we have our second Inventor's Challenge coming in ten weeks, just prior to the end of winter session. For this challenge, you are allowed to include a single magical augmentation."

Everson's brows raised at the statement. The students surrounding him chatted with each other as they discussed possibilities. Leveraging what they had learned in Chaos Theory offered new possibilities to what they might create.

Nindlerod's grin remained. "I knew you would be excited about this one." He rubbed his gnarled hands together. "I cannot wait to see your ideas come to fruition."

The bell rang and students began heading for the door. As Everson stood, Donnell tapped his shoulder.

"Can we work together again? We made a good team, right?"

Everson glanced toward Ivy, whose face reflected hope.

"Me too?" she asked.

Recalling their previous creation darkened Everson's thoughts. "You two realize that the last invention didn't go so well, right?"

Donnell shrugged. "It was a great idea. The judges even said so. If we had a bit more time to perfect it, we would have won."

Everson thought of the timekeeper and the modifications he had made to it since the competition. He considered telling them that it now worked flawlessly but decided to hold back for fear of having to reveal his secret.

A soft hand touched his arm. "I...like working with you, Everson," Ivy said in her shy voice, her eyes downcast.

After a moment, he nodded. "If you two are set on it, we can work together."

"Wonderful!" Donnell patted Everson's shoulder. "Now, what are we going to build?" When Everson didn't respond, Donnell's eyes narrowed. "You have a plan, right?"

"Yes. I have a plan," Everson said. "If it works, this will be unlike anything ever created."

Everson found Jonah staring with the gleam of longing in his eyes. With a chuckle, Everson turned toward the front of the class, toward the target of his roommate's attention.

Leaning over her desk as she recorded a note, Master Alridge stood and faced the class. Her friendly smile lit the room.

"We are now past the mid-point of the school year. Thus far, you have learned numerous Chaos runes and their applications." With her hands clasped before her, she strode down the center of the classroom. "You understand how Chaos can turn a simple rock into a bright light, how it can increase or decrease the gravitational effect on an object, how it can turn something solid into something brittle, and how a Chaos augmentation can bring an inanimate object to life. Today, we begin to delve into the more dangerous runes."

Reaching the back of the classroom, she spun about and resumed her lecture. "The Chaos rune for Power is among the most useful, yet it can be dangerous. With this rune, the kinetic energy of whatever receives the augmentation becomes many times more powerful than its original state. Apply a Power rune to a catapult and it may reach a target miles away rather than the typical range of a thousand feet or less.

"The danger comes in abuse. You see, Power is among the runes we can use on a human being. I can tell you from experience that a super-charged warrior is a frightening thing, able to perform feats that might seem unimaginable. A well-trained fighter with such an augmentation can become a killing machine, able to face and defeat dozens of trained soldiers."

Images of magic-powered warriors danced in Everson's head. The concept brought a sense of awe – tempered by an overarching fear. He raised his hand.

"Yes, Everson?" Alridge nodded toward him.

"This ability to augment the power of a soldier…couldn't that be used against us by an enemy as well?"

The Arcane Arts instructor's face turned grim. "Yes, that is truly a risk, Everson. Chaos can become a weapon, or, in this case, turn people into weapons of mass destruction."

She paced down the aisle again, her hips swaying as she walked. "Hundreds of years ago, the Ministry decided that the threat of Chaos was worse than the positives. Their response was to take drastic steps to eradicate it." A few students in the room nodded at the idea. "All knowledge of its use was destroyed," she paused, her voice becoming somber, "as were the people who could wield it."

Everson gasped at the thought. Images of the systematic murder of anyone who possessed the ability flashed in his mind. "These people were murdered because of something inside them, something they did not choose?" he blurted. "Without having acted with ill intent, they were killed for something they *might* do?"

Sadness reflected upon her face. "Again, you see to the heart of the issue, Everson. Regardless of what justification they proclaimed, what the Ministry did was an act of genocide…an act far worse than what any arcanist has ever committed."

She strolled to the fore of the classroom and began to relay applications for the Power rune. Everson's thoughts drifted as he imagined ways he could use this new augmentation to enhance various inventions. It was not long before he found himself eager to test the results.

—⊕—

Everson leaned close to Donnell. "Cut it here and here, just like the drawing. Keep the edges clean and don't damage them."

"I don't understand why you need cork." Donnell complained. "What are these disks for anyway?"

With a shake of his head, Everson replied, "I told you already. You can help me build this, but I'll not reveal what we are creating until I'm ready."

"We've been at this for weeks, crafting parts for who-knows-what." Donnell glanced across his bench, meeting Ivy's gaze. "Do you think this is fair?"

She shrugged and turned toward Everson. "While I'm curious, when we agreed to help Everson, it was under the condition that he could keep the purpose a secret for a while." She lowered the magnifying lenses over her eyes and turned her attention toward the thin strip of metal she was working. "I suggest you accept it and stop torturing yourself, Donnell."

A frown crossed Donnell's face, and he threw a disgusted glance toward Everson, who laughed as he rose to his feet and shuffled away.

After crossing the room, he approached the metal band he had formed in the forge, inspecting the steel now that it had cooled. As his father had taught him, the iron ingot had been heated with coal and beaten, stretched, and shaped in controlled heat. Now cooled, the thinned metal remained strong, yet flexible.

He put it aside and turned toward the utility door. A longing drew his attention toward it. He stood and shuffled to the door. When he pulled it open, he found himself squinting at the bright snow-covered Foundry Yard. The air was cold, but not bitter cold. Now on the backside of winter, a few warm days would melt the remaining snow. Those days couldn't come soon enough, for something out there called to him. It waited in the quarry, the key to his new creation.

With a sigh, he closed the door and shuffled back to his workbench, where he pulled out the drawing for the next component he was to craft.

31

ESTEEMED GUESTS

"...**A**nd while the positive end of a magnetic field attracts a negative field, it repels another positive field. Behold."

Master Nindlerod moved one magnet close to the other. The second magnet lurched away from the first, sliding across the benchtop each time the two drew close to one another. Nindlerod cackled in laughter as the last lurch launched the second magnet off the benchtop.

Everson craned his neck and watched in interest. He immediately began imagining practical applications for magnetics and found himself wondering if a magnetic field could be charged to a high degree.

The bell rang, interrupting the thought.

"Before you leave, remember that the winter Inventor's Challenge is two weeks away. Finish your projects and prepare your demonstrations." Nindlerod rubbed his palms together in anticipation. "I'm looking forward to the new creations you plan to present."

Students filtered out the door with Everson trailing behind. When he stepped into the hallway, he found Donnell waiting for him.

"You heard Nindlerod," Donnell said. "We only have two weeks left. Are we going to get it done in time?"

Everson considered the work remaining as he shuffled down the corridor. "We are nearly done crafting the components. In two days, assembly should begin." Images of the components coming together flashed in his head, with the most critical ingredient missing. "However, there is one key item that I must procure."

Donnell frowned. "Procure? What are you talking about?"

Everson shared a smirk. "I'm talking about the element that brings our creation to life."

A sigh came from his friend as they turned the corner. "Why must you forever be cryptic? Besides, you have yet to tell us what we are building."

"I know, I know. When we begin assembling it, I'll explain the whole thing."

As they drew near the main hall, Everson discovered a crowd gathering. Judging by the students' behavior, something was happening – something exciting. When he neared the rear of the crowd, he found Ivy and nudged her to get her attention.

"What's happening?"

She turned toward him, her eyes alight with excitement. "It's a king."

"What?" Donnell asked.

"A king is here, right up ahead."

"Which king?"

"King Brock of Kantaria."

Donnell's eyes widened and he began pushing his way through the crowd. Eager to get a glimpse of royalty, Everson trailed in the larger boy's wake, careful to stay close to Donnell before the gap he created closed behind him. Some students became upset at the pushing, but they were soon left behind. When Donnell reached the front, Everson slid in beside him.

A line of guards – dressed in black armor marked by a red starburst insignia – stood before the crowd, keeping the students in check. Beyond the guards, five men were in discussion. A grim-faced guard stood among them, along with Headmaster Ackerson, and Master Hedgewick. One of the last two men leaned hard against a cane, his thickly muscled arm trembling violently. With a bald head, graying goatee, and a white scar across one temple, the man appeared to be a former soldier, now crippled by something that affected his leg. The fifth man, Everson decided, must be the king.

He stood shorter than the other men, even slightly shorter than Master Hedgewick. In his thirties, the man possessed an athletic build, brown hair, and intense green eyes. An Order rune marked the man's forehead, eclipsed by the Chaos rune of a red starburst – a rune Everson had never seen on a forehead. While the man's form-fitting black leather coat appeared dashing, he did not appear very king-like.

When the discussion finished, the man shook Ackerson's hand and then headed toward the crowd where Everson stood watching. Two of the guards who held the crowd in place stepped forward and began using their arms to create a gap – a gap that placed Donnell to one side, Everson on the other. More guards passed by, leading the way while the others walked toward Everson. As the king passed, his eyes locked with Everson's for a moment, accompanied by a smile and a nod. Star struck, Everson found himself unable to respond. Then, the man was gone, sliding through the crowd as the limping soldier and grim-faced guard followed behind.

Despite the sense of awe that lingered, Everson immediately liked the man. That brief moment of connection left him feeling like Brock was a man of compassion, not just another faceless ruler who ignored those beneath them.

Everson's gaze shifted toward Donnell and found his friend staring toward the king's back, his eyes narrowed and lips pressed together so hard, they had turned pale.

Everson and Jonah entered the dining hall the next morning and found the room buzzing with excitement. In addition to King Brock, the king of Torinland, the queen of Ri Starr, and the leader of the Tantarri had arrived. Anxiety and concern tainted conversations filled with conjecture. Everyone wondered what could possibly draw half the rulers of Issalia to the school.

When Everson discovered that Duchess Mae was among the visitors, he recalled Quinn's tale of meeting the woman. The thought made him wonder if the subject might be related to Vinacci's attack of Cinti Mor.

Just before breakfast was to end, Headmaster Ackerson entered the room with a female student at his side. The girl rang the bell with vigor, the clanging chime echoing noisily and ending all conversation. With the students quiet and all eyes on Ackerson, the man addressed the room.

"As you have no doubt discovered, we have some highly esteemed guests visiting us. Meetings will take place for the next few days, meetings that will require my attendance as well as a number of academy instructors." His gaze swept across the room. "As a result, all classes are cancelled until further notice."

The buzz of voices rose at this news. Ackerson nodded to the student with the bell, and she rang it again until all attention had been restored.

"Please be respectful of the meetings and do not cause any trouble. I suspect you recognize the value of free time, and I suggest you make the most of it."

Turning about, Ackerson swept out the door with his assistant trailing behind.

"No class today." Jonah gave Everson a sidelong glance. "What should we do?"

Everson grinned. "I have a plan. Let's go back to our room to grab our cloaks and I'll tell you about it."

They left the dining hall and headed down the long corridor that led to their room. Once there, both boys donned their grey wool cloaks and then Everson pulled a pack from the wardrobe. The contents inside the pack clinked, drawing Jonah's attention.

"What's in the pack?"

"Caffe mugs," Everson responded.

"Why?"

"We need to collect something with them," Everson said with a shrug.

Jonah's eyes narrowed in thought. "You're after more chunks of that black rock."

"Good guess."

With an eye-roll, Jonah opened the door. "Fine. Let's go."

They traveled down the long corridor and found a cluster of people before them as they passed the Infirmary. Guards in the black and red of Kantaria, joined by guards dressed in the dark green of Torinland, formed a half-circle around a pair of doors that led to the Hall of Truth.

The space between the guards and the wall opposite from the doors remained empty, with a crowd to either side. Everson shuffled into the nearest crowd and found himself beside Donnell, who stared in silent observation.

Master Alridge emerged from the crowd beyond the guards, and gave a small smile as she walked past them. Everson's gaze shifted to the man with her – the mysterious man in black. As he hobbled past, leaning on his cane, the man gave a small nod toward Jonah, a nod that Everson thought he saw Jonah return.

"Do you know him?" he asked with a frown.

Jonah turned toward Everson and blinked. "What? No. How would I know him?"

When Everson turned toward the doors, the man passed through them. A brief glimpse of the room beyond revealed a table at the far end, resting upon a dais. At the table, King Brock sat in discussion with Master Hedgewick. The door closed and Everson found his curiosity piqued, wishing he could get closer to discover what was to occur within the room. Clearly, the guards were stationed to prevent that from happening.

"Come on." Jonah crossed the open space before the guards and slid through the crowd.

As Everson followed his friend, he wondered what had happened to draw the rulers of Issalia together...and wondered if King Ulric was among them.

When they reached the Foundry, Everson was surprised to find it quiet and empty of students. With the Inventor's Challenge approaching, he was sure that there was work yet to finish for every team. *The distraction of the visiting rulers must have drawn everyone's attention.*

Jonah opened the utility door and led Everson outside. The sky above was gray, threatening to rain as it had every day for the past week. The result of days of rain was immediately apparent.

With the snow gone, the gravel of the Foundry Yard was visible everywhere but for a few rogue snow piles along the north side of the building. Puddles, wide and shallow, small yet deep, dotted the yard. Once they passed the outbuilding, the gravel gave way to the soggy turf of snow-trampled grass. The effect caused Everson's canes to sink inches into the ground and frequently become stuck. As a result, Jonah reached the quarry far before he did.

Everson stopped at the quarry edge and found Jonah below, squatting beside the rock. When Jonah reached toward the boulder, Everson held his breath, anticipating…hoping. A crackle of red energy arced toward Jonah's finger and he yelped, jumping backward and nearly falling when his boot slipped in the mud.

A grin crossed Everson's face, and he shuffled down the rocky incline. "I'm surprised that you subjected yourself to that."

Jonah pulled his finger from his mouth and looked at it. "I thought that maybe…maybe the energy had dissipated." He shook his head as he stared at the rock. "I can't believe it lasted all winter."

Everson settled beside Jonah and slid his pack off his shoulder. "I'm glad it did. Otherwise, my idea wouldn't work."

Jonah gave him a half smile. "Are you going to tell me what you're up to?"

A chuckle was Everson's response. He pulled the pick from his bag and handed it to Jonah. "Just break off a few more pieces for me."

Jonah moved closer to the rock and swung the pick. After a dozen strikes, a section of the rock shattered, spilling chunks into the mud. When Jonah turned toward Everson, he found a mug waiting.

"Use the pick to push a chunk into each mug."

Jonah snorted in response, but did as requested. As he filled each mug with sections of the black rock, Jonah handed them to Everson, who carefully slid them into his pack. Once finished, Everson tied the pack closed and shouldered it, noticing how the weight had increased. Both boys then climbed out of the quarry and retraced their steps back to the academy.

As they neared the school, Everson spotted someone climbing up a tall ladder that leaned against a wall of the Foundry.

"Isn't that Donnell?" Everson asked.

Jonah's gaze shifted toward where Everson pointed his cane. "Yes. I think you're right." He watched for a moment and then turned toward Everson. "You go back inside. I'll find you later."

When he angled toward the rear of the Foundry, Everson called after him. "Where are you going?"

"I want to see what he's doing."

Everson frowned at the thought. His braces made him capable, but climbing a ladder was beyond that capability. Besides, the Foundry roof was three stories up. He shuddered at the thought of falling such a distance.

Rather than wait, he headed back to the Foundry to begin the final assembly of his greatest invention.

32

TRUTH UNTOLD

Hours passed with Everson working alone. Periodically, he would glance toward the utility door and wonder about Jonah.

"What's taking him so long?" he complained.

His growling stomach informed him that mid-day was approaching. He finished attaching the actuator, securing it tightly with a bolt, and decided it was a good time for a break. He opened the storage crate his team had been assigned and placed the partial assembly inside, joining the pack he had taken to the quarry that morning. After closing the lid, he secured the lock, pocketed the key, and grabbed his canes.

As he made the journey across the Foundry and into the hallway, Everson considered the work that remained. *The two assemblies should be complete within a week. Then, it's time to test.* Raw excitement filled him, causing his pulse to race and stomach to flip.

A commotion in the main hall pulled him from his reverie. His brow furrowed as he tried to grasp what was happening. A crowd had formed a circle near the doors, many with their heads downcast, some resting upon a neighbor's shoulder. He shuffled between two clusters of students, navigating toward the middle. Girls were crying; the boys' expressions were somber. When he emerged from the crowd, Everson saw a sight he would remember forever.

Lying on the floor was a body, for the twisted pose and angle of his neck made it clear that the boy was dead. His eyes stared toward nothing, empty and lifeless. Blood coated the side of his face, capped by a nasty gash across his brow. Rena knelt to one side of the boy, Torney on the other – both with eyes downcast.

"What happened?" Everson blurted.

Torney looked up and shook his head. "He's dead, Ev. There's nothing we can do."

Everson stared down at his friend's lifeless gaze and felt an emptiness inside. Loss. Like a hollowness that he didn't know how to fill.

"I don't understand. I just saw him a short time ago. What happened?"

Rena wiped the tear from her eye. "Some students found him beside the main hall. We think he fell off the building."

Everson swallowed when he recalled seeing Donnell climb the ladder and Jonah following. He tried to speak, but the words got caught in his throat. After a swallow from his dry mouth, he cleared his throat and tried again.

"What about Jonah?"

Torney frowned at Rena, who shrugged. "Jonah? We haven't seen him. Was he friends with Donnell as well?"

An ugly thought stirred inside Everson, a thought too horrible to voice. He stared down at Donnell's twisted body in fear – fear that Jonah had something to do with Donnell's death.

With his hunger forgotten, Everson headed back to his room. Lost in a haze of loss and disbelief, he found himself at his door without noticing the journey. He unlocked the door and entered. There was no trace of Jonah, nothing to show that he had been in the room since they had left early that morning.

He settled on his bed and relived the morning outing with Jonah, trying to remember anything that seemed odd. Up to the point where they had spied Donnell on the ladder, he couldn't think of anything noteworthy. Everson recalled Jonah's demeanor changing dramatically in that moment, going from glib to focused resolve.

A soft knock sounded from the door. Not wishing to get up, Everson called out.

"Come in."

The door opened and Ivy peeked in. Her face was blotchy, her eyes puffy. She slid inside and closed the door behind her.

"You heard about Donnell?" she asked in her soft voice.

Everson nodded. "Yes. I...saw him."

Kneading her hands, she looked away. A tear streaked down her cheek.

"I don't understand." She sobbed. "Why was he on the roof? How could he fall?"

Everson bit his lip as he considered what to tell her. He glanced toward Jonah's bed, and his insides twisted at the thought of his room-mate – his friend – as a murderer.

"I...don't know." He shook his head, unwilling to say the words that bounced in his head.

Ivy removed her spectacles and rubbed her eyes dry. She appeared a mess.

"Come here. Sit. Please." He patted the bed.

With a nod, she sat beside him. Unsure of what else to do, he tentatively put his arm about her shoulder. She leaned into him, her head bowed as she sobbed.

The door opened, startling Everson awake. When he moved, Ivy lifted her head from his chest and straightened her glasses. Jonah stepped in and paused, appearing surprised when he found Ivy in the room. A glance toward the window informed Everson that it was late afternoon and that he had fallen asleep for more than an hour, perhaps two.

"I'm sorry," Jonah said. "I hope I wasn't interrupting."

Ivy shook her head and rose to her feet. "No. It's fine, Jonah. I must be going anyway." She moved toward the open door and spoke over her shoulder. "Thank you, Everson. I'll see you tomorrow."

As the door closed, Jonah sat on his bed and let out a sigh. Everson stared at his friend, trying to decide where to begin. Before he knew it, the words blurted out.

"Donnell's dead. Did you have something to do with that?"

Jonah's lips pressed together in a thin line as he stared at Everson. After a moment, his eyes shifted away. "It's not what you think."

"What is it, then? What happened?"

"I…can't tell you."

Everson blinked, his jaw hanging open. Disbelief became anger – anger that flared within him. "He's dead, Jonah. Dead! Tell me it was an accident. Please tell me that you didn't mean to kill him."

"It *was* an accident. Killing him wasn't my intent. It just…happened."

"You need to tell Headmaster Ackerson. If you explain it as an accident, I'm sure you'll be fine."

Jonah shook his head. "I'm sorry, Everson. The mystery surrounding his death must remain as is."

Everson's anger came to a boil. "Why?"

"I…cannot say." Jonah stood and put his hand on the doorknob. "Let it be, Everson. Remember your friend well, but let it go. We will not speak of this again."

The door opened, and Jonah stepped outside, leaving Everson frustrated, confused, and alone.

33

THE SPARK

An energy filled the Arena; an ambience of excitement that Everson held fast to his heart, hoping that it would lift his spirits. As he gazed at the crowd, he recalled the last time the school had gathered.

It had been a dreary spring day, overcast with the threat of rain looming. A brisk wind blew down from the mountains, causing the students to wrap themselves tightly in their woolen cloaks. Those who had neglected the extra layer shivered with arms stiff by their sides, dressed only in their double-breasted academy coats and breeches.

The entire school had come out, although only a fraction of the students knew Donnell. In fact, Everson found that nobody beside himself and Ivy even considered Donnell a friend. Still, the death of an academy student warranted attention, despite the unexplained circumstances.

Ackerson finished speaking – the man's words sliding past Everson like so much fluff – and he moved aside. Master Alridge stepped forward and rested a disk of wood atop the sheet that covered Donnell's body. Moments later, a red glow emitted from the disk and it burst into bright flames. The sheet and surrounding wood caught fire, the pyre rapidly growing into a raging inferno. Despite a distance greater than ten strides, Everson was forced to hold his hand up to ward his face from the intensity.

A moment of silence fell over the crowd, filled only by the crackling flames. The headmaster and other academy instructors in attendance then headed toward the school, trailed by somber students. Everson stared at the flames, thinking about Jonah and his role in Donnell's death. It hurt him that Jonah wouldn't discuss what happened. The issue had created a gap between them, one as deep and wide as the valley that surrounded the school.

The flames faded in Everson's eyes and his thoughts returned to the present.

Master Nindlerod stood from his seat among the other judges and shuffled to the center of the Arena floor. Mid-day sunbeams shone upon him, bathing him in light. He lifted a cone-shaped device to his lips and shouted "Silence." The crowd quieted while Nindlerod waited. With the ruckus fallen to a hush, he addressed the audience.

"Welcome to the winter Inventor's Challenge. Once again, we gather to discover what innovations our young engineering students have created. I'm sure you know to expect the unexpected."

Nindlerod held his arm toward the other masters seated at the far end of the Arena floor, opposite from the contestants. Everson noted that Headmaster Ackerson was missing, and he realized that he hadn't seen the man since Donnell's funeral, the same day King Brock and the other rulers departed. Everson waited for the announcement. After all, he had requested it.

"For the first team, I call upon the teammates of Donnell Banks, who honor their fallen comrade." Nindlerod turned toward them. "Ivy Flue-rien and Everson Gulagas, please come to the center and present your invention."

The butterflies sleeping in Everson's stomach suddenly burst into flight, stirring his innards and quickening his pulse until he nearly fainted. He nodded toward Ivy, who stood and circled behind the cart. A grunt slipped from her lips as the cart – with Everson sitting on it – lurched into motion.

All eyes were upon Everson as curious comments echoed throughout the room. He didn't need to hear them to know that people wondered why he sat upon the cart with a blanket over his lap and his canes gripped in his hands. The curiosity was something he expected. In fact, it was something he desperately wanted.

Everson had spent his entire life feeling incomplete. His dependence on others left him wishing to be more than just a burden. While his braces and canes offered mobility he would have otherwise lacked, most would never appreciate the gap that remained between him and someone with functioning legs. Every time he met someone with a cane, he felt a connection. They understood a piece of what he had lived every day of his life. He desperately wanted the audience to appreciate that perspective, for only that would give them a true appreciation of what he had accomplished.

When the cart reached the center of the floor, Ivy stopped pushing and shifted to stand between the cart and the judges. The crowd quieted, and she addressed them.

"We lost a teammate and a friend two weeks ago. Without his assistance, the invention we are about to present would not exist." She gestured toward Everson. "So, Everson and I dedicate this moment to the memory of Donnell Banks."

Applause echoed throughout the room. With the funeral fresh in everyone's memory, Donnell was well known, despite having barely existed in their minds before his death. When the applause faded, Ivy continued.

"Throughout history, there are moments that change the course of humanity. From the discovery of fire to the invention of the wheel, these things impact our lives today despite having been discovered many centuries ago. Today, you will witness the next great change. A discovery that opens the door for new ideas, a whole new world of possibility."

Ivy turned toward Everson and grinned. "Despite my help and any contribution from Donnell, the ingenious invention you are about to witness came from Everson, as did the amazing discovery that makes it possible."

Everson frowned at her statement – something outside of the agreed script. All eyes turned toward him and he realized that the moment had come. He took a deep breath…and bared his soul.

"Like the rest of you, I was born with legs. However, mine are…

useless. With the help of braces to keep them straight and canes to support me, I have been able to get by. The gap between getting by and actually walking is wider than the sky, farther away than the stars. Accordingly, when I discovered the means to capture and harness Chaos, I put my mind to the task of crossing that gap." He tossed his canes to the floor and watched them bounce and roll across the dirt. "Behold what Chaos Conduction can do."

With a flourish, Everson yanked the blanket from his lap and tossed it aside. He looked down at the mechanical assemblies that encased his legs, the polished steel bands gleaming brightly in the sunlight streaming through the windows above. When he pushed himself off the cart, he landed with a thud. Straightening his hips, the actuators attached to them triggered the Chaos core in each mechanism, and his legs straightened, leaving him standing tall, grinning.

Everson crossed the floor, taking lumbering steps as his mechanical muscles whirred noisily. When he reached the wall, he turned from the crowd, squatted, and leaped.

There are moments that define individuals. There are moments that define generations. And then, there are moments that transcend such narrow views. This was Everson's moment, a moment that every student and faculty member would forever remember. This was a moment that would alter the course of history…at least it was as Everson saw it.

The glass-paneled ceiling stood four stories above the floor. Yet, at the apex of his leap, Everson nearly reached the thick wooden beams that held the glass panels in place. Arching through the rays of sunlight, he focused on the floor as it quickly approached. With legs extended, he flexed his hips as his feet made contact and the mechanical legs bent, the air in the cylinders expelling in a rapid hiss. A puff of dust billowed up from his feet, clearing as he stood upright and turned toward the judges. The stunned looks he found on the master's faces drew a smile on his own, satisfied by the effect.

Using his cane, Nindlerod pushed himself to a stance and hobbled toward Everson. Master Hedgewick rose from his chair and passed the old man.

"Did someone give you a Chaos augmentation?" Hedgewick demanded as he stared at the mechanical legs.

"Um…no, Sir." Everson shook his head. "Not exactly."

"What powers them, then?" Nindlerod asked.

Everson reached down to his thigh, fumbling with the latch for a moment. When he swung the metal plate open, he moved his hip slightly and the actuator engaged with the chunk of rock. Red sparks of energy crackled in the opening when the pump engaged. He flexed the other direction and the pump reversed itself, again crackling with energy as air hissed out from it.

"Amazing," Hedgewick muttered as he stared at the sparking rock. "What do you call this power source?"

"Chaos Conduction. It's raw, unharnessed Chaos stored within an inanimate object. Certain materials seem to conduct it, while others appear immune." Everson shrugged. "In fact, I am only using a slight bit of the power available. When conducted properly, this tiny piece of rock is far more powerful than a steam engine."

A grin formed on Nindlerod's face – a grin that evolved into laughter, cackling noisily until it was drowned by deafening applause.

34

CHAOS CONDUCTION

"Once the mechanical legs were fully assembled, Ivy and I began testing them. In an effort to keep our invention a secret, we agreed to meet in the Foundry late at night when others were sleeping."

The masters seated at the table stared back in rapt attention as Everson spoke. His attention shifted from Master Hedgewick to Master Nindlerod. Seeing Nindlerod, Everson recalled how surprised he had been when the man approached him after the Inventor's Challenge concluded.

"Well done, young man," the Engineering master had clapped him on the shoulder and eyed the mechanical legs resting on the cart beside him. "It has been years since a student astounded me so soundly." He turned toward Hedgewick, who was having a discussion with another master. "Your prize was well-earned."

"Thank you, Master Nindlerod." Everson glanced toward Ivy, who kneaded her hands in silence. "However, I did not do it alone."

Cackling laughter came from the old man, and he clapped Everson on the shoulder again. "Humility as well." He nodded. "Very good." The man's jovial expression grew serious. "I would like you to join a few of us in Ackerson's office. We desire additional details regarding your discovery."

Ackerson's office is where Everson now found himself. The headmaster was joined by Masters Alridge, Hedgewick, and Nindlerod. In addition, the man in black watched on, a man introduced as Master Firellus. Something about the man's eyes put Everson on edge, as if the man peered into his very soul. Looking at the table, Everson collected his thoughts and continued with his response to their question.

"When I first strapped the legs on, any movement I made caused me to lurch about in fits and jerks. The first time I tried jumping, I overdid it and almost crashed into a forge, thankfully saving myself by latching onto a pulley hanging from the ceiling." He shuddered at the thought of landing in the forge coals.

"We then began to make adjustments – reducing the size of the conductors wrapped about the charged chunks of stone, tweaking the length of the actuator arms, and other minor modifications. By the third night, I was able to walk. By the fifth, squatting, jumping, and even running became possible."

Master Firellus leaned forward, and his eyes narrowed. "That's all well and good, but can you again describe how you captured this raw Chaos you speak of?"

"Well, as I told you before, my friend Jonah used an augmentation that resulted in a simple rock turning a dull black."

"What augmentation? Which rune?"

Everson realized he couldn't hide the detail he had been avoiding. "We aren't sure, but it has to do with heat."

Master Alridge leaned closer, frowning. "Where did you learn of this rune? We haven't covered it yet in Chaos Theory."

"I know." Everson's gaze flicked down toward his lap. "We discovered the rune ourselves. It's marked on the plates inside the kitchen ovens."

When he looked up, he noticed Alridge glance toward Firellus.

Ackerson tapped on the table, drawing Everson's attention. "Why, exactly, were you looking inside the ovens?"

Everson sighed. "We were after the secret of enchanting. There was a rumor that the ovens always remained hot, without the need of a fire. After discovering the rune, Jonah and I decided to test it. The rock he used it on burned bright and hot and lasted for only an hour."

Everson frowned as he recalled Donnell's funeral. His eyes narrowed as he realized that Alridge had used the same rune to ignite the funeral pyre. When the woman nodded, he continued.

"It became obvious that our experiment didn't work, yet the idea of enchanting – the idea of a permanent augmentation – continued to pull at me. The applications for such augmentations in conjunction with the right inventions could yield world-changing results. Therefore, I dragged Jonah back out to the quarry a few weeks later. When he tried the same rune on the same rock…nothing happened. Or, so, we thought.

"When we tried to touch the rock, red energy lashed out from it. At first, we didn't understand the implications. When we returned weeks later, we discovered that the energy remained. That's when I suspected the truth – the first augmentation had changed the rock in some manner, such that the subsequent application of Chaos resulted in the rock absorbing the energy rather than it being trapped within the rune."

"Incredible." Master Firellus said with wonder in voice. "After all these years, it was right in front of our face, only requiring the right series of events."

Nindlerod patted the man on the shoulder. "Such is the way of discoveries, Elias. In hindsight, they may appear simple, but thinking of them the first time requires the right mind and a stroke of luck. With only one or the other, it remains undiscovered."

Ackerson spoke. "I think we have the information we need. I'm sure you're hungry. Get yourself a meal. If you ever come across anything of note again, my door is open to you."

Everson nodded. He leaned forward, flexed his hips, and straightened into a stance with a resounding hiss.

Ackerson shook his head as he stared at mechanical legs. "Brilliant. Simply brilliant."

Everson walked toward the door and looked back one last time, finding all eyes staring at the invention strapped to his legs. He suspected that he should feel self-conscious, but instead he experienced a sense of wonder. Even Firellus and Nindlerod, who both used canes to help them walk, would never know the joy Everson felt at taking a few simple steps across the room.

After eating, Everson returned to his room. When he sat on the bed, he pulled the gold medal from about his neck and stared at it. Pride hummed within his chest, and he wished his parents could have seen his moment of triumph. He reached out to hang the medal from the bedpost, but missed. With a clink, it bounced on the floor and rolled beneath Jonah's bed.

With a sigh, he groaned. "Smooth move, Everson."

He stood and squatted with a hiss, but was unable to reach the medal. Shifting, he bent one leg further and attempted to kneel but lost his balance. The impact of striking the stone floor drove a sharp pain through his shoulder. He lay still for a moment and wondered at his ability to recover, fearing himself a turtle turned up on its shell. Noticing the medal now within reach, he swept his arm out and grabbed it. In that moment, he noticed something else.

Between the wooden slats that supported Jonah's mattress, were sheets of paper, the edges bent and hanging free. He reached out and gripped the free corners. With gentle tugs, careful not to rip them, he pulled out a small stack of papers. He then rolled over and put the papers and the medal on his mattress. With his hands free, he was able to push himself off the floor and get one mechanical leg beneath him. Rising and settling on his bed, Everson began looking over the papers in his hand.

Notes of how *Chaos* functions and the runes they had been taught in Chaos Theory were scrawled upon three of the sheets. On the fourth and fifth sheet, he found a journal of sorts, along with something that caught his eye.

Upon my arrival at the school, I was able to ferret out and befriend a loner as we had planned. His name is Everson Gulagas. He hails from Cinti Mor and his family moved from the city the very day that we captured it. I chose him because he needs my help, despite his brilliance. The boy is crippled, and my ability to fully function makes me an asset to him. As a result, I have been able to blend in and am gathering the information we need, while also receiving training that will offer value to the new Empire.

Everson stopped reading as the words blurred in his vision. A sweep of his fingers wiped the tears away, but new ones replaced them. *All this time, I thought Jonah was my friend.* He sobbed and tears dripped on the papers in his hand. Betrayal. It hurt far worse than he had expected – soul crushing to the point of breaking him.

After a few minutes, he wiped his face dry and gathered his resolve. *Jonah will not get away with this. He will find that he betrayed the wrong person.*

Standing, Everson walked to the door with the papers in hand. After slipping into the corridor, he locked it behind him and headed toward Ackerson's office.

35

WHAT LAY BENEATH

"Academy leaders found themselves at a loss," Quinn said to her captors. "After interrogating the male cadets, they still hadn't found the murderer. Lacking any leads, the investigation stalled.

"Even without Darnya's influence, Chuli remained my only friend. Others seemed reluctant to trust me." Quinn frowned at the memory. "The academy leaders acted as if nothing had happened. My innocence had been proven to them, but I don't think the girls saw it that way.

"The next ten weeks passed without any events of note." Quinn felt the ropes around her wrist beginning to loosen. "Chuli and I continued to train in secret, and our skills improved. On sparring days, I would win handily, and she often did the same. As my abilities and my confidence improved, I found myself longing to test a true set of blades.

"Our monthly ranger outings continued, but their nature changed with the weather. Dressed in white cloaks and grey furs, we would hike through the snow, moving at a pace less than half of what we had grown used to. Even so, the effort of climbing mountains in waist-deep snow made us long for it to melt. The only aspect of those trips we found improved was the hunting. Tracking became far easier, while the lack of leaves and the white backdrop made it easier to spot game.

"Horsemanship training continued, and we learned the dangers of ice, which can prove as much a threat to a horse's footing as a human's. While my skill at riding paled compared to Chuli's, I found myself one of the better riders among the female cadets.

"In archery, we found new challenges. They would rotate our days in the range, waiting for those days when the wind blew stiffly. When the cold breath of winter rolled down the mountains, drifting snow would blind us and sting exposed skin. In these conditions, we learned to account for the wind, keeping our arrow flight flat and compensating for drift. At first, I thought they were torturing us. However, as time went on, my perception began to change. By the end of winter, I found myself able to adjust on instinct – sometimes even before I shot the first arrow. Again, my skill was not as strong as Chuli's, but it was better than most of my squad mates.

"When the weather turned and the snow began to melt, Goren made an announcement that set the school afire."

Running as fast as she dared – far faster than when she had first tried it, Quinn crossed the series of beams high above the sparring room floor. She had realized months earlier that the trick was to see the beam and not the drop below it. Reaching the end, she leaped across the gap to the narrow ledge, careful not to hit the wall too hard and fall backward off it.

She scaled down and dropped to the floor. When she turned, Vi called out "Forty-two counts."

While still collecting her breath, Quinn grimaced in frustration. It was her fastest time yet, but another overshadowed her personal achievement. She glanced at Yvette and found a smirk of satisfaction on the girl's face. Possessing a compact frame, the brunette was fast and agile. It wasn't that Quinn didn't like Yvette. She just hated losing.

"Formation!" Jasmine barked.

Quinn and the other first-year cadets stood in one line, the second-year girls in another, five strides apart. As usual, Jasmine examined them as she strode down the gap. When she reached the far end, she commanded them.

"March to my lead."

She led them out the door and down the corridor. Turning, the squad followed her to the door to the Coliseum, where she paused to face them.

"Go in and find a seat. Captain Goren has an announcement to make. Be respectful. You will regret it if you embarrass me."

She pulled the door open and held it as the girls entered the massive building. When Quinn passed through the door, she found the male cadets occupying the front rows, so she and the other girls took seats in the open benches behind the boys.

The building had undergone a change...one that was still in progress. A layer of partially constructed block wall covered the wall that separated the Coliseum from the baths. A single level of scaffolding stood beside the wall, while additional scaffolding sections waited at the other end of the Coliseum floor. The sight left Quinn wondering what the changes might mean, but the thought stalled when Goren strode to the center of the floor. He gazed upon the stands and addressed the crowd.

"The Arena Championship is a competition with a long and illustrious history. For over a century, it has been a means to measure the top fighters against one another, rewarding one individual as the best. However, we have decided that the original intent of that competition no longer serves our needs."

The man's voice bellowed throughout the building as he continued. "Since this institution was founded five years ago, the training that cadets receive has expanded beyond the artistry of close combat. Accordingly, we are introducing a new competition. The TACT Games will commence four weeks from today. As in past years, a series of duels will again occur in the Coliseum. In addition, we will hold events in archery, agility, horsemanship, and hunting. The winner of each will receive a medal and one gold piece. Where the competitors place in each event will also help to determine this year's TACT Games Champion. In the event of a tie, the individuals involved will face each other in a game of Ratio Bellicus to decide the winner."

Reaching into his waistband, Goren removed a sheet of paper. Unfolding it, he continued. "Your squad leaders have selected those whom they feel are best suited to compete in this challenge. I have here, a list of ten first-year and ten second-year boys in addition to six first-year and six second-year girls. When I call your name, come down to the floor and assemble behind me."

He stared down at the paper and began announcing names. Quinn found herself considering who among her fellow first-year cadets might be included. Hirna, Chuli, and Yvette all seemed obvious. Beyond those three, she hoped to hear her name called.

Hearing a familiar name called, it drew Quinn's attention. Her eyes grew wide when Iko rose from the crowd, trailed by Percy as his name was announced next.

Something quivered inside Quinn as she watched Iko descend the stands. The feelings she had for him had been buried beneath the winter snow. Seeing him felt like the spring sun rising, melting the snow and warming what waited beneath. She stared at him with her thoughts jumbled, twisted by the feelings stirring inside until Chuli poked her.

"Ouch. What?" Quinn complained.

"Goren called your name."

Quinn blinked and heard Chuli's name called next.

Standing, Quinn led Chuli down the stairs. When they reached the floor, she followed Hirna past Goren and found a spot behind him. Quinn looked at Iko, his eyes following her as a smile stretched across his face. Refusing to respond in kind, she remained stoic. When all names were called and the competitors had gathered behind Goren, he addressed the crowd.

"The thirty-two cadets standing behind me will meet in this very room in four weeks. For five days, they will give their best, fighting for their pride as if fighting for their lives. When the contest ends, we will have our very first TACT Games champion.

"You are dismissed."

Applause rang throughout the room, but Quinn ignored it. Her mind was elsewhere. She headed toward the stands and blended in with the cluster of students filtering out of the building. Rather than heading directly to the mess hall, she stepped aside and waited. When Iko passed by, she grabbed his arm and pulled him to a corner.

"Ouch!" he appeared startled. "Um...hello, Quinn."

"You remember me?" The sarcasm in her tone was thick. "How touching."

He blinked. "I…I'm happy to see you."

"When did you get back?"

"Last night."

"A night and a day pass, yet you couldn't find time to see me, time to let me know that you're safe."

"It was late when we arrived and…today was difficult. Sergeant Khallum woke Percy and me early and ran us though extra sessions to ensure we remained in condition." He smiled. "You were concerned for my safety?"

"Don't change the subject. You were gone the entire winter and never sent word. When you returned, you neglected to find me. I thought you cared for me."

He moved closer and put his hand on her shoulder. "Quinn, I'm sorry. If I had the means, I assure you I would have sent word. I told you why I didn't see you until now. Come and eat dinner with me. We can talk there."

The fire inside Quinn began to quell. His response seemed logical, but she didn't feel like being logical – which made her irritated with herself. With a reluctant nod, she walked with him to the mess hall.

"So, how is your mother?" she asked.

His brow furrowed. "My mother?" He paused and blinked. "Oh. Sorry, my mind was elsewhere. While the temple healer was able to help her, she will not walk again. She now lives with my aunt, likely bedridden for some time, perhaps forever."

Quinn felt unsure of how to respond. Iko must have noticed her expression because he grinned and changed the subject.

"At least I was able to avoid the harsh winter weather while I was away."

Quinn snorted. "Yes. You missed some painful ranger outings."

"Speaking of which, I wonder what they'll task us with for the TACT Games events."

As Quinn led him toward the kitchen, she considered the topic and decided that she had better focus on her training. She didn't plan to merely compete. She planned to win.

36

THE GAMES BEGIN

It was a beautiful spring day. The sun shone brightly, its warmth balanced by a cool mountain breeze. After three weeks of steady rain, several days of clear skies had dried the puddles away and had drawn fresh young leaves from the trees in the valley. A stray cloud passed before the sun, temporarily dimming the brightness and giving extra weight to the chill in the wind. Quinn shivered, but her stance remained true.

The twelve female cadets and twenty male cadets who were among the competitors stood in rows four persons deep. With chests out, stomachs in, and arms at their sides, they remained still as Captain Goren announced their names to the crowd. Seating had been erected between the archery range and the riding fields to hold spectators for the first two events. The cadets who were not competing filled the stands, along with a smattering of officials from both schools.

"To commence the first ever TACT Games, we begin with archery." Goren gestured toward a woman dressed in greens. "Our Master Archer, Zina Hammerton, will announce this event."

Tall and lithe, the dark-haired woman stepped forward and gave Goren a nod. "Thank you, Captain." She turned toward the crowd. "Archery consists of nothing but a person, a bow, an arrow, and a target.

This is an individual competition where each bullseye is worth three points, the rest of the target worth one point, and any other shot results in zero points.

"We begin with static targets at fifty paces. The sixteen top scorers advance to round two, the top eight to round three, and the last four top scorers move on to the finals. When I call your name, take position before a target and make ready. Do not loose an arrow until I call for it."

She read off eight names. While Quinn was not among them, Chuli's name was. The Tantarri girl moved forward and chose a target, as did the other seven cadets. When the competitors stood ready with bows raised and arrows nocked, Hammerton hollered, "Release!"

A staccato of *twangs* sounded, followed by the *thumps* of arrows striking. Repeatedly, Hammerton called for them to loose their arrows. Most arrows found their mark, but a few fell short or buried themselves into the hay bales stacked behind the targets. Amazingly, nine of Chuli's shots found the small red circle on her target, the tenth landing just outside the edge. The archery assistants ran onto the field and collected arrows as they tallied scores. While most of the other competitors fared well, none came close to Chuli's leading twenty-eight points.

Another group of names were announced, this time both Iko's and Percy's landing among them. Quinn watched in curiosity. She knew Iko was skilled with a sword, but she had never seen him shoot. At the same time, she recalled Percy mentioning his skill with a bow and was eager to witness it for herself. Like Chuli, Percy shot with alarming accuracy, placing all ten arrows in the circle in the center for a full thirty points. At the same time, most of Iko's arrows struck the target, with four landing within the bullseye. The score put him among the leaders, but far behind his friend.

With the group finished, Quinn knew hers would be among the names called. As she approached her mark, she took a deep breath and fought to calm the fluttering in her stomach. Raising her bow, she drew an arrow, nocked it, and took aim. "Release!" She released the arrow. With a shallow arc, the arrow's path bent a hand span to the left by the time it struck the target's outer edge. When they sighted the next arrow, she considered her observation and shot. It struck a bullseye. With the following arrows, she did her best to repeat the results. By the time her ten arrows were spent, eight were buried in the target with three bullseyes.

The following round took place at a hundred paces. While Percy's and Chuli's shooting remained constant, each with eight bullseyes and two others on-target, the other cadets scored much worse. Among the eight who advanced to the third round were four girls and four boys - Quinn, Chuli, Hirna, Yvette, Iko, Boykin, Oliver, and Percy.

The archery assistants removed the eight targets and began hanging new targets from a rope that ran across the field.

Hammerton strolled onto the field and turned toward the stands, shouting as she addressed them. "Now down to eight, we will challenge these cadets to determine their true skill. Rarely does a target remain still in the real world. Accordingly, they are now tasked with shooting a target that moves."

She turned toward the remaining eight with a heavy gaze. "When your name is called, stand at the center mark. You will shoot at fifty paces, like the first round. However, this time you must launch at will. The target will only pass you once."

Hirna's name was the first called. She took position, and Hammerton called out. The assistant at the far end began to crank a wheel, winding the rope in and taking the target with it. Hirna began to loose arrows in a slow and steady rhythm. When the target passed the midpoint, she still had seven arrows in her quiver and only one in the target. Realizing her dilemma, she began to release arrows faster, but none hit the mark. Dejected, her head hung heavy as she returned to stand with the others.

Percy was the next called. As Quinn expected, he fared much better with nine arrows in the target, six of them bullseyes. Yvette, Boykin, and Oliver each took turns. While Yvette was able to get four arrows to stick, Boykin and Oliver both failed to hit the mark more than twice.

Quinn turned toward Chuli and Iko as she realized that they were the last three to shoot. Iko's name was called first. Quinn felt anxiety twisting her insides as she watched him shoot, striking the target four times with one bullseye. Hers was the next name called.

She approached her mark and drew three arrows, nocking one as she held the other two between other fingers. The move was difficult to execute, but she decided to chance it in hope of getting more arrows launched while the target was in range.

Hammerton shouted and the target began to move at a steady pace from left to right. Quinn took aim and considered the wind and movement speed, leading the target just a bit. She released the first arrow and nocked the next before it struck. The second launched, followed by the third. She then drew one arrow at a time, loosing them the moment her sight was set. When the target faded behind the wooden panel at the far end, she found her final arrow in her hand. She had shot nine with five striking the target, two in the center. The response from the crowd filled Quinn's heart. A smile forced itself upon her face as she retreated.

A pat on the shoulder awaited her as Chuli gave her a nod. "Impressive shooting, Quinn. Your skill is much improved."

"Thank you," Quinn replied as Chuli slipped past her. "Good luck, Chuli."

The Tantarri girl turned and smirked. "Luck is not needed when skill will suffice. Regardless, I thank you for the sentiment."

As Quinn expected, Chuli was correct. Not only was she able to shoot all ten arrows, but nine struck the target with five in the center ring. The crowd cheered voraciously, clearly impressed by Chuli's skill.

The final four, Quinn, Chuli, Iko, and Percy, moved to the hundred-pace mark as fresh targets were attached to the rope. While Quinn had made it to the final four, at longer range, her shortbow left her at a disadvantage to the longbows used by her competitors. She was able to strike the target three times with one in the center, beating Iko's score of three, but landing far behind the two leaders. Chuli hit eight times with four bullseyes. Yet, Percy edged past her, striking the target nine times and landing five bullseyes.

The four finalists joined Goren and Hammerton on a small platform before the crowd, with each receiving a medal. Percy was awarded four points for first place, Chuli three for second, Quinn two for third, and Iko one for fourth.

As the applause faded, Goren made a final announcement. "We now conclude the first round of the TACT Games. Join us here tomorrow for our horsemanship competition."

Quinn put her plate on the table and sat on the bench. A groan slipped out, driven by the pain in her back.

"Still hurting?" Iko asked with a grin.

"Yes."

He snorted and glanced toward Percy. "Well, you made it further than I did."

Chuli sat beside Quinn. "I still don't understand why you people behave as if horses are foreign to you. It is nothing to guide them so."

Quinn sighed. "I realize that things are different with the Tantarri. However, most of us cannot afford a horse of *any* kind. Tantarri horses cost as much as a house."

"That is so sad." Chuli shook her head. "I don't know how you can put a price on a horse."

Percy and Iko chuckled at the comment, earning them a frown from Quinn. "I think you misunderstand my meaning. What I intended was…"

"I know what you intended." Chuli smiled. "I was casting a joke."

The boys laughed harder.

"I think you meant that you were *making* a joke," Quinn offered.

Chuli tilted her head as she considered Quinn's words. "No. I like casting better. It is as if I were fishing for laughs."

That earned Chuli laughter from the entire group. When the laughter subsided, Quinn recovered the lost topic.

"Anyway, I'm glad that the riding competition is through and that I didn't crack my head open on that fall."

Percy grinned. "Your fall *was* quite spectacular."

Iko nudged him. "Stop it." He took Quinn's hand, his face reflecting overacted sympathy. "I was concerned that you had been seriously hurt."

Quinn snorted again. "I wasn't the only one who fell. Both of you took a spill as well. In fact, I think only three cadets did *not* fall."

Iko shared a knowing smirk. "At least I made it over the fence and the wall. It was the river crossing that caused me trouble."

Quinn arched a brow. "As I recall, your horse stopped dead before it, and you almost crossed by yourself."

The comment left Percy and Chuli chuckling.

Iko's expression appeared pained. "That landing hurt, you know… and that water was cold. Weren't you concerned for me?"

Quinn reached across the table and patted his hand. "I'm sure your ego is quite damaged. However, it was perhaps a bit too bright and shiny before. A few dents and blemishes should balance things out."

Percy burst into hard laughter and clapped Iko on the back. "Ha! Your ego is now beyond repair!"

Iko elbowed his friend again, this time hard enough to earn a heavy grunt. Quinn gave Chuli a sidelong glance.

"You appear to be the girl to beat, Chuli. With nobody else collecting more than four points after two events, you have a three-point lead."

Chuli shook her head. "Such is not the case. While I do have a lead, the first two events are the ones at which I excel the most." She sighed. "For the others, I'm afraid, my skill is average."

Iko leaned closer. "Tomorrow, we move indoors for the agility challenge, and the next day will be filled with duels." Iko glanced at Percy. "The last event is hunting. Goren said that it was a team event. Percy spent much of his life in the forest and is an able tracker. The four of us are the best with a bow. Perhaps we should combine as a team. We would surely win."

Quinn looked at Chuli as she considered the idea.

"You don't have to answer now." Iko stood, as did Percy. "Think on it."

Quinn watched Iko as the two boys walked away. His suggestion made sense – his reasoning sound. Yet, something nagged at her, refusing to allow her to relax.

37

A MEMORABLE WIN

Cheering students filled the stands, eager to see how the competitors would fare. Quinn looked up in awe, amazed at the transformation that had occurred in recent weeks.

A new wall had been constructed inside of the wall that led to the changing rooms. Similar to the escarpment, this wall included oddly spaced rocks that jutted out from the others, providing foot and hand holds. Looming with an ominous presence, the wall ran nearly to the ceiling, forty-feet above. Climbing the wall was just the beginning of their next challenge.

When Captain Goren took to the center of the Coliseum floor, he presented Sergeant Jasmine as the event host. The woman took Goren's place and explained the rules.

"What you see before you is a course constructed to test the strength, speed, and agility of our contestants. Beyond that, it shall test their courage. We will run a series of heats, with the winner of each advancing."

She turned toward the cadets, addressing them. "We shall begin with the girls, four competing at a time.

"Quinn, Chuli, Jinny, and Hirna, you are up first. When you reach the top of the wall, choose a track. The first to cross the finish line wins."

Quinn lined up beside the other girls and took a calming breath, trying to settle a stomach that twisted like a loose rope in the wind. She stared at the wall just a dozen strides away and sought out her first gripping point. Time seemed to slow, the moment stretching as she waited for the signal. And suddenly, it happened.

"Go!"

She and the other girls darted forward and began their ascent. After racing up the Escarp twice a month, Quinn knew she was the fastest climber among the girls, and she counted on gaining an early lead. As the wall sped past her, she worried about the remainder of the course.

Her fingers found a grip of the ledge atop the wall, and she glanced to the side as she pulled herself up. Hirna was five feet behind her, matched with Chuli while Jinny was slightly past half way. Quinn shuffled to the side, grabbed ahold of the handles, and jumped.

The pulley above her squeaked rapidly as it sped down the rope, across the building to a platform two hundred feet away. She found herself laughing at the thrill – the speed, the height, the sense of freedom. The pulley slowed when it neared the other end, but Quinn still had to lift her legs and brace herself as she collided with the wall atop the platform.

Turning about, she released the handles and found Chuli and Hirna speeding toward her. Not wishing to lose her lead, she scrambled down to the next platform, twelve feet above the floor. Without hesitation, she ran across a narrow beam, twenty feet long, and jumped when she reached the end.

In her haste, she almost missed the rope that dangled from above, but she was able to grip it and swing to the next beam. Her foot slipped and she teetered, her arms waving as she tried to maintain balance. Once set, she again hurried across the beam and began scaling down the ladder at the far end.

There, another platform waited for her, with a pit of mud below and metal rungs above, each rung spaced a stride apart. With a jump, she grabbed the first rung, and then the second, allowing her momentum to carry her from rung to rung until she cleared the mud. When she dropped to the ground, she heard the crowd growing louder. A backward glance showed Hirna at the middle rung and just seconds behind her.

Quinn darted forward and stumbled, her palms skidding across the dirt, her face through a cloud of dust. Rather than standing, she crawled forward the last ten feet and entered the hollow log. The fit was tight, but Quinn lacked the bulk that some of the girls and most of the boys carried, so she was able to squirm through quickly. When she regained her footing, she spotted the finish line fifty feet away. Sprinting with all her energy, she crossed it first. When she looked back, she found Hirna struggling to escape the log. By the time the girl cleared it and began to run, both Chuli and Jinny had emerged. Jinny crossed the line second, followed by Chuli, with Hirna last and appearing quite upset.

With a pat on the shoulder, Quinn gave Chuli a nod. The Tantarri girl gave her a grin and returned the favor.

"You can win this, Quinn. You have skill in this area."

"Thanks." Quinn said between gasps for air.

Hirna's face appeared a storm as she stomped past. Jinny shrugged.

Quinn had done it. She had advanced to round two, but the competition was sure to grow more difficult.

$$\rightarrow\!\!+\!\cdot\Phi\cdot\!+\!\!\leftarrow$$

The second round found Quinn matched against three boys, including Percy. While the boys had an advantage in strength, their added weight and size worked against them. One fell from a beam and broke his arm, only to be healed by an awaiting ecclesiast. Percy's hand slipped, and he fell from a rung into the mud pit for an instant disqualification. The last competitor, a short boy named Evran, proved to be a true challenge. Although she had a lead going into the rungs, the boy caught up and almost beat her to the finish with Quinn edging him by a half step.

The other group from the second round followed, consisting of two girls and two boys. The round was competitive, with Iko doing well despite his size. Nonetheless, he could not compete with Yvette, who ran the beams as if they were ten feet wide and slid through the tube as if it had been greased. She won by three strides, leaving Iko second and the other two an obstacle behind.

While Iko and Evran raced to decide third and fourth place, Quinn took a drink from her waterskin and glanced toward Yvette.

The short dark-skinned girl climbed like a spider and could balance like a bird on a clothesline. Yet, Quinn could find no animosity in her heart for Yvette. Despite how badly Quinn wanted to win, she decided that having Yvette win was something she could accept.

She walked over to the girl, attracting Yvette's attention.

"I wanted you to know that I am proud of us making it to the finals." Quinn said. "I also wish you luck."

Yvette's eyes narrowed, her tone accusing. "Are you trying to get into my head?"

Quinn shook her head. "Not at all."

Rebuffed, Quinn turned and walked away. As she neared Chuli, the girl gave her a nod. "You show honor, Quinn. It makes me proud. Sometimes, I almost think you are Tantarri."

Quinn was taken aback and considered how to respond but was interrupted by the cheering crowd. Evran crossed the line two steps ahead of Iko, and the crowd roared with applause. The pulleys were towed back into position at the other end of the Coliseum and Sergeant Jasmine returned to the center of the floor.

"With third and fourth place settled, we now turn to our final two contestants, who will vie to become champion of the agility challenge. Quinn Gulagas and Yvette Bumburro, take position at the line!"

Quinn took a deep breath as she strode to the line. A glance to the side showed Yvette standing three strides away with a hard gleam in her eyes. That look of determination stirred something inside Quinn. She pressed her lips together and turned toward the wall she was to climb. Her nerves settled, her focus attuned to the task before her.

"Go!"

With rapid and fluid movement, not one motion wasted, the way Quinn scaled the wall would have made a lizard proud. She reached the top and grabbed the pulley handles with a thrust, her legs swinging wildly out as her momentum carried her down the long rope. She reached the end, spun and scrambled to the platform below with Yvette a breath behind.

Without regard for safety, she sprinted across the first beam and dove for the rope, swinging to the next beam before resuming a run. When she flipped down to the next platform, she found herself in lockstep with Yvette, both of them flipping from rung to rung in sync as if they were performing a rehearsed dance.

Landing, they each dove into their hollowed log, with Quinn scrambling through as if her feet were on fire. As she exited the log, Quinn found Yvette doing the same. Quinn sprinted toward the finish line with everything she had when an image coalesced in her head – one of Everson hanging on the edge of a cliff, his fingers slipping as he screamed for Quinn to save him. The threat to her brother provided added urgency and she ran faster than ever before.

Quinn suddenly came upon the Coliseum wall, slowing too late to avoid colliding with it. The impact drove the wind from her lungs and she heard a hollow thump as her vision went black. Pain flared in her forehead and a rolling chime rang in her ears. Struggling to inhale, she found only resistance as her lungs refused to acquiesce. She rolled on her side and coughed before sweet air entered her body and she blinked at the blur surrounding her.

Within the haze, a face surfaced, grinning. "You or your brother," Torney said. "I'm not sure who is worse."

His hand gripped her arm and a shock of cold swept through her, forcing a chill and leaving her gasping for air. She blinked and realized that her head no longer hurt.

Torney put his hand out. "Here. Let me help you up."

Still confused about what had happened, Quinn allowed him to help her stand. She looked toward the cheering crowd and found them clapping and shouting her name.

With a pat on the shoulder, Torney flashed her a grin "Congratulations. When you win, you make it memorable."

"What?"

Jasmine approached her and grabbed Quinn's hand, holding it high as she turned toward the crowd.

"Next time, you can stop running when you cross the line."

Quinn looked down at the finish line, thirty feet from the wall. Realizing what had happened, she felt her cheeks grow flush. The entire school had seen her folly.

"Impressive win, though." Jasmine said as she lowered Quinn's hand. "I would have bet on Yvette, but there's something in you. Something I can't quite define. We shall see if it happens again tomorrow."

Quinn turned toward the crowd again. They would be back tomorrow, and they would be expecting blood.

38

A SOUR TASTE

The healer sped down to the arena floor and ran to the boy's side. Sergeants Khallum and Jasmine joined him. From her seat beside the changing room entrance, Quinn could see the white of his bone sticking through the torn breeches. Hearing the scream when Khallum reset the boy's leg gave Quinn a chill, and she grit her teeth. Moments later, the healer stood and stepped back. The boy sat up, rose to his feet, and thanked the healer before heading off to change, crossing directly over the spot where a mud pit had stood the day prior.

Once it was filled with dry dirt, rolled and packed hard, there was no evidence of the mud pits existing. In addition, the wooden platforms and beams had been removed, leaving only the new climbing wall as a reminder of the agility challenge.

As the healed boy passed her, Quinn stared at the hole torn in his breeches, the opening surrounded by fresh blood. Her gaze shifted to Iko, who approached with a relaxed smile. When he sat beside her, she turned toward him with narrowed eyes.

"I am quite impressed. I watched you spar once before but didn't grasp your skill. You never mentioned how good you are with a sword."

He shrugged. "You never really asked. I'd rather not boast unless forced into it."

Sitting back, Quinn turned the thought over in her mind. A piece of her struggled with the thought that he kept it a secret, as if he were hiding the truth from her intentionally. That piece of her also noted how easily it came to him. She didn't know which bothered her more. Still, he had a point about boasting. Nobody loves a braggart.

Iko put his hand on her knee, the warmth coming through her thin sparring breeches immediately. "It appears that I'm not the only one. You have handled your opponents with ease as well."

Flashes of her match against Jinny danced in Quinn's mind. Knowing that her opponent tended toward a conservative approach, Quinn's brazen attack was intended to cause discomfort. The result left Jinny on her knees with broken ribs and a quick win for Quinn. Her subsequent round against Hirna was quite different. The larger girl held an advantage in strength, Quinn in quickness. Skilled with her shield, Hirna repeatedly blocked Quinn's attacks and often returned the favor with a strike of her longsword. After a few volleys, Quinn feinted a high strike with one sword and was able to get beneath Hirna's shield with the other. A solid strike to the midriff caused Hirna to clutch at her stomach and allowed Quinn a solid strike upside her opponent's head. With eyes rolled back, Hirna fell to the floor in a heap. Quinn stepped back and rubbed her wrist, sore from striking her wooden sword on the metal helmet. However, she had again won.

The images faded, and Quinn turned toward Iko with a shrug. "Only the best duelists remain as we enter the finals. I'm sure the next match will offer a greater challenge."

"What if we are forced to face each other?" Iko asked with a half grin.

"I suspect you will do your best to win, and I will do the same." She pressed her lips together as she considered the idea. "If you cannot tell, I am not fond of losing."

His grin widened. "Neither am I."

Sergeant Khallum waved from the center of the Coliseum and the crowd quieted.

"The field is now down to eight. We will have one more round and then break for lunch. The final battles commence this afternoon."

"Round three will begin with Jacquinn Gulagas facing Chuli Ultermane."

Quinn turned toward the girl sitting beside her. Their gazes locked. While they had always known it was possible, they had both dreaded this eventuality. Only one of them could advance to the final four. Only one could earn points from this event.

Chuli gave Quinn a nod, and they both stood and strode across the floor. Quinn slipped her sparring helmet on, as did Chuli. Upon reaching the circle at the center, each girl took position opposite from the other.

"You two know the rules. Prepare to fight." Khallum stepped backward until he stood beyond the ring. "Go!"

Quinn gave her friend a nod and edged forward. After a nod in response, Chuli raised both the small shield strapped to her forearm and the wooden sword held in her opposite hand.

The first attack came from Quinn, lunging forward with both swords coming in an arc from one side – one sword high, the other low. Chuli ducked the high sword, blocked the other with her shield, and spun about with her sword coming at Quinn's midsection. Quinn spun away and thrust her leg backward with a kick to Chuli's thigh. The Tantarri girl grunted and jumped back.

As they again faced each other, Quinn thought of the many times she and Chuli had sparred in private. While Quinn usually got the better of Chuli, many of those victories came when Quinn invented a trick or a risky move that caught the other girl by surprise. However, she discovered that new ideas grew more difficult to capture for each one spent.

Chuli slid forward and stabbed with a thrust. Quinn twisted sideways and returned the thrust with her forward arm, which struck Chuli's shield. Rather than drawing her sword back, Chuli swiped upward, Quinn reacted, but a hair too late when Chuli's sword clipped the tip of Quinn's nose.

With her eyes watering from the pain, Quinn staggered backward. A wipe of her wrist across her nose revealed bright red streaks. She stared at the blood and her expression became a grimace – an anger filled her and hardened her resolve.

Darting forward, Quinn leapt high. As expected, Chuli raised her sword to block Quinn's leading sword and her shield to block Quinn's other strike. Both connected and deflected Quinn's blows, but neither stopped her momentum. A hard kick struck Chuli in the chest, driving her backward. A momentary stumble joined Quinn's landing before she drove forward with a flurry of slashes that Chuli urgently deflected, the action driving her backward yet again. With a feint, Quinn spun below a high swing and thrust her foot backward into Chuli's thigh. The Tantarri girl stumbled backward, her foot stepping outside of the circle. The crowd cheered, the match was called, and Quinn was declared the winner.

Breathing rapidly from the exertion, Quinn pulled her sparring helmet from her head and shook her damp hair loose. "Good match."

Chuli removed her helmet and wiped her forehead dry. "I did not realize how close I was to the ring edge. That is not something you have tried in our sparring matches."

Quinn wiped her sore nose, again leaving streaks of blood on her hand. Touching it hurt. A lot.

"It may be broken," Chuli noted.

The two girls walked toward the benches at the side of the floor as Rena descended from the stands and met them.

"Do you need any healing, Chuli?"

The Tantarri girl shook her head. "My wounds are bruises at best, the worst of which is to my pride."

Rena chuckled at the response. "Well, someone has to lose."

"True." Chuli gave Quinn a sidelong glance. "However, there is little honor lost when you lose to someone of exceedingly strong character."

Quinn rolled her eyes and turned toward Rena. "My nose may be broken."

Rena shared a sideways smile. "If you saw your nose, you would say there is little doubt. You look terrible. Unfortunately, that means I must set it before I heal you."

"Just do it." Quinn moved close to the girl and waited.

With her fingers pressed to either side of Quinn's nose, Rena pressed them firmly together. Quinn felt a pop and winced at the pain that caused her eyes to water again. Rena then placed her palm on Quinn's forehead and closed her eyes. The deep chill that Quinn was expecting struck and drove the air from her lungs, leaving her gasping for air. Thankfully, her face no longer hurt.

"Thanks, Rena." Quinn said as the girl removed her palm.

As she handed Quinn a hard roll drawn from her pocket, Rena smiled. "Anytime. Congratulations on making the final four. Good luck in the next round."

Rena returned to the stands, Chuli headed toward the changing room, and Quinn found a seat on the bench while Khallum announced the next pairing.

Iko sat beside Quinn, the two of them the only cadets remaining on the bench. He took a deep drink from the waterskin and wiped his mouth dry.

"Good match," Quinn said.

"Thanks. He was tough."

Quinn snorted. "It didn't seem like it. You beat him in less than a minute, just like the others you faced today."

"Bilchard is strong. Blocking his swings hurt – shook my bones."

"You blocked, what? Perhaps four strikes?"

He shrugged. "Four *hard* strikes."

She rolled her eyes and looked across the Coliseum floor. Khallum stood to the side, in discussion with Jasmine. In a few minutes, he would return to the center ring and announce the final duel.

"I don't know why you're giving me a hard time," Iko said. "You handled your last match with ease as well. Perhaps more so than mine. I think you embarrassed Percy with the quick win."

Fighting against Percy and his quarterstaff had required Quinn to adjust her strategy and offered the opportunity to unveil a new move she had been perfecting. After attacking with a quick flurry of sword strikes that Percy had blocked, Quinn made a wide swipe with her swords that left her back exposed. He took the bait and swung his staff in a hard sweep. When Quinn back flipped over Percy's strike, it left him overextended, his backside unprotected. A quick thrust under his arm connected with his ribs, cracking them and giving her the win.

With the memory passed, Quinn glanced at Iko beside her and shrugged, "I got lucky."

Iko chuckled. "That flip you executed shocked everyone. It takes more than luck to pull that off. While it won't work on me now that I've seen it, you certainly caught Percy by surprise."

Khallum strolled to the circle at the heart of the floor and the crowd quieted. In opposition to the lessening noise, the anxiety within Quinn grew stronger.

"We have reached the final match," Khallum announced. "The winner of this duel will decide the day and claim the title of sparring champion.

"I now call to the floor Ikonis Eldarr and Jacquinn Gulagas."

With a final glance toward each other, Iko and Quinn slipped their helmets on, rose to their feet, and strode toward the ring. Reaching the center, they squared off five paces apart and waited.

"This is it," Khallum said. "Win and you are champion."

He moved outside the circle and shouted. "Fight!"

Quinn stared into Iko's amber eyes – eyes that normally held her captive, eyes that had hooks in her heart. Those eyes sparked with intensity. In this moment, he was the enemy.

Easing forward, Quinn held her swords ready. Unlike other fighters, Iko held his longsword in his left hand, his shield strapped to the right. When they drew within three paces, he struck. Blinding fast swings slashed at Quinn, strikes that she slapped aside, ducked, and dodged.

Quinn was used to having an edge on quickness, but with Iko, she found herself at a disadvantage. Protecting herself became her sole focus, leaving her unable to counter attack. His sword snapped, swung, stabbed, and struck again and again, pressing Quinn in a way she had never been pressed before.

She focused on his sword, watching every motion, twisting, dodging, blocking, strike after furious strike.

Iko suddenly darted forward and thrust his shield into her as she slapped his sword aside. The impact was thunderous – his size, weight, and strength lifting her off her feet and launching her into the air. Her head and shoulders hit the ground hard. Blackness hollowed her vision into a narrow tunnel. Dark spots appeared, shifted, and faded, only to return.

Shock, confusion, and pain flooded in. With her thoughts slow to form, as if wading through muck, Quinn tried to regain her senses. She blinked and gasped for air and found herself on her side, her helmet off, her face in the dirt. A shadow loomed over her, joined by a distant voice that was lost to the ringing in her ears. She felt someone grab her arm.

The intense chill of healing shocked her senses and drove the wind from her lungs as the sound of the cheering crowd replaced the ringing. Her vision cleared, and she found Rena kneeling beside her. Quinn sat up and realized she was lying outside the ring. Within, Khallum held Iko's hand high, the duo turning slowly to the cheering crowd. Quinn frowned, knowing that she had lost. Rena held a hand out and helped her stand.

"Thanks again," Quinn said.

"I'm glad you're all right. That hit appeared…very bad."

Quinn looked toward Iko and found his attention toward the crowd as he drank in the applause. With the sour taste of defeat on her tongue, she retreated toward the girls' baths. Rena may have healed her physical wounds, but deeper wounds bled with fury.

39

A TEAR OF BETRAYAL

With heavy breaths, Quinn followed the two shadowy forms before her as they jogged up the slope. The glow of the brightening sky offered a hazy view of the trail – a trail she knew well. They emerged from the brush and crossed the meadow that led to the saddle.

They crested a ridge and the eastern horizon came into view – a jagged divide defined by shadowy peaks below a bright blue aura that threatened to consume the stars above. Iko slowed to a stop, as did Percy, Quinn, and Chuli. They each withdrew a waterskin, taking eager drinks in between their gasps for air.

"We did it. The sun's not up yet." Percy noted.

Quinn gazed over the valley behind them. "I can't believe we let you talk us into going this far." She looked at Percy as he was taking another drink. "You know we'll have to carry whatever we kill back over this saddle."

Iko moved closer to her. "Let the others try to hunt squirrels or whatever other pathetic game they can find in that valley. If we want to win, we need larger game." He pointed east. "We'll find it down there."

Quinn frowned. Hearing his reasoning again didn't change the fact that it seemed insane. She wondered if any other teams would try to hunt beyond the valley where the schools resided. She capped her skin and shifted her pack.

"We had better get going, then," Quinn said. "The bigger the game, the longer it will take us to haul it back. If we arrive after nightfall, it's all for nothing."

She glanced at Chuli, who gave a firm nod.

"Right," Iko agreed. "We'll rest again at the bottom, and then we can hunt."

Without another word, Iko broke into a jog, following the trail that led to the valley east of them. Quinn sighed as the sun edged over the horizon and a bright ray of light shone upon her face. She broke into a run, following the boys as the three of them descended into the shadow-covered valley.

Percy knelt among the underbrush, examining the forest floor. To Quinn, there was nothing to see but leaves and strands of yellowed grass. After a moment, he stood and nodded.

"It's a deer, big enough to be a stag. The tracks are fresh, too."

As Percy gazed through the surrounding forest, Quinn and the others did the same. Bright green buds of new leaves obscured the view, making it more difficult to see than recent visits to the valley.

When Percy slid his bow off his shoulder, Quinn and the others did the same.

"If I remember right, there are clusters of pines ahead. There's a good chance that the deer is among them." Percy spoke softly, staring into the woods the entire time. "We should split up, come from opposite directions in case he bolts."

Iko replied, "Good idea. One group might flush the deer toward the other."

"Chuli and Percy are the best with the bow. We should split them up," Quinn suggested.

Percy waved to the side. "Iko and Chuli, you two circle around to the east. Quinn and I will circle to the west. If you shoot, make sure it's not at one of us."

Iko patted Percy on the shoulder as he passed by. "We'll try, but we can't make any promises."

Chuli glanced at Quinn with a shrug, drew an arrow, and followed Iko through the brush. As their footsteps faded, Percy turned toward Quinn. "Are you ready?"

She drew an arrow from her quiver and gave him a nod. "Let's go find a deer."

Flashing a grin, Percy turned and slipped through the trees. As Quinn trailed behind, she tried to emulate the boy's movements – the way he eased past branches without touching them and how his footsteps slid beneath the leaves rather than crunching through them. After walking a couple hundred yards, Quinn spotted a copse of pines to her right and another ahead. She suddenly recognized the location they were approaching. Her thoughts darkened…the shadows of those dark trees becoming ominous. Despite their need for stealth, the words refused to remain unsaid.

She whispered to Percy. "This is where it happened…where Simone and Darnya were killed."

He glanced back at her with a furrowed brow. "I know. Now, be quiet."

As he raised his bow and eased forward, she stopped. A frown crossed her face as she stared at his back. Gaps began to fill…an incomplete picture assembling into something recognizable. Her eyes widened, but she held the gasp back – instead raising her nocked bow and pointing it at Percy.

"It was you." She didn't whisper this time.

Percy turned toward her with his bow held low with one hand, arrow in the other. "What are you talking about?"

"You killed them. You know this is where it happened because you killed them."

He stared at her for a long moment with his brow furrowed, lips pressed together.

The events and details sped through Quinn's head. "You and Iko didn't duel that day, claiming to be sick. And when they questioned the other boys, you two were away from the school." She frowned. "Iko's mother isn't truly sick, is she?"

Finally, he spoke. "You don't understand, Quinn."

She held her bow ready, watching him closely. He was fast and an amazing shot, so she planned to shoot at any movement.

"I understand well enough. You murdered our fellow cadets and then tried to kill me."

Percy smiled and shook his head. "You've seen me shoot, Quinn. You'd be dead if that was what I wanted."

Quinn frowned, knowing that was true. "Why did you do it?"

"It's...complicated." He shrugged. "Besides, I thought you'd be happy to see Darnya dead."

"While Darnya and I had our issues, I never wanted her dead."

"Well, be that as it may, it was necessary." Percy shook his head. "It would have been too obvious if I had only killed Simone."

Quinn's eyes narrowed as she considered his words. She heard footsteps and turned to the side to find Iko and Chuli approaching. His arm was about her neck, his knife pressed against it.

"Drop the bow, Quinn," Iko called out.

"Iko? What are you doing?"

He continued forward, Chuli with him, his amber eyes intense – glaring. "You should have let it go, Quinn."

Quinn frowned, her focus shifting to Chuli and found her eye blackened, her cheek bleeding. "Are you all right?"

"I am well." Chuli grimaced. "When we saw you with your bow aimed at Percy, he hit me. I...was not ready for it."

"Quinn." Her attention shifted to Iko as he spoke. "Drop the bow. Don't make me kill your friend."

She stared into his eyes and found nothing of the usual warmth, no hint of emotion at all. If she shot Percy, Iko would kill Chuli. An attempt to turn her bow on Iko would allow Percy to shoot her.

With a sigh, Quinn lowered the bow and tossed it to the leaf-covered forest floor.

"Should I kill her?"

Quinn turned toward Percy and found his bow raised, arrow nocked and aimed toward her. When she looked back toward Iko, her eyes met his in a long and silent moment. *He's actually considering it*, she thought.

It was a thought that hurt badly. She had given a piece of her heart away, a part that he had nurtured and cared for…only to now crush with a single look.

Finally, he shook his head. "No. Their deaths would serve no purpose. We cannot go back without them. It would raise too many questions."

He grimaced and pushed Chuli forward, the girl stumbling but managing to maintain her balance.

As Chuli moved beside Quinn, Percy shuffled toward Iko, keeping his nocked arrow pointed at the girls the entire time.

"You could join me, Quinn," Iko offered.

She frowned. "Why did you kill them?"

He shook his head. "You wouldn't understand. There's more at stake here than the lives of two girls. The world is changing, Quinn. A new power rises, one that will make things right again."

Quinn glanced at Chuli and found confusion in her eyes, the same confusion Quinn felt inside. She turned back toward Iko. "Any cause that forces you to murder innocents cannot be worthy."

Iko smiled, an expression that contained no hint of joy. "Your innocence is among your more endearing qualities, Quinn. However, naiveté can be dangerous…it may even kill you one day."

She frowned. "I'll not be part of whatever conquest you support…not for the price you would have me pay."

He grimaced. "That's too bad, Quinn. We could have been something special." He stepped closer. "Toss me your pack and quiver. Yours too, Chuli."

The girls swung their packs and quivers off their shoulders before throwing them toward Iko. Quinn's fell short – very much on purpose. When he bent to pick it up, she lunged forward and kicked him in the face, her toe connecting with his nose with satisfying force. He fell onto his rear with a cry of pain.

"Argh!"

His hand went to his nose and came away bloody. Percy drew his bowstring back but Iko called out.

"Don't!" He rose to his feet with both packs and quivers gripped in one hand. A wipe of his wrist across his bent and bloody nose left crimson streaks on his sleeve. "Why challenge me, Quinn? You know I would beat you. I proved that in the Coliseum."

"This isn't the Coliseum. Drop the bags and have Percy lower his bow. I'll show you a beating."

Iko glared at her as blood dripped from his nose. "Maybe next time."

"I look forward to it," Quinn replied with steel in her voice.

His eyes narrowed, glaring at Quinn as he began to back away. "Leave them be, Percy. We have their food and water. They'll have a long, thirsty hike back, and then they can go on with their lives."

Iko circled around Percy, who still had his bow aimed at the girls. He then turned to look back, his eyes locking with Quinn's. "Have a good life. Don't try to follow us, or we'll be forced to kill you."

With that, he took off at a run, heading east. Percy lowered his bow, spun about, and scampered after Iko. As their brown coats faded into the forest, Quinn felt a single tear run down her cheek – a tear of betrayal.

Quinn stopped reciting her tale as she felt the knot loosen. A sigh of relief slipped out as she pulled her hand free. However, she kept it behind her back and squinted into the light, toward her inquisitor.

"I'm thirsty. Can I have a drink of water?"

The man who had been questioning her replied, "Give the girl some water."

She heard shuffling from behind her and felt someone leaning over her shoulder. Turning her head to the side, Quinn saw a woman's hip behind her, a knife strapped to her thigh. From her other side, a woman's hand appeared, gripping a cup that she raised to Quinn's lips. The water was welcome because she was truly thirsty. As she finished drinking and the cup lowered, Quinn's hand darted out, grabbed the knife hilt, pulled it free, and sliced through the rope strapped around the chair and her chest. At the same time, she had a grip of the woman's wrist. The cup fell as Quinn stood, the metal clanging when it hit the floor. A forward lunge lifted the woman's body over Quinn's back, flipping her to slam hard on the floor, right into the glowing rock.

Shouts and cries of surprise rang through the room.

Quinn spun around and picked up the chair with her free hand, swinging it like a weapon as she smashed it into one of the other two captors who had been standing behind her. The man fell to the floor as the chair shattered, leaving a broken leg in one of Quinn's hands, the knife in the other. She thrust the chair leg into the stomach of the other man. When he bent with the blow, she cracked him over the head with the knife hilt, driving him to the floor.

With the three captors behind her down, she spun toward her questioner. The shroud had fallen, and she now saw him as a man in his late twenties, with an average height and athletic build. He drew the sword at his hip as a guard standing behind him did the same.

"Bravo, Quinn. I commend you. If your responses hadn't made our decision clear, your ability to free yourself and take out three guards would have done it for sure." He waved his sword toward her. "Now, drop the weapons. We won't harm you."

"Where's my brother?"

"He's in the room next door. Just put down the weapons and we'll take you to him."

She frowned as she considered his statement. "Why should I believe you?"

The man sighed and sheathed his sword before holding his hands up. "You gave us the answers we were seeking. We never meant you harm. We merely sought the truth, and in seeking it, we determined that you possess something else we seek." He pointed toward the floor. Quinn's gaze followed and settled on the rune still marked on the stone. "Remember the Truth rune? You would know if I were lying."

Quinn stared and knew he was correct.

Another person materialized from the shadowy corner, a boy Quinn recognized the moment his face appeared in the light.

"Torney?"

Torney nodded. "Do as he says, Quinn. Everything will be all right."

With narrowed eyes, Quinn considered her options, not wishing to give in. Everyone fell still for a long moment before she relented.

"Fine," she sighed before dropping the chair leg, the wood bouncing and rolling noisily on the hard floor. With a flip of her other hand, Quinn drove the knife into the seat of the broken chair. The three captors she had attacked groaned and began to rise to their feet.

The man who had addressed her stepped forward and held his hand out. "Hello, Quinn. My name is Delvin. Welcome to the team."

40

A BIT OF LIGHT

Everson paused to gather himself. The wounds inside him remained fresh, no scabs yet covering them. Less than a day had passed since he had discovered the truth about his roommate – now knowing that Jonah merely considered him a pawn, not a friend.

He blinked and took a breath as he fought to retain his composure. With himself collected, he resumed his tale.

"When I arrived at Ackerson's office, I found the man working despite the late hour. I knocked and he let me in. After taking a seat before his desk, I handed him the notes I had discovered beneath Jonah's mattress. His face was grim when he read them. He thanked me for coming to him and promised to handle the issue as he walked me to the door. I returned to my room and went to bed. The next thing I knew, you people grabbed me and put a bag over my head."

The room fell silent. Everson realized that the bright light had dimmed, the energy of the augmentation waning. Knowing that runes began losing their effectiveness after an hour informed him of how long he had been telling his story.

"See! I told you!" A voice Everson recognized said the words, bringing a frown to his face. "It wasn't my fault."

"Yes, Jonah," the questioner replied. "We see the truth of it now."

"Jonah?" Everson asked.

"Sorry, Ev. I couldn't tell you," Jonah's voice came from a dark corner of the room.

A door opened behind the man seated before Everson, the light beyond exposing a better view of the room. A figure eclipsed the doorway, one he knew well.

"Everson!" Quinn exclaimed as she rushed into the room.

"Quinn? Are you well?"

She knelt before him, wearing naught but her cream-colored shift. "Don't worry about me. Are you all right? Did they hurt you?"

He shook his head. "No. I'm fine. Just cold."

Standing, she turned toward the others in the room and kicked the shroud behind the glowing rock. Immediately, faces coalesced into view.

The man in black, Master Firellus, was the man who had been questioning Everson. Behind the man were Jonah, Master Hedgewick, and Master Nindlerod. Another man stepped through the doorway, young and athletic with dark hair, a thin goatee, and intense eyes – a man Everson had never seen before.

"Now that you cowards cannot hide in the shadows, I suggest you apologize to my brother," Quinn demanded with steel in her voice. "And for Issal's sake, get him a blanket. It's cold in here, and he has only his smallclothes."

Master Firellus frowned at the other two masters as Nindlerod broke into cackling laughter. The man in the doorway crossed his arms and leaned against the frame with a smile.

"She is certainly bold," the man in the doorway said. "You should have heard her story." He grinned. "I like her...a lot."

Master Firellus rose from his seat. "Untie the boy. Let's get them both clothes and a meal." He then spun about, limping toward the doorway as he leaned on his cane. "Jonah, can you two please explain things to them while they eat?'

The man in the doorway moved aside as Firellus limped past him, followed by Masters Hedgewick and Nindlerod.

Clothed and seated in a room across the hall from the cell where they had questioned him, Everson took a bite of warm bread and washed it down with a long drink of water. Quinn sat across from him, eating as eagerly as he was. The room was empty other than the table at which they sat, joined by four chairs, and some bookshelves along one wall. A glowlamp suspended over the table – hanging from a thick wooden beam that ran across the ceiling – lit the small room.

The door opened, drawing his attention as Jonah entered with a bundle in his arms. Jonah shuffled forward and poured the cloth-wrapped load onto the table with a grunt. A sigh escaped his lips as he plopped down into an empty chair.

"Whew." Jonah wiped his brow. "Those are heavier than I expected."

Everson stared at the bundle of gray cloth, bulky and over three-feet long. "What is it?"

"Rather than grabbing your canes and braces, I thought you might prefer your new invention." Jonah glanced across the table. "I'm sure Quinn will be interested to see it."

Everson found himself grinning at the idea. He popped another chunk of bread into his mouth and reached toward the bundle. When he pulled the blanket aside, the metal of what lay beneath reflected the blue light of the glowlamp. With a grunt, he lifted one of the mechanical legs and lowered it to the floor, spinning in his seat to slip his leg into it.

"What is that?" Quinn asked.

"You'll see."

The trousers they had given Everson were a bit bulky and required him to wrap them tight to his leg for a proper fit. He then began securing the metal bands that held the contraption to his leg and his foot.

"I'm glad that's over with," Jonah said. "Hiding the truth from you was killing me. I…value your friendship, Everson. I hated having secrets divide us like that."

Everson turned the words over in his head as he finished securing the last clamp. Jonah's secrets had caused him pain…along with the notes he had found under Jonah's bed.

"What really happened with Donnell?"

Jonah nodded. "Yes. I suspected that would be among your first questions." He sighed and his eyes glazed over as he recalled a memory.

"As you know, I followed him up on the roof that day. Once on top, it took me some time to locate him. When I did, he had his ear against one of the upper windows that look down into the Hall of Truth. You might recall that some of the masters were meeting in that hall with the kings of Torinland and Kantaria, along with Queen of Ri Star and the Duchess of New Kardis."

Everson frowned, wondering why Donnell would do such a thing… beyond uncontrolled curiosity.

"When Donnell heard me approach, he attacked me. We scuffled for a bit, and I realized just how strong he was…certainly stronger than me. He tried to push me off the front edge, but my training kicked in and I was able to use his momentum against him. When I peeked over the edge and saw how he had landed, I knew he was dead.

"After climbing back down, I immediately went to his room and picked the lock. Inside, I found a series of missives he had prepared – the same notes you found under my mattress."

"Donnell?" Everson asked. "Those were written by Donnell?"

Jonah put his hand on Everson's shoulder. "I'm afraid so. He wasn't who you thought he was."

Everson looked at Quinn and found her eyes narrowed as she focused on Jonah. He turned back toward his roommate. "I don't understand."

"Don't worry. You'll get to hear it all explained in detail. As soon as you two are ready, I'm to bring you upstairs and we'll cover everything."

Reaching across the table, Everson grabbed the other mechanical leg.

"Where are we, anyway?" Quinn asked.

"You're in the basement below the Arcane Ward. By the way, you'll be glad to have those mechanical legs. This place has *so* many stairs."

41

A WARDEN'S PURPOSE

Everson followed Jonah down the corridor, each of his footsteps heavy despite the leather soles on the bottom of his feet. When they reached the stairs, Everson climbed them – two steps at a time – without effort. He glanced at Quinn and found her grinning.

"Your new legs are wonderful, Ev."

He smiled. She knew how difficult stairs had been for him, having watched him methodically shuffle up stairs – one step at a time – his entire life.

They turned the corner at the landing and continued upward to another corridor, lit by glowing beams overhead and glowing stones below. Jonah led them down the hallway, past numerous closed doors, and to a pair of double-doors at the end. They passed through the doorway into the largest indoor space Everson had ever seen. He gaped at the sight, as if the Foundry had grown four times the size and had sprouted amazing new creations with it.

The shape of the room was square, three-hundred feet in width and length. Three stories above, a grid of massive beams supported a ceiling held up by thick columns spaced at wide intervals. The columns glowed with the strength of a fully charged glowstone, as did the heavy beams overhead, bathing the space in blue light. A dozen forges spaced along one wall glowed orange and the clanging of hammers shaping metal filled the air.

The trio walked past a flying machine in mid-construction. Stretched hides covered its metal frame and runes marked every piece. Everson spied Reduce Gravity runes on passive components and Power runes on the parts that moved. Two men were busy bolting flat blades on a spindle while a woman stared at a rune that glowed with a faint red light.

"Is she…"

Before Everson could even finish the question, Jonah replied with a nod. "Enchanting? Yes."

Everson turned toward the contraption with a look of wonder. "So… it's real."

"Oh, it's real. I'm sure you'll think up some crazy ways to use it, too."

The workers paused and stared at Everson, one man nudging the other as he pointed toward Everson's mechanical legs. Everson grinned with pride, an odd feeling compared to the shame he normally felt under such circumstances.

They continued forward, passing a group of four workers – two male and two female – who were busily assembling a catapult with four launch arms. Everson frowned at the small size of the launch baskets.

"Why four launch arms? And why are the baskets so small? They'll never be able to launch a projectile heavy enough to do damage."

Jonah chuckled. "I wouldn't be so sure. Just remember, we have access to magic here…for the siege engine and for its projectiles."

In the next work area, they passed a group assembling an oven like the one he and Jonah examined in the academy kitchen. On and on, they walked, passing other inventions and components that were being crafted, assembled…and enchanted. When they finally reached the far end, Everson's head was spinning with ideas.

Jonah opened the door and the siblings slipped past him, into another corridor. He again took the lead, walking past a window that revealed the pale light and long shadows cast by the rising sun.

Quinn sighed. "We've been awake for hours and it's only dawn? I get the feeling that this will be a long day."

Everson turned toward her. "Aren't you curious to see what this is all about?"

"Oh, I'm curious for sure. But where will it leave me with Sergeant Jasmine?"

Jonah stopped beside a door. "Don't worry about her. You're done at the academy now anyway."

Quinn frowned at his statement. Jonah's knuckles banged on the door three times, the sound echoing in the hallway.

"Yes?" A voice came from inside the room.

"It's Warden Selbin. I have them with me."

"Come in, Jonah."

Jonah turned the knob and stepped aside. Everson walked past him and into a large office with Quinn a step behind.

Shelves filled with books covered one wall and a desk sat beside them. Upon two of the walls were tapestries, one with the symbol for Order and other with the symbol for Chaos. Black curtains covered the wall opposite the door, slivers of light leaking through gaps and seams here and there. Glowing statues lit the space and made it easy to see the people seated around the table in the center of the room.

Masters Firellus, Nindlerod, and Hedgewick all turned toward Everson, as did the man named Delvin. To Everson's surprise, two other men sat at the table as well, one of whom Everson knew well, the other not at all.

"Come in, Everson, Quinn," Headmaster Ackerson said. "Have a seat."

Everson walked to the table, his legs whirring with each step. With all eyes on him, he felt self-conscious. His stomach churned with anxiety as he realized the magnitude of the moment. These were important people.

He sat upon an empty chair with Quinn to his right and Jonah to his left. Everson searched the faces in the room and found all eyes on him… except for Delvin, who appeared focused on his fingernails.

"I'm afraid your time at my school has ended, Everson," Ackerson said.

"What?" Everson felt his gut wrench. "But…I've done nothing wrong."

Ackerson chuckled. "You misunderstand. This is a graduation of sorts. Your education will continue, but with a different focus."

The man unknown to Everson leaned forward. He had close-shorn brown hair and a trimmed beard to match. His physique was that of a warrior, so it didn't surprise Everson when he addressed Quinn.

"You are also finished at the military academy, Jacquinn." He looked around the table. "Things have changed…we must accelerate our plans and adapt. Accordingly, you and a few others will move on."

Quinn frowned. "What, exactly, does that mean, Captain Goren?"

A piece of paper rested on the table before Goren, one he picked up and stared at briefly before reading out loud.

"Sol Polis has fallen, and with it, Kalimar is ours. A new regime rules the east coast, one with new laws – laws that restore order to Empire citizens.

"The borders between your lands and ours extend from Yarth, to all of Vinacci, to the east coast of Hurnsdom. Any attempt to reclaim these lands will be treated as an act of war, as will the mere presence of an armed force approaching our borders. All trading between the Empire and the kingdoms of Issalia will cease until amicable trade agreements have been negotiated with each nation.

"Furthermore, know that we have reinstated the Choosing ceremony and have formally outlawed the use of the dark magic tied to Chaos. Anyone found to have the inherent ability to channel Chaos will be imprisoned. Any demonstration of this forbidden magic inside our borders will be met with swift execution.

"Take heed of these warnings. They are the last you will receive."

The room fell silent. Everson's brow furrowed as he sifted through the message, replaying it in his head.

Master Hedgewick spoke, drawing everyone's attention. "This message arrived three days ago and copies have been sent to the leaders of Kantaria, Torinland, Ri Star, western Hurnsdom, and to the Tantarri."

"What does this have to do with my brother and me?" Quinn asked.

Master Firellus turned toward Jonah. "You didn't tell them?"

Jonah shook his head. "No. We didn't get that far. I merely explained Donnell's death."

Elias turned to look Everson in the eye. "You have a unique mind, young man – a mind that could save lives…or take them." His gaze shifted to Quinn. "You, on the other hand, have other traits that we need. Fierce determination, quick thinking, and a strong will to survive are not things that we can teach. My associate here," he gestured toward Delvin, "believes that they are critical for the wardens we put in the field."

"Wardens?" Everson found himself asking, not even realizing the word had slipped out until it reached his ears.

Goren nodded. "Yes. Wardens…agents who fight for the rights and safety of our people."

Nindlerod snorted. "Enough dancing around the subject." The old man turned toward Everson. "A few years back, a secret organization was formed, known as the Issalian Clandestine Operative Network…or ICON.

"The need for such a group became apparent after a series of assassination attempts made toward the rulers of Issalia. Most of these attempts failed…despite some unsavory side effects. King Cassius of Torinland suffered permanent damage from his poisoning, but he still lives. King Brock avoided the attempt on his life, but his general did not. General Budakis suffers from permanent nerve damage, much like King Cassius. However, King Talvin of Vinacci was not so lucky. After his murder, the government went through a time of turmoil. He was eventually replaced by a council of rulers who refused to meet with the leaders of other nations. Last fall, King Ulric of Hurnsdom – your king – was killed when Cinti Mor was captured by Vinacci soldiers. Based on the letter Goren just read, we must now assume that King Pretencia of Kalimar is dead as well.

"We have enemies hiding among us, operating with subterfuge. Protecting our rulers has become a challenge, one we dare not fail any longer. With this new Empire rising to the east, we find our backs against the wall and at a disadvantage. They presumably know much about us, while we know little to nothing of their actions or intent. This is why King Brock first came to us to form ICON."

The names of kings and secret agencies were spinning inside Everson's head, coalescing into something complex, a new problem to solve. Still, gaps remained.

"I still don't understand what this has to do with me or my sister."

Goren clenched his fist. "We need wardens: agents who can help us combat these unseen, secretive enemies. We plan to train Quinn and others like her to become field agents who can delve deep into enemy networks behind false identities. We will prepare them to infiltrate their network and gather information. We will prepare them to become who and whatever they must. We will prepare them to defend themselves and to kill when necessary. In the end, wardens must do whatever is required in order to protect our people."

Hedgewick leaned forward, looking at Everson. "Field agents, like your sister, will need special tools, gear, weapons, new means of transportation…anything that people like you might create. You can help save lives, Everson. Your discovery of Chaos Conduction is likely to become a critical advantage in the war to come."

"War?" Everson glanced about the table in concern.

Goren held up the missive from the Empire. "You heard the message. This new Empire has captured a third of the continent with the intent to rule it as they see fit – twisting the law to their own purpose despite the discrimination and potential genocide that may come of it. Killing kingdom rulers and taking their lands by force were already acts of war. It is time we acknowledge it."

The room fell silent for a moment until Quinn spoke.

"What if we say no?"

Frowns and grim stares were enough response.

Delvin sat back with his hands clasped behind his head, appearing at ease…relaxed. "I highly suggest that you say yes. Things will be far easier that way." He smiled. "Besides, I heard your story, Quinn. You were born to be a warden."

"It all comes down to purpose," Nindlerod stated. "We seek those who have an inner drive, an agency that makes them ideally suited to become wardens. For Everson, it is his need to be useful."

Everson gasped at the insightful comment.

Delvin said, "Quinn's purpose is to defend those who cannot defend themselves. That and her determination make her perfect for the job."

Quinn pressed her lips together as she stared at Everson. "My brother won't be at risk, right?"

Everson grit his teeth. "I can take care of myself, Quinn."

Nindlerod laughed. "While I'm sure you are capable, Everson, you will best serve ICON with your mind. Create things that keep people like your sister alive, and all will be well." Nindlerod stared toward Quinn as he spoke. "Your brother would remain here, safe in the Ward."

"The Ward?" Everson asked.

Elias nodded. "Yes. You two will live here now, as will the others we plan to bring in. It won't be easy. Your training will increase three-fold, and you will find yourself pushed to your limits…and beyond. We need to have you and others ready as soon as possible."

42

WARDENS

Jonah waited in the corridor with the door held open. Quinn watched her brother exit the room and walk past Jonah, staring at Everson's mechanical legs the entire time. She shook her head in wonder. *I still can't believe he did it. He can walk.*

"Just remember, our room is next door if you need anything," Everson said.

Quinn gave him a nod and a half grin, a nod Jonah returned as he pulled the door closed.

She turned and looked about the apartment...her new home. A table with four chairs stood to her left, along with a small counter that had food stored above, plates and other eating utensils below. A sitting area waited to her right, with a desk and bookshelves along the wall. Moving slowly, she crossed the room, her hand running along the back of the leather sofa. Turning, her gaze landed on the two open doors beyond the dining table. One of those bedrooms was hers, the other for her room-mate...once one was assigned. As she approached the glass-paned doors at the far wall, she opened one and stepped outside.

Looking up, she realized that outside was an inaccurate term. A glass-paneled dome stood between her and the mid-day sky, five stories above. As she stared up at the white clouds drifting eastward, two consecutive fireballs flew past. Appearing like shooting stars, she stared at them until they passed beyond her view. The image brought back memories of her carriage ride with Iko – a precious moment that was now forever tainted. A sigh slipped out and she blinked the memory away, choosing to think on other things.

Stepping onto the balcony, she rested her forearms on the railing and looked down to find her room four stories above a courtyard that was hundreds of feet across and just as wide. Below that courtyard was the Forge and the odd creations she had seen when passing through it with Jonah and Everson. She suspected that Everson would be spending much of his time in the Forge. The thought made her wonder what inventions he might concoct now that he would have access to enchanting.

The courtyard was largely an open space made of square stone tiles, almost like a giant Ratio Bellicus board brought to life. Complex structures occupied portions of the space – a conflagration of rails and beams and ropes that reminded her of the agility course from the TACT Games. Surrounding the entire area were the tall walls that contained it, each with rows of balconies like the one she stood upon – nine stories worth. She wondered at how many people lived in the Ward…and how many more would be joining her.

A motion below drew her attention and she spotted two warriors – a boy and a girl dressed in gray sparring gear. The two ran toward each other with incredible speed, and when they were a hundred feet apart, they both leaped and soared upward, impossibly high. Quinn's mouth dropped open, gaping as the two figures rose into the air above the balcony where she stood. As their arcing leaps met, both swung their sparring weapon in a terrible collision that oddly made no more than a muffled thump. The girl spun with the impact and dropped toward the ground while the boy struggled to remain upright, flailing wildly as he tried to bring his feet beneath him. Quinn held her breath as they plummeted toward the courtyard floor, fearing that they would be killed from falling such a height. The girl landed gracefully, the thump of her impact meeting Quinn a second later. Conversely, the boy got his feet beneath him just in time, squatted with the landing, and rolled with his momentum. Amazingly, neither appeared hurt as they turned to face each other for another pass.

The sound of a door opening behind her drew Quinn's attention. She turned to find a familiar face entering her room.

"Chuli!" She ran inside, toward the smiling Tantarri girl. They hugged each other tightly for a long moment until Quinn finally released her embrace, stepped back, and noticed the pack on the floor beside Chuli.

"What are you doing here?"

"Can't you see, Jacquinn Gulagas? I have been assigned to this room."

A grin spread across Quinn's face. "You're my roommate?"

A nod and a sigh accompanied Chuli's response. "It appears so. I'm still unsure of what this means, but I believe it is a good choice after what happened with Iko and Percy."

Quinn's grin faded upon hearing Iko's name. The scars from his betrayal were fresh, raw, and painful.

Chuli stared at Quinn with concern. "Last night, I heard the sounds of a struggle coming from your cell in the infirmary, and I feared what had become of you. Nobody would tell me. I remained locked in my cell until after breakfast today, unsure of what would happen. Then, two men appeared, carrying my things. They told me I would be safe if I agreed to come with them. While they brought me here, they said this was my new home and that I was to train with you. They would not tell me why. What happened?"

Quinn shuffled to the sofa and sat with a sigh before gesturing toward the chair across from her. "You should sit. There is much to explain."

Chuli appeared concerned, but she did as Quinn suggested.

Quinn stared toward the Ratio Bellicus pieces and game board on the table. Events of the past day churned in her head as she considered where to begin.

"After we returned to the school and informed Jasmine and Goren of what happened with Iko and Percy, that information triggered other events. Guards came for me in the middle of the night, as you heard. However, I wasn't the only one. They took my brother from his school as well. They put us in separate cells and tied us up to interrogate us. Thankfully, the truth set us free – set us on a new course.

"When I told my story, detailing my time at the academy and my interactions with Iko, the people who run this place were able to guess at the reason behind his actions.

"They believe that Iko and Percy are spies, as was another boy at the other school who had befriended my brother. The assumption is that these spies were sent to gather information to use against us. When Percy told me that killing Darnya was necessary to throw off suspicion, what remained unsaid is why he had killed Simone.

"It turns out that Simone was undercover, posing as a student to help find and recruit new wardens…and to seek out any spies. Iko and Percy must have discovered her true role, so they killed her.

Alarm reflected in Chuli's eyes. "They killed Darnya only as a ruse to hide suspicion?"

Quinn shrugged. "Apparently, hiding the truth was all the reason they needed."

"I'm sorry, Quinn." Chuli leaned forward and took Quinn's hand. "You allowed yourself to get close to Ikonis. He took that trust and betrayed you."

With a deep breath and sheer will power, Quinn kept her tears at bay. "Thank you."

The two girls fell silent for a moment until Chuli spoke.

"In case you are curious, the school settled on a winner for the TACT Games. Well…two winners."

"What?" Quinn blinked. "Who?"

"You and I tied for first, despite not scoring any points in hunting."

"Tied?" Quinn frowned as she glanced at the game board on the table. A grin appeared. "Didn't Goren say that ties would be addressed by playing Ratio Bellicus?"

"Yes. I do believe you are correct. Perhaps we should play a match."

Quinn sat forward and eyed the black pieces on her side of the board, considering her first move. "I thought you might never ask."

After a moment, Chuli asked, "What came of the spy at the other school? Was he using your brother as well?"

"Yes. My brother is…special. Donnell realized that, seeing Everson as a way to gain information. My brother has always been extremely curi-ous...and brilliant. By befriending Everson, Donnell had access to someone who would chase mysteries for him and would teach him things beyond what he might learn in the classroom. It appears that Donnell was caught spying and was killed in the process. Thankfully, the warden who killed him was able to intercept the information Donnell had acquired before it left the school.

"Something is happening, Chuli. Things are changing, and there are people behind it who are willing to kill anyone along the way. They have already assassinated three kings and have taken control of the entire eastern coastline. There is a fear that, given time, the entire continent will fall under the hand of this new empire. We have been recruited by an organization that was created to prevent that occurrence and to protect many innocent lives in the process."

"What is this organization you speak of?" Chuli asked.

"It is a group called ICON. We are no longer training to become soldiers. They promise to make us something more. They plan to make us...wardens."

EPILOGUE

The guard wrenched Iko's arm, pulling it backward as the shackle clicked together. A tug on his other arm elicited a grunt as it, too, was placed in a shackle behind his back.

"Come along now. Don't give us any further trouble," the guard grumbled.

Iko glanced at Percy as his friend rolled his eyes. A push from behind sent Percy stumbling forward and Iko braced himself for the same treatment.

With a guard in the lead and two prodding them from behind, the boys crossed the spacious courtyard. The blackened remnants of a hedge maze stood in the heart of the space, beside a charred fountain surrounded by a sprawling plaza. Iko heard the gurgle of flowing water as he passed the fountain, the sound reminding him of his thirst.

The guard leading them – a middle-aged man dressed in mail covered by a white tabard marked by the blue symbol of Order – carried an arrogance in every word, in every movement, in every strutting stride. Iko longed to test the man, longed to knock him down a peg.

They approached buildings at the core of the complex, including three tall towers – two marred with black scorch marks while the third shone with the pale stones that marked it of new construction. Built of the same stone as the tower and the rest of the Citadel, they approached a massive alabaster building at the center of the complex.

A series of tall arches stood in front of the building, supported by pale columns that lined the top of the stairs they climbed. Once beyond the arches, they passed through an external hall and a wall of oversized doors. The four guards stationed outside gave the escort leader a nod as he opened a door and led his captives inside.

The interior hall was bustling with activity, a conflagration of disorganized organization. As people moved this way and that, the guard led Iko around the interior fountain, through the traffic, and up a flight of stairs at the far end of the space. When they reached the fifth floor, the man approached the two guards blocking the second door and addressed them. As he spoke, Iko glanced toward the window to his other side and saw the massive hole in the Citadel wall – a section twenty strides across. A crew of mason workers were in the process of rebuilding the wall, the new stones appearing two shades lighter than the old ones. Opening the door between the guards, the man led them inside.

The room was spacious with a balcony on one end, a fireplace and bookshelves along one wall, and a desk at the center. A man looked up from the desk, rising as the guard led them into the room.

"General Kardan," The guard saluted the man.

"Why are you here, Sergeant Mollis?" General Kardan stood and circled the desk. Tall and muscular in a lean way, the man appeared quite capable despite his age.

"I caught these two trying to sneak into the Citadel," the sergeant replied.

Iko sighed. "I told you we weren't trying to sneak in. We simply walked through that massive hole in the wall."

The man turned toward Iko, sneering. "You were armed, trying to enter unchallenged and without a writ."

Percy muttered, "Here we go again."

Iko pressed his lips together, restraining his frustration. "Will you just tell the General what we told you? Or, is it too much for you to handle?"

Mollis' eyes bulged as if they were about to burst. After a moment, his reddened face relaxed and he turned toward Kardan.

"They recited an odd passcode, Sir." Mollis turned toward Iko, frowning hard before continuing. *"Mankind is lost without Issal's hand to guide them."*

General Kardan stepped forward and stared Iko in the eye. "I see." A long moment of tension held everyone motionless…until he spoke. "Unchain them. You may also return their weapons."

Mollis looked at Iko with a furrowed brow. "Are you sure? They appear unseemly."

Iko sighed again. "How would you appear if you spent three weeks traveling, without money for a decent place to sleep?"

Mollis stared at Iko, his frown deepening as he took his keys out. Iko turned his back toward the man and waited as his shackles were removed. With his wrists freed, he accepted his bow, quiver, and hunting knife from one of the other guards. The moment Percy was freed and his weapons were returned, General Kardan addressed the sergeant.

"You many leave us Sergeant."

Mollis gave Kardan a salute and exited the room, closing the door behind him.

Iko shook his head. "How do you deal with that man? He is insufferable."

"He is an asset. As with anyone who possesses skills, I will use those skills the best I can. In this case, he is good at managing his men and keeping them in line. There is little else required of him, so I can look past his deficiencies." Kardan moved closer. "It's good to see you again, Ikonis."

The man's arms wrapped about Iko in a powerful hug that compressed his lungs and forced air from him. When he let go, he turned to Percy.

"Percilus. It's been…what? Four years?" Kardan hugged Percy, driving a breath from the boy.

When Kardan released him, Percy replied, "Five, actually."

"That long?" Kardan turned and strolled toward his desk. "Your time with Martin was well spent, I assume?"

Percy nodded. "Yes, Sir. I dare say that I learned everything he had to offer before I left."

"Good." Kardan turned his attention on Iko. "And the time with your uncle?"

"He taught me well, Kardan. None in their military academy can stand up to me in the arena." Iko glanced toward his companion. "Percy has proven to be the best archer and among the best hunters at the school as well."

Kardan sat at his desk. "Very good. I assume you are not here just to exchange pleasantries."

Iko moved closer to the desk. "Actually, I am here to give a full debriefing. But first, I need to know if she's here."

"You can see her now if you wish."

After a glance toward Percy, Iko nodded. "Let's do that."

Kardan rose from his desk and approached the door at the side of the room. After a knock, he waited.

"Yes?" A female voice rang from beyond the door.

"I have someone who needs to speak with you, Archon."

"Send them in."

Kardan opened the door and stood aside to allow the boys past him.

While Kardan's office was spacious, this room was immense. The suite was broken up into sections including a sitting area with a fireplace, a bath with a copper tub and an oval mirror, and a four-poster bed at the far end. The nearest section, the one Iko and Percy stood in, contained a desk and shelves filled with books. Sitting at the desk was a middle-aged woman with black hair pulled back into a bun. She was dressed in white clothing and had a gold cloak over her shoulders, the metallic nature of the cloak reflecting sunlight that poured through the open balcony doors behind her. The woman paused writing and looked up, her eyes locking with Iko's – eyes that matched his own.

"Hello, Mother."

The woman stood and gave him a warm smile. She circled her desk and took his hand. "Ikonis. You have grown so much." Her eyes examined him from head to toe. "I bet you are a fine warrior."

"Yes, Mother. The best at the academy."

She smiled. "Wonderful." She turned toward Percy. "Percilus. You look well."

Percy bowed his head. "Thank you, Archon Varius."

When Varius' eyes fell on Iko again, he said the words he dreaded sharing. "I have failed, Mother. Percy and I were discovered. We had no choice but to flee the academy."

She frowned. "And when did this occur?"

Iko sighed. "Three weeks past. We were forced to take an unused route to avoid discovery, and then we headed toward Vingarri. Of course, you were not there, and we were unaware of the campaign in Kalimar. Once we learned you were in Sol Polis, we came here straight away."

"While your failure is disheartening, I believe we have Issal to thank for it. Now that we have Kalimar under our wing, the new Empire stands on firm ground." Varius turned and circled her desk to stand behind it. "Four weeks past, I sent a missive to the kingdoms of the west, claiming the east coast as Empire lands and pronouncing our position. We move into the next phase, inviting those who fear Chaos to join us. Sol Polis is once again the capital of the Empire. It is only a matter of time before we rule the entire continent."

Iko nodded. "Yes, Mother. The Hand shall once again guide the people of Issalia, as was meant to be. And one day, we will see the end of Chaos."

The adventure continues in **The Arcane Ward**, Wardens of Issalia Book Two.

NOTE FROM THE AUTHOR

A Warden's Purpose is merely the beginning of a thrilling new adventure. With most characters I write, I feel as if Everson and Jacquinn are part of me — fragments come to life within the words on the pages. They return in book two of the series and are joined by others who play critical roles in the struggle to come. *The Arcane Ward*, book two of the *Wardens of Issalia* series, is now available for your reading enjoyment.

Best Wishes,
Jeffrey L. Kohanek
www.JeffreyLKohanek.com

ALSO BY JEFFREY L. KOHANEK

Fate of Wizardoms

Book One: Eye of Obscurance

Book Two: Balance of Magic

Book Three: Temple of the Oracle

Book Four: Objects of Power

Book Five: TBD

Book Six: TBD

* * *

Prequel: Legend of Shadowmar

Runes of Issalia

The Buried Symbol: Runes of Issalia 1

The Emblem Throne: Runes of Issalia 2

An Empire in Runes: Runes of Issalia 3

Rogue Legacy: Runes of Issalia Prequel

* * *

Runes of Issalia Boxed Set

Heroes of Issalia: Runes Series+Rogue Legacy

Wardens of Issalia

A Warden's Purpose: Wardens of Issalia 1

The Arcane Ward: Wardens of Issalia 2

An Imperial Gambit: Wardens of Issalia 3

A Kingdom Under Siege: Wardens of Issalia 4

ICON: A Wardens of Issalia Companion Tale

* * *

Wardens of Issalia Boxed Set